The GENDER *of* FIRE

by John Yearwood

Other Books by John Yearwood

In the Icarus series:
 The Icarus Jump
 The City and the Gate
 The Gender of Fire

Forthcoming novels:
 The Lie Detector App
 Detritus of the Sun
 The Jar of Pennies

Printed by Kindle Direct Publishing, Seattle, WA
Available from Amazon.com and other online stores.
Available on Kindle and other devices

Library of Congress Control Number: 2019917036
CreateSpace Independent Publishing Platform, North Charleston, SC
Copyright © 2019 The John and Stephenie Yearwood Management Trust
All rights reserved.
ISBN-13: 9780997104172
Design by Bill Carson Design

"Few novels take on the fraught relationships of political power between women and men through Western history as imaginatively as does The Icarus Jump."

"Told with narrative alacrity, with sex scenes as vivid as its battle scenes, this book is an engaging read for anyone who has pondered (and who hasn't?) the variants of human sociability tried in prehistory."

"What a leap of imagination! Yearwood's mixture of 21st century technology and Greek mythology grabbed me from page one..."

"I can't recall the last time a book has stolen and kept my attention like this...I looked forward to getting in bed at night so I could cruise through a few of the relatively short chapters."

"This book is definitely a page turner! Between the sci-fi, action, history and romance I couldn't put it down. I can't wait for the sequel!"

"Know how when you finish a really good book you feel like you are missing something because it is over? This book will make you feel that way too. Well written and enjoyed every word of it!"

"Great book! Great author! Would definitely buy sequel."

"Enjoyable. I'd even call it a "page turner". Very entertaining. Now a few weeks later, I still think about it."

Reviews of John Yearwood's other books:

"A non-stop adventure, filled with constant conflicts and continual, careful planning for coming conflicts. As physical battle after battle unfolds, Army Ranger Charles Shelby also must battle his own 21st-century male stereotypes about women and hierarchy and power, while torn by his attraction toward two very different types of female 'warrior.'"

"Great read with plenty of action. Cannot wait for the next one. Great author with great writing skills. Must read!"

"Wow! I loved it. I know that I was not going to get started on the second book; but I had just a moment of free time, and I thought that I would just get started. Well, I was hooked from page one, and every free moment I was reading a page or 20... until I had to get up and do something. I loved that there was a wonderful story with romance and action while having some very deep thoughts mixed into it."

FOR STEPHEN, IN HONOR OF HIS ETERNAL QUEST

Brute beauty and valour and act, oh, air, pride, plume, here
Buckle! AND the fire that breaks from thee then, a billion
Times told lovelier, more dangerous, O my chevalier!

—Gerard Manley Hopkins, "The Windhover"

ONE

T he wooden funeral pyre for King Phorbus rose twenty feet above the city army's camp, his armor-clad body lying regally on a bier of black pine heavy with pitch. Melia, Kratos, and Eurymedon, the king's surviving children, touched their smoking torches to the tinder, and fire crawled relentlessly up the stack. When the fierce flames ignited the olive oil–soaked bier and black smoke billowed into the clear morning air, Melia raised her arms and began a quiet, sad song. Kratos, the burly warrior, added his own tuneless rumble, and then Eurymedon with his melodious tenor joined in. After a few minutes, Rhodia stepped up behind Melia in a slow, weaving dance around the pyre as they sang.

Throughout the camp, their dirge spread among the thousands of soldiers kneeling in sorrow, watching the fire reaching into the sky, their spears like a barren forest spreading as far as the eye could see. The hundred female warriors called the Meliae, in black with their curious crossbows slung across their backs, encircled the pyre, slowly dancing in the opposite direction, adding their soft voices full of passion and grief. Tears streamed down their battle-hardened cheeks.

Melia's clear voice floated over the assembly, as befitted a priestess, blending with the crackling of the fire. Her voice undulated as the flames gained and fell back, gained and fell back, growing louder and louder, until the flames were white-hot and the song powered over them.

Former US Army Ranger Charles Shelby, called Icarus by Phorbus and his people because these archaic Greek speakers

7

could not pronounce the "ch" or "sh" of his name, stood silently at attention outside the circle of Meliae, facing the pyre. He had seen a lot of death in his time, much of it caused by him, but the somber majesty of these final respects for the legend-worthy king moved him deeply.

From time to time, he would execute a sharp right or left face, march twenty paces, stomp his foot, do an about-face, and march back. Like so many others, as a young recruit he had day-dreamed of serving as a sentinel in the honor guard at the Tomb of the Unknowns in Arlington, and he imitated the sentinel watch now. But he would never see Arlington or the Tomb again. At least he hoped he wouldn't. By some fate he vaguely understood, the mysterious intervention of this people's goddess wrenched him from time's boring logic—in the twenty-first century—and brought him here, four thousand years into the past to a purpose and a destiny that mystified him.

But here he was, marching a path of sorrow before the pyre of the greatest leader he had ever known. Intimately known and loved and by his people and honored above all others, King Phor-bus was a soldier unknown to history.

By sunset, it was over. Nothing remained of the body or the pyre but gold-vermillion coals smoldering in the cool autumn air amid beds of ashes and one blackened finger of wood pointing toward the evening sky. Phorbus was gone. His armor was gone. His sword was gone. The legend of his life had drifted skyward in the fading sparks of the fire.

His children took one final look upward, following the flight of his story drifting into ever thinner smoke. Then they turned and walked hand in hand back to the large tent, their heads bowed and hooded in their grief. No one spoke, no one wailed, for death, like life, was the gift of their goddess, and to wail would be to insult her gift. But their sorrow was deep, and its tears carved their furrowed faces.

The thousands of city soldiers filed slowly by the smoking pyre, each bringing a stone to pile on the ashes. Some brought stones the size of bowling balls, while others, moved more deeply by love and respect, struggled under stones of enormous weight. By twilight, a tumulus had risen over the dead king's ashes, and the camp had fallen silent for a night of quiet mourning. It was over. Phorbus's smoke, his last earthly form, had drifted on the evening breeze across the battlefields toward the distant city, blending with the smoke of the solitary altar still burning before the goddess's idol on its acropolis.

The summer was slipping away like the drifting smoke and the darkening day. The night air wafting from the surrounding high hills and cliffs chilled the burly arms of the soldiers cooking their meager dinners around small campfires. Behind their camp, glowing in the lavender evening, the grain stood ripe for harvest, the grapes ready for picking and crushing. Though the Achaean invaders could be seen by the pale gray pollution of their fires just a mile north, the city's outnumbered defenders hoped this pesky war would end soon so the more important work of salvaging a year's worth of food could begin. The longer the barbaric Achaeans remained, the more likely they would steal the crops and burn what they could not eat. This night, the soldiers would rest and weep, and at dawn they would begin the final, brutal work of sweeping the Achaean vermin from their valley, land their ancestors had inhabited and farmed for a thousand years.

Then they would migrate. The earthquake had wrecked their peerless city, released poisonous gas into its streets, and the population had fled south, away from battle and buildings too dangerous to inhabit. The soldiers would demolish the northern heathen invaders, then reap, then follow their wives and children laden with the riches of the earth to begin their lives anew in some peaceful place to which their goddess would lead them, a land not wracked by earthquake nor invaded by bloodthirsty bandits.

In the glowing west, the constellation Scorpio pursued the setting sun. Its red heart, Antares, the "not-Ares" star, the "anti-Mars," throbbed in pursuit of Helios. In a few weeks, the scorpion's claws would close around the sun god, and the year's light would begin to fade into winter, bringing cold rain. They must reap the crops before the rains began or the damp weather would bog down the scything and make threshing impossible. Like the pyre, their time was burning out.

TWO

"**A**lcestis," said Dolios, the slave boy who belonged to Shelby, "where is Melia?" He sat down with the younger girl in front of the big tent, near the fire, and shared his blanket with her. As a slave, she was naked but for a gold collar. He wore a slave's collar too, but Shelby insisted he also wear clothes. He was the only slave of the thousands belonging to the city who wore clothes.

"Did you not see her up at the altar, sacrificing to our goddess?" she asked.

"She's still up there? She's been gone a long time."

"I just came down the hill. When I left, she was still in her trance. Some older women are with her, and a group of the Meliae."

She shivered a little. "Thanks for letting me share your blanket," she added, keeping her eyes on the fire.

"The Meliae are good warriors," he said, moving closer to her to share their body heat. "I didn't see them at the citadel when they rescued Phorbus, but I heard them tell about it. They killed hundreds of Achaeans with those bows of theirs. When they ran out of bolts, they picked up Achaean arrows and fired those. It was quite a slaughter. Then they dropped the whole mountain on top of the Achaean reinforcements."

"Exciting," she said without enthusiasm.

The two watched the logs shift in the campfire. She spread the blanket a little to catch more of the heat from the fire.

"They look like warriors, now, not like the girls they were

when they left," she said. "You can see the veins sticking out over their muscles. No fat on them at all. It's not natural."

Dolios nodded. "They scare me," he said, staring ahead. Alcestis looked at him. "Why?"

"Because of the things I've seen them do. It makes me uneasy to be around them. I mean, I trust them, but then I don't trust them."

"Girls can be mean, Dolios," she said. "They might look all sweet and soft, but they can be deadly."

"When men fight, they bluster and yell and try to scare the other fellow into giving up," Dolios said. "It's always personal. But with the Meliae, they just kill. No passion, no caring. It's not even a triumph for them. It's just something they do, like sweeping the litter out of a tent. Kill a few dozen Achaeans, then sit down to breakfast as if nothing has happened. I tell you, it's scary."

"Not so scary if you understand women," Alcestis said. "Women don't think about things the way men do. For a woman, a threat is a threat, not a challenge. We don't care about the challenge, only about getting rid of the threat."

"I wish I could believe you," he said, "but sometimes they take real delight in killing, too. Sometimes it's all business, but then sometimes they seem to enjoy it."

"You say they kill without passion as if it were a normal thing like sweeping a tent, and then you tell me they enjoy it. Which is it?"

"See, that's what scares me. I can't tell from one minute to the next. One minute they're emptying the trash, and the next they're laughing and having fun while they gut Achaeans and throw their bodies onto a fire. I don't get it."

"How old are you Dolios?"

"I'm about fifteen harvests. Why? How old are you?"

"I'm fourteen harvests, but I think I have more experience than you."

The logs shifted again, and a new set of sparks twisted into the air.

"Have you been crying?" Dolios asked.

"Yes." She wiped her eyes. "I miss Phorbus, and my family, and the city."

"But you're a slave, like me."

12

"I still have a family. I worked at the palace as a slave. My father promised to buy me back when I'd learned enough, and my mother was to let me marry to one of her friend's sons. But now the city is empty, my family is gone, and here we are in the middle of this camp. I don't see life ever going back to how it was before."

"It won't."

"When Phorbus returned, we were so happy, because it meant we could go back to the city and to being civilized again. Get out of these dirty fields and have baths and food. But now he's dead, and the warm stones of his burial mound grow cold in the night, and Melia is withdrawn and silently mourns her father. Everyone is so sad about his murder. And we don't know what's going to happen. And the Meliae's behavior seems so unlike who we were as a people. Everything has shifted, like in the earthquake. Everything is changed."

"Maybe you should sleep with me tonight. I could protect you if the Achaeans attack."

"You? Protect me?"

Her incredulity wounded him. "Just a thought," he said. "Icarus is teaching me how to be a warrior."

"But I thought you were working with Hestia, learning to become a craft master."

"I am. She's teaching me all her tricks with metal, and we're making a new weapon that no one is supposed to know about."

"That big log with a sling? Everyone has seen that. What's secret about it?"

"How it works and what it can do. You'll see."

Alcestis stood up and got more logs for the campfire. Two soldiers on the far side of the fire, red-eyed with grieving, nodded at her appreciatively.

"Whose slave are you now?" Dolios asked when she sat back down next to him. "Are you still working in the kitchens?"

"That's where I worked in the city. It's all mixed up out here. No kitchens, really, though we have cooks. No laundry, but lots of clothes washing. I have plenty of work and stay busy, so no one seems to notice. I think I'm everybody's slave."

"Icarus needs a slave girl now that Ino's dead."

"Were you there when they found her in that big jar of olive oil?"

"I'm the one who saw her first. Icarus moved the lid, but it was too dark to see inside. Then I held up the light, and there she was, staring up through the oil."

Alcestis shuddered. "How awful." She blinked away a tear.

"It's been a hard time," Dolios said, reaching a hand over to hers and clasping it with a friendly squeeze.

She shook off his hand and looked away. "Do you think Icarus would have me?"

"I think the choice is up to Melia," he said. "She is in charge of the slaves. I don't know if she has time to think about it."

"I guess that's settled then." She sat still as a stone for a few more minutes, then shrugged out of the blanket and stood up. "I'm going in," she said, and she disappeared through the flaps of the tent.

D espite her grief at the loss of her father, after a few weeks Melia discovered it had become easier to slip into a trance as she prayed in front of the midnight sacrifice. The fragrant smoke of roasting meat billowed upward, and the crackling fat was the only sound disturbing the dead night. She bowed her head to the bare earth before the stack of stones that served as an altar, her arms spread out toward the palm-sized golden idol that belonged to her mother, the seated goddess with her arms crossed beneath her breasts.

Images began rushing into her mind. At first one by one, and then by twos, and then in multitudes as the earth in its secret passion opened its heart. She saw her mother, Metis, embracing Phorbus with her little sister, Kalista, clinging to his hand. She saw her brothers Ophion and Iapetus locked in combat, but Ophion was smiling at Phorbus as though to say, "Look father, I caught him and will never let him go!" And then so many others thronged around her dead family, acknowledging her, speaking to her of their fears and hopes—and then of her own. She could not hear them, but she could read their lips.

In a silent arc behind her stood twenty of the Meliae in their black uniforms, nearly invisible against the night. Their crossbows were held ready in their arms. They were prepared to intercept an ambush, if the Achaeans dared.

But the Achaeans did not dare. Nor did the golden jackals, native to that part of Europe, nor the bears, nor the wolves, although in their lairs the predatory beasts must have smelled the blood of the sacrifice.

Sometimes Melia's trances were brief, and sometimes they lasted all night. The Meliae would wait for her, no matter how long it took. They were under no illusions about the threat of the filthy, barbaric Achaeans from the north. Even here, a mile away, they could smell their enemy's encampment, the rank odor of dirty men and maggot-infested meat buzzing with flies. "See a fly? Expect an Achaean." It was a saying as old as their valley, and they had never known it to be wrong.

These women warriors had been trained and honed by Shelby into a dangerous guerilla force. Working with Hestia and the other crafters, he had designed the intricate compound cross-bows they carried. The bolts were single-cast bronze shafts with blood gutters down the side that penetrated Achaean armor and shields. No other warriors in the world had such weapons.

On the battlefield, no one was safe from the Meliae. Achaeans were still a threat because Shelby had managed to train only a hundred of the women warriors, and the crafters had only pro-duced an equal number of crossbows. They were wracked trying to keep up the supply of more traditional weapons for the many thousands of city troops already in the field. You could see smoke and hear the hammering from the forges for miles. During active warfare, the forges and crafters had no time to produce more crossbows.

But there was no hammering while Melia was in her trance. Noise might distract their goddess, and then Melia would not have the visions that allowed her to see into the future to lead them. Everyone in the camp respected her need for silence and waited with bated breath for it to end.

* * *

Shelby was sitting in the big tent with Eurymedon and Kratos, but they were poor company even two weeks after the funeral. By this time of night, the two brothers were thoroughly drunk and weeping silently into their goblets. It was appropriate, Shelby thought, to send off their father this way, but it was not getting the war won. The enemy were encamped close enough for midnight forays despite a battlefield still littered with dead warriors from the preceding days. Unless both sides called a truce to clean up their dead, the ground would become fouler than ever by the following afternoon.

He reflected that it would have been only a matter of time for Phorbus, anyway. The king had lost the will to live after he learned that his son Iapetus had murdered his own mother and sister, throwing their still-struggling bodies onto the burning altar on the acropolis. Phorbus's sadness had been palpable, weighty, dragging on him. The assassin who had crept into his room likely had done him a favor by shortening his grief, reuniting him with Metis at the underground pool of the dead.

Shelby rose and put a hand on each brother's shoulder in turn, then left the tent silently. He passed Dolios sitting alone by the campfire, signaled him to follow, and made his way up the hill to where his wife, Melia, had erected her altar within distant view of the sacred city. She was still there, motionless, her head bowed to the earth and her arms outstretched. He stood for a time watching her, then went forward through the arc of Meliae and knelt behind her. In the chilly midnight air, he drew the tattered lion skin he wore closer around him. It was warm in the tawny fur as he waited on the praying Melia and watched the great wheel of stars wandering toward the western marches of the sky. Three paces behind, Dolios knelt with his head bowed, the blanket over his shoulders.

Melia began heaving and sobbing, and then she gradually drew herself up, backing out of her trance, tearing herself away from the enigma of the divine. To leave too soon was death; to stay too long was death. Yet who could tell the difference between life and death in the presence of the immortal?

Witnessing Melia's agony as she regained the present world, Shelby wished it were easier for her. He helped her to her feet. Her sweaty face was ashen and drawn, and her hair was bedraggled from her struggle. She was groggy but alert, exhausted but refreshed, dead but alive, and partly divine herself. Shelby was familiar with this daily ritual, and he silently helped her as she regained control of her body and moved back into reality, brushing the dirt from her forehead and nose. Normally beautiful and radiant, her face was drawn and ashen.

The Meliae, silent and fatal, gathered around them as they walked, and the attendants rushed to section the smoking carcass and turn the pieces of meat while they were still edible.

After some twenty paces, Melia spoke. "I saw the birth of fire," she said. "I saw its womb, hotter than a forge, brighter than the sun. It destroyed everything in its path."

She shuddered and gripped Shelby's arm more tightly. "It is coming at us," she whispered. "Let us put the Achaeans between us and the coming fire."

Shelby held his tongue. He knew from experience that she would start making more sense in a few minutes.

Judging by the stars, it was well after midnight. They walked back down the hill, gradually losing sight of the moonlit valley, the ancient but ruined walled city, and in its middle, the white speck of the temple on its acropolis.

She shuddered again and shifted her grip. "I do not know how long we have," she said, her voice almost normal. "Our goddess doesn't pay much attention to time."

"That's the way of these eternals," he replied. "Time means nothing to them."

"All I know is that the whole valley will be devastated. I don't know if it will be tonight or tomorrow or a thousand harvests from now. Only that it will become a burning cauldron. Many people will die. We may not, if we heed the warning. I've never seen anything like this." She wiped her hand over her face. "I've never known her so angry. The assassination of my father has enraged her even more than the death of Metis. None of us are safe."

"It's hard to flee from a god," he said.

"Her anger makes sense," she replied, "after all that has happened. This is no longer a safe place. Our memories of these events will curse it forever. She's right. Only purifying fire can cleanse those horrors."

"I wish I thought it would be easy for our armies to slip away," Shelby said, "to disappear over these high hills into the west, but that takes time and makes noise."

"I'm done grieving for father and mother and Kalista, and yes, for Ophion, and even for Iapetus. I'm done. We have new perils. Let's eat something and then begin moving our baggage into the hills. Tomorrow we will fight a defensive battle while some of the troops harvest the fields at our back and gather what grapes they can."

"Dolios," Shelby said, "run ahead and prepare a meal for us. Then send Hestia to me. I will rouse Eurymedon and Kratos, and by dawn I expect to see wagons heading west."

"In an eye blink," said Dolios and sprinted away.

"He's a good kid, but he thinks I need a slave girl to help with my clothes and bathing, and he's found one for me."

"He has, has he?" Melia sounded amused, fully recovered from the ordeal of her vision. "More like he's found one for himself and wants you to be his excuse."

"Maybe. Her name is Alcestis, and she's fourteen, he thinks. From what he tells me, she's not specialized in anything but has skills."

Melia leaned in close to him, sniffing. "She would need to be able to clean those clothes," she said. "I like the Icarus smell, but you reek of battle."

"It may be this lion skin. I've been wearing it into battle nonstop for about three months. It's been rained on, dragged through dirt and mud, and splattered with blood and guts. I've done what I can to brush it off, but it's getting old."

"Yes, it's the skin, but it's also those strange clothes of yours. What do you call them? A tee-shirt? What is that supposed to mean? Tee-shirt. 'Tee' as in 'tau'? Why not a tau-shirt?"

He was glad to see that she had recovered some of her good humor. They went on toward the big tent, murmuring and joking with one another while the silent Meliae followed, deadly as black mambas and silent as shadows.

FOUR

T he day dawned at last, finding Shelby standing on the earthwork that guarded the city camp from the Achaeans. He
did not see any movement in their camp and suspected
they would be happy for another day off. As he debated giving
it to them, the clinking of a wagon distracted him. Hestia and
Dolios came into view with a load of bronze weapons, most bent
or broken.

"Ah!" he said when they were in earshot. "There you two are."

The old woman grinned up at him through the wrinkled road-
map of her face. "Good morning, Icarus. Thank you for loaning
Dolios to me. We have been gathering old weapons to melt down.
It saves a world of trouble when we do not have to dig the copper
and tin ourselves."

"Good morning, Hestia. And good morning, Dolios. You have
been busy."

"A full load, as you can see," she said. Most of this Achaean
metal is cheap stuff. Not much tin. But costly. It cost men's lives."

"Do you have tin to add to it?"

"We have a store of tin, but by the time we melt all this down
we will not need to add much. Then it's just a matter of pouring
out and waiting for it to cool."

The two mules pulling the wagon slowed of their own accord
as they drew closer. Shelby suspected they did not like the scent
of the lion skin.

"Did Dolios tell you that we will begin moving west this

evening? You will need to pack up all your tools today. You may not have time for much casting."

"The workers have the furnaces going already, see?" Hestia pointed to the heavy smoke plumes at the rear of the camp. "These will be melted down before noon, then cast. While I wait on the melt, I'll direct the packing. We'll be ready to move by nightfall."

"Melia warns that fire will be born in the valley and destroy all in its path. But she doesn't know when. It could happen today, tonight, or next year. Pack your most important tools first. You might need to leave in a hurry."

"I understand, Icarus," she said.

Dolios hopped down as the wagon rumbled past, the mules skittish but obedient.

"Did you ask her?" Dolios scrambled to the top of the earthwork to stand with Shelby.

"She agrees that somebody needs to do a better job of keeping me clean and getting the stink out of this lion skin. But she believes you have an ulterior motive for Alcestis."

"What's a, uh, 'terior' motive?"

Shelby began walking toward the big tent. "She thinks that maybe you want to have Alcestis around so you'll have a friend and also so you won't have so much to do."

"I try to be friends with Alcestis, it's true," the boy said, "but she doesn't want to be friends with me. Or with anybody, I guess." They heard Kratos's deep voice as he bawled at his men to pack up.

"I wonder if Eurymedon has aroused yet," Shelby said.

"He was up before I was," Dolios said. "He has his cavalry already packed and ready to move out. He's just waiting on the word."

"Go and find him. I'm going to speak with Melia about convening a council. It's not wise to put off acting on her visions."

"Yes, master," Dolios said and hurried away.

"If you see Kratos on your way," Shelby called after him, "send him to me."

In the tent, he found Melia talking quietly to a thin teenage female. The girl was kneeling in front of her, head bowed, her hands folded in her lap. Shelby did not think she was at all attractive, with her long angular face and narrow nose. Though he could not see her body, he assumed the thin arms and legs would be attached to an equally thin trunk, and her breasts were barely breasts at all.

"Ah, Shelby," Melia said when she saw him. "Just in time. Alcestis here says she wants to be your slave girl. I don't know this girl well, and I might have chosen someone else. But here she is. This is a good time for me to teach you a lesson about choosing slaves."

Shelby didn't like her tone. It was hard-edged, superior, judgmental. He suspected that she was not happy to be interviewing a female slave to take care of him. Her voice made him uneasy, and it was having a similar effect on the trembling girl.

"Actually," Melia continued, "I've been waiting for you. You brought it up, so you get to go through this. Just so you'll know."

"I'm not sure that's a good idea," he said. "I have some important business to do if we are going to break camp."

"Sit down and observe!" Melia said. "First, Alcestis, show me your left hand."

The girl held out her left hand. It was trembling.

"You always examine their left hands first. Do you know why?"

Shelby shook his head.

"I thought not. You examine their left hands first because those are the hands they clean themselves with." To the girl, "Turn it over and spread your fingers."

She leaned forward to examine the hand, smelled it, and then turned it over again and inspected the nails. Satisfied, she sat back up.

"Rule number one," she said. "You do not want a slave who does not know how to clean herself."

"Thank you for this instruction. I think I should leave."

"No. Stay and learn. Alcestis, stand up."

Shelby was right, he saw. No hips, a long flat waist, almost no pubic hair. A pointy chin. A thin face with tiny, thin lips, high cheekbones, little eyes set close together, thin lashes, untended eyebrows, straight bobbed hair of an indistinct brown. She was still a girl, and not the beauty that Ino had been. But then beautiful Ino had a lover who turned out to be fatal to her and to many others. To the whole city.

"Is this the girl you want serving you?" Melia asked.

"It's your choice," he said. "Only if you think I need someone." Melia grunted. "Alcestis, go and stand in front of Shelby!"

She did.

"Turn around and bend over," Melia said. "Put your hands on your knees. Shelby, spread her and tell me what you see."

"I don't need to spread her. I can see fine."

"Touch the girl, Shelby, and spread her and tell me what you see."

"She looks clean to me."

"Right then," Melia said. "Alcestis, lie on your back on this rug and lift your knees but keep your feet on the ground."

"What now?" Shelby asked, increasingly resentful of the procedure and the manner in which she was carrying it out.

"Watch and learn," Melia said, spreading the girl's legs. She pushed them up until the girl's knees were even with her hips, then pressed the knees against the floor. Alcestis had to be incredibly limber to take it.

"That's a start," Melia said, running her eyes over the girl's body. "I bet you never tried this with Ino, did you," she said. "She might have surprised you if you had. She could do it too. All young women slaves take stretching instruction to keep them limber."

Shelby felt his face reddening and saw her eyes twinkling. Still holding her down, Melia began to question Alcestis about her sexual experiences. When the girl protested that she had never had sex, Melia deftly reached down and spread her labia, holding a lamp nearby to take a look.

"Hmmm," she said, "it looks like you're telling the truth. How did a slave girl of fourteen harvests remain a virgin?"

She sat back on her heels and pulled the girl's legs down, then reached down to take her by the hand and help her to sit up.

Scarlet with embarrassment, Alcestis dropped her head. "I don't know, my lady," she whispered. "Just lucky, I suppose. I think people don't notice me."

"I could make a lot of money selling you to the Achaeans," Melia said.

"Oh please," cried the girl. "Not that! Please not that!"

Melia patted her hand. "I'm only teasing. But don't worry. We buy women slaves from the Achaeans; we don't sell them."

"Shelby," Melia said as she lifted the girl's head and turned her face side to side. She parted the girl's lips and looked into her mouth. "Do you want her?"

"What do you think?"

"I think she could help Dolios take better care of you. Maybe. You've been giving Dolios to Hestia, and he was already out of his depth caring for you. But I also think she would cause Dolios trouble."

"Oh no, lady," said the girl. "I don't care for Dolios."

"Oh?"

"No, my lady. My father promised to buy me back when I had learned enough, and mother wants me to marry someone she has in mind, if I like him. But I don't know where my parents are."

"Does Dolios know this?"

"I told him."

"And he still suggested you to Shelby? That's interesting. What do you think, Shelby?"

"I think you and I should talk about it later," he said, studying her. "I need your advice."

"Ah, good answer, Lion," she said, smiling. "A good answer indeed. Alcestis, you may go. You've passed the inspection, and I will let you know what we decide."

He liked that she had said "we." That was a positive sign. And he suspected that they would be so busy in the next few days that all question of assigning the skinny girl-child to him would be forgotten. Still, now that she'd mentioned it, he was sure he could smell the rotten odor of the lion skin and the foul stench of his poorly washed clothes. Maybe the girl would be a help.

FIVE

A round midmorning, the clashing of drums and loud cries of men began in the Achaean camp. Thousands of soldiers beat their shields with their swords as they streamed out onto the plain. Two prongs of chariots swept around the mass on either side, arraying themselves for a charge, and the army began moving toward the city's camp, calling and threatening.

Shelby's troops were ready. They left off their packing and took up position on their earthworks. An archer stood between every armored foot soldier, arrow notched. When the Achaeans charged, they would have first shot, then step out of the way as the armored foot soldiers rushed onto the field. The armies were evenly matched in numbers, but the city troops averaged eight to ten inches shorter and fifty to seventy pounds lighter. No one in their civilization was much taller than five feet, so their survival depended on discipline, tactics, and unity.

When the Achaeans had closed within a hundred yards, they stopped, and the chariots wheeled around in front of the mass of men. Then the displays started. First one chariot and then another would approach the camp of city troops, and its fighter, its "hero," would taunt them and dare them to come out against him, one to one. As the morning wore on with no response, these taunts grew more vicious and the so-called heroes approached closer and closer to the earthworks. Shelby felt the tension in his men up and down the line, but he was proud of them for restraining them-selves, for waiting for the command to move out.

Meanwhile, unseen by the Achaeans, Hestia had wheeled the new weapons—four trebuchets—into position. They were loaded and ready to fire on command. She had then returned to supervising the casting of the recovered bronze into swords and spear points and to packing up her workshops. They would sharpen the new swords that night, after they crested the first of the western hills.

When the sun was at high noon, Shelby mounted the earthwork in his lion's skin, his head crowned with the crystal-eyed lion helmet. In his right hand, he held the RMJ Shrike tomahawk he had brought from the twenty-first century. Under the skin, he wore the modern Kevlar body armor he'd also brought, which his own troops had not seen. It had proven useful in the past, deterring swords and spears and deflecting arrows.

The enemy Achaeans spotted him standing high on the breastworks, daring them all, and surged forward, pushing the chariots closer to the camp, diminishing their maneuvering room. Shelby appreciated the lack of discipline that threatened to bog down the chariots. It would make his job easier.

One of the chariots came within thirty feet of him, and its hero began his tirade, threatening and sticking out his chest, spitting, and patting his rump. He became increasingly infuriated as Shelby silently watched him. With deliberate insult, Shelby yawned.

"Come down here and fight me like a man," the Achaean yelled. "You're no lion. You're a coward." He turned to his army. "This lion is a coward!" he shouted. "They're all cowards. Don't you see?"

He whirled around and threw his spear. Shelby saw the cocked arm and watched the flight of the weapon. He moved sideways half a step and caught the spear in his left hand. He held it up for his troops to see, and they broke out in great laughter and cheers. He then snapped the spear across his knee.

At his feet, prone on the breastwork, a hundred Meliae with their deadly crossbows were hidden to either side of him. He nudged Rhodia, their leader, with his foot. She shot the hero dead with a bolt to the head, and another cheer erupted. Shelby raised his tomahawk high and then dropped it, and the four trebuchets fired their massive stones into the Achaean army. With bloodcurdling cries, the first of the city troops stormed over the earthwork and down into the field, where they assembled into a phalanx formation. The group behind them assembled into Kratos's dodecas, the deadly fighting squares with twelve men to a side.

From the cover of the hills to the west, Eurymedon's cavalry swept down with shouts toward the Achaean rear, unleashing deadly barrages of arrows. The Achaeans responded with their own arrow volley, and the sky darkened with stones from slings and javelins and discuses thrown from both sides. Another hurl of the trebuchets sent two-hundred-pound boulders smashing into the Achaeans, splattering their blood across the yielding earth. Then the trebuchet artillery changed to collections of ten-pound stones that scattered like grapeshot farther and faster as the Achaeans surged forward.

The dodecas moved into position, and the phalanx fell back to protect their rear. As the dodecas attacked, Achaeans toward the back hurled thousands of small jars filled with flaming oil. The city's troops had advanced too far into the battlefield for the trebuchets to fire without endangering them. The flaming oil broke the ranks of the dodecas, and the city's warriors scattered, trying to wipe the oily flames from their burning hair and bodies.

For every dodeca that scattered in the flames, a hundred or more of Shelby's troops were cut down by the physically larger Achaeans. The slaughter gave the barbarians heart and spurred them on, bloodlust inflaming their rage. For the first time, it looked as though they would win a battle against the city's army. They regained the ground they had lost and surged in their screaming masses toward the last line of defense, the earthwork upon which Shelby stood. Advancing at a run, they overwhelmed the city's infantry, destroying what remained of Shelby's united fighting groups. Soon it was every man for himself, and the city's troops scrambled to regain the relative safety of the earthwork.

The Achaean chariots wheeled out of the way to either side of the battle as the armies clashed head-on. With Shelby's troops routed, those chariots attacked the flanks of the fleeing soldiers, mowing them down.

Eurymedon's cavalry galloped toward the Achaean rear, his fury driving the enemies harder toward the city's emplacement, despite the many who fell from his archers.

Dangerously low on arrows, he moved his cavalry to the left flank of battle and attacked the chariots. It was a desperate move and deadly to both sides. The mounted warrior had to ride up on a chariot and leap to the moving platform to engage the fully armored Achaean with his charioteer and spear bearer in hand-to-hand fighting. Sometimes they missed and were trampled by chariots coming toward them. Sometimes their legs were caught by the tall moving wheels, and many were speared as they leapt.

Eurymedon raced his horse through the charging chariots until he spotted the Achaean warrior who appeared to be the leader. Crouching on the back of his galloping horse, he thundered behind the chariot. He timed his stallion's speed and then flashed through the air, hitting the chariot's hero on his back. Slashing downward with his bronze sword, he severed the Achaean's spear hand, and blood spurted over the charioteer's legs. The huge man pulled Eurymedon off his back with his remaining hand, and the spear carrier, standing to the hero's left, thrust a spear at him, slicing his left side. In the tangle of bodies and mess of blood in the speeding chariot, Eurymedon lost his footing, falling against the chariot's right side. The Achaean hero struck him with the stump of his right arm, blinding him with blood and knocking him backward off the bouncing chariot into the path of others rushing toward him. The momentum of the chariot prevented him from regaining his footing, and he rolled and tumbled across the battleground. A chariot's bronze-bound wheel missed his head by half an inch. And then he was up, clutching his side and gasping as he watched another chariot bearing down on him.

His cavalry had followed him into the charge, and one of his riders leapt onto the lead horse and reined it aside while two more gained the floor of the chariot and engaged the Achaeans. Eurymedon had been saved for the moment, and the moment was all he needed. He jumped onto the back of the nearest Achaean horse. Using his uninjured arm, Eurymedon hacked the horse free from its harness, and urged it on, away from its two companions and up the low hill of the camp's earthwork. His cavalry followed as the trebuchets resumed their barrage against the Achaean hordes.

Many brave soldiers from the city died in these daring maneuvers, but it turned the tide of the chariot onslaught and gave the survivors time to regain the earthwork, to rally and defend. It was the deadliest day of fighting the war had seen. Thousands lay wounded or dead on the field.

During the last desperate attack against Shelby's retreating city troops, the Achaean ranks fired a barrage of missiles. A discus caught Shelby on the side of the head, and he went down on one knee, and then fell over Rhodia, unconscious. Squirming to get onto all fours beneath him, she bore him to shelter at the base of a towering ash tree nearby.

"Dolios," she gasped, "get a healer. Get Melia. We must stay on the barricade to protect the camp." She ran to her position on the earthwork as the slave boy sprinted away, returning moments later with a healer. Dolios adjusted Shelby's head inside the lion's skull that served as his helmet, picking bone fragments out of his scalp as the healer went quickly over his body.

"Get cold water, wash his face," the healer said. "He will recover or not, but I cannot help him. He's not pale, not bleeding. It's all in his brain." She hurried away to tend to other injuries.

Melia came moments later, carrying the blue bottle of magical salve, a gift from the goddess that Shelby had brought back from the labyrinth on his trip through from the twenty-first century. She knelt over him, listened to his slow but steady breathing, and kissed him on the forehead. His mouth fell open, but his eyelids did not flicker.

"Stay here and protect Icarus," she said to Dolios. "I will send others. I will check on him again when I can. I heard that Eurymedon was wounded also." She hurried off through the mass of retreating soldiers scrambling over the barricade, their panicked shouts blending with the buzz of stones hurling through the air from the trebuchets and the higher pitch of whizzing arrows and javelins.

SIX

K ratos, five feet one and two hundred pounds of solid muscle, knelt next to Shelby and rubbed his friend's shoulder. For the first time in his life, Kratos had not enjoyed a day of battle. It had been an awful day, full of reverses. The Achaeans had routed the city troops, something they had never done. He expected the trebuchets to turn the tide against the Achaeans and send them scattering, but the Achaeans had come on more strongly with an innovation of their own. Where had they gotten all that oil and those little, fragile jars? How had they set the oil afire and kept it lit? Kratos hoped Shelby would soon wake up and help him figure out what to do.

Dolios brought wine and fresh bread and knelt next to them. The fighting was over for the day, the Achaeans gone back to their own camp dragging some of their wounded companions with them, but the wailing of dying men was incessant beyond the earthen barricade, a fading opera of anguish and pain blending with the songs of scavenging jackals and the distant howling of wolves.

Although a slave, Dolios had learned from Shelby that he could speak before spoken to, and even ask questions. "It's important to learn," Shelby told him. It had taken little effort to get out of the slave's habit of being invisible and silent.

"What happened out there?" he asked Kratos.

Kratos looked off to the top of the barricade and then around at the tree line. He pulled off his helmet and shook his bushy red hair and beard, slinging a shower of sweat. Once again Dolios was reminded of the man's huge strength, shoulders so muscled that he had almost no neck.

"They threw fire on the dodecas," Kratos said. "Under our shields, we were protected from their rocks and arrows, but not from fire."

"Why not?" Dolios asked.

"It dripped through the roof of the shields and set the men on fire. The shields became too hot to hold. Then their chariots rode us down."

"What are you going to do?"

"I don't know. We can go back to using the phalanx alone, but it is not as effective."

It was not Dolios's place to make suggestions, but part of the solution seemed obvious. The woods were full of cork trees. Some of the soldiers wore helmets made out of cork. If his master's helmet had been lined with cork, he might not be lying here unconscious. Cork would have absorbed the discus blow, and it would have insulated the dodecas. But the burning oil could still drip over the sides of the shields and scorch their bodies. He wondered how they would solve that problem.

Shelby began to moan. His eyelids flickered but did not open. "He was hit badly," Kratos said. "A discus?"

"I only saw him fall over Rhodia," Dolios replied. "She crawled here on all fours with him on her back."

"She's a tough one," Kratos said. "I like that." He got a far-away look in his eyes and began grinding his teeth as he pondered, his thick, blood-splattered red beard working side to side. He finished the jug and threw it against a nearby tree trunk, shattering it.

"Where's Hestia?" he asked.

"She's moving her workshops west," Dolios said. "Icarus told her to be moved by tonight."

"You're working with her now, aren't you?"

"Yes," said Dolios. "I think master believes I will be more useful as a crafter than as a soldier. He says that I'm smart enough, but that I'm not strong enough. I'd like being a soldier, though," he added hastily, seeing Kratos's glance.

"We have many soldiers," Kratos said gruffly, "and many

laborers in the workshops, but we do not have too many crafters. Who knows? You might be better at it even than Hestia. Apprenticing you to Hestia was a kind thing for Icarus to do for you. Make the most of it."

Shelby stirred again, sat up, and vomited. He groaned and lay back with a sigh, his eyes closed, his hands clutching his head. "Who's there?" he asked, his eyes closed. "Jesus, my head hurts."

"Kratos and I are here with you, master," Dolios said, bending low over him to wash his face with cold water. "We think you were hit by a discus. Your lion's helmet was smashed."

"Oh!" Shelby kept his closed.

Neither of them could tell if he had understood what he'd heard.

"I'm going to check on Eurymedon," Kratos said. "I hope Melia has enough of that magic salve stuff left to treat him. If not, he is in for a long bit of rest and healing."

"Shall I come for you when Icarus awakens?" Dolios asked.

"No need. I will come back here, and then I think we will move him into a better shelter. Night is coming on."

He moved away, followed by the six attendant guards who stuck by him everywhere he went. They had fought with Phorbus for decades, and now that the old king was gone, Kratos had inherited them. Their battlefield choreography was invaluable, and today it had kept Kratos alive. They were good at their job.

* * *

Melia used a flattened stick to dip the last of the salve from the blue Nalgene bottle. Shelby had brought the bottle from his own time and carried it through the labyrinth, where he fought the guardian, the insect-like creature that haunted the vast tunnel network. The monster punctured the bottle with its stinger, leaving some of its venom inside. With so many thousands badly wounded, the bottle was almost empty.

She kneeled beside Eurymedon. "They sliced some of your muscles, and I can see bone where they cut you. If I do not have enough salve to cover the entire wound, maybe I'll bind this stick to your ribs until tomorrow. It has a little salve left on it."

Eurymedon was grim, exhausted, and pale with pain. "Do

what you can, sister," he said, breathing heavily. "I will heal in time, regardless. I always do."

When she finished, the healers applied bandages to his open wounds and then washed him and dosed him with less magical concoctions of their own: opium poppy, tea made from willow bark, other herbs. Soon he was resting peacefully, and he began drifting off when Kratos entered the tent.

"Hello brother," Melia said, rising and turning to him.

Kratos embraced her, the strong clove-like odor of his manhood almost as powerful as his arms.

"How's little brother?" he asked.

"He has a nasty cut on his right side. You can see the rib bones, but his lung is not punctured. I'm more worried about the bad bruising where he tumbled from that chariot. He also took some heavy blows to the face. Overall, I don't think he's in a lot of danger, but he cannot function now."

"Will he be able to ride tomorrow?"

"We'll see what the guardian's salve does for him. He got the last drop."

"Should we send someone back into the labyrinth for more?" Kratos sat down heavily next to his snoring brother, looking at the secure bandages.

"Icarus could only have come through that labyrinth if the goddess led him, and that is a path I do not know. Not even I would be able to find the guardian again. Plus, he might have destroyed her when they fought."

"Why do you suppose our goddess placed that guardian in the labyrinth?" Kratos asked. "And why do you think Icarus was allowed to pass?"

"My guess is that the labyrinth is a gate between our world and his. Remember, he also found the black pool where the spirits of the dead reside. Metis spoke to him. She might have wanted him to travel that way to bring us mother's message."

"I guess we too will one day enter the afterlife and see our mother and father again," he said. "And Kalista."

"And Ophion."

"And Iapetus, I suppose, but I do not want to see that one again unless I can strangle him. He has caused all this trouble."

"Maybe he was only the excuse for the trouble. Our people

have lived in this valley for a thousand harvests. We built the city that was the envy of the world, we have been wealthy and well fed for ages. I hate to think that we brought all this trouble on ourselves, but we are human. Iapetus could not have been successful without help from other citizens of the city, persons who knew or who suspected him and said nothing. Remember that even before the betrayal, the worship of Zeus had been growing among our citizens."

"Do you think the Zeus worshippers were behind the treason?"

"Some of them were, certainly. But many more converted. It was just a matter of time. When people change gods, they change themselves, and we were not alert enough to those changes. We were too comfortable in our wealth and bounty."

They listened to Eurymedon's easy breathing until the twilight began to fade.

"I wonder if Icarus can move around yet," Kratos said.

Melia beckoned an attendant with a wave of her finger. "I'll send this woman to check," she said. "Perhaps we should have some men carry him back here to rest with Eurymedon. At least everyone will be in the same tent."

"Phorbus married you to Icarus just three weeks ago," Kratos said, "and you haven't had much time together yet. Perhaps you should keep him to yourself."

"What?" she exclaimed. "Spend the night with an unconscious man? I think not. I'll put him in here, and then perhaps we can talk about today's battle."

"He might not be much help," Kratos said, "and Eurymedon's not going to talk tonight."

"I'll get Rhodia in here, too," Melia said. "I want to know what happened in the field with the dodecas, and what you think we can do."

* * *

The attendant returned a few minutes later with Alcestis in tow. "He's sitting up," she said, "but his right leg is numb, and he doesn't trust standing on it. His head hurts him badly." Melia glanced at Alcestis.

"She wanted to come where you were," the attendant said.

Melia noticed the girl's goosebumps. "Sit over there and warm yourself," she said.

She turned to Kratos and said, "She's a virgin."

Kratos looked the child over. Then he looked away. Virgins were not important in a society ruled by a goddess, where fecundity was a religious duty and protected by law. "Could be valuable," he said, "but she's not very pretty. What are you going to do with her?"

A look of alarm appeared on Alcestis's face.

"I'm going to keep her with me," Melia said. "I will use her to help take care of my husband."

Kratos's ruddy face broke into a huge smile, showing all of his gapped teeth. He laughed aloud. "Keep her?" he exclaimed. "Keep her to help with Icarus?" He laughed again, until tears streamed from his eyes.

"And why, dear sister, do you want a virgin — of all people — to help you with Icarus?" He tried to control his laughter but failed. "So you will know when he sleeps with her?"

"Alcestis," Melia said with a sour look on her face, "go fetch Eurymedon's twins. Then see if you can help Dolios bring Icarus here. It's about time those Persian harlots of Eurymedon's helped with his care."

The naked girl nodded and hurried from the tent.

"I do not need a virgin to look after Icarus," Melia hissed at Kratos. "Thank you very much."

Still mirthful, Kratos knew when to concede a point and said nothing. Melia was a forceful presence and apparently not in the mood to be teased. He swallowed his laughter along with more wine and wiped the back of his hand across his mouth.

"Well, sister," he said.

"Well, brother," she replied, still cross.

They sat silently for a few minutes, until Kratos made to stand.

"Where are you going?" she asked.

"To see to the troops and to check on Hestia. I need to be sure she is well protected. We can't lose her."

"She's fine. Sit down."

Kratos, a man who killed on average twenty Achaeans every

day in hand-to-hand combat, whose tree-trunk legs could propel him vertically to the height of his head and whose hands could snap a neck, sat and waited.

"What happened?" asked Melia.

"They threw fire on the dodecas," he said. "Lots of fire. It burned our people and they could not hold their shields."

"I know that," she said. "What I want to know is why we did not know they were planning this."

"Our spies are not telling us much," Kratos replied, somber now with the tragedy of the day weighing on him again. "We had no idea they had that much oil in their camp, much less the willingness to use such a valuable food in this way."

Rhodia entered the tent and divined the conversation while taking in Eurymedon's condition. She gave Melia a questioning glance. "I heard he was very brave on the battlefield today," she said. "The soldiers are making up songs about him around their campfires."

"I'm glad to hear there's something for them to sing about," Kratos said.

Kratos's bodyguards came through the flaps of the tent, carrying Shelby on a stretcher made of spears. His lion skin, tattered and filthy, was draped over him.

"Gently," he muttered. "Put me down gently. My head is killing me."

"How is your leg?" Kratos asked.

"It tingles, like it's been asleep. So does my right arm and my whole right side. Half an ounce more force and I would have been paralyzed."

The bodyguards eased him down, and Melia sat beside him.

"Would it help for you to put your head in my lap?" she asked.

"Yes," Shelby said, "but it would help more for me to keep my eyes covered and not move."

"You were unconscious a long time." She stroked his black hair, tenderly feeling the bruised side of his head above his left ear. "This was a wound your body armor would not protect you from."

"Better padding," he said, with an effort.

After the bodyguards left, Dolios, Alcestis, and two high-breasted, dark-haired Persian twin slaves entered the tent.

They cried out when they saw Eurymedon, and crowded around him, whimpering, rubbing their breasts against him and stroking his legs. Dolios's look clearly conveyed that he thought them the most useless creatures on the planet, but Rhodia's expression was unreadable. She and Eurymedon had been lovers for many years. Though the Persians participated in that relationship, no one doubted that Rhodia would have cut off their heads in an instant.

"Now, Kratos," Melia said. "Let's talk about battle."

Shelby roused. "Battle?" he asked. He flexed his right hand and struggled into a sitting position, his eyes fully open and focused.

"No, no fighting right now," Melia said. "We want to talk about it."

Shelby looked around the tent. "Everybody out!" he ordered. "Not you, Dolios, you stay. You twins, out. Girl, out." When they had gone, he beckoned Kratos and Rhodia to move closer.

"What are you doing?" asked Rhodia.

"If we are going to discuss battle," Shelby said, "then we will discuss it only among ourselves. No one but we three will hear, and Eurymedon when he joins us again, and Dolios, whom we trust. We do not know that they are spies, but they have mouths, and they talk."

He raised a hand to his head and grimaced again. The change in blood pressure from sitting up caused his head to pound.

"Drink this," Melia said, handing him a large jug of cold water. "Dolios, go and get a healer. Now that Icarus can sit up, it's time to treat him."

"I'm glad to see you awake. How's the right hand?" Kratos asked.

"Better, brother, but still numb. I can flex it." Shelby finished off the water.

A healer stepped through the opening in the tent. "I brought willow bark tea," she said. "I added a very little drop of opium dissolved in wine. It should help his pain."

"Not too much, I hope," Melia said. "We don't need him to sleep."

"Not too much," the old woman replied. "Just enough."

The tea was bitter but warm, and it went down easily enough. Within minutes the pain abated in Shelby's head, and he became hungry. Then the hunger passed, and his brain seemed to clear.

"Tell me what happened after I was knocked down," he said to Kratos. "And then we will plan."

SEVEN

W hen the night was at its darkest, Rhodia and the hundred Meliae slipped from the city encampment. They were dressed entirely in black: black leggings, a clothing idea they had taken from Shelby's twenty-first-century shorts, black head covering that left only their eyes exposed, and black sleeves. They'd blackened their hands with powdered coal and grease. Ten feet from the earthen embankment they were invisible, and from twenty feet even their movement in the dark night could not be detected.

They stepped gingerly and silently toward the Achaean camp through the litter of the battlefield, with its severed limbs and corpses, sometimes scaring off packs of jackals. The wooden barricade of the Achaean camp was irregular, sloppy, and temporary, and they could see enemy soldiers lounging or sleeping near their campfires, some walking around, others gambling. A few were urinating.

"Looks like they don't plan to come out tomorrow," whispered Rhodia to Amalthea, her lieutenant.

Amalthea was smart, fearless, and blessed — or cursed, depending on your point of view — with massive muscles. She could have been an Olympic champion weight-lifter if she lived in Shelby's time. She alone of the Meliae was an equal match in strength and ferocity for any Achaean.

"Motherless scum," whispered Amalthea. "I could peg one through the gap in their ridiculous wicket."

"I think they put up the barricade to keep out the jackals," Rhodia said. "Not us."

The Meliae split into two groups, Amalthea leading one and Rhodia the other, circling the huge camp, observing. Rhodia was attracted to heavy smoke billowing from one part of the camp. She and the fifty warriors stayed low in the trampled grass, moving without bobbing their bodies up and down, keeping a steady, smooth path that attracted no notice, the way big cats stalk prey, the way Shelby had taught them.

* * *

The Achaean camp did not have a defined rear. Wagons and camp followers were scattered randomly, with campfires crowded by sleeping workers and soldiers. The stench of the place was increasingly revolting to the Meliae as they crept closer through the shadows. Soon they were less than fifty yards from one of the kilns, where they could see thousands of small clay jars lined up for firing. Khloe, appointed next in command to Rhodia, looked at her, telegraphing a question with her eyes. Rhodia shook her head and moved on.

Amalthea's group had also moved into the rear of the camp, where they came upon a work squad of slaves supervised by burly Achaeans with whips. They were shocked to recognize some of their own city people, their backs bare and bloody with lash marks, bent to the tasks of gathering reeds, stripping them, and cutting them into uniform lengths. Some were putting the reeds into the clay jars filled with oil that were lined up by the hundreds. One of the Meliae lifted her crossbow to take out an Achaean who was beating an old man, but Amalthea stayed her hand.

"Let's go on," she whispered. "We'll be back before the night is over."

They moved through the shadows toward the glow of large fires and the clacks of many hammers. Sneaking through the wagons they came upon a sleepy Achaean woman squatting to urinate. The woman looked up with surprise as Amalthea came into view, but one of the Meliae shot a bolt through her throat, knocking her backward onto the wet earth. She gurgled, thrashed a little, grabbing at her throat, and then lay still.

As Amalthea's group approached the center of the activity, they saw six long poles with massive, head-high wheels on each end. In the center of the poles was a modified chariot. The poles extended ten feet to either side of the chariot and were studded with fixed blades of different lengths and at various angles. Amalthea studied the contraptions from the shadows. The horses standing nearby in groups of eight appeared to be fitted with modified tack. Some had already been harnessed to chariots redesigned for only one rider, though workers continued to hammer at the rotating blades. Suddenly the meaning of the contraptions came clear to her. The Achaeans would drag these bladed poles across the battlefield, the rotating blades slicing through everyone and everything in their paths.

She doubted that the horses could be controlled, or the poles clear all the obstacles on the battlefield. Still, if it worked, it would be a powerful assault on the dodecas.

She signaled to her team to withdraw. Kratos needed to know about this right away. Only Eurymedon's cavalry would have the speed and maneuverability to defeat these rolling blades.

* * *

Two hours before dawn, the scream of horses stampeding awoke the Achaeans. Their stable hands were dead, and the horse corrals and fencing had been destroyed. Their stores of oil blazed. They next discovered that the slave teams were gone and their drivers dead and castrated, the signature of the city's women.

* * *

"Who will lead the cavalry while Eurymedon is unable to fight?" Shelby asked. He and Kratos were meeting with Amalthea and Rhodia soon after the Achaeans awoke to the chaos in their camp.

"One of the Meliae is an expert horse handler," Rhodia said. "But she has never worked with the men before."

"We need someone who understands how the men fight," Kratos said. "No one can lead who does not know that."

"Maybe we will wait for Eurymedon to awake," Shelby said.

"Maybe I will lead them," Kratos said. "They will follow me."

Shelby looked at him steadily. "Then who leads the foot?" he asked.

"You. Get your armor on," Kratos replied.

"No," Melia said, returning from the morning sacrifice. "I'm going to war. He's staying here to meet with Hestia and the others, and to rest. Tell your bodyguards to stay with me today."

EIGHT

From the tall lookout tower over the western gate of the city, Eumaeus squinted at the dust cloud generated by the departing city troops. He did not need to read the signal flags from Icarus to know what was happening. By the evening, the Achaeans would be encamped around the city, possibly even assaulting it.

A dark grin spread across the furrowed crags of his face. He was ready for them.

When he was five or six, Achaean pirates attacked and burned Eumaeus's village in Crete and took him as a slave. King Phorbus rescued him in a daring raid on the pirates' encampment at the beginning of his world tour with Amphinomus and Arktos, and the little boy went with him around the known and unknown world. Eventually, Phorbus freed him, and Eumaeus became the trusted head of the elite palace guard. Short, compact, and hard as nails, he was a professional soldier with a bitter hatred for weakness, excuses, and Achaeans. Humorless and unbending, practical and stern, what he lacked in imagination he made up for in loyalty and commitment. He was what Melia's people called an ash-hard warrior.

"Arda," he said to a nearby soldier, "run up to the acropolis altar. Tell our governing matron, Agala, it is time to put the final plan in motion. We will get everything ready for the Achaeans and meet her in the tunnels just at the moment the sun touches the western hills. Return to me with her reply."

"Yes sir," the young man responded. "Tell Agala it is time to start the final plan." He sprinted up the long exterior wall. It would have been shorter to go through the city, but the troops had learned to avoid the interior. After the earthquakes two months before, the streets were tangled with debris and still harbored pockets of deadly hydrogen sulfide gas and methane. The city was dead, and the population safely evacuated, but Eumaeus and his five hundred had kept up the appearance of occupation to fool the Achaeans.

No one could think of a more fitting end to the war than to let the Achaeans swarm in and be blown to pieces by exploding methane gas. At last, the trap was about to spring.

Eumaeus breathed deeply. At forty feet above the city streets, the air was fresh and pure. He struck his chest with his fist. "For Phorbus and the goddess," he said. "Death to the Achaeans, and life to us."

He was glad to leave the ruined, stinking, fatal city. Glad to leave behind the horror of Iapetus murdering his mother and his sister. Glad to leave behind the panic and pain and sorrow. It was time.

NINE

❦❦❦❦❦❦❦❦❦❦❦

Eurymedon rolled over on his left side and groaned. The Persian beauties stirred, and one rolled with him, spooning him, reaching her hand gently, sleepily, to his bandaged chest, drifting down over his bare stomach, its male contours and hard muscles. Then she fell back to sleep. But Eurymedon's eyes popped open, and he stretched. Outside it was full daylight, and he ached from yesterday's battle. Surprisingly, he did not ache as much as he thought he would.

"Get up!" he said, sitting up, dislodging the hand between his legs and slapping one of the women on the rump. "I need food. And water."

He made to rise and felt something shift in his wounded side. It burned, as if his skin were pulling apart. He cursed and rolled over onto all fours to push himself off the floor of the tent, straddling one of the girls. She smiled up at him brightly and reached to pull him down, but he shook his head and sat back, resting on her bare legs. His swollen penis argued with his full bladder, as it did most mornings, and the bladder was going to win. But he took a moment to enjoy the sight of the sleepy, dark-haired slave, the compelling curve of her waist and her delicious breasts. Maybe after he peed.

"Hmmm," he said. "I love how you look in the morning." He buried his hand in her dark pubic hair and turned to kiss her twin deeply. He called them Delta-one and Delta-two. Kratos sometimes kidded him that he should have named them Lambda-one and

Lambda-two because that letter looked more like spread legs. He liked the delta connotations more.

He removed the gentle hand from his penis and got up to go outside and urinate in the sunshine. It was the perfect way to start a day.

"Can't you do that in private?" Rhodia asked as she approached.

"Why?" He shook his penis at her, grinning. He and Rhodia had been friends since infancy and on-again, off-again lovers since their teens. Their lusts and temperaments matched. He knew she would ask him to marry her eventually, but he also knew that, as leader of the Meliae, she'd discovered a passion for killing men.

She snorted at him, contemptuously. "And your Deltas? Are they awake yet?" She brushed past him as she headed toward the tent flap.

"They were waking up," he said, following her in. "The camp seems in an uproar. What's happening?"

"Icarus and Kratos set a trap for the Achaeans," she said, going in to toe the slaves up. "Delta-one, get food. Delta-two, bring hot water, wine, and a healer." She too enjoyed looking at the pretty girls, and she enjoyed playing with them, but they did not much move her to tenderness or sympathy. Delta-one pouted at her, and Rhodia grabbed the girl's mouth, squeezing it, puckering the lips. She bent over and kissed her roughly, taking the girl's lips entirely into her own mouth and biting them gently. "No pouting," she said, releasing the girl's face and patting her on the cheek. "Get moving. We are packing up to leave as soon as Eurymedon's wounds are re-bandaged."

"Move?" Eurymedon asked. "Move where?"

"To Arktos's garrison in the western hills," said Rhodia. "But first we are going to trick the Achaeans. Icarus and Kratos set it up last night while you slept. Sit here while I take off your bandages. I want to see how well you healed in the night."

Eurymedon did as he was told. It did not pay to argue with Rhodia. Still, while she worked on him his hand went first to her exposed thigh and then gently to her breast, which was barely covered by her chiton.

"Stop that," she said, slapping his hand away. "We don't have time to waste."

"It's not waste," he said.

"Yes, it is," she said. "Right now, we are trying to move thousands of people west and trick the Achaeans into believing that those people are soldiers. They will think we've abandoned the battlefield."

"We got hit hard yesterday," he said.

"We lost a lot of good soldiers, and our formations broke, but we were busy last night. I think the Achaeans will learn this morning that most of their horses have scattered through the valley." She smiled grimly as she loosened the wet bandages. Eurymedon had bled freely in the night.

"Looks like the last of the guardian's healing venom didn't do you much good," she said. "Let me help you down on your side. Don't bend," she warned. "It will open up again."

"It felt fine during the night," he said, "but this morning I moved and felt a burning pain. I might have opened it up already."

The spear had caught important shoulder and back muscles, as well as laying bare a portion of his ribcage. She was surprised that he could move his right arm at all, but it was obvious he could not fight today. Those sliced muscles might take weeks to knit and regain their strength.

"You will have a bad scar," she said with mock sympathy. "Your youthful beauty has been ruined."

"Nah," he said, "they missed the important part."

"A little to either side would have killed you," she said. "It would have either punctured your lung or severed the artery in your arm. I'm glad you made it back."

"He hit me hard. Right in the side seam of my breastplate. I'm going to need new armor before I can fight again."

"You're going to need to rest and to keep from moving for at least a week. After that, we'll get you more armor. Icarus thinks the war will be over before then."

"Listen to Lady Rhodia," the healer said, entering the tent. "If you insist on moving that arm, I will bind it to the side of your body. You must rest this wound." She knelt and examined him, shaking her head.

She removed the flat stick Melia had attached to his side.

"This is not good," she said, mopping up the fresh blood that welled up from the deep wound. "I need to clasp the skin together and then sew it with boiled linen. It won't be pleasant, so you best distract yourself. After I sew it, the best we can do is bind it tightly. You must not pull it apart again. So far, there's no infection, but it could be coming."

"What can I do to help?" asked Rhodia.

"I need somebody responsible to distract him while I sew him up," the healer said. "And then someone will need to keep him still while his body knits back together."

"Eurymedon does not take orders well," Rhodia said, "and I'm going to be too busy to tend to him. If we dispose of the Achaeans today as we hope, then I will tend him—with a bludgeon." She shook her fist under Eurymedon's nose. He grinned at her.

"We will move him and Icarus together. Perhaps they can watch for one another."

"Is Icarus wounded too?" asked Eurymedon. The huge man seemed to be indestructible.

"He was struck in the head by a discus, we think," the healer said. "His right hand and foot continue to tingle, and he's still dizzy. We're not letting him fight today. You and he can move into the hills together in a baggage wagon."

"Are you implying that I am baggage?" Eurymedon snorted.

"Any man who cannot work or fight is baggage," Rhodia said. "Useless. We will let you live because we think you will heal. Otherwise . . . ," she said sternly, reaching down and taking his scrotum in her hand, pulling it out from his groin to be easier to amputate. She drew her finger across it and sneered at him.

"Dolios will pack Icarus and then come here to help you," the healer said. "Tell your slaves to get started." She looked at them with disgust. "If they will do anything useful," she added.

"They are good at distraction," he said, grinning, easing Rhodia's hand away.

"Well, then, you two, get busy distracting him. Rhodia, hold his arm up and keep him from moving. Put your feet on his shoulders to give yourself leverage. This is going to hurt."

CHAPTER

TEN

The Achaeans caught enough horses to pull five of their new scythes and fifty chariots. To each three-man chariot they added another four of their best soldiers to ride along, overloading each chariot with seven soldiers. By midmorning, the force was moving rapidly toward the rising ground of the west, pursuing the apparently fleeing city army. The five eight-horse teams pulling the scythes struggled to keep up. The chariots behind the scythes spread out to either side to avoid the choking dust kicked up by the whirring blades, which made a dangerous-sounding hum. They pulled far ahead, leaving the scythes behind.

The gap did not escape Kratos's notice, where he sat astride his stallion among his intent cavalry. He shouted a few quick orders, pointing with his sword. The flanking squadrons acknowledged with raised spears and eased off in opposite directions. On his command, they would thunder down the hills from the cover of trees and attack the chariots. Melia and her troops were poised behind him, hidden behind boulders and low hills. Archers to their rear crept forward, then hundreds of warriors with slings and rocks. Behind them were the four trebuchets, loaded with hundred-pound boulders. All kept silent, letting the ignorant Achaeans advance into the trap. Like Eumaeus on the city wall, anticipation showed in their grim faces.

* * *

Two or three miles to the rear of the chariots, the mass of the Achaean army divided into three hordes and moved away to storm the city walls, abandoning the chariots and the scythes, which scurried on to their doom. When the Achaeans advanced to within half a mile of the city, they were astounded to discover that thousands of soldiers were silently waiting for them. The spears were four and five deep, unmoving, crowded together along every foot of wall. Behind the walls, lines of smoke from cooking fires rose into the evening air. Atop the acropolis the white temple gleamed in the late afternoon. The altar in front of it blazed high with the fat of the sacrifice, dark smoke rising and drifting northward toward the high mountains. Banners fluttered from the towers, and the gates were shut, impenetrable.

The Achaeans thought the south wall of the city would be the easiest route for invasion since it had collapsed in a massive explosion months before. The largest horde chose to prepare their assault there, while the two smaller hordes arrayed against the still sturdy west and north walls. They carried all their siege engines into position, ready for the charge: ladders, ropes, grapples, battering rams. Years of planning and seven months of war had led to this moment. They were eager for the assault and the rape that would follow, jostling one another, vying for position, restless. The first over the wall and into the city had his pick of the females and the plunder. It was the ancient way. It was the path to glory and wealth. Everyone knew that, and everyone wanted as much as he could get.

* * *

It was an emotional moment when Agala removed her small golden figure of the idol from its niche in the sacred room beneath the idol. It was her symbol of office as a governing matron of the city. Eumaeus took her arm to help her make her way down into the underground tunnels beneath the acropolis, but she shook him off, instead climbing into the idol's vast lap. She would not leave until it was time. Eumaeus had his work to do, she had hers, and neither were finished.

* * *

The Achaeans had used fire pots on the dodecas. Now they would get a dose of it themselves when Eumaeus opened the flood gate of burning oil at the altar and the fire spread over the whole acropolis. The soldiers the Achaeans thought were lining the walls were actually several thousand straw-stuffed and pitch-covered mannequins ready to explode into flame. When the Achaeans stormed in, they would mire themselves with the pitch and oil of the mannequins on the walls. Those who did not burn instantly would ignite when they descended into the city streets where the pockets of methane were ready to explode at the slightest spark. His two hundred men, still hidden in the blocked towers, would speed along the walls spreading fire, and the mannequins themselves would crown the city with fire, shutting off the Achaean escape.

Eumaeus knew that the immolation of her enemies would be a fitting final sacrifice to the goddess in this sacred place. His men knew it as well, even though it could be a suicide mission for all of them.

ELEVEN

The constant jolting of the cart nauseated Shelby and he hoped the ride would be over soon. He'd have to teach these people about springs and shock absorbers. Arktos's garrison on the rim of the western hills seemed like a long way from the battlefield and already the sun was sinking. It would be dark long before they arrived.

Next to him, Eurymedon and several other wounded soldiers also bounced along amid rug-covered hay. One of the soldiers, a man with a tightly wrapped broken leg and badly burned head and face, moaned at each bump. The healers had left instructions to keep the bandages that covered most of his face moist with the boiled water carried by the cart driver. The foot of another soldier had been crushed beneath a chariot wheel, and the thigh of another had been impaled by an Achaean spear. Theirs was just one of hundreds of carts carrying the wounded to safety, but they were the last in line. Shelby had insisted on it.

"How's your head?" Eurymedon asked after one of Shelby's dry heaves.

"It hurts like a motherfucker," Shelby said.

"Oh, friend, you must not say 'motherfucker' in such a tone. That is offensive."

"Right. Sorry. Then it hurts like a devil is chewing on my brain."

"Better. Like a harpy or other evil spirit."

"Just like that."

"But you can move your jaw, and you can talk, so that is a good sign."

"How about you, little brother?" Shelby asked, trying to lift himself up to a sitting position to cushion his head from the bumpy ride.

"My side hurts like a motherfucker," Eurymedon said with a grin. "I think it is okay to say 'motherfucker' if you say it with a smile and a pleasant tone. After all, our goddess does not object to mothers being fucked. It is a religious duty." He chuckled. "I can lift my arm, but I have no strength to pull with it. I cannot shoot a bow or swing a sword. Today I am useless."

Shelby was confused. Hadn't he been speaking this country's archaic Greek? "Motherfucker" was surely a modern English word, and English would not emerge for almost another three thousand years. Yet Eurymedon had understood the word and then said it himself. Had these people come to understand him so well that he could speak either language? Or was his mind playing tricks on him? He decided on the latter.

He watched the countryside as the cart jostled along. The stands of ancient forest gave way to extensive vineyards. He closed one eye and tried focusing on objects near and far. He could do so with his left eye and then with his right eye, but the eyes did not focus together, and that increased his sense of nausea and vertigo.

He wondered if bruising or swelling in his left inner ear was causing his nausea. If so, drinking that willow bark tea would increase the likelihood of bleeding. He would ask the healer for something else, maybe a small amount of opium or a few seeds from a poppy plant. Maybe they had a mushroom of some kind they could dose him with. They must have something that would work.

"I assume you wanted us to ride in the last cart so you could see the Achaean chariots pursuing us," Eurymedon said with a jolly tone in his voice. "I am not sure we will do much good. You cannot stand, and I cannot fight, and these others," he nodded at the three soldiers lying in the cart with them, "probably would not be much use either."

"Have you not noticed the Meliae guarding us?" Shelby asked. The black-clad women rode silently through the woods and by-paths, avoiding the main trail but keeping abreast of the line of carts.

"So nothing is wrong with your brain, either," Eurymedon said. "Your mouth works, and your brain works. I think you will be healed by tomorrow."

"I hope that is not too late," Shelby said as Rhodia appeared on horseback from the field.

"The Achaeans have done exactly what you thought they would do," she said to Shelby. "They have encircled the city. We expect they will wait until nightfall to attack, which is even better."

"Like a mouse in a trap," Eurymedon said, with a large grin. "They will go in, and they will never come out again."

"If it all works," Shelby said. "I will not rest easy until I see that Eumaeus and Agala and the others have gotten away safely. How long will it take for them to reach the garrison?"

"About three days on foot," Eurymedon said. "On horseback, about half a day. They may have caught some Achaean horses, since Rhodia set so many of them free."

"We'll wait for them," Shelby said. "We'll abandon no one, and we'll search for them as well. But we'll also begin the harvest once the Achaeans are safely inside the city. Do you think Agala followed my instructions about the wine and grain?"

"If they make it to the acropolis through the city, they will find it. The city will be burning behind them," Rhodia said.

"Goddess willing," Shelby said. He almost nodded but caught himself.

"Have you seen the Persians?" Eurymedon asked.

"They are up ahead, sitting on top of a pile of luggage," Rhodia said. "Don't worry, boy, we will keep our toys." By her tone, she seemed annoyed.

"Keep us informed," Shelby said. "And if you see Dolios, ask him to join me at the garrison."

She nodded and rode off, giving Eurymedon a parting glance that would have pierced a more sensitive man.

Eurymedon grinned. "Motherfucker," he muttered through a broad, white-toothed smile.

ᗷᗷᗷᗷᗷᗷᗷᗷᗷᗷ

T he cart rumbled to a stop where Dolios stood waiting. From the high hill, Shelby could see out over most of the valley and had a fine view of the city. In the fading light, the distant Achaeans looked like black ants swarming toward a mound, the ground dense with them.

"They will not wait for dark," Eurymedon said. "Look how excited they are. If their officers do not drive them over the walls, they will go over on their own."

"Eumaeus has been ready for weeks," Shelby said. "The fire is burning, the altar is set up, and, if Agala did her job, the grain and wine are ready. Let them go."

"Motherfucker," whispered Eurymedon, shocking Dolios. Shelby saw the boy's look and put a hand on his shoulder. "It's a joke between me and Eurymedon," he told him. "What do you have to report?"

"The first wagons should be at the garrison now and will be returning by the other route, as you insisted. From a good spot lower down, I watched Kratos attack the chariots."

"How did it go?" Eurymedon asked, grimacing as he shifted his arm.

"At first it looked like Kratos would have a difficult time. The chariots carried archers as well as extra soldiers, and they shot back at the cavalry. Some of our horses were wounded or killed. Then the blades mounted on rolling logs came. Some of our soldiers shielded themselves next to the fallen bodies of the horses. Blood sprayed as the scythes rolled over them. I don't know if the soldiers were safe."

"That doesn't sound good," Shelby said.

"Lady Rhodia was closer," Dolios said. "She may have seen it more clearly."

"What happened next?" Eurymedon asked.

"With Kratos in the lead, the cavalry charged straight at the chariots. That's when the trebuchets let their boulders fly. Some struck the chariots and others fell in their path. Kratos seemed to concentrate his firepower on the rolling scythes and dropped the lead horses of all of them. That created havoc. The scythes either swerved out of control or rolled to a standstill and were run into from behind by the charging chariots. Then Melia's troops came out of hiding and charged in."

"A good plan," Shelby said. "How did they do?"

"It was a bitter fight, but the Achaeans were outnumbered and in chaos. Melia ordered our own men into the chariots, re-harnessed the rolling logs, and forced the remaining Achaeans toward the city."

"She will drive them over the walls," Eurymedon said, "as soon as they realize those chariots do not carry their own men."

"She cannot encircle all the soldiers with just the chariots," Shelby said. "I hope she knows what she's doing."

"Kratos has finished chopping off enemy heads and follows with the cavalry," Dolios said. "They will drive the Achaeans toward the city and slaughter them as they assault the walls."

"The signal flags have been going," he added, "so Kratos and Melia must know what each is planning. And Eumaeus, if he's still on the walls."

"By now, Eumaeus should be on the acropolis at the altar, lighting the fires," Shelby said.

"Look!" Dolios said, pointing at the distant city. "The Achaeans are going up the walls now."

The dust of Melia and Kratos approaching from the west could be seen driving the Achaeans more tightly against the city walls, which were dark with troops scrambling up ladders and ropes.

A great flare arose from the acropolis. Within minutes, the lines of smoke from the fake cooking fires began to grow heavy and dark. It billowed upward first from houses near the acropolis and then farther down, along the walls.

"It's working!" Shelby said, holding a hand over his right eye to better focus. "Eumaeus has done it! Let's hope he gets away in time."

"He is the bravest man we have," Eurymedon said. "That is why my father made him captain of the palace guard."

Melia's chariots reached the rear of the Achaean armies and drove them harder. Those who did not fall to her troops' spears scrambled over the walls. The entire Achaean army had been driven into the city, into the trap.

Everyone had stopped to watch the battle at the city walls. When at last the walls were clear of the frantic dark ants, those who could do so cheered. The Achaeans were bottled up, and the harvest could begin, at last.

THIRTEEN

T he path up the hill became much steeper after the overlook, and thick stands of pine cut off their view of the distant city. The carts slowed, sometimes coming to a standstill, as the drivers navigated the numerous switchbacks. It took them longer to traverse the last five miles of the path up from the valley than it had to travel the previous fifteen miles, but eventually they entered a clearing, where they could see the outlying pickets of the hilltop garrison ahead.

Arktos, the garrison commander, was waiting for them, and Dolios hopped down from the cart to make room for him. Arktos was one of the largest city warriors. His hair had been as thick as fur and coal black in his youth, but now that he was older—he and Phorbus had been the same age—it had turned silver. Patches of hair protruded from his shoulders around his armor, waving in the night breeze. His bushy beard doubled the size of his face and almost completely hid his mouth. A powerful, compact man, he had an air of authority and a resonant, commanding voice.

"Little brother," he cried, putting his hand gently on Eurymedon's uninjured left arm. "Smile at me. I want to see if you still have all your teeth."

Eurymedon grimaced, showing his teeth. Shelby could tell that it cost him great effort. The young man's wounds had become increasingly painful as the healer's medicines wore off, and jostling in the cart had not helped. Shelby, on the other hand, noticed that his head was hurting less and the tingling was almost gone from his right hand. In his right foot, he could feel the sharp fire, like ant bites, that precedes a limb coming back to life.

Arktos turned to Shelby. "And who are you? The lion? We have not met."

"Yes," Shelby said. "They call me Icarus. Phorbus married me to Melia before he died."

"Ah, yes," Arktos said. "You do not look as resplendent here as you did when I last saw you. You rescued Phorbus from the citadel and returned him to his family. What was left of it. Even I owe you a debt for that. Phorbus was my oldest and dearest friend."

"I had plenty of help," Shelby said. "The Meliae made it happen."

"You trained them, did you not?" It was more of a statement.

"I harnessed and focused them," Shelby said. "They did the rest."

"We have never seen our women harnessed at anything, especially fighting," Arktos said. "I think Phorbus was right. You are a remarkable man to be able to lead them."

Shelby smiled. He liked Arktos. He seemed to be a trustworthy, open, and honest man. "How is your garrison?" he asked.

"We are well stocked, and the western border is secure. Kratos did a lot of damage to Achaeans on both sides of these hills when he was up here. I think the path west will be fairly open, though you may find some Achaean settlements along the way. I should warn you of an unknown terror rumored to be farther to the west, in the steep lands before you reach the sea."

"We will enslave or kill all in our way," Eurymedon said. He grimaced. "I can't wait to get out of this bouncing cart."

"It's a bad wound," Shelby said. "How long to the camp?"

"About an hour from here," Arktos said. "I have already laid a feast of wild boar and my honey wine for you. I assume that will be to your liking."

"I have had little to eat since this time yesterday," Shelby said. "This head injury has me feeling nauseated, but it seems to be getting better."

"Our healer will help," said Arktos. "I'm afraid the healers you had lower down were mostly accustomed to women. Up here, we do not have women. It is a man's camp."

"I see," Shelby said.

"The women prefer the easier life of the valley," Arktos explained. "I like the clean air and the bright light on these hills and the distant views. From the front door of my hut I can see the entire valley, from the city in the east to the citadel in the north. A lookout tower lets me see even farther. Some days when the air is clear, I tell myself that I can see across the dark mountains all the way to the sea, though probably I cannot. It's too far. I loved the sea in my youth, with its wind and the brilliant splash of the waves breaking white. Since we are moving from the valley, maybe the city will release me to return to the sea."

"We may all go to the sea," Shelby said. "I know of beautiful, fertile lands across that sea to the west. When we are ready, when the harvest is gathered and the wine made, we will move in that direction, and one day I hope we will arrive in a land where we can prosper in safety."

"I have learned one thing, my young friend," Arktos said. "No place worth living in will ever be entirely safe. Others will always try to take what you have—your crops, your women, your children, your life. Always."

"Yes," Shelby said, "that's true. We can only have peace through strength."

Twilight faded into a gentle purple glow in the west as the cart pulled to stop in front of Arktos's round hut. Though low and smoky, the building was large enough and warmed by a fire in the middle that sent a column of smoke up through a hole in the roof. Taking a last long look at the city ablaze like a torch, thirty miles to the east, Shelby ducked into the hut. Muffled rumbles of distant explosions followed him in.

"The gas pockets are blowing up," he told Arktos. "Achaeans are dying by the thousands in those flames."

"Why don't they leave through the gates?" Arktos asked.

"Eumaeus and his five hundred bricked up the gates on the inside and filled the towers with dirt and sand so they could not be opened," Shelby said. "A solid sheet of fire now prevents the Achaeans from going back over the walls."

"Now that's a sacrifice worthy of the goddess," Arktos said, turning back to admire the sight. "We will miss the city, but we can build another. We will not miss the Achaeans."

"We evacuated the city down the southern outfall," Shelby

said. "If my geography is accurate, our first refugees will come out of the highlands conveniently located to take sail for Crete."

"How close will they be to the Eurotus River Valley?"

"Close enough to settle there. That country is low and brushy, however. It does not have these vistas."

"Do you think the matrons will choose that valley?"

Arktos had obviously been through the Eurotus river system and could visualize the possibilities. Shelby knew that in a millennium the Eurotus Valley would be home to the great city-state of Sparta.

"I don't know," he said. "My concern is to settle Melia and our troops. The matrons took twenty males for every hundred people. For all the work that needs to be done to settle the people and to defend them, that may be insufficient. Still, it is what it is. They are alive for now, and they are free. And all the other males are with us."

"And for the time being, we have stopped the southward surge of the Achaeans," Arktos said.

"The Meliae sealed the passes through the northern mountains and dropped a mountains on the citadel," Shelby said, sitting at the low fire in the middle of the hut at Arktos's bidding. Eurymedon was helped to a spot next to him. He grimaced as he lowered himself. Arktos poured him a large goblet of honey wine and sent one of the attendants for the healer. Eurymedon nodded his thanks but set the goblet down, his hand shaking, and reclined, his eyes clenched shut.

"The only way for more Achaeans to enter the valley is to climb over the citadel's rubble or to come by way of these western hills," Shelby added, his concern for Eurymedon clouding his face.

"These hills go all the way to the sea, Icarus," Arktos said, handing him the tender foreleg of a boar and then filling his goblet with honey wine. "Achaeans can climb over them, and have done so, but not very quickly and only with limited baggage. Still, they come. I wonder what drives them out of the north."

"It could be population pressure," Shelby said, "or perhaps they are tormented by invaders descending on them just as the Achaeans descended on us. In my time, we could trace the pressure back to horsemen from the steppes of Asia who pushed west and south. Probably, it is a combination of factors: drought, famine, disease, and invasion. It's hard to tell what drives them, but it's not hard to tell why they envied us this valley with its cool, clear water, its fertile fields, and its mineral wealth. This place has been a kind of paradise."

Arktos nodded as he watched the healer help Eurymedon sit up so he could sip opium–infused wine.

"He will sleep now," Arktos said. "At least up here, above the valley, we can heal in safety."

FOURTEEN

᭡᭡᭡᭡᭡᭡᭡᭡᭡᭡᭡᭡

T hree weeks passed as the troops streamed up to the garrison, leading wagons loaded with grain and pressed grapes. They had collected much of the harvest not destroyed by the competing armies, but the grain needed to be winnowed before it could be ground into flour. Soldiers and farm slaves worked shoulder to shoulder, casting the rubbed grain high into the gentle breezes with their flat baskets, leaving long trails of chaff that could be seen from the nearby hilltops. Vast numbers of amphorae filled with wine seethed with the action of the yeast, happy with the extra oxygenation of its rough passage up the hills. The golden days of autumn were upon them, the sun warm during the day and the nights chill under starfire brilliant as glittering diamonds.

Three weeks of rest were enough for Shelby to heal completely, and he resumed his predawn fitness regimen. The Meliae who were not on guard duty accompanied him. The slap of their sandals on the dirt tracks in the cool morning and the dust they raised awoke the rest of the camp. When they returned from their hour-long run in the steep hills, they stretched and performed the strengthening exercises Shelby taught them. For this morning ritual, the trim Meliae wore "bikinis" made of a band of cloth crossed over their breasts and tied behind their necks, and a swath of cloth tied between their legs and around their hips. It would have been easier to wear nothing, but clothing was a sign of status. In the rosy dawn, their sweaty bodies glistened and the striations of their undulating muscles below their smooth skin were very beautiful, drawing all the male eyes in the camp in admiration.

The distant city had burned for days, smoke lingering over the acropolis. Shelby was confident that any Achaeans who remained alive were still penned among the ruins. Melia thought that more than three-fourths of them had perished in the fires, and others had probably died from the poisons Agala left behind in the remaining stores of wine and wheat.

"It's not a soldier's way," Kratos said, joining them with the last of the retreating city troops. "It's not entirely honorable. I prefer to face my enemy, then cut off his head. Still, the war is over. We lost the city and the valley, but we did not lose the war."

"The world is large, Kratos, my brother," Shelby said. "If only one in ten of the Achaeans survived, that is still a formidable force. They could cause trouble."

"What have the survivors been eating these last three weeks?" Eurymedon asked. "Each other?"

"That is the kind of people they are," Arktos said, "but my guess is that they are eating their horses and mules before they start on one another. Still, I imagine those who remain may be going without sleep. I know I could not sleep if my comrades were thinking about eating one another." He grinned. "If they eat all of their horses and mules, they'll be on foot when they come out to fight, and Kratos will have his chance to finish this business."

"We hope this war is over, brother," Shelby said. "My guess is that bread and wine make a healthier army than the rotting flesh of one's dead companions, so we are certain to win any future encounter."

"I don't want to hear this kind of talk," Melia said. "I want to remember our city as a sacred place that was blessed by our divine goddess."

"Let them talk, sister," Eurymedon said. His youth and the tiny drop of healing venom had worked wonders on his wound, though his arm looked withered from lack of use. "They are not hurting us with such talk."

She looked at him sharply but said nothing. No one thought that he had changed her mind, but then no one wanted to cross her, either.

"We have laid in the stores of the harvest as best we can," Arktos said. "I say we should stay here in the hilltops until winter has passed before trying to move west."

"What is winter like here?" Shelby asked.

"We have snow and bitter cold," Arktos replied. "Sometimes the snow is as deep as my waist."

"Then your suggestion is a good one," Shelby said. He glanced at Melia. "If Melia approves, we will camp here until warmer weather in the spring."

"I don't know if our goddess will allow it," she said. "But she has allowed the harvest, so she may let us stay. Her prophecy of coming destruction by fire was unusually specific and frightening, and we risk our lives remaining close to the valley. I also remain concerned for the Achaeans in the city. Will they stay there? Did we kill them all? Or will they get stronger during the winter and then break out to make war on us? We have divine warning and the Achaean threat. These dire futures we can avoid only by going away. But with winter upon us, moving may be as deadly as remaining."

"Either way," Arktos said, "the Achaeans cannot harass us here. We are safe from them, and my line of forts stretches almost to the old citadel. No one will circle us or threaten our rear, and no one will get up here. This is the best place for the army to recuperate. And maybe we are far enough from the valley to have time to move away from the firebirth."

"Yes," Melia said. "Divine fire is our greatest threat. But your efforts here over the years have been a significant benefit to the defense of our goddess and her city. Your people owe you much."

"Bah!" he said. "Thank you, Melia, but it was Phorbus who convinced me I would be happier up here, and he was right. The women do not come, and I have always liked that."

"One of your great strengths is your willingness to speak your mind," she said with a tone just shy of sarcasm. She turned to Shelby. "Join me and the Meliae in our barracks when you are ready. It is time to plan a route west."

She rose and then the men rose, waiting respectfully for their priestess to exit.

"All of the Meliae!" Eurymedon said when Melia was out of earshot. "You will be sleeping in the same room with all of the Meliae. Now that is an experience for you, my lion." He smirked.

"Master, do I need to stay with you?" Dolios asked. Shelby thought the lad was trembling. The idea of trying to sleep in a room with a hundred feared female warriors must have been too much for him.

"Send Alcestis to me," Shelby said. "And no, you can move in with Hestia. It will be better for both of you."

The trembling slave boy went to the ground, clasping Shelby around his knees. "Thank you, master, thank you!" he exclaimed.

Eurymedon and Arktos looked on, confused. "They frightened him one time," Shelby explained.

Kratos reached over from his sitting position and put a hand on the boy's head, rubbing it. "When you are older," he said gently, "you will understand women better. Now, it is wise to be terrified. Stay with the men."

"I will not force him to be alone with them again," Shelby said.

"Just so."

"Women do not take well to harness," Eurymedon said. "They almost never listen to men or to what we think is reason. That Icarus made them into a fighting force at all is remarkable. I'm terrified of them, too."

"Truly," Arktos agreed. "It is a wise man who is terrified of women."

"Women can do anything men can do," Shelby said, "but they almost never get the training. If you train women to fight, they learn to be deadly. That's all I did. What they do with the training lies much deeper in their minds than anything I could teach them. You might remember that, little brother, when you cuddle up with Rhodia. She is soft and sweet and alluring, but she is also deadly, scheming, and powerful. Just like you. She is just like you."

Kratos laughed. "Not exactly," he finally managed to sputter. "She's not exactly like him."

"You would notice that," Shelby said. "The parts are different; the will is not."

"The parts are pretty significant, Icarus," Eurymedon said. He laughed so hard the tears streamed from his eyes.

"Icarus is right," Arktos said when Eurymedon had laughed himself out. "The parts of our bodies do not make us who we are. And as for me, my body parts say it is time for bed. Perhaps your body parts say that you wish to lie with your beautiful Persian twins. I cannot tell what Icarus wishes to do, though I think he will drift after Melia until the world melts away if he can. So," he said, rising, "I go to rest and to dream of Phorbus and my youth. You young men enjoy what rest your youth allows you." He left the room to settle into an antechamber. His soft snoring was soon the only sound in the hut.

Kratos looked at Shelby and then Eurymedon, then back to Shelby and nodded at Dolios.

"Go on, Dolios," Shelby said. "Find Hestia, and if she is awake, ask her to come in here."

"You said at one time that you had ideas about defensive structures," Kratos said after Dolios had left. "We will build a new city in the next few years. Let's talk about what you know and how we should plan. I fear our matrons will be scattered and unable to help with design." He took a gulp from the jug of wine and passed it to Shelby just as Alcestis entered the hut, a timid look on her face.

"Ah, Alcestis," said Shelby. "Come here and rub my right foot. The tingling returns when I am tired."

"Elevate it," she said, "like this." She placed cushions under his knee and leg, and then began massaging the foot. "Let me know if this helps."

As the slave girl worked on his leg, the three warriors spoke long into the night about the wise design of their lost city and ways to improve it. An hour before sunrise, Shelby woke to the snoring of his comrades. During the night, little Alcestis had curled against his shin and rested her small face against his knee. She too had fallen into a deep sleep.

Standing in the hut door, with a golden shield in front of him in both hands, was Eumaeus.

FIFTEEN

bbbbbbbbbb

"**E**umaeus!" exclaimed Shelby, shaking the girl from his leg and springing up.

Kratos, startled awake by Shelby's cry, vaulted into the air from a dead slumber and came down in a crouch, his knife drawn, ready to attack or defend.

"Oh," he said, straightening up. "Eumaeus, you startled me."

"I'm glad to see you have not grown soft," Eumaeus sneered, striding into the tent. "Here, Icarus, is the golden shield given to you by Phorbus that you left in my care, and the goat-skin bag that protects it."

"Eumaeus, I am so glad to see you!" Shelby said, going to receive the shield and putting his big hand on the shorter man's hard shoulder. "Come in. Sit and rest. Tell us about your journey. You and your men did a beautiful job with the city. Excellent. Extraordinary."

Eurymedon, shaking his head and yawning, patted around him on the bedding until he realized his twins were not there. He looked groggily at Eumaeus. "You're here," he said, wiping his hand over his face. "I didn't expect you."

"I traveled across the steep country through the forests in the south," Eumaeus said. "Agala came with me as far as the sacred pool. At her instruction, I left her at the top of the cliff where the path goes down."

He remained standing even though Shelby and Kratos both beckoned him to take a seat.

"She will not get far," Shelby said, sitting and shooing the girl out to bring breakfast. "One of the earthquakes blocked the inner temple where the women always went to worship the goddess. It is open at the top, just enough to crawl through, which is how I came here. But unless Agala has special gear, she is not going to get into it. It is as good as sealed."

"Besides," Shelby added a moment later, "once inside, she would find the bodies of Iapetus and Ophion where they killed one another."

"She told me to leave her," repeated Eumaeus, his stern face unsmiling. "She did not ask me to accompany her. I saw her making her way down the cliff to the pool, and I waited for her for three days, but she did not come back. I left her as she instructed. I came by the road where I met you that day you were first here, with Metis and Kalista. We have been many miles in these months since you arrived in our valley, Icarus, few of them happy."

"Tell us how the trap for the Achaeans worked," Shelby said. "Did all go as planned?"

"I sent all but two hundred men out through the tunnels when I saw your signals," he said, "even forcing Agala's attendants to go with them. Then everything was ready. You were accurate in thinking the Achaeans would attempt the ruins of the south gate first, and those never made it inside. We were ready for them, and our engineering worked perfectly. The rest of the wall collapsed, pushing them into the pit left by the tower when it blew up.

"Then my men hidden in the other towers let fire loose on the walls and made their way over the housetops, spreading fire as they ran to the acropolis. All those cooking fires: that was a good ruse, Icarus. You read the Achaean mind. They thought the population was still in the city."

He paused, looking around the hut. Arktos had come in to listen to his tale, carrying a jug of cold water, which he handed to Eumaeus. The ash-hard warrior took a long drink.

"Keeping out of the streets was the key," Eumaeus said. "Agala and I both thought the gas had seeped up and pooled in the low spots. When the houses started blowing up, we knew it. Sometimes the explosions would knock my men down, raining stones on everyone around. We burned the marketplace, all those big trees that had grown there for five hundred harvests or more, and we made it up to the altar at last. Agala was waiting for us, sitting in the lap of the big idol and smiling and waving a leafy olive branch."

Eurymedon had risen, and now he went to Eumaeus and put his good arm around the man's shoulders.

"Agala said she would wait for the Achaeans and instructed us to go on. I sent everyone else but told Agala that I would wait with her, to die at the foot of the goddess in the center of the world. She became angry and ordered me to leave, but I told her I had been ordered to stay in the city to protect her. Phorbus told me to do that, not you, Icarus," he said, looking squarely at him. "You also asked me to do it, but Phorbus had ordered me to do it the final time I spoke to him." He swallowed hard before continuing.

"We listened for a long time to the roaring fires and the thumping of houses exploding, the fall of stones and roof tiles, and finally a small group of thirty or so blackened Achaeans made it up to the acropolis. By this time, it was late at night, but we could see them clearly in the light of the flames. They paused when they saw us, then raised their spears and charged. Agala stood then and held out her olive branch at them. I don't know what she said, some ancient curse, but it stopped them. She waved the branch around her head and then thrust it down at them again. They fell to their knees and then facedown. The altar flared, and I could see that they were bleeding from their skulls. I lit the final fires, the big cauldrons we had stored in the temple, and fire poured out over the acropolis like a flood. The Achaeans flamed and sputtered, and that's all I saw. The next I knew, Agala was leading me by the hand through a dark tunnel."

"Amazing story," Arktos said. "Those old matrons have powers you do not want to test."

"Mother could do things like that," Kratos said, "but rarely. It drained her, and she was low for days afterward."

"I've felt Melia do it to me," Shelby said. "But she did not kill me, of course, and I did not bleed from my skull. I thought I would, though. It hurt as much as the blow from that discus."

"She has not done it to you yet, Icarus." Eurymedon smiled. "Not yet. She may be the most powerful matron the city has ever had, though you're lucky she is so young. Those powers come later, after their time of childbearing."

Tears had appeared in the corners of Eumaeus's eyes, and he wiped them away angrily, clinching his jaw. He stood silently.

"Eumaeus," Arktos said, "in the name of Phorbus, sit down." He nodded to Alcestis, who had returned with food. "I will send this girl to bring Melia here, and you will tell your story again. But before she gets here, tell us, did you find others from the city? How were they, and where were they going?"

Eumaeus sat. When he spoke again, it was directly to Arktos.

"My troops overtook the last of the citizens," he said, "heading toward the Eurotus River Valley. They thought they might go on to Crete, but they doubted that our cousins there would welcome so many. I think they mean to settle along the river. If you will permit it and Melia will release me, I would like to rejoin them."

Arktos nodded, knowing it was not his place to grant wishes or to give orders to this captain of the palace guard.

"Were the people healthy?" Shelby asked. "Were they well stocked and well led? I worry about them."

"They are organized into eleven tribes with each matron at the head," said the old warrior, sitting ramrod straight, his legs folded beneath him. "Agala was the twelfth matron, and she had sent her people with the others. When we parted at the pool, she called me her son." He turned away from the others to hide his face as emotion welled up within him.

Melia entered a few moments later, and Eumaeus rose and repeated his story, his voice with a new, hard edge in it. He pointed to the shield as he explained returning it, and at the end of his tale he said that Agala had sent him to Melia bearing a gift.

Melia's hand went to her heart and she knelt, tears seeping from her eyes.

Eumaeus went to his knees before her, and from his kitbag he took a small golden statue, a copy of the temple's idol. He dropped his eyes as he handed it to her.

"You are now the twelfth matron and spirit of the spring moon," he said. "Long may you live." He collapsed in tears before her, his face buried, the sense of all that had been lost washing over him, dissolving the steel of his soul.

CHAPTER

SIXTEEN

T he days shortened, the skies darkened with the rains of autumn, and then came snow. Hestia and Dolios ventured farther and farther into the battlegrounds of the valley scavenging bronze, until finally, one cold day when the switchback paths down the hills had frozen over, they stopped going. The hilltop garrison with its thousands of troops settled into a routine of quiet industry, preparing for their exodus to the west and healing from their injuries.

One morning in the dark, Melia awoke wide-eyed and sat up, the bedcovers falling from her lovely breasts. "Today, the sun begins his return to us," she announced. On the floor around the bed she shared with Shelby lay the hundred Meliae, snoring quietly under their warm furs, snuggled together to share body heat.

No one paid attention to her.

"I say," she said louder, "this is the day. Spring is coming. The sun is bringing back the warmer weather."

"That's nice dear," mumbled Shelby, reaching for her. She had moved the covers off his shoulders, and the cold in the room was waking him up. If she weren't so much fun to sleep with, he would avoid this room full of the scent of physical women. Its tang was overpowering.

"Also," she said, throwing the covers off of him, "you better get out of here. It's that time."

"Wha—?" he blinked. He did not object to getting up early; he'd awakened plenty early many times.

"Get out," she said. "This is no place for a male right now.

Take Kratos and Eurymedon and leave the garrison. Go hunting! I don't care what you do, just get out of this room and get out right now."

They had enjoyed a lusty night full of passion, more or less ignored by the Meliae though some had enjoyed the sight. Melia had explained that the Meliae, as did all the people from the city, respected their lovemaking as a symbol of a healthy future full of passion and love for them all.

"They look to us for everything," she had said. "They take every cue about how they will spend their day and what tomorrow will be like from how we act in front of them. They interpret everything. I will show you," she had told him in the dawn of their marriage. She then had tied a ribbon around her head, making a bow in the front on her forehead. "It might look awkward for me to wear a bow like this on the front of my head, but I will wear it all day, and all day tomorrow. Watch what happens."

Sure enough, the following day several other women and most of the Meliae were wearing bows on their foreheads. By the end of the week, even some of the soldiers were doing the same.

"See," she'd said later. "They watch everything. Nothing we do is private, or just between us. Let us be kind and passionate with one another and absorb ourselves in one another and make our poor exiles happy."

It took some getting used to, this public exhibition, this life as a symbol. On the plus side, it gave the people a way to cohere, to act with one will, and for so many thousands of soldiers and attendants this was a good thing.

"Out!" she shooed him, her voice bringing him back to the present. "Out! And send Alcestis to me with warm water and bread for us all. We will not leave our quarters today, but if we do, it would be better for you and the other men to be away."

Living in a society governed by women had taught him a thing or two. When he left, he saw attendants bringing in stacks of clean linen cloths. She was right, he reasoned, we need to go hunting for a week.

Wrapping the bedraggled lion skin around himself for warmth, he walked toward Arktos's hut in time to see Eurymedon's Persian slave girls hurrying off.

Sure enough, at Arktos's hut the two brothers were up and

packing for a trip into the hinterland far from the garrison. They knew from past experience when it was time to become scarce.

"A week's worth of wine," Kratos hollered. "Lots of wine. And bread. Bring bread and meat!"

"You think of everything, brother," Eurymedon said with a smile. "I will go and prepare horses for us."

"Perhaps we should make an excursion to the city to check whether the Achaeans are recovering," Shelby said.

"That's a good idea," Kratos said, "but the three of us will hunt wild boar today. I can taste it already."

"We could send a scouting party," Shelby said. "Don't we already have a scouting party down there?"

"We did, but they retired when the snows came. They reported that fires were still burning in the city, but also that they heard sounds of men working. We obviously did not kill all of them."

"If that's the case, then when spring comes they will cause us trouble."

"Perhaps. Perhaps not. I have been scouting to the west for the last two months, and I know our path. If we leave them alone, I think they will not bother us."

"If you say so," Shelby said, something stirring in him uneasily. You never turn your back to an enemy, especially not one you think you have defeated. On the other hand, how many Achaeans survived? Maybe, he hoped, only a few hundred remained. Maybe fewer. And he was sure very few of their camp followers had made it over the city walls. With few skilled laborers and probably no women, he doubted the Achaeans who still lived were a very happy bunch.

"Nope," he muttered to himself, remembering the warm embrace of his recent comfort with Melia. "Not a happy bunch."

"What?" asked Eurymedon, reentering.

"Just talking to myself," he replied.

"Icarus, brothers, I am coming with you to hunt the boar," thundered Arktos entering from his partition in the hut. "I cannot stand it up here anymore. I need fresh air."

Everyone smiled. They all knew the allure of the clean air of the upper hills, fresh blown snow, and the thrill of the hunt. But they also knew of the advantages of life in the city, with warm and happy women.

Later, the silence and the fresh cold were refreshing and cleansing, and the four warriors traveled much of the day without talk, followed at a distance by a few attendants and preceded by the gentle white puffs from the nostrils of their horses.

Shelby felt happier than he could remember feeling in his own time. He didn't miss the screech and continuous thunder of twenty-first-century Ramstein Air Base, the purposeless bustle and unrewarding frenzy of indefinable policy. "Oh, Goddess," he prayed, "never send me back to the twenty-first century." This act of prayer was a major shift for his so-called modern mind.

SEVENTEEN

W ith time on their hands during the long winter months, the refugees in their hilltop fortifications tended to their tools and possessions. They repaired armor and sharpened blades, and despite the enforced confinement of the lingering cold weather, all were happy to know that the days were gradually getting longer. The cold weather would persist for another month at least, and then the frozen hills would turn to mud. In the valley, a thousand meters below, they could see the energetic sun melting snow off the fields where the stubble of the last harvest remained. A smoky pall lingered over the distant city, thirty miles away, and the once pure-white temple was now blackened by oily smoke. Sharper eyes could see that a corner of its roof had fallen.

When he was not training himself and the Meliae in regular daily exercises of combat and calisthenics, Shelby conferenced with Hestia. Dolios had become Hestia's right hand, and she re- lied on the slave boy more and more to supervise and execute the many production queues she managed. She always included him in the conferences.

"He is a good boy," she said. "He is learning. Not everyone can learn."

Shelby took a father's delight in this. He was proud of Dolios, a present to him from Melia's mother, Metis. He was also more than a little amused by the lad, whose age since the last harvest was now considered to be fifteen. And he grinned to himself whenever he saw Dolios trying to speak to Alcestis, who invariably ignored him or shut him down.

Alcestis was a strange girl, with her long, rectangular, almost horse-like face and her dark eyebrows. True, in the months she had been helping to care for him she had begun to acquire more feminine attributes, to fill out. Most days he made her work out with the Meliae, because, frankly, he didn't have anything else for her to do, and the strengthening and flexibility exercises seemed to have a pleasing effect on her body. She had hips now, and her shoulders were far less bony. Her breasts seemed to be swelling. One good thing the exercise had done was make her more grace-ful. She no longer seemed to walk locking her knees with her full weight coming down on her heels. He assumed she was still a virgin, though he really didn't care. But he was sure Dolios cared, from the way he followed her with his eyes even while listening to Hestia and himself, his unsuccessful attempts to attract the naked girl's attention, and the widening of his pupils when she moved.

Every day shortly after noon, just as Shelby was toweling off from the morning's exercise, Hestia and Dolios would ar-rive, and for an hour or so they would discuss innovations and inventions. For a full week, they discussed creating chimneys to generate more heat for their furnaces, and Shelby explained what he knew about making iron from iron ore, which was not much. Hestia was not sure why they needed iron until he showed her his Shrike tomahawk and explained that iron could lead to steel. She grasped the potential.

"The hotter the fire, the more advanced the civilization," Shel-by told her. "You melt the iron ore in the chimney, not in the coals beneath it, because you get higher temperatures in the chimney. If you orient the furnaces on hilltops facing the prevailing winds, then you get better heat from the improved draft. Add slaves working the bellows, and you should be able to do it. If you keep melting and re-melting the iron at a high enough temperature, it can become steel which is far stronger."

Weeks passed, and one day she came and took him by the hand to lead him up to a hilltop where she had created the chim-ney from fired bricks. He helped her pack it with stacks of char-coal and more bricks, and all day and into the night they kept the fire stoked. Two days later, the fire had cooled, and he went back with her to help disassemble the chimney. There was a lump of blackened iron, still hot. She used thick leather pads to lift it and lay it on a flat stone. Sparks flew from it as slaves beat it with heavy flint rocks.

"Those sparks are called the 'fleas of hell,'" Shelby told her. "They will burn through flesh. Dress your slaves in thick leather aprons and leather coverings for their feet."

Shelby watched as the very first lump of steel in the history of the world was gradually beaten into a long rod, reheated in the fire, and folded many times under his direction. Finally, Hestia hoisted a thirty-inch-long blade of Damascus steel, her wrinkled old face and hawk-like eyes glittering with excitement. The joy in her face drove hundreds of workers to laughter.

"What do you think, Icarus?" she asked gleefully.

"Sharpen it, and then you will know," he said. "Then let's think about other uses for this metal. Meanwhile," he added, "come back with me and let us talk about steam engines."

"When will you teach me to fly?" she asked, on the way back to her headquarters.

"Now that's a good idea," Shelby said. "That's as much a weaving problem as anything. I'll talk to Melia about it. She spends her afternoons supervising the city's weavers."

"Why weaving?" She had grasped his forearm in her muscular, wrinkled hand to keep his attention.

"For the parachute," he said. "We may not ever get to fixed wing gliders, but we can make paragliders if we get the right material. Linen might make a good material. It won't be soaring with the birds, but it will give you a chance to ride the wind while coming down from a mountaintop. We'll see."

"You always say that," she said. "This 'we'll see' thing. I can already see, Icarus. I can see it in my mind, just like the trebuchets. You tell me clearly, I will see it, and then, I will make it."

He looked at her with genuine love and admiration. "Yes," he said, "with the fire in your mind, you will."

EIGHTEEN

E very day, the chief topic of discussion in the camp was their migration westward. Kratos led scouting parties in search of the easiest passes through the hills because they were in largely unknown territory. Though the city had existed for a thousand years in its peaceful valley, few citizens had traveled much beyond its boundaries. Villages and tribal areas in the immediate vicinity were well known, of course, but only a few soldiers had fought wars at greater distances, and the majority of the camp's occupants had never been so far from the city.

Kratos's forays west were through rough country, sparsely populated and rarely explored. Shelby urged him to probe the land for a path to the western sea, toward Italy. Deep down, he felt something prodding him to move this people into the rich land that would one day be known as Tuscany. He dreamed about it, heard a voice in his head whispering it, no matter how often he dismissed it. When he told Melia, she said Mother Goddess was speaking to him, and he should pay attention for once. He did.

Kratos's reports on his scouting expeditions were discouraging. He'd found twisted defiles, steep hills dead-ending into blind canyons, and no easy travel anywhere.

"Deep in the mountains, we found vicious natives, too," he reported. "We watched helplessly from a distance as they ambushed and killed one of our men with their spears, then dragged his body off into the brush with them, laughing in their guttural way. The left behind his weapons and horse, and their track in the brush quickly disappeared though we searched for them.

They were very large men with huge jaws, but we could not get close enough to see them clearly. We should avoid these people if we can. I fear they are cannibals."

"Would they be useful as slaves?" Melia asked.

"They are worse than Achaeans," Kratos replied. "They are very rough, and primitive, wearing nothing but unbelted skins over their privates, and apparently have no metal or cloth. We saw no females or huts, though smoke from their fires drifted above the trees in some valleys. You can smell them from a great way off. Perhaps they are the terror Arktos spoke of."

"It doesn't sound like the kind of slaves we want," Eurymedon said, casting an eye toward his little Persians huddled together, their delicate fingers busy with needles and thread and giggling to one another.

"No," Kratos said. "We might be able to beat them into sub-mission, but I don't know. I worry about moving our people through their territory. We might fight them for every foot, even at night."

"I'm going up to the watchtower to sit quietly for a while," Shelby announced." I want to think about the best way for us to move west."

"It's cold on the watchtower," Melia said. "I'll stay here and start sorting and packing. When we see how big our train is, we'll know more about who goes first and how to sequence the trip. The days will begin warming enough to travel in a few weeks."

* * *

Shelby rose, added a layer of fur under his lion skin and wrapped his head and face. She was right. The wind blew down from the northern mountains night and day at this elevation, and the cold cut into your skin like so many blades of fire.

The day was overcast as well as cold, with clouds obscuring the tops of surrounding mountains. He could see the city sitting on its hill in the middle of the valley, far away and strange now. Smoke still rose from it, possibly smoldering fires or perhaps the Achaeans' cooking fires. The mostly level plains around the city were patched with snow where herds of horses moved along, pawing at the frozen grasses. Beyond, in the distant east, the stark barrens of jagged mountains lowered over the still scene. A single crow flew over the valley from the south. Shelby thought he heard its caw, but he wasn't sure if it was his imagination. He decided it must be a trick of cold air.

He knew that everything was not as it seemed. Spring was coming, but midwinter had just ended. The days were longer, but not warmer. He had no idea how many Achaeans survived in the city. They could have a few or they could have thousands. If Eumaeus truly filled the gate towers with dirt and stone to block the gates, as he said, then their only way out would be over the walls, or through some of the tunnels, many of which might still be filled with poisonous gas. If they climbed down the walls, they would be exposed to the arrows from the scouting parties. Surely by now they had filled the pit left when the south gate blew up, and that means they could ride out when they needed to. If they were eating horses, then they were well fed and would remain a formidable threat. He couldn't determine if it would be safer to stay and finish the war with the Achaeans or to migrate to Italy. He hadn't counted on the hill people.

Shelby stood brooding until Alcestis came up to the roof directing Dolios and some other male slaves carrying blankets, braziers, and stacks of wood. One of the men placed a chair for Shelby.

Alcestis carried a loaf of warm bread and a jug of wine. She stood barefoot on the frozen stone deck, lifting one foot and then the other. She wore loose furs around the core of her thin, shivering body.

While Dolios directed the others to make fire in the braziers, Shelby sat in the chair and beckoned Alcestis over. He took the jug and loaf of bread and pulled her into his lap helping her curl up her skinny legs. He wrapped her tenderly, and rubbed her nearly frozen feet. He knew she did not like to be cuddled, but she seemed to welcome the warmth. And her extra body heat kept him warm, too. He brushed away the crumbs he dropped on her head as he ate the bread. He pulled her head against his chest. She squirmed, all elbows and knees, uncomfortable until he finally told her to be still. She remained tense.

He liked the familiar smell of her, but her inability to relax was distracting. He glanced at Dolios, squatting on his heels near a brazier out of the wind, and beckoned him over with a nod of his head.

"Take her downstairs and put her next to a fire. When her feet are no longer cold, come back up. I'm staying here in the clear air for a while."

Dolios muttered something about her feet never getting warm, no matter what, but it was indistinct. And then Shelby was alone, staring out over the dull winter landscape at the muted grays of the overcast sky blending shadows and shapes.

In his mind's eye arose the image of eternal war, of peoples from the north and east moving into the land, of Xerxes with his millions invading the Grecian peninsula, and then the Muslims, and then the Ottomans, of David slinging rocks against a giant. Forever and ever, centuries of bloodshed.

Then the vision shifted to the funerary sarcophagus from Etruria he saw in the Louvre, of a man and woman smiling in death, reclining together and looking outward at a world in peace. "I was bred to make war," Shelby said to the vision. "I'm good at it."

The air had stilled as these thoughts raced through his head. The smell of baking bread rose up the turning stair and wafted across the roof of the watchtower. He heard the laughter of women from below, the distant moo of a stabled cow, the faint screech of a turning wheel on a cart.

"All of the country in this part of the world is folded into north-south valleys by tectonic plate collisions," he said aloud. "The whole world is folded up here. Moving west means climbing innumerable hills, up and down. If we moved north or south we would climb far fewer hills."

A ray of sunshine broke through the clouds in the east, playing briefly over the jagged mountains. Another crow passed overhead, this one flying east to west. Perhaps the earth was talking back to him.

The core belief of Melia's life was that the earth spoke to her, and her duty was to listen to it. To her. To a goddess. To the universe.

Shelby felt confused, uncertain, and it worried him. He was not accustomed to such feelings. Life had been so simple: you learned how to fight, then you went out and killed your nation's enemies. What came after that was not your concern. But he'd become something like the king, leading the remnants of an ancient civilization to new lands and advising on its defense.

It was not a role he wanted or had trained for, but one that came to him by default. And, he realized, by love. Melia loved him, and she was not alone. Rhodia loved him, too. As did many of the Meliae, or what passed for love with those warrior women. Khloe. Iphigenia. Adelphi. Ochne. He guessed it would be impossible to sleep every night in the same room with a hundred physically fit women, making love to only one of them, without some kind of bond arising with them all.

In the distant eastern mountains, the sky lifted again and a strong ray of sunshine danced over the tooth-like peaks, bringing his attention back to the present.

"We could go north up the valley," he said aloud, knowing that no one would hear him. "We could take the whole baggage train north to the ruined citadel and then find a way through the rubble and into the northern plains where the Achaeans came from. But we could not take the horses or the wagons. Everything would need to be disassembled and carted through the passes, over the broken boulders."

Dolios came back up the steps onto the roof and tended the weakening fire in the brazier. Then he squatted again to be near the warmth. Shelby took a long pull on the jug of wine, felt it warming him inside, and then drew the back of his hand across his stubbly mouth. He should shave again.

He stayed up in the cold air for a long time, until the day began to fade, and finally Melia came to find him.

"Your face is blue beneath your stubble," she said. "Come down and warm up. Get some food. Talk to me."

"Yes ma'am," he said.

She cocked her head to one side and looked at him quizzically. Then she turned and led the way back to the staircase.

Before he stepped off the roof, he took one more look to the east and thought he saw, in the gathering darkness, a faint red glow in the hills.

NINETEEN

"In order to reach the land where I will take you," Shelby told the assembly one night during dinner, "we must travel over the water. We do not have boats to travel in, and we are too numerous to find the boats we will need. Therefore, when we reach the shore, we will spend a year building boats and learning to use them."

"We've traveled by sea before," Kratos said. "Some of us. Our cousins still live in Crete, and we have visited them. I traveled a good deal by boat on my tour."

"I've never been in a boat," Eurymedon said. "Is it fun?"

"Sailing is a popular sport in my own day," Shelby said, "but it has a long and distinguished history in the development of the world."

"War?" Kratos asked.

"Yes, war, commerce, exploration. Very important. The Phoenicians were especially good at it. I think they may be distant relatives of yours. If we can find some of their sailors, maybe they will sell us ships or teach us to build them."

"I sailed in a Phoenician ship when I traveled back from Libya," Kratos said, "but we also saw many reed rafts made by the Egyptians and others. Most of the merchants travel by those. They are not really rafts since they have sails, but the master of our ship said that they had to be rebuilt every six months or so. They depend on the buoyancy of the reeds to stay afloat, whereas the Phoenician ship was planked with wood. The reeds become waterlogged after a time."

"Most boats travel up and down the coast," Shelby said, "never getting too far from land. But that would make our voyage too long. I will teach you how to navigate over open water and then you will be masters of the sea and be able to compete with the Phoenicians in war and trade. I think you will like that."

Since their migration from the city, the people at the garrison had become accustomed to dining together without much ceremony or regard to rank, everyone mixed together. The Meliae tended to sit together, though many of them had family members. The garrison's rooms were not large, however, and several hundred people crammed together into a hall meant that there was a good deal of noise from talking and laughter. Shelby sat back on his chair looking out over the short, healthy, and happy people, Melia at his side. She put her hand on his thigh and smiled up at him, and he leaned down and kissed her.

"What is involved in this navigation you speak of and how do we make the boats?" she asked him in his ear.

"Where's Hestia?" he called out in response.

"Here I am, Icarus," the old craftswoman replied from the rear of the room. "Coming."

"Dolios, take some slaves and fetch me a large bowl of water. I want to show something to you and Hestia."

When that was done and Hestia was sitting at his feet, her legs crossed and her old gnarled hands in her lap, he took out his knife and dropped it into the water.

"Why did the knife sink?" he asked.

"Because it is heavier than the water," she said.

"Hmmm," he said. He reached over and took a copper olive oil lamp from the table. It was fairly deep, capable of holding about a quart of oil. He handed it to Dolios and told him to empty the oil into another lantern. When Dolios returned, Icarus asked Hestia to weigh the knife and the lantern in her hands and tell him which was heavier.

She held one of the objects in each hand and quickly determined that the lantern was heavier.

"Let's see if it floats," he said. It did.

"Why did it float?"

"I don't know," Hestia said.

"What makes it float?" he persisted. "It is heavier than the knife, and the knife sinks."

"Because it is wider?" she asked.

"Why would being wide make it float?"

"I don't know," she said, "but I think I see how to find out."

"I thought you would," he said.

"It does not float completely. Some of it is in the water." She used the knife to scratch a line on the lantern marking the level of the water.

"Why are you doing that?" asked Shelby.

"I'm just observing," she said. "I'm not really sure. I've never worked on this question before."

"You've worked with all other materials," he said, "but not water. If we are to cross the sea, you must learn to work with water."

Her eyes twinkled with that inner fire of intelligence he loved about her. She sent another slave running to her workshop to bring back a set of scales and her weights.

While they were waiting, Shelby asked Dolios, "Does wood float?"

"Yes, master," the boy replied.

"Does it burn?"

"Yes, master."

"Alcestis, do you know why wood floats?" Shelby asked.

"Some wood does not float," she said. "Some wood is water-logged and sinks. Also, if you take a stick and throw it into water, it floats on its side, but if you put it straight down it does not float as well and always seeks to float on its side."

"Good observations," he said. Hestia looked at the girl with new interest.

The slave returned with the scales, and Hestia weighed the knife and the empty lantern. The lantern indeed was heavier. Then she weighed goblets from around the room until she found two that were the same weight.

Next, she put the lantern back in the water and began filling it with water. When it sank, she lifted it out and poured the water into one of the goblets and weighed them again. She witnessed that the goblet filled with water was much heavier than the empty goblet.

"What have you just proved?" asked Shelby.

"I don't know," she said.

"You've proved that the water has weight. How much weight does that water have in relation to the copper lantern?"

"A lot," she said.

She stared at the experiment for a time, took a long drink from a goblet of wine in front of Shelby, looked at his face, looked back at the wine, took another drink, looked at his face again. "The water fills all the space into which it is poured," she said. "If it is poured into the lantern, the lantern sinks. But the lantern keeps the water out, and so it floats."

"Yes," he said. "What does that have to do with the weight of the water?"

"Oh!" she exclaimed and leapt to her feet, grabbing the wine goblet and holding it high over her head, twirling around on her old bowed legs "It's the weight of the water that's kept out!"

"That's not all," said Shelby.

"What?" she asked, dropping down again. "What more is there?"

"The knife pushes aside a weight of water also," Shelby said.

"Oh, yes it does," she said.

She mused for a time and then stated, "It's the shape. It's the shape relative to the weight of the water. The weight of the water that is kept out by the lantern's shape must be greater than the weight of the lantern, or it will sink. When I add weight to the lantern, it sinks when it reaches the weight of the water it has kept out."

"Yes," Shelby said. "What does that mean?"

"It means that as long as I can remove the water, I can make a vessel of any size out of any material and it will float, as long as the weight of the water that's kept out is greater than the weight of the vessel."

"That's right," Shelby said. "And if you can get it to float, then you can sail it."

"Now we know that boats do not need to be made out of wood," she added. "We could make them out of copper. Or bronze. Or even that steel you showed us how to make."

"You would rather use the wood for sturdiness and convenience," he said, "but you can put copper on the outside to seal them from the water and to protect the wood from creatures in the sea that love to eat wood. Wood is plentiful, copper requires mining and smelting and other labor, as does the steel, but copper ore is also plentiful. Remember that both the knife and the lantern displaced a weight of water, yet the knife sank. Why?"

"Because of the shape?" she asked.

"What about the shape?"

"The wider the shape, the more water gets moved aside," she said.

"The reason the knife sinks and the lantern does not is—?"

"Because of the shape?"

"Think about the shape for a moment. While you do that, let me tell you a famous story."

The hall fell silent at his words. The people loved to hear him tell stories, many of which they did not believe. Still, he made them think.

"What weighs more, bronze or gold?" he asked.

Hestia knew immediately. "Gold," she said.

"Yes," he said. "Now here's the story. There was once a wealthy Achaean king who asked a craftsman to make him a gold crown. He gave the man a quantity of gold he had weighed, and the man went away."

"Was it an Achaean craftsman?" Rhodia asked, sniffing. At her gesture, all the people laughed.

"Yes, it was," Shelby said.

"My guess is that he stole the gold and was never seen again," said Rhodia.

"Close," Shelby said, "but no. He made a crown, and he presented it to the king. The king put the crown in a scale, and it weighed exactly what it was supposed to weigh. The king was pleased. As he studied the crown for several months, however, he became convinced that the man had stolen some of the gold, but he did not know how to prove it."

"He called his most famous adviser and told him to prove that the crown had not been made with the correct quantity of gold. The adviser went off and took a bath."

"An Achaean took a bath? When did that happen?" Rhodia asked.

"It's a story," Shelby said, laughing. "The Achaeans will one day learn to bathe."

"Not very likely," Melia said.

"We will kill them all first," Rhodia said, slipping a knife from her chiton and testing the sharp blade with a knowing look at Shelby.

"When the Achaean got into the tub, he saw that the water rose. That made him think."

"Again, Icarus, you test our ability to believe you," Rhodia smirked.

"Know your enemy, Rhodia. Of course, he can think."

"Maybe," she retorted.

"Their brains make them easy to kill." Kratos laughed and then drained every goblet of wine within easy reach.

"The adviser thought and thought, and finally he realized that it was not his weight that displaced the water and made it rise, but his volume."

"What does that mean?" Hestia asked.

"It means that a human body, like everything else, has a certain volume. Placing it in water displaces a certain amount of water equal to the volume of the object, whether it is a body or a crown. When he took the proper amount of gold by weight and put it in water, it moved a certain amount of water. Because it is so much heavier, that is, so much denser than copper, it has a smaller volume than an equivalent weight of copper. Let me show you."

He took out one of the gold coins he had picked up during his battle against the Achaeans and asked Hestia to put it in one scale of her balance. Then he instructed her to balance the scale with a handful of pebbles. When the two were in balance, he carefully marked the level of the water and then dropped the coin into it. He noted on the side of the container how high the water rose. Then he removed the coin, made sure the container was refilled to the exact same level it had been before he dropped in the coin, and he dropped in the pebbles. The water rose higher than the gold.

"See how that works?" he asked. "The gold does not have as much volume as rock, even when it weighs the same. That was what the king's adviser discovered. When he took the crown, it moved more water, because the gold had been mixed with copper. Since copper is lighter than gold, the volume of the crown had to be greater if it was mixed with copper in order for it to weigh the same. That proved that the workman, who made the crown of the exact correct weight, had cheated the king because the volume of the crown was too great for the weight of the gold. The difference in the volume between the original gold and the crown was equivalent to the amount of gold the craftsman stole."

"What happened?" Hestia asked.

"When the king understood, he cut off the craftsman's head," Shelby said. "Everything occupies a certain volume in relationship to its weight. No matter how you arrange the thing, either as a long rod or as a cube, it displaces the same volume of water. Once you understand that, then you understand how shaping the object to exclude a certain weight of water means it will float."

"So why does wood float?" Dolios asked.

"Because it has air trapped inside it," Shelby said, "and that makes it lighter than the water it displaces. If you remove the air, as Alcestis pointed out, by saturating the wood with water, it sinks."

"Why does the stick sink when point down and try to float on its side?" Alcestis asked.

"Did you understand what Hestia discovered?" Shelby asked. She nodded.

"Then I will let you think about it. If you think you know, go and visit with Hestia and ask her. If you do not come back from Hestia for a time, I will understand, isn't that right, Hestia?" he asked

Hestia smiled up at him, fairly dancing with happiness and nodding. "If it works for water," she cried out, "does it also work for air? Is that how to fly?"

He smiled at her. "Yes, he said. "But how you displace the air makes a difference, and we will talk about that for years to come. You will learn to work with air after you have learned to work with water."

He rose and took Melia by the hand. "Come with me," he said, pulling her to her feet. "You get the first lesson in flying."

TWENTY

T he snows melted off the valley floor first, turning the ground to mush. Chill winds still blew from the northern mountains, roaring down the long valley, but greenery appeared in the bushes and grasses and the valley filled with early spring's gentle fire of returning chlorophyll in hues of faint lavender and greenish gold.

The wagon trains were organized, and troops of soldiers were appointed to guard them. Advance guards had already departed along the routes scouted by Kratos, clearing roads for the wagons. For weeks, Eurymedon and his riders had been rounding up strayed horses in the valley and driving them up the hill toward the garrison. A number of mares were beginning to foal, but Shelby expected that would not prove too great a hindrance to their travels. Many of the women among them were also pregnant, but most would not give birth until late in the fall. The long, cold winter had not been a time of idleness, in more ways than one. Melia, too, was pregnant.

As far as he could tell, none of the Meliae were expecting. They appeared to have stayed away from the men. Shelby was puzzled by it until Melia explained about some of the ancient medicines developed over centuries by the Matrons. Besides, he had plenty of other things to think about. That his fighting force was intact was a pleasant bonus.

It could take most of the spring and summer to arrive at the sea, months to travel two hundred miles, Shelby reckoned. Much of the way would be tortuous and likely beset by tribes of wild men, through steep inclines and declines, over rocky paths with possibly little in the way of food to scavenge from the land. Still, it was time to leave.

* * *

One evening a few days before they were to set out, Shelby climbed the watchtower to look out over the valley. Despite the daily reports from scouts, he was compelled to see the cold country for himself. In the distance, he saw Achaeans gathering outside the city's walls but without apparent purpose. Possibly they were working on the towers, trying to get the gates open again. He could see masses of men climbing and swarming like ants but not individuals. It was too far.

Let the Achaeans do what they wanted. They fought for the city, a poisoned and shattered place. They could have it. It was no city for women and children.

Tragedy scarred the entire valley. The betrayal of Iapetus, who stabbed his mother and his little sister and then burned them on the altar, was a dark stain, a pollution, in the hearts of the people. How would they ever again eat the sacrificial meat cooked on that altar? It had been desecrated — they had all been desecrated — by that act. Those old Greek writers were right about moral pollution: It must be expunged through sacrifice and prayer and more sacrifice, or the people would sicken and die. If they did not sicken physically, they would sicken morally. The city was polluted with the ruin of earthquake and the poisonous gases, and eroding morality. The pollution could not be washed away by sacrifice or blood or prayer. Their only hope was to abandon the spot and rebuild somewhere else, far away.

Melia joined him on the watchtower, standing close under the shelter of his arm to ward off the chill in the air. Neither spoke for some time.

"I love the coming of spring in the valley," she said finally. "All the hues, the blush of the earth awakening from its winter sleep. Mother loved it so. She could stand for hours gazing at the fields coming to life, watching the storks returning from the south, weeping for the sheer beauty of this place. I will never look out over it again without thinking of her."

"And of her murder," he added.

"Yes."

"Ready to leave?"

"Yes. This was a beautiful place once. Now its beauty only reminds me of horror. Still, I love watching the spring return. We will do that in some other place next year."

He hugged her to his side, and she snuggled into him. As the twilight faded, they could see torches twinkling from the distant city walls, moving like so many tiny fireflies. Shelby's heart grew heavy as he watched the distant enemy. He felt a sense of doom descending with the night.

"I think we better leave tomorrow morning at first light," Melia said. "We must not try the divine patience. Now that I am carrying our child, I can hear her much better. We have a stronger connection. I am so deeply in love with you and with her and with this child to be, but I think she wants to finish the job here, cleanse this place of all memory, beyond any cleansing we can do. She is waiting for us to begin, so we may not have much time."

"Tomorrow it is, and we will go without looking back." Shelby shifted on his feet, looking down at Melia, seeing how her thick, long hair was braided off the back of her head and pulled around in front to hang between her breasts. "Our goddess has violated the order of time already once by bringing me to you."

"Look how the birds are flying this way from the east," she said a little later, watching the clouds of birds catching the last light high above the shadows cast by the hills. "And what is that moving on the valley floor?"

"Where?" he asked.

"There. Far to the other side of the city. Can you not see it?"

"Horses, maybe?"

"Perhaps," she said.

The valley floor was now dark except for patches of unmelted snow glimmering in the dying light. Shelby couldn't see what Melia was talking about, but a sense of oppression began to well up inside him.

In the distant nighttime, a chorus of jackals began, their bone-chilling songs drifting through the dark trees that picketed the high hills. The animals had fattened on the rotting bodies of dead Achaeans all winter. Closer jackals answered as they emerged from their nasty dens, called into the night by their comrades.

"Once that would have been beautiful to me," Melia said. "They have such a range of music in their calls, but I do not find their songs beautiful tonight."

"They are not hunting," Shelby said. "They are alarmed. Something is not right."

"Our people have always said that the songs of jackals open the gates of night and of death," she said quietly. "Metis could hear the goddess singing in their voices. I never have."

"They are moving this way," he observed. "Thousands of them. I did not know so many lived in the valley. You never hear more than one or two at a time."

"Everything in the valley is moving this way," Melia said.

A large red stag came crashing up the hill and ran past the watchtower, fully visible in the torch light that now shone on all sides of the structure.

"That stag looked panicked," he said.

"Come on!" she said urgently. "Time to go. Let's get everyone moving. Our mother is about to cleanse this place."

Even as she was speaking Shelby could see a glow beginning in the eastern mountains, and then he felt the tremor as an earthquake began. The tremor built in intensity, a shock at first, followed by harder and harder shocks. He swayed, fighting to keep his balance.

"Go!" he urged. "Get everyone out of the tower. It will be the first to fall!"

They hurried down the stairs, calling for everyone to get clear, to get away from walls that could fall on them.

Just as they reached the ground, a sudden jolt tossed Shelby into the air and he fell, sprawling. He looked in alarm for Melia. She and Eurymedon were steadying themselves in each other's arms.

"Like riding a stallion," he called, a huge smile on his face. And then one of the eastern dragon tooth mountains blew up. Hundreds of deer, jackals, and bears flooded toward them from the valley. Through the bird-dense air Shelby watched as the mountain erupted, spewing fire and smoke straight at heaven.

It was the cannon fire of gods. The goddess had struck back at Zeus.

Moments later, the roar of the eruption reached him, accompanied by more heavy shocks. The deep, sharp crack of earthquake and volcano, the shifting of the earth, and the brilliantly lit plume of the eruption seemed to pummel the cloud palaces of the Olympians, towering up into the sky in wreaths of lightning.

From what Shelby hoped was a safe distance, it was stunning. Beautiful, frightening, magnificent, threatening. It was like a mighty arm with a terrible fist striking the sky. He watched the ash cloud rise through lightning and begin to drift northeastward toward the ancestral homes of the Achaeans and Mount Olympus. The shadow of that cloud and its outfall would destroy the crops and lives of hundreds of thousands, snuffing them out in a suffocating blanket. Spring would not come to those lands.

Melia found him and stood beside him, staring at the wrath of the volcano, clasping his hand. "What if it comes this way?" she asked, her voice raised over the shriek and roar.

"If the wind shifts and blows the ash toward us, we will die from suffocation," he said. "Already you can see stones cannonading the valley twenty miles from the eruption. If we were there, those rocks would kill us just as they are killing the Achaeans. It is a beautiful sight, but we need to move while we can. I hope we can put many miles between us and that mountain by morning, and that might not be far enough, depending on the wind. We will be lucky if we can move everybody at least five miles."

"What will it do to the valley and the city?"

"Bury them," he said, "in fire." He took her hand and led her down the hill into the night.

CHAPTER
TWENTY-ONE

🔥🔥🔥🔥🔥🔥🔥🔥🔥🔥🔥🔥

S helby stood on a high overlook watching the long line of people and wagons wending west through a twisting valley. They'd spread out along the path. Some of the gaps were a mile wide, leaving room for an enemy to dash in and surround the travelers.

"We've got to close up the line and keep it that way," he said fiercely to Garanus, the thin, stork-like lieutenant who was one of Kratos's trusted friends.

"Yes, Icarus, I know. Kratos knows. All of us are concerned, but the terrain is our enemy now. We can't improve our line unless we improve the terrain."

"I know, Garanus, I know," Shelby said. "I'm just worried. It's taking much longer than I thought, and I worry about the city's safety."

Even without their city as such—the buildings and the square and the gates—the people continued to refer to themselves as "the city." Shelby admired the concept, the way it separated the physical existence of a place from the spiritual and psychological sense of belonging to one another. They were a community, certainly, and for many of them the lack of walls was not a significant hindrance to their idea of city. Good for them.

"Perhaps we should rearrange the line so that the slower-moving units are in front," he said. "Or we could disperse them and mix them with the faster units."

"It's the terrain, Icarus," Garanus replied. "Going downhill is faster than going uphill. Horses move faster than mules. Wagons mire in soft earth, and roads must be cleared for them to pass. Herds of horses must be tended to protect them from wolves, bears, lions." He paused. "People," he added, looking doubtfully overhead at the dark ridges and dense pines. "The wild men come every night hunting for meat, but they take anything we are not guarding. And remember that they stole a slave last week. We found the slave's head, but the rest of his body was gone, as you know. Some of us worry that they might have eaten him."

Shelby nodded. He knew about the guard who lost everything except his head.

"I fear it could take ten of us with spears to conquer just one. A guard told me he saw a wild man leap completely over a horse and its rider without touching either. They are broad, strong, agile, tall, and dangerous. We should avoid them if we can, but it is impossible to tell where their territory is."

"They're not civilized," Shelby said, "and I don't think we can negotiate with them for safe passage. Has anyone tried to talk to them?"

"I heard a couple of them speaking softly in the brush when we passed, but they didn't show themselves and I couldn't see them. They have a language of sorts, at least they have a series of grunts and clicks that passes for language among them, but we do not recognize it. No one among us can make the same sounds." He shifted his long spear to his other hand and reached up behind his right ear to scratch. "Kratos has decided to kill them whenever he finds them."

"Has Kratos killed any? I'd like to see one up close if he has," Shelby said. "This is our new enemy, and I'd like to see a representative."

"I don't think Kratos has killed any," Garanus replied. "I think these wild men are too sly for him. Maybe for all of us."

"Perhaps we will muddle through," Shelby said, "but I still don't like these gaps in the line, and I especially don't like the way the line thins down to only one or two abreast going through the narrow places. We are too vulnerable at those times."

"We have lost scouts in the higher hills," Garanus said. "They follow your instructions to fan out and search a wide span on either side of our line, but some never return. Probably they are ambushed by the wild men."

"I will speak with Kratos. We should increase the number of scouts, though that could leave even more of the line exposed."

They watched the slow progress of the city for a time, the hot sun overhead, burning off the mists and shadows of the valley.

"If the next valley is broad enough and has a good supply of water, perhaps we should stay there for a week to rest," Shelby said. The hills seem to be getting a little lower. Maybe the path will get a little straighter too."

"I hope so, Icarus. Our supplies are running thin."

"How much do we have?"

"We need to be where we are going in a month. Many of our people already are foraging as we go, digging roots and gathering berries."

"That's part of the reason we are moving so slowly."

"We must pitch camp somewhere in the fall and stay through the winter. We should also try to plant a crop to harvest before winter, so that pushes our need for a camp back at least two months before cold weather. Also, some of our women are pregnant, and the babies will arrive after the equinox, during harvest if we can have one."

"I hope we find the sea with enough time to have a harvest. It will take us all winter and maybe all next year to build boats and learn to use them."

"I am one for the shore," Garanus confided. "I've only been on the sea one time, when my parents took me to see relatives in Crete. A storm came up unexpectedly, and we were all sick. When we finally arrived, we were not particularly welcome. Pirates had been attacking our relatives, burning their boats, stealing children and everything else. I was glad to return home, but the sea journeys were hard."

"It takes a while to get used to the constant motion of the water," Shelby said. "But you do, in time. I hope Kratos has found a way down to a harbor, where we can find boats or build them."

"I've not seen him for ten days, but the troops speak of him. The men rotate in and out of his scouting party, so they remain refreshed, but he is now three or four hard days' ride ahead of us."

"Kratos never tires," Shelby said. "He is the most amazing warrior I have known."

"Look! Do you see the wolf?" Garanus pointed up the hill into a stand of black pine. "If you watch, you will see the movement. From the way she moves, I think she is a female. She appears to be alone, but females are almost never alone, so I don't know for sure. I've been watching her for weeks. When she comes into the open and skirts a stand of trees or crosses the valley to avoid a certain area, I think it is because wild men are hiding there."

"That is a valuable observation, friend," Shelby said. "Let's feed her from time to time. Kill a rabbit, leave it for her. Perhaps we can train her to be a scout for us."

TWENTY-TWO

A mile ahead of the two men, Melia and Rhodia were walking together beside a wagon. Dolios was driving the wagon and also scanning the countryside for potential threats. He was nervous about the wild men and expected at any moment to be ambushed by a party of them. With several of the Meliae asleep on top of the piles of blankets and treasures in the wagon, he was not worried for his safety, but he was alert, watchful.

Rhodia and Melia were bored with the trudging pace of the wagons and wandered off toward a nearby stream, out of earshot of the wagon train.

Dolios glanced over his shoulder at Alcestis, who was sitting among the Meliae, quietly mending the lion skin where it had been torn and punctured.

He liked Alcestis, but he couldn't tell whether she liked him. Perhaps she needed more time. Perhaps she would never like him. He was well aware that pushing her would be a mistake, a sure way of losing her. Meanwhile, he would continue to be kind and to look out for her. Without her parents to buy her back, she might remain a slave forever, just as he might. In that case, unless he could win his freedom and enough wealth to buy her, their lives would never be their own.

He loved her narrow face, her bony arms and legs, her pointed nose and her small mouth. Most of all, he loved her intelligent eyes. And she was a thinker and a learner. Her brain was gorgeous to him. Like Hestia, she had a beautiful mind.

Hestia's work progressed slowly, because she could only work at night, when the wagons stopped moving. She was creating a new set of armor for Shelby, a gift. And she was excited to be exploring many other things, making little copper boats, contemplating iron. How do you cut and shape iron, she wondered.

Besides, Hestia had many other things to do just to keep the wagons functioning. New wheels, new harnesses, new crosstrees as well as preparing and repairing armor—all chores she happily supervised during their evening stops. For larger projects, she would sometimes stay a day or two behind as the main caravan moved slowly on. Then they would ride all night to catch up, always guarded of course, their way lit by the ingenious brass lanterns with parabolic reflectors that she and Shelby had created for nighttime signaling.

Dolios, meanwhile, should have been helping her, but his skill at wagon driving kept him occupied and allowed his thoughts to settle on the strangely quiet and not-so-pretty image of Alcestis. The miles were brutal, delaying all of them from getting on with the more vital parts of their lives.

Shelby also used the lanterns and trumpets for nighttime signaling all up and down the line. The ravines through which they passed were always narrow with overhangs where the wild men could ambush them, but the lanterns gave a sense of security in knowing that help could be sent when needed, even at night.

For several days, the wild men had not stolen from them, leading more optimistic people to believe they had moved beyond the savages' range. Only the lone wolf, ghosting along in the dusk, was known to be lurking away in the shadows.

CHAPTER
TWENTY-THREE

A s the column advanced, so did the season, growing warm in the spring sun. Melia and Shelby took to sleeping outside under the stars. When the air grew damp and cool in the hours before dawn, she would roll next to Shelby to draw warmth from his slumbering body.

She loved lying awake, pondering those bright specks of light in the dark sky and running her hands over her swelling belly. Shelby often disturbed her with his explanations of what the stars were. She preferred the old stories she had grown up with, the idea that they were windows into the homes of the million divine sisters, an eternal city full of love and compassion. She did not like to think of them as huge balls of fire scattered across the sky, burning like the sun. She could not fathom the distances and the sizes he told her about, or the double stars and the star clusters and the galaxies. He had pointed out the blur of the Andromeda Galaxy, so distant and so huge that it sounded infinite, and yet he said there were billions and billions of such galaxies.

He'd point out constellations and tell her about navigating by the stars, sketching out a tool he called an astrolabe, a star taker. It was a funny name for a tool. Nobody could take a star. She knew Shelby meant that it took the position of the star, not the star itself. But why didn't he come up with a word that meant star positioner? That's the way the tool was used. What would it be, an astrothemis?

Sometimes she could hear the soft voice of the goddess singing to her from the stars and the hills. Until she became pregnant, most of her communication with the goddess had been through visions delivered during her trances. The visions were full of imagined or forgotten things rushing silently toward her from the dark. Very occasionally she'd heard distant voices, but they were indistinct. Now, though, she could hear her goddess speaking. That first quiet voice: "Fire is coming. Get ready to go, child." Almost immediately she'd realized she was pregnant.

"Tell me, Mother Goddess," she said aloud, low and quiet so as not to disturb the others. The baby stretched in her, then curled again in sleep. She lay silently staring upward in the soft night, emptying her mind of thoughts, deepening her awareness of the world, straining to hear the singing of the stars beyond the snoring rustle of the camp.

"What?" Shelby asked, drowsily, not really awakening. Then he was fully awake. Something was watching them; he felt it. He eased his hand to his tomahawk and slowly drew the cord around his wrist.

Melia felt him tense and turned her head from the stars to look at him, inquiring with her mind into the sudden tension in his body—his careful, alert breathing. She, too, became tense.

A wolf howled nearby, a short yowl, and she heard it rustle in the undergrowth. She reached her hand out to Rhodia nearby, intending to poke the girl in the ribs to alert her as well, but she wasn't there. Maybe she had gone to pee, something Melia also needed to do.

Shelby reached over and held her still, shifting on the bedding. Then suddenly he was up and off, moving low to the ground in the shadows.

The wolf yipped again, farther away.

"Who's there?" challenged a sentry, not far from them. Melia sat up, looking around for the Meliae. Adelfi was gathering her huge body beneath her, getting ready to spring. Khloe cocked her crossbow, and Iphigenia uncovered her spear. The snoring petered out as the others awakened and quietly armed themselves. They moved low to the ground, assembling in a protective shield around her.

Melia cocked her own crossbow and then lay still, on her left side, waiting.

A dark shape lifted out of the shadows nearby, indistinct and threatening. It was as large as a bear. But what bear ever walked into a group of humans? They avoided the trouble of humans. Beyond it, at the edge of her vision, were more shapes. A dozen, perhaps more.

Behind her to her left, she heard the rasping noise of a sword being drawn.

"Wild men," whispered Rhodia. "Close. Hard to see in the dark."

"I see them clearly now," Melia said. "I smell them, too. I can sense the heat of their bodies."

"Your eyesight and nose are better than mine tonight."

"Adelfi," called Melia loudly, and the shapes dropped out of sight again. "Bring light."

Soon the group was surrounded by blazing torches, but no wild men were found. Shelby stayed out hunting them the rest of the night, scouring the perimeter and trying to track their movements without success.

In the morning, they found the disemboweled body of a sentry, his legs and arms missing, his buttocks cut away. The remainder of his carcass lay in a pool of muddy blood.

And both Alcestis and Dolios were missing.

TWENTY-FOUR

"Do you think they ran off together?" Rhodia asked.
"Out of character for Dolios," Shelby replied, searching the ground for clues. "Although, I know he's attracted to Alcestis. A guy can change when it comes to a woman he loves."
Rhodia snorted and moved away.

Garanus and a group of his soldiers were scouring farther up-hill. Shelby saw the crane-like man drop to his knees to examine the ground. When he stood again, he signaled to Shelby.

"I think we found something," he said. "It doesn't look good."

"Rhodia, make sure the Meliae are positioned to protect Melia and the others in case these savages come back while we are away. Then you can join me again up there with Garanus. Also," he added as she turned to go, "send some riders ahead to alert Kratos. I will find Dolios and the girl. Or what is left of them."

"I will also instruct the train to construct defensive barricades and to draw together," Rhodia said. "I wish Eumaeus was still with us. He was good at that."

"Yes," Shelby said. "I miss him. I hope he prospers in the Eurotus valley."

"What do you think?" Garanus asked. "It looks like there was a struggle here."

"I'm not sure that sandal belongs to Dolios, but it is one of ours," Shelby said. "Usually Dolios doesn't wear sandals. He'd rather go barefoot."

He turned the sandal over in his hands, examining it closely. It was the kind of footwear Hestia made her workers wear to protect their toes. It had a few small burn marks on it, little pin-holes where the leather had been struck by sparks of hot metal. "If it does not belong to Dolios, then it belongs to one of Hestia's workers," Shelby said. "Any other evidence?"

"We also found a trail of footprints and dislodged stones going up the hill," Garanus said.

"If it was Dolios who was taken here, I don't understand why we heard nothing. Surely he would have cried out for help." Shelby looked around. "And what was he doing up here this far from camp anyway?"

"The girl?" Garanus asked.

"Maybe, but unlikely. It's not the kind of thing Dolios would do."

"Perhaps she's the one who left," Garanus said, "and he followed her."

"Maybe," Shelby nodded, "but it's not like her, either."

"That sentry was killed and cut apart," Garanus said. "We might find that others are gone as well. I wonder if they were going for the women and killed the sentry to get closer to them."

"Almost certainly," Shelby said. "And if they have Dolios and Alcestis, they're going to take them back to their tribe. They'll eat him and keep Alcestis alive to breed. I'll bet they ate the sentry's heart and liver on the spot last night and are carrying the body parts back to feed the others."

They made their way up the hill, spotting broken branches and scuff marks in the dirt where a body or bodies had been dragged. Then the scuff marks disappeared. As they went down the far side of the little hill, they saw a single line of footprints gradually fading away toward dense forest high up on a ridge.

"Fan out," Shelby said to the other men. "Stay close, but examine a broad stretch of land. My guess is that they've made for those trees up there, and we will eventually see evidence of it. But I don't want to miss anything in case my guess is wrong."

They toiled up the rising slopes, following wandering paths that likely had been made by animals through head-high brush and over rocks, moving farther away from their camp. Shelby spotted the print of a large dog, possibly the wolf he called Calu, after the Etruscan god of death.

Calu had become more trusting as Garanus and his men

continued to feed her, but she wasn't comfortable enough to approach within a hundred yards of them.

He spotted deer prints and larger cloven hoof prints that could be boar or ibex. They found only one human footprint, but it was too small to belong to the wild men or to Dolios. He hoped it was left by Alcestis, because it seemed to be alone. If it were hers, then she was on foot and not being carried. Maybe the wild men had not captured—or eaten—her.

After another hour, they rested. No one had brought water or provisions. Two men returned to camp for supplies and horses and more men to aid in the search. Shelby leaned back against a shady rock to puzzle over the mystery of the youngsters' disappearance. For the last hour, they'd seen no evidence of the wild men. But the wild men were apex predators and in their own country. Tracking them might be harder than tracking any other animal if they didn't want to be followed. He remembered tales of tracking Apaches or Comanches in the western United States in the early days of that republic: you didn't know you'd found them until you were about to die.

He closed his eyes and wiped the sweat from his forehead. Garanus leaned over and whispered, "I see movement above us on the hill."

Shelby's eyes popped open, and he squinted into the distance. "Where?" he asked quietly.

"See that cracked boulder, the big one? Something moved past it. It could be an animal."

Shelby stared a minute more, and then he saw the wolf, low to the ground, creeping forward. "The wolf?" he asked.

"No, ahead of the wolf. I see the wolf now, too."

Shelby's eye caught Rhodia's, and she moved over to them. He explained what they had seen and told her they were going to investigate.

"I want to go, too," she said, swinging her crossbow around to make sure it was loaded.

"We need you to direct the troops here, keep them safe. I'll signal when you should come up."

"I'm quieter than you, and I have a better sense of smell," she replied. "Also, I'm restless. I don't like sitting here."

"Go with Icarus," Garanus said. "I'll watch for your signals."

Shelby sighed internally. Of all the headstrong women he had known, Rhodia could be the most difficult. He was not sure he himself could survive a fight with the wild men, and he knew that Rhodia could not. She was strong, lithe, deadly, and a good shot, but if what he'd learned about the wild men was accurate, she'd only get off one bolt before they were on her. And then they would eat her, because she would do too much damage to them if they tried to breed her.

Besides, all in all, he'd rather live in a world without Garanus than without Rhodia. The hot-tempered little redhead was fun, in a dangerous kind of way, creative and sexy, and it was obvious that she was strongly attracted to him. But here she was, staring up at him with her blue eyes and waiting for him to move.

They'd go. Maybe it wouldn't be as fatal as he feared.

TWENTY-FIVE

B efore they reached the cracked boulder, Shelby saw
Alcestis. The skinny, naked girl was crawling slowly on
her hands and knees, moving quietly from bush to bush.
Nearby, the wolf was also creeping along. They looked like a
team working together, not like the wolf was hunting her. Their
extreme caution suggested that they were alert to something he
could not see.

He and Rhodia dropped to the ground and continued quietly
up the hill toward the boulder. When they reached it, Alcestis and
the wolf were gone, but they found a narrow gully that was about
ten feet deep and just wide enough for a single file of men. The
gully, a watercourse in wet weather, cut a twisting and turning
path uphill, its bottom layered with dried silt washed down with
the rains. It was packed hard with large human footprints.

Rhodia started down into the gully, but Shelby pulled her
back and signaled her to follow him. He crept along the edge to
avoid being pinned between attackers. Fighting just one of those
wild men would be difficult.

The pair moved slowly, and they were soon out of sight of
Garanus and the others. Shelby considered going back to bring
Garanus up to date but rejected the idea. The urgency he had
seen in Alcestis's movements alarmed him. She must be following the wild men, and they probably had Dolios with them. He
reasoned that she would not try to follow them if she didn't know
Dolios was alive.

He picked up the pace a little, trying to preserve their silence.

But nobody moves completely in silence, and that bothered him. These wild men survived because they were superior hunters, and that meant they spent lifetimes sneaking up on prey. Possibly they had bows, or atlatls, and rocks were abundant. Everyone knew they had spears. They could damage at a distance if they wanted. They would be attuned to every nuance of the land and would listen for movement in every branch and leaf. They could remain motionless and invisible, like all good hunters. They could attack swiftly, and they probably were hyper-vigilant and suspicious all the time. Against such a band, Rhodia's single crossbow and his tomahawk would be next to useless.

After thirty or so minutes, they heard voices and shuffling ahead and caught a glimpse of a figure rounding a bend in the gully. It was a large man, and they only saw his back, but they also saw Alcestis. She nodded at Shelby, and he nodded back. She nodded at the wolf and then looked at him again. He nodded to her again and put his hand out palm down, signaling her to lie flat and still. She did, and he and Rhodia crept up to her.

Alcestis pointed over the edge of the gully and slowly backed away. Shelby took her spot and then moved ahead until he could look down. The gully widened out here and he saw Dolios on his knees in the middle of nine wild men squatting on their heels. He was gagged with a thick rope of twisted leather or sinew and the gag was tied to his hands behind his back. One of the men was holding the sentry's severed leg over his shoulder, a sandal still strapped around the foot. At his feet lay two severed arms.

Shelby sensed Rhodia creeping up and put a hand out to stop her. Just sitting there was like trying to hold your hand inches from a hornet's nest without being attacked. No matter how cautious she was, it wasn't worth the risk. A slight change in air currents could waft his scent down to them, and they would swarm up the gully walls.

"Take Alcestis and go back to the cracked boulder," he whispered to Rhodia, "and signal Garanus to bring up his men. I'll ease uphill and wait for them to pass."

She nodded and moved off, Alcestis behind her. Calu, thirty or forty yards away, watched the women move away, and then fixed her yellow eyes on him.

He heard grunting and eased back up to the edge of the gully.

A wild man was hauling Dolios to his feet. The boy collapsed, and one of men kicked him. He tried to stand, staggered, and fell again. Shelby saw the bruising on his face and knew the boy had put up a fight when he was captured.

It was the first time Shelby had seen the men in daylight, and they were formidable. They were easily seven feet tall, and they had to weigh well over three hundred pounds. Maybe four hundred. They were broader than National Football League linebackers. They were the size of grizzly bears, with muscles like rodeo bulls. They wore light fur aprons in front, and nothing else. Their buttocks were uncovered, except by the dark hair that grew all over their bodies. They had full beards and long, gorilla-like arms. Their broad noses were flat against their faces, and when they opened their mouths to grunt at one another, Shelby observed prominent canine teeth. The sun had turned their skin dark, and they seemed to all be tattooed. But it was their movement that impressed him most. They were swift and deft, with no wasted motion.

One of them finally picked Dolios up and slung him over his shoulder, and the man with the sentry's leg came up behind, threatening Dolios with it.

One of Dolios's sandals was missing, so the one Garanus found probably belonged to the boy.

He had no idea how poor Dolios could be rescued. He wondered if he himself would need rescuing before the day was out. He glanced around for Calu, but she was gone.

TWENTY-SIX

For some time, he followed the gully after the men, dismayed and anxious. Gradually the ravine deepened where it cut through a composite terrain of hard clay and rocks, the debris of a long-dead volcano. But it also narrowed, squeezing the men into a more restricted passage. A flash flood at this point would kill all of them, but under the clear sky and hot sun he doubted that could happen.

Still, it gave him an advantage. He could push rocks down on them, or he could jump into the gully and fight them one at a time. Perhaps both. Alternatively, he could just continue to follow them until he found their lair, where he supposed a hunting band of nine would have at least other individuals to care for: women, children, perhaps some elderly, possibly more men. If they were approaching that home base, then no doubt some of its residents would be watching for them. They might see him following the men, and then all hell would break loose when they raised the alarm.

They were less than a mile from the wooded ridge when he spotted the wolf on the opposite side of the gully. Had she been following all along? Alcestis crept along behind her, stooped over and close to the ground. What the hell was she thinking?

Rhodia came up behind him. "Garanus and his men are almost here, and reinforcements from the camp," she whispered. "We should have a hundred or so on horseback soon."

He nodded to her and then, with a questioning look, he nodded toward Alcestis across the gully.

"Later," she whispered.

Despite Rhodia's information, he thought he might be forced to act before they reached the ridge. Here the gully was deep and narrow, but it would broaden, and then who knew what kind of additional problems they might have. And even though reinforcements would soon arrive, it might be too late. The sooner he and Rhodia took action, the better. But where, and how?

They cut across a thin peninsula of land and ended up ahead of the band. He made up his mind. He would block the gully and fight them one on one, and Rhodia could shoot at them from behind. He signaled to her, and she seemed to understand. She wiggled backward and then down the path to a lower point. Across the gully, the wolf crept forward, her teeth bared, her ears back. Alcestis was nowhere to be seen.

As quietly as he could, Shelby slipped into the ravine ahead of the band, around the sharp bend, and stopped under an overhang of rock. Beneath it, with his back to the gully wall, they wouldn't be able to get him from behind or above. He might be able to take them on.

Then he heard them, padding along, speaking quietly in guttural tones interspersed with clicks. A shift in the shadows of the gully, a kicked pebble, and the first man rounded the corner and came face-to-face with him.

Shelby struck him in the chest with the prong of the tomahawk, and the man staggered backwards, surprised and enraged. His powerful legs propelled him into the air, and Shelby hit him again as he came on, striking his left shoulder with the blade of the tomahawk. With his right hand, the man drove his spear at Shelby as he came down, thrusting again and again with lightening-like speed while behind him the other savages, raising deafening howls of rage, crowded forward to see what was going on.

The man charged him again like a wounded bull, head down, furious, his strength undiminished by two blows that would have killed other men instantly. Those behind shoved forward with great clamor, their sheer size forcing their wounded comrade ahead. Shelby parried jab after jab of the spear, and then dodged a thrown spear that ricocheted off the gully wall.

A shadow appeared from overhead, and a large rock dropped onto one of the men. Then another and another. It wasn't Rhodia.

It must have been Alcestis. The rocks knocked one man down, but other men picked up the dropped stones and heaved them at Shelby, who was still struggling with the first man.

Never in his life had Shelby been so out-muscled and out-fought. In the narrow gully, he did not have room for any of his well-practiced martial arts maneuvers. He could kick forward, but not sideways, and it was impossible to twist. Bleeding heavily from cuts and bruised badly, only sheer luck kept him from being seriously wounded, and he knew his luck couldn't last. If Rhodia could not kill them from behind, he would be overwhelmed, rocks or no rocks from overhead.

Alcestis was strong for her age and worked consistently with the Meliae in their calisthenics and training, but she was unable to pick up and carry stones large enough to do real damage. And the wild men had no problem picking them up and heaving them back at her.

And then, it was over. The last man dropped forward, his gapping mouth with its large canine teeth digging into the dirt. The deafening noise dropped, replaced by the groans and growls of the dying. He scanned the area. Some of the men were still moving or twitching, and one was glaring at him, his fearsome teeth bloodstained and his lips drawn back to bite, but he was also gurgling for breath. He could not rise, but Shelby drove one of the stone-tipped spears into the man's mouth anyway.

Rhodia came into view from the rear. "Easy shooting," she said. "They didn't even know I was there. I decided to hit them between their shoulder blades to make them drop their weapons. I think some of the bolts passed through and struck the men ahead. You, however, look awful. Can you walk?"

Too exhausted to speak, he nodded and leaned against the rock and clay wall, his head falling back as he panted. He wanted to sit down, but he wanted to find Dolios first. That had been the whole point.

They heard horses overhead, and Alcestis came up through the gully to join them, her eyes still full of rage. "Where is he?" she asked. "I saw him just when the fight started, but then I lost sight of him in the bodies."

"Down here, Garanus," Rhodia called, and the angular lieutenant joined them in a scatter of rocks, landing feet first on one of the dead men. He looked around at the narrow defile, surprised, then impressed.

"All of them?" he asked.

"Yes," Rhodia said.

"Did you see the wolf up there," Alcestis asked. "She was not happy to be this close to so many people."

"I saw her stealing off through the brush, just the tip of her tail," he said. "The horses gave us away, I'm sure. And I know they smelled the wolf."

Shelby was still gasping, and he was beginning to hurt. A cut on his cheek bled freely, and blood dripped off his chin.

"Dolios is under here somewhere," he gasped to Garanus. "I'm going to need help pulling these bodies away until we find him." He gasped for air, then panted. "And I'm going to need help getting out of this gully. I don't have the strength to climb up." Garanus nodded and shouted some commands up the steep bank.

Soon ropes dangled over the edge. Rhodia and Alcestis tied them around the bodies, and the horses overhead made short work of uncovering Dolios from under his huge captors. Alcestis removed a sharpened piece of flint from the hand of a corpse and cut the leather thong out of his mouth and then from his hands. Dolios leaned over and vomited.

"I thought Achaeans smelled bad," he said. "You have no idea."

"Yes, I do," said Rhodia. "Alcestis and I will finish the job of killing them, and then let's go back to camp."

Shelby raised a hand weakly, and then let it drop. What was the point? These city females would castrate every dead enemy. Wild men were the enemy, now.

"Be sure they're dead before you touch them," he warned, putting a hand on Garanus's shoulder. "Give me a boost up?" he gasped.

"Use a rope," the soldier said. "We'll tie a loop for your feet and another for your hands, if you think you can stand long enough to be pulled up."

Shelby nodded, and a minute later he lay sprawled at the top of the gully. He closed his eyes on the brilliant sky.

TWENTY-SEVEN

S helby rested briefly, worried that the fight would awaken the wild men's camp and bring their companions. But for a moment, he really could not move. He sprawled in the dirt recovering, catching his breath, feeling his loss of strength. Then, with Garanus's men helping him to his feet, he got on a horse for the ride back to camp. During that time, he grilled Dolios and Alcestis.

Alcestis had awakened and seen that Dolios was not yet back from Hestia's forge. She couldn't sleep, and she thought she'd go and wait for him.

And Calu? Alcestis had begun carrying scraps of meat out to the wolf every day at dawn and dusk during the winter, when they were still camped with Arktos at the western garrison. She would place the scrap on the ground, speak in the direction of the wolf, and then go back inside. When she looked again, the scrap would be gone.

It took two months before Calu allowed Alcestis to see her and another month before she grew easy enough to allow others to see her. Now Calu seemed to follow her whenever she left camp, though never very close.

Calu was her only friend, she said. Except maybe Dolios, who was mostly self-absorbed.

Dolios explained that he had not expected to see Alcestis, and certainly not the wolf, but when he heard Calu yip, he stood still. That's when a wild man came at him out of the dark. He struggled, bit, and kicked, but the man held him tightly over the mouth and carried him away.

"I saw the wild man grab something," Alcestis said. "It looked like Dolios in the dark. You know, short, not much there. And the wolf had warned me. When the wild man began to carry him away, I knew I'd lose them in the dark if I didn't follow. I thought if I stayed up with them, I would be able to come back here and tell you where they had taken him. I had no idea they would butcher that poor sentry and sit around on their heels eating his insides. That's when Calu appeared. We kind of understood one another and followed them when they ran off."

"You're lucky they didn't eat you," Shelby said.

Alcestis turned suddenly. "Calu just went down the hill," she said. "Is another group of wild men heading this way?"

"Maybe," Shelby said. "They will not be happy when they find their brothers. We need to get back to camp."

The ride was easier and faster than walking, but it was just as arduous. Shelby was afraid he would pass out from the exhaustion of the battle, reminding him once more that he had become more vulnerable, perhaps more mortal, since the discus hit him. They were almost to camp when the chilling screams of wild men penetrated the noise of the horses' hooves. They had found the corpses. He wondered briefly if the rest of the band would eat their dead brothers and sons. He somehow doubted it, but he was certain they would want revenge. He couldn't face them again anytime soon. Tonight would be very dangerous.

* * *

"I'm glad you're back," Melia said when they rode up to the camp. From the expression on her face, it was clear she had been worried. "It must have been rough."

He dismounted with difficulty, stumbling on weak legs. He had to lean on her to make it to the tent. On the way, he explained what had happened.

"Kratos has been alerted," she said. "Or will be, if the riders get through. Tell me what you think will happen next."

"My guess is that the rest of the band will come after us," he said. "Probably tonight. The sooner we are away from these mountains, the happier I will be."

"Is it safer to move, or to stay and defend?" she asked.

"I don't know," he said. "If we can't keep the wagons and people defended, if they get too strung out, then it will be more dangerous to move."

"Do you think we should send Garanus back with a stronger force to confront them?"

"Rhodia shot nine of them in the back," he said, "but if we can't get easy shots, then no, we can't stop them. They are very tough and hard to kill. They are skilled at camouflage, so you can't see them until they're on you, and a blow that would kill an average man only infuriates them. When they are coming at you, they can move so fast that you might not be able to get a shot off. They have spears and can throw large stones. I don't think they have bows, but in this brushy country our bows are little use against them."

"Hmm," she said, tending to her bruised husband. "I wonder if they've had much wine in their lives."

Shelby broke into a smile. "Sometimes, lady," he said, "sometimes you think of everything."

"We have a lot, but if we leave it out then our own people could get into it. Especially now. They are tense and afraid. Let's think about this and consult others."

"How we did it would be important," Shelby said. "If they have no experience with wine, then they might not know what to do with it."

"Maybe we will need to teach them," she said, grinning broadly. "I bet the Meliae could figure that one out."

"Perched up on wagons in firelight, dipping goblets into barrels of wine and carousing?" asked Shelby.

"Something like that. Maybe they also need to be naked."

"So they can get away?"

"Possibly they would not want to get away." She grinned. "You cannot always tell with women."

She went through the flap of the tent, and Alcestis came in, carrying refreshments of wine and bread.

"I hope master is not angry with me," she said, her face down.

"No, Alcestis, I am impressed by your forethought and your courage. You did absolutely right." He reached out and took her hand, pulling her closer. In her awkward way, she resisted.

"Thank you," he said. "You saved Dolios, you led us to him. He would be somebody's dinner if you had not followed."

She blushed, drew away from his light grip, and darted from the tent with her hands over her face.

TWENTY-EIGHT

"If they like the wine, we might not be able to get them to go away," Garanus said later that afternoon. "And how could we deal with a crowd of drunken wild men?"

"What about wild men with hangovers?" Rhodia asked. "That could be worse."

"I think we should kill as many as we can and then get as far away from this place as we can, and that's that," Eurymedon said. "We can send out archers on horseback, run them down, and get away."

"These are huge, immensely strong men. We can't kill them head-on, except with the crossbows, and we may not have enough of those," Shelby said.

"That brings us back to wine," Melia said. "Or trickery of some kind."

Alcestis came and went, bringing wine and food to where they sat on a rug, planning. Dolios, still too beaten and exhausted to move, was tended by one of the healers, who cleaned his wounds and instructed him to rest. Shelby felt the same way.

"I hit that guy square on his trapezius," Shelby said. "I hit him hard, as hard as I could, and it should have chopped through to his collarbone, but I'm sure it didn't. That prong in his chest just made him mad. I know it hurt and the prong went all the way in, but it didn't stop him. When I pulled it out, the cutting edge made a nasty gash. Still, on he came, as dangerous with one good arm as with two. He staggered but didn't stop. I don't think the prong penetrated his pectorals into his lung. That's how big and muscular they are. That spear of his nearly killed me. A similar blow to an Achaean would have ripped his whole chest open, but with these guys it's worse than fighting a lion. Our best chance with the wild men is to get the hell away from them."

"We can't," Melia said. "We can't move this vast train far enough or fast enough."

"We can't even circle up the wagons for defense," Shelby said. "The ground and the brush are too rough. We have almost no maneuverability."

Alcestis set down a tray of refreshments and turned to him. "Master," she said, "we have fire." Then she left.

"She's right," he said. "We have fire."

"Of course, we have fire," Rhodia said, disgusted. She glared at Alcestis. "So what?"

"Garanus," Shelby said, "for what's left of the day, have your troops clear brush. Pile it about a hundred paces away in an arc around the camps and set fire to it as a defensive barrier as we move out. I see no other solution. We will continue to set fires as we go, unless the wind shifts to blow the fire back toward us. As long as it blows like this, we will be safe behind the barrier of flames."

"I like the wine idea," Melia said, "but Rhodia is right. Even if I drug it, we might have a bunch of drunken wild men to deal with before they pass out."

"It would take a lot of wine to get to them," Shelby added, "even if it's drugged. And they might metabolize it faster than we do. It might not even affect them. It seems to me our best defense is the fire barrier."

"And we can keep the wine for ourselves," Melia said.

"I'll help Garanus, and we'll get all the wagon groups to do the same," Eurymedon said. "At least we are not just sitting here waiting to be attacked in the night."

"Let's go to work," Shelby said. "I'll rest up a bit longer and try to think of ways to improve this plan. I'm especially worried about Hestia and her forges. We cannot lose her. She's irreplaceable."

"If they are as tough as you say," Melia said, "then we must use spears and not arrows on them, Eurymedon. Or crossbows."

"I've said all along that we needed more crossbows."

Eurymedon stood. "Not that many people listened."

"We haven't needed them up to now," Shelby said, reaching up a hand. He pulled himself up with the help of Eurymedon. "But you're right, we need a thousand of them now."

"I will sacrifice at sunset," Melia said, also rising. "Perhaps the mother will clarify our situation. Perhaps not. The wild men are as much her creation as we are, so she may not interfere. Still, she certainly helped us against the Achaeans." Melia stood splay-footed for a moment, her hands behind her on her lower back, the posture revealing her swelling belly. "Ooof," she said. "The child is restless tonight."

"So are the natives," Shelby said, receiving a quizzical look from Melia. "That's a saying we have in my country. The natives are restless. It means there will be unpredictable trouble."

"We can predict this accurately," Garanus said. "They are still howling out there."

TWENTY-NINE

〰〰〰〰〰〰〰〰

A fter the sacrifice and her trance, which seemed to go on and on, Melia was too exhausted to stand. Rhodia and several of the Meliae helped her back to the tent she shared with Shelby, and she collapsed.

"Our mother goddess told me that we would continue to have troubles until we saw the sea," she said. "She did not offer any help or suggest how we could escape our present difficulty. These men belong to a time long before our own, when all people were this way. That worries me."

"I'm more worried that the brush won't burn well enough or long enough to keep them away," Shelby said.

"At least we will be able to see anyone moving toward us. That approach last night scared me."

"Me, too," he said. "They got too close. And they killed that sentry so quickly that he didn't have time to alert anyone."

"Killed and then ate," she said, "while sitting on Dolios. The boy had a difficult time of it. I've given him something to help him sleep through the night. He will still be groggy tomorrow."

"I wish you could give me something," Shelby said, pulling his body armor over his head. "This twenty-first-century armor gave me a big boost last year against the Achaeans. I never wore out. The Guardian's venom kept me in top shape. I wish I felt that way again."

"It wasn't venom," said Melia. "It was a gift, and it had healing powers that helped us win against the Achaeans. You demean the gift of the goddess through that Guardian if you continue to call it venom. It's sacrilegious. Stop it."

He broke into a smile. "You'd have called it venom if you'd seen the stinger it came out of," he said, reaching out to stroke her hair. "But I will obey. Not because you're right, though you may be, but because I love you, and that's good enough."

"Good enough," she affirmed, taking his hand. "Go and do what you can to protect us, Lion."

He armored up again and prepared to go back out to confront the terrors of the wild men and the night. Stepping out of the tent, he saw Alcestis preparing an evening meal. "Don't interrupt me when I am speaking to others," he told her. "That is not permissible behavior, and you know it."

"I'm sorry, master," she said, "but it seemed to me that everyone was missing an obvious answer." She hung her head.

"But you angered everyone in the meeting. Rhodia might have killed you."

"If not her, then the wild men," she said. "I wish I could be as free as the wolf."

He squatted next to her. "You did turn the course of the conversation," he said, "and we are putting fire to use tonight. I'm glad you spoke when you did. We need to think of a way for you to participate in our discussions without disturbing the other's sense of propriety." He patted her knee. "I'm not mad, just embarrassed that you spoke like that. Let's try a signal next time. If you need to speak to me about something you think I should know or think about, place two fingers to your lips, like this." He showed her. "Then I will excuse myself and go outside the meeting to listen to you. That way, no one takes offense. If there is something I need to speak privately to you about, I'll do the same. Got it?"

She nodded.

"And I would also like for you to be as free as the wolf," he said, standing, "but then you would be like the wild men. That might not be a good thing, in the long run."

"Yes, Master."

"Stand up," he said, reaching down for her hand. When she stood he pulled her to him in a hug. "You have been the most important person in the camp today," he said. "You tracked the wild men, you led us to rescue Dolios, and you have suggested a defense while we are moving away from this place. Tell me more about the wolf. She is a beauty, and one of the most dangerous creatures on the planet."

"She is expedient and wily," Alcestis said, pulling away. "She wastes nothing. No energy, no sleep, nothing. I wouldn't say we have much affection for one another. In fact, there's no real connection at all. But she has been useful because of her superior senses. I can read her motions, and they tell me if wild men are around, or game, or somebody who is not dangerous. So I continue to feed her. I hope you don't mind."

"Extraordinary," he said. "Of course, I don't mind."

"You won't let the soldiers kill her, will you?"

"Not if I can help it. Should I speak to them?"

"They are fearful of her, and I've heard them talking."

"I'll pass the word. No killing of wolves."

"We might lose a horse or a sheep or something," she said. "Not even then?"

"Alcestis, I owe you that much for what you've done today. If a wolf takes one of our animals, it will be because we were not paying close enough attention. Meanwhile, feed her, and perhaps she won't hunt our cattle."

"Yes, Master," she said, dropping her eyes. "I think that is a good plan."

He turned to go but turned back.

"How soon can Melia's part of this camp be ready to move out?" he asked.

"We can leave here in less than an hour," she said. "Well, we can. I don't know about the others, but Melia and her household can move quickly."

"Good idea," he said. "Get ready to move out. Darkness and smoke may be our best opportunity to escape."

THIRTY

lllllllllllll

"Fire will drive all the animals toward the wild men," Melia observed. "They will have excellent hunting for a time. That may distract them from us."

"Maybe they will forget their slain brothers in two days," Shelby said, "if they have plenty to eat."

The entire city population knew of the wild men's attack the preceding night. And they were well aware of the constant howls echoing down the valley from all directions. When word came to spread fire in the valley as widely as possible and to move out, everyone was on edge and ready.

The wagons jostled over the night-darkened land, leaving the flaming hills behind. Every wagon camp had followed orders, spreading fire in a huge arc, and lucky breezes blowing up the valley floor carried the smoke and flames away from them. They moved as quickly as they could, urged on by fear and the eerie howling.

They soon realized they were not completely protected. The fire did not move quickly, and vagaries in the breezes seemed at times to stall it out and shift its position. Even though gaps occurred in the fire-line large enough for groups of the savages to pass through, Shelby hoped the ground would be covered with coals and hot ash that would burn their unshod feet. The tactic had bought them time to put a few miles between them and the wild men. That was something.

The following morning, the sun rose red and dusky through the plumes of smoke, and the howling of the wild men receded into higher reaches of the hills behind them. Everyone kept a constant eye out for any movement in the brush, which they set afire as they passed.

Despite his exhaustion, Shelby continued on horseback well into the morning hours, encouraging the mounted troops and the archers on the wagons to remain alert. He did not want to stop for anything, and all that day drove them relentlessly. When Melia complained that she needed to stop to conduct the sacrifice, he refused. His fear of the wild men had combined with his war experiences in Afghanistan four thousand years in the future, and he was running. He wanted everyone to run. Run. Just run. Demons at his back, demonic howling, the scent of wild men, hairy and huge, like grizzly bears blending with the unwashed assassins of the prophet. His anxiety was uncontrollable. He knew, he just knew, they would be attacked and have no defense.

The fire began to burn down and go out behind them as the daylight faded. And no matter how hard they tried, they could not get it to spread fast enough to cover them, leaving them exposed to ambush from the sides. In his mind's eye, Shelby could see the wild men following them, looking for weakness, waiting for a chance for revenge. His anxiety for Melia and their unborn child drove him beyond exhaustion well into the evening, when she made him stop.

"You are killing the horses, Shelby," she shouted at him as he rode by. "Do what you can to protect us, but unharness the horses, feed and water them, and let us rest, or all of us will be dead before dawn."

He stared at her, angry, driven by his fear and anxiety. "Rest," she whispered in his mind. "Rest now."

He spurred past her to the end of the train, those closest to the wild men and presumably most vulnerable, and urged them to keep up. Then he rode again on his laboring horse toward the front. He ordered the wagons to stop and take up defensive positions, to deploy guards armed with spears, and to build large fires on their perimeters.

He rode back to Melia. "We will close up the gaps," he said. "We will draw everyone together for the remainder of the night and rest, as you insist. I don't like it, because I think we are pursued, but you're right. We cannot continue. Perhaps they cannot continue either. Seek guidance from our mother when we stop, and Garanus, Eurymedon, and I will set our defenses for the night."

"Use women as well as men for sentries," she said.

"And some of us can fight," added Rhodia riding up. "Melia, ahead perhaps twenty minutes' ride is a nice spring with fresh water and a protected dell. It will be cool during the night, but at least we can place the Meliae around it to protect from ambush. I suggest you go there."

"Good idea," Shelby said. "I will dismount there and walk back to the rear. You're right about the horses. This one staggers."

"Dolios can go with you," Melia said. "He's recovered, and Alcestis has ridden with me all day. She can walk, too. Take her."

"I want Hestia and her workers as close to you as we can get them," he said. "At the core of our camp."

"Shelby, you are too frightened," Melia said. "The wild men may be dangerous, but they are not plentiful. We can stop them if they attack and we are prepared for them."

"As long as they do not eat you," he replied angrily, "we will survive."

He turned his back on her wry look and walked off into the dark, followed by Dolios and Alcestis. He handed Alcestis the SOG knife to keep on a strap across her shoulder, since her narrow hips could not hold a belt. Dolios carried a spear, a bronze sword, and across his back one of the extra crossbows. Shelby also carried a crossbow, though he wondered why he had not thought to get one for Alcestis. He was on the point of sending her back for one of the four or five extras, when he heard a horse riding up behind him.

"Icarus!" called a soldier. "Icarus, Kratos has returned to join us. Will you come back to meet him, or do you want him to meet you here?"

"Better send him to Melia," Shelby said. "We may have savages pursuing us. Does he have fresh horses?"

"He has unridden horses, but they have been traveling over broken ground all day."

"Then we will move forward to meet him. Let's not kill his horses from exhaustion, either. And the same for you. Dismount and walk with me, lead your horse. My heart is much easier with

Kratos here. Tell me, did he bring men?"

"Yes, everyone. They are all with him. He has stories to tell, I hear, but he waits on you."

Shelby smiled for the first time in two days, and he picked up his pace. This was good news indeed. Kratos back, that fierce fighter, with his hundreds of seasoned warriors. They might survive if the wild men attacked.

No machine guns. No guns of any kind. No grenades. No mortars. No RPGs. No cannon. No armored vehicles. No bombs. No claymores. No landmines. No night-vision goggles. No radio communication. No satellite GPS. No rockets. No helicopters. No drones. No air support. No M1A1 Abrams tanks. No endless supply lines. Nothing of the twenty-first century was available for use in this dark prehistory of Europe except the SOG knife, his Shrike tomahawk, and his Kevlar body armor. And the Shrike was nothing against a foe like the wild men. He had nothing but his training and his heart. And now he had Kratos.

Maybe that would be enough.

THIRTY-ONE

ratos was chuckling with Melia, drinking wine from a large
goblet, when he saw Shelby approaching. "Icarus!" he
boomed, springing to his feet. He rushed to give Shelby a
hug and then drew back his head to give him a friendly butt in
the chest.

"Kratos, my friend," Shelby replied, unwinding. The shorter
man's hug relaxed him more than anything.

"I've found the sea, Icarus," Kratos beamed. "It's a day beyond
this valley. I went close enough to see a small village on the coast
where we may be able to trade. I saw boats there."

They sat with Melia. "Good news, Kratos," Shelby said.
"Good news. Maybe this long trek from our city is about to enter
a new phase."

"We could sack that village with little effort," Kratos said.
"I'm certain. But perhaps they would be more useful as friends.
Besides, there's not much village. It looks like a poor place."

"Were you able to talk to any of the locals?"

"No, the ones I saw from a distance do not appear to be
Achaeans. Arktos said he had been there with Phorbus, though."

"Eumaeus once told me there was a story about how Phorbus
got that shield, but he didn't tell it to me. It had something to do
with a seaside village."

"Arktos led me to believe it was a legend worth remembering," Kratos said, "but he didn't tell it to me, either. Mother said it
was father's most treasured possession."

"Do you know what language they speak?" Melia asked.

"The bigger question, Kratos, is this: Do they eat bread?" Shelby asked.

"Their fields are poor and unattended, so I think their meager crops mostly feed rabbits and ibex. But they have crops."

"That's a relief," Shelby said. "We've just come through a country where the men eat each other."

"As Melia has been telling me," he said, his face becoming grim. "Very large men, larger than you."

"Much larger and stronger and faster than me. They are the size of oxen."

"But there are not many of them," Melia said. "Our goddess mother has shown them to me. Theirs is a savage, brutal existence, short-lived and almost childless."

"We didn't see them when we came through ahead of you," Kratos said. "Maybe they were hiding, or maybe they were somewhere else and my smaller group slipped through unnoticed."

"Does this coastal village have walls?" Melia asked. "Does it have a harbor? Is there a river flowing into it? Are there hills around it? Tell me everything. But before you do, perhaps you could sit a little farther off. You've been in the field without a bath for a long time." She grinned at him, holding her nose. "Pregnancy has made my sense of smell more acute."

Kratos laughed. He rubbed his hands in his armpits and smelled them. "Ah, the odor of a true man," he said, grinning. But he got up and moved a few feet away.

"No, truly," he said. "This is a poor fishing village with no more than a dozen or so stone houses built above the tide. A spit of land extends out into the sea on one side to make small bay, but the rocky beach makes poor anchorage for large ships. I did not count the fishing boats, but I doubt they have more than a dozen. Of course, some of them could have been out. The place looks too poor to have the kind of gold that went into that shield, or even the goats to provide its goatskin case. I counted ten conical stone huts surrounded by a wall topped with a bramble picket—I guess to keep out the wild men, though how it could do that is a mystery. It would barely be a hindrance to us, and Eurymedon has horses that could clear it."

"Perhaps the wall is a mystery to the wild men," said Shelby. "They may not understand what a wall is."

"I think you're right, Shelby," Melia said. "The wild men have no masonry construction skills, and do not comprehend things like walls and houses. Those are outside their experience."

"Killing is not outside their experience," Shelby retorted. "Or cannibalism."

Cries rang out behind them and surged up the wagon train, thousands of voices raised in alarm.

"Let's go," Kratos said, leaping to his feet, pulling his helmet over his bushy red hair.

"Icarus, Icarus," said a breathless messenger on horseback, "the wild men have attacked the last group of wagons!"

Shelby glanced at Melia and she rose to her feet, the firelight reflecting over her hair like a crown of flames.

"Go!" she said, raising her hand.

Rhodia and the other Meliae crowded around her, an impenetrable wall of one hundred armed women. Some took up positions around the little dell, crossbows ready. Others formed a tighter perimeter.

"Hestia!" Shelby called back to her. "Get Hestia!" Then he and Kratos were astride horses and riding toward the rear, followed by Kratos's bodyguards who were scrambling to catch up.

* * *

It was worse than he feared. This time the wild men had come to kill in vengeance. They had not taken prisoners or eaten the slain. They were like coyotes in a pen of sheep, chasing fleeing slaves and citizens alike, the naked and the clothed, slaughtering the ones they caught. Anyone who left the relative safety of the wagons was killed. Those who cowered beneath were plucked out and bashed. Others were crushed beneath a loaded wagon a wild man had overturned. The wild men were still at it when Shelby and Kratos arrived.

"Plan?" asked Kratos.

"Straight at 'em?" asked Shelby.

"Better if we fight together, brother," Kratos replied. "Try not to get pinned between them."

Eurymedon came up behind with some cavalry.

"Surround them," Shelby said. "Kratos and I are going in."

149

"Garanus," yelled Eurymedon, "take the cavalry and surround them. I'm going with Icarus and Kratos!"

"Bodyguards," Kratos shouted. "Keep our backs!" He plunged forward followed by Shelby and Eurymedon.

Almost immediately the three of them came upon a huge savage bashing a slave by his leg like a rag doll. When the savage saw the three approaching, he dropped his still breathing quarry and turned to face them, blood dripping from his teeth.

"This is bad!," Kratos exclaimed.

"Charge!" yelled Eurymedon, spurring his horse at the man, his lance leveled. The other two spurred after him, but the savage eluded them, leaping sideways and then toward them. A blur of active danger, he was impossible to target. He collided with Kratos's horse, felling the animal and tumbling Kratos to the ground. Shelby drove at him with his tomahawk slashing downward, fearing he would have little effect, but the wild man jerked his head back and the tomahawk buried itself into his skull. Shelby was pulled off his saddle as the man went over backward. The wild man gripped Kratos even as the blow to his skull was killing him. Kratos buried his sword in the man's chest as the hold loosened, the savage's mouth snapping open and shut. Shelby could not wrest the tomahawk from the wild man's skull until he sat on the ground with his feet on the savage's shoulders and pried with both hands.

Finally the tomahawk began to budge, and then eased out, drenching him in blood just as two more wild men bounded toward them, leaping, thrusting with their spears. Even crouched to attack they stood as tall as Kratos and easily matched him in agility and speed. Eurymedon turned his horse in time to impale one of them on his lance, but the lance broke and his horse lost its balance. The lance did not kill, and the man yanked it from his massive chest and went for Eurymedon, who leapt clear. Kratos's bodyguards closed in on the whirring, frenzied wild man. The lance wound increasingly slowed the savage, and he finally succumbed to multiple spear punctures in his upper body. Eurymedon went at the second wild man just as Shelby got back to his feet. The dangerous savage whirled on Eurymedon but Kratos caught the man's foot with his blade as he leapt, and Shelby buried the spike of his tomahawk in the man's back as he came down. He realized that the spike was just too short. At three inches, it did not penetrate vital areas in these huge men.

"Fight smart," he muttered. "Fight smart."

Eurymedon finished off the crippled man by driving his back-up lance into the wild one's chest. Two more wild men moved from the shadows into the firelight. One was the largest human Shelby had seen, almost eight feet and easily five hundred pounds or more of solid muscle.

The larger man stood slightly ahead of the other one, his spear in his right hand off to one side. He stared at Shelby, who was wearing his lion's skin and Kevlar, the lion's discus-crushed skull tied to his head. Speaking without turning his head, the huge savage said something to his companion, his words sounding like guttural cicadas, full of contempt. The companion silently stared at the three warriors. Kratos's guards backed the three brothers with their bronze-tipped spears at the ready.

Shelby, Kratos, and Eurymedon stared back. Eurymedon made to move forward, but Shelby stopped him and stepped forward himself, folding his arms over his chest, his tomahawk in his right hand.

Around them, people were screaming and weeping, brush fires were glowing against the fading sky, and cavalry thrashed through the underbrush with shouted orders and answering cries. But here before this overturned wagon and its slaughtered occupants, the savage and the civilized faced one another in silence.

The largest wild man glared a heartbeat longer, then raised his voice and pointed back over the mountains, shouting at them. Though his words were unintelligible, the meaning was clear. Kratos elbowed Shelby aside, beating the front of his shield with his sword.

"Leave my people alone," Kratos bellowed. "Leave my people alone." He moved toward the huge man, followed by the body-guards who spread to either side of him, their spears with blood-guttered points held toward the man. "Leave my people alone," Kratos roared again, his deep battlefield voice carrying over the melee. Then he charged the savage.

The second wild man moved to protect the larger savage, but Shelby saw the movement and he and Eurymedon rushed to engage him.

The huge wild man laughed at Kratos and then lunged with his spear. Kratos batted the spear aside with his shield and spun, leaping inside the wild man's outstretched arms and slashing downward with his sword, bellowing all the while. He cut the man from his shoulder to his groin, severing the breechcloth, which fell in a stinking heap. The wild man recoiled, regained control of his spear and then stooped to advance at Kratos, his mouth grimaced to show his large canine teeth, his arms spread.

The bodyguards were trained to hit high, middle, and low alternately, to keep step and surround, but their main purpose was to protect Kratos. They struck simultaneously as the wild man advanced, then Kratos ducked inside the spear again and thrust upward with his sword. It caught the savage on the underside of his chin and the blade came out through his mouth. The savage reared back, pinning Kratos's hand to the hilt of his sword and pulling him clear of the ground. The bodyguard plunged spears into the muscular body, and Kratos fell to his feet leaving the sword impaled through the savage's mouth. He struck his dagger deep into the man's inner thigh, the blade seeking and then finding its target. The savage's femoral artery exploded in a spray of blood over the ground, and the man went backward, the spears plunging into his still-struggling corpse over and over.

While Kratos and the bodyguards were occupied with the huge man, Eurymedon spotted a group of five wild men bounding toward the scene. He sent Garanus and the cavalry to head them off, and he and Shelby closed with the second savage.

Distracted by Kratos and the attack on the larger savage, the second wild man did not see them approach but whirled and grimaced at them, showing his teeth and tongue and glaring fire from his eyes. He vaulted into the sky, intending to come down on the short Eurymedon, who raised his lance to impale him. At the last millisecond, the savage saw the upraised lance and twisted his body aside in mid-air, falling heavily to the ground and rolling away, springing up again to his feet in a graceful arc. Shelby anticipated the move and was close enough to bury his Shrike in the savage's back, aiming at the spot where the kidney was, but the man's muscles were too thick for fatal internal damage.

He spun on Shelby, and Eurymedon drove his lance into the

side of the man's chest, slashing it side to side to sever as much lung as possible. Blood poured from the man's mouth. Shelby brought the spike of the tomahawk down onto the man's clavicle, feeling the reassuring crack as the bone broke under the blow. Wrenching backward, he tore as much flesh as he could. With his strength failing, the dying wild man grasped for him, trying to pull him close enough to sink his teeth into. The fire died out of his eyes, his jaw drooped, and he fell forward on his face, releasing Shelby.

With a foot on the man's ribs, Eurymedon pulled his lance from the huge chest and turned to look for more trouble, but suddenly it was over.

"Leave my people alone!" bellowed Kratos at the shadows of the great giants fading into the brush. "Leave my people alone!" His voice boomed like the deep fire of cannon over the smoking landscape.

THIRTY-TWO

T he death toll on the city was large. In the confusion, it had been impossible to know how many wild men were involved. Some said a dozen, others a hundred. But at least forty citizens had been killed or seriously mauled. Some of the most dreadful wounds were from teeth, as though savaged by wild animals.

"We are not familiar with these kinds of attacks," a healer confided to Shelby. "Dogs, of course, occasionally a jackal or even a bear. But these kinds of bites are new to us. Look how the flesh was ripped and torn. Bites on necks were deadly, but these other bites, these were for punishment."

Melia arrived to supervise moving the maimed to triage, and to witness the carnage for herself.

"This poor slave's forearm was crushed by a bite," she said. "He may lose it."

"We will try to keep it from infection, but yes. I'm not sure we can help his bones knit back. He will be crippled," the healer replied. "We've seen hands, even a foot bitten this way. They were punishing us."

"Well, shit," spat Shelby, shifting his shoulders and wiping the blade of the Shrike on his tunic.

"No," Melia said, reading his mind, "we will not chase them. Didn't you say the big man gestured back over the mountains? Well, we can't go back. But we will not make this worse by hunting them."

"It's already worse," Shelby replied. Kratos nodded, anger

flaring in his eyes. "We just want them to leave us alone, but look how this has escalated. They killed a sentry and kidnapped Dolios. When we rescued Dolios we got this. We must retaliate, or they will keep this up, and that's a price I don't want to pay."

"Calm down, Shelby," Melia said. "Just calm down. They're gone for the night. I can feel it."

"They will judge our response," Kratos said. "If we do not respond with greater force, they will continue to attack unless we turn back. And then they will harass us as we go. We cannot leave it alone."

"Kratos is right, sister," Eurymedon said. "Icarus is right. These are bullies and we must teach them a lesson, or they will get us all."

"What do you think you can accomplish?" she asked. "Do you think you can exterminate them all? Is that what you want? And next time they might bring women. You really do not want to fight their women."

"I don't want to fight any of them," Shelby said. "I want them to leave us alone."

"They lost how many in this fight?" she asked. "One? Two?"

"The brothers and I killed three," Kratos said.

"And it took all of you to do it, right?" she asked.

"It was a surprise attack."

"How was this a surprise?" she asked. "We've been listening to them howling for two days. This was no surprise. We had plenty of warning."

"I know, damnit," Shelby fumed. "I know. I've been trying to get us away from here. I thought the fires might help to protect us, but they didn't. We're too strung out and vulnerable, and the ground won't let us congregate in tight formations. We are fighting terrain as much as we are fighting them."

"Besides, sister," Eurymedon said, "look how strong they are. I saw one wild man—just one—turn over that cart and pluck up the people hiding underneath."

"You will not hunt the wild men," she said. "Do what you can to protect us here, but do not leave the wagons to go off through this rough and brushy country. That is the end of this discussion." She turned to Rhodia. "You and the Meliae are returning with me to our spring, where we will defend ourselves while these men try to get their wits about them."

She walked off, clearly furious.

"Eurymedon," Shelby said, "round up the cavalry if they haven't been eaten and get them to circle this scene. We will escort the wounded and salvage what wagons we can. Get the undamaged wagons tied together around the camp, all the people inside the circle of wagons. Turn the wagons over to present a wall to the savages. It's the best we can do tonight. Tomorrow we will improve our picket lines around the camp. Everything else, dead people and broken pieces, into the fire. Kratos, do you agree?"

"I don't agree with any of this," the burly warrior replied, "but I don't see any other choice. Let's get this mess cleaned up. Guards, watch the shadows and do not sheathe your weapons. Alert us to any movement."

"I think we should scout the countryside from horseback when it's light in the morning," Eurymedon said. "We might be able to see why they have become so much more violent."

"Perhaps they have a settlement nearby," Kratos said. "Maybe they feel threatened as well."

"Maybe the fire will go wild and spread through the country," Shelby said. If it doesn't drive them away, at least it will deplete their hunting where the ground has been burned. Maybe we can starve them away, make them want to go elsewhere to hunt."

"They might think they can feast on our citizens," Kratos said. "That's what it looks like to me. If we kill off the game, they'll just eat our slaves and horses. Or Eurymedon. I despair of keeping our cattle safe." He chuckled. "I think you are safe, though, Icarus. They won't like your taste, which I imagine is somewhat between rancid boar and rotting lion." Grinning, he punched Shelby in the arm.

"These bites, though," Eurymedon said, "what was it the healer said? They're for punishment? I don't get it."

"I don't understand everything that's going on," Shelby admitted. "I don't know what their motivation is, except that they can get away with it. Apparently the attempt is worth the risk to them."

"Even hornets try to avoid conflict," Eurymedon said. "These wild men go looking for it. Did they think we would just let them eat our people without responding?"

"If we hadn't pursued them two days ago, we would have lost only a sentry and that skinny boy," Kratos said. "Now look how many we've lost. Even more maimed."

Having surrendered their horses to help transport the wounded, they fell in behind the last row of litters bearing the wounded in a somber parade back to the larger camp. Afraid of the dark and the dangerous savages in the shadows, everyone carried burning sticks or torches.

"These savages are not like the Achaeans," Kratos said after they had trudged for a while. "They don't really fight. They swarm and maul and maim, and then they drift away like smoke into the brush. Despite their size, they are nearly invisible. At least with the Achaeans you always know where they are."

"That dying guy pulled my horse over," Eurymedon said. "We've got to figure how to avoid contact and fight them from a distance."

"More crossbows," Shelby said.

"More crossbows," Eurymedon said.

"I hate to admit that you're right," Kratos said. "A real man fights face-to-face, up close and personal. I like the smell of my enemy's last breath. Until now, I've thought those crossbows appropriate for women, not for real men, but I haven't fought with a foe like this before. They are not honorable men, not as we understand honor, so killing them with treachery or from a distance is not dishonorable. We need more crossbows."

"How can we use the Meliae with their crossbows better?" Shelby asked. "We might not be able to make more crossbows right now. It's an intricate process and requires a lot of labor."

"We can train them to shoot from horseback," Eurymedon suggested. "At least they would be able to see further over this brush."

"Tall trees rise above the brush, and in places it is thick and dark, even during daylight," Shelby said. "I hope we can set it afire as we go, protecting our flanks and our rear. But I like the idea of shooting from horseback. It works on open ground. Maybe if we put them in into groups of four, they can protect one another if they are attacked."

"What if the wild men attack the front of the caravan?"

Kratos asked. "What then? They could cause a huge amount of damage with a frontal assault, especially if they just blended away into the brush and did not wait around for us to fight back."

"The train is too long and too spread out," Shelby said. "We need tighter formations, faster road building, wider roads, more fires, and more protection. This is a huge problem of organization and order. Who will supervise it?"

"Melia," Kratos and Eurymedon said simultaneously. "She will order it and the women will do it. Just tell her."

"I like the idea of the Meliae on horseback, Eurymedon," Shelby said. "I hope we have time to train them. They are deadly shooters already and fearless."

"But a wild man will just tackle a horse and pull it down, or leap over it. If she doesn't have time to shoot her crossbow or misses on her first shot, she's dead."

"Yeah. Yeah," Shelby said, thinking. "Yeah, you're right. Honestly, fire is our only defense, and it's only good while the brush lasts."

"Still," Eurymedon said, "you can see more from a horse than from the ground. We didn't see these wild men coming, but it was dark."

"They are master hunters," Shelby said. "It's how they survive. I don't mean to romanticize it, but they must learn from their infancy how to blend into the earth, to be one with it, to use its contours to creep up on game."

"Then we must be better at it than they are," Kratos said. "No noise, no obvious movement, no odor. We've got to be better hunters than they are, so we can find them before they find us."

A sharp scent of wild thyme drifted to them from bruised plants as the horses passed. It stirred something in Shelby, something deep and dangerous, reminding him of cordite and the hills of Afghanistan, something beckoning him to fall again into the black hole of his memory, to be consumed by his terror and disgust. Kratos slapped him on the shoulder, squeezing him.

"Icarus, my friend, my brother," Kratos said. "Icarus, we are nearly back to Melia. Tell her what gnaws you."

"Thanks, brother," Shelby responded, shaking his groggy head, trying to shake off the visions that snapped at his heels like demon dogs, or like wild men. "Sometimes, you know—"

"Yes, brother, I know," Kratos said. "I know." He gave Shelby a big hug, partially lifting him, taking some of the burden of his mortal weight. "I know."

* * *

Melia met him in the sheltered dell, hands on her hips.

"Don't even speak," she said to him, holding up her palm. "Not a word. Alcestis, take this exhausted man over to the spring and wash him. It would be a good idea to hold his head underwater for a bit. The cold water will do him good."

"Can't Dolios do that?" whined Alcestis.

Melia's withering look changed the girl's mind, and without a word she took Shelby by the hand and led him over to the shallow brook at the bottom of the dell. Down there the odors of sage and oregano smelled like sweet, spicy tea and Shelby began to relax as the slave girl struggled to get him out of his battle gear. She untied the lion's skull helmet, draped the skin on the soft grass at the water's edge, and then set about undoing his buttons and zippers until she had him stripped down. She drew him into the water and pushed him to lie down, rubbing him all over to stimulate his skin and smooth away the dirt and sweat.

The water melted away his fatigue, it's cold finally conquering his troubled rage. He began to relax. Alcestis rubbed his face, especially around his eyes, then held his head underwater and massaged his head, loosening years of dreams.

Underwater, he had a flashback to his first experience in Melia's time, when he plunged boots down into a cold mountain pond after his extraordinary failure in the Gryphon gliding parachute device. Had he traveled through time during the jump, or was it after the submersion in the pool? Was it the whole process, or was it the cold water washing over him? What moved him from the twenty-first century AD to the twentieth century BC? Was any one point in that jump from the belly of the C-130 the transition? Was his momentary loss of consciousness after leaving the plane the point of transition? Was it finding the cave with the ancient, mysterious rock paintings of women, women doing everything? Would this plunge into cold spring water take him back to twenty-first century Ramstein Air Base?

He struggled to sit up, but Alcestis held him down. She reamed out his ears with her fingers, then eased off, helping him up into a sitting position. He stared around the darkened dell to make sure he was still home, still with Melia and the others. Still with Alcestis and not some girl in a Kaiserslautern flop house. Still home.

"Thank you Alcestis," he muttered, shivering in the water. "Good job."

She helped him out and back to the low fire where Melia still sat, fuming, then dried him off with rough linen cloth and draped dry clothes over him.

"Why are you angry?" he asked, taking the jug of wine from Alcestis.

"Why?" she asked. "Why? Why do you think?"

He looked at her without expression, then took another long pull of wine.

"I'm tired," he said. "I'm going to lie down and rest. Don't get yourself eaten while I sleep." He stretched out on the ground and wrapped the cloth around his damp head.

"I'm angry because you are making excuses and not thinking," she said, shrilly. "I'm angry because we lost some good people. I'm angry because we should have known better than to try to move in the dark through their country. We couldn't see them until they were already on us. You should have thought of that. You would have thought of it if you had not let yourself be driven by your irrational fear. That's why I'm angry. I told you that you were too scared. I told you to rest. But oh no, you had to drive and drive and drive, and exhaust everyone and nearly kill the horses, and what happened? We were too strung out trying to move in the dark. That's why I'm angry."

"Is that all?" he asked, his voice muffled by the cloth.

"No, it is not," she said, struggling to her feet. She went around the campfire and sat down on him, hard.

"What?" he asked, regaining his breath, his chest lifting her. "You want to fight?"

"No," she said, "I want you to listen to me. Don't pretend I'm not talking to you. Don't ignore me. When I tell you to stop, you stop. When I tell you to go, you go. Understand? Listen to me. If I tell you that you are too tired and you need to rest, then stop and rest. I know what I'm talking about."

He jerked the cloth off his head, grinning.

"I love you so much," he said, putting a hand on her leg.

She brushed his hand away. "If you had stopped when I told you to, the last group of stragglers would have caught up with the rest of us and the wild men might have reconsidered their attack. You cannot outrun them, Shelby. They pursue. They can run for days. If you had rested, you would have been able to think." She reached forward, shifting her weight on his torso and rapping her knuckles on his forehead. "I know more than you do," she said. "Listen to me."

"Yes'm," he said, continuing to grin. He loved seeing her ablaze this way. He was wary, certainly, but he knew it would be all right. Everything would be all right. He put his arms around her, but she struggled to get up.

"No," she said, "close your eyes and go to sleep. The Meliae will surround us tonight and we will be safe."

He yawned, the exhaustion descending on him like a blanket. "Okay," he said, closing his eyes. "Okay. Tell them to watch in shifts so some of them stay rested." He yawned again, "And—" Yawn. "A…ler—" He was out.

THIRTY-THREE

ⅅⅅⅅⅅⅅⅅⅅⅅⅅⅅ

Howling awoke them a few hours before dawn, and most were unable to fall back asleep. They stumbled in the dark toward the center of the camp, getting as far from the burning perimeter as they could.

Shelby was already awake when Dolios knelt beside him, eyes wide with horror. "Master," he whispered urgently. "I'm scared. Some of the people say the wild men would have gone away if I had not been rescued." His lower lip trembled, and tears filled his eyes.

An angry mob started chanting just out of sight: "Give us the boy! Give him to the wild men! Give the boy to the wild men!"

Shelby felt his temper igniting. "Stay next to me," he said to the boy. "They envy you your clothes, for one thing," he continued. "They know you are a slave and they don't like to see a slave wearing clothes. They also envy your intelligence and the favor you have from me and Hestia. Envy is powerful with ignorant people and logic is weak. But this camp does not run on mob rule. You will not be sacrificed."

Melia had dozed off, but now sat up, wide awake, her hair standing out like some auburn-headed Medusa.

"Are those our people?" she asked. "What do they want?"

"They want us to sacrifice Dolios to the wild men, because they think that will make the savages go away."

"But what about that?" Dolios asked. "Would they go away?"

"No, Dolios, they will not."

"I wish they would shut up," Melia muttered. "This baby

makes enough kicking and punching without all that stupid howling."

"Sorry, dear," Shelby said, patting that luscious curve of her hip.

"Go tell all of them to shut up," she said, pulling the light covering over her head. "I'm going back to sleep." She yawned. "Also, I love you." She moved his hand away and jammed the cover down.

"You heard her," he said to Dolios, rising and helping the boy to his feet. He pulled his Shrike tomahawk onto his wrist, thinking how useless it had been against such foes, and wondered what weapons they could use against the wild men. Maybe slings. Probably atlatls. Crossbows, certainly, as long as they hit vital spots: kidneys, necks, knees, diaphragms, heads. Despite their firepower, crossbows might not penetrate thick abdominal walls.

He knew a pro football player whose girlfriend shot him with a pistol at close range, and the bullet had not penetrated his muscles. Eight to ten inches of muscle is tough. It had hurt the guy, though. He began treating her with respect, part of which meant giving up football and becoming a security guard with regular hours and more time at home. He got a part-time job at the gym where Shelby trained, and Shelby had seen the scarred dimple next to his belly button where the guy was shot. Spotting for Shelby one day as he bench pressed, they got to talking about being shot. One thing, he admitted, was it got your attention.

Shelby didn't want more attention from the wild men. He wanted a lot less, and now he had the problem of terrified people in the camp to deal with.

Dolios followed him past a ring of guards around the tent to confront a throng of angry people muttering to themselves. They quieted when they saw Shelby and the boy, but one older woman pointed her crooked finger at Dolios. "Icarus, send the boy out to the wild men. That's all they want," the old woman said.

Others in the group echoed the sentiment. "He's just a slave like the rest of us," said one. "It's his fault they're trying to kill us," yelled another. The crowd's voices raised in volume as their hysteria spread. They bayed like so many dogs, barking out words without thinking.

He understood their terror. He realized he might have been

partially responsible for it, given how he had driven himself and all of them over the last two days. Was it too late to resume control? Could he reposition himself as their leader, having shown his fear yesterday?

"These savages are simple," he said, raising his voice to be heard. "They want two things. They want us out of their land, and they want more to eat. Dolios here will not feed them for long, so they will be back. And they will continue to prey upon us until we leave them behind. So settle down!"

"But they'll go away if they have the boy!" an old man yelled. "He's the reason they came on us to start with."

Internally, Shelby sighed. Where the hell was Kratos when he needed some backup?

"Tell you what," he said to the man, "you go out there first and ask them to go away."

"Not me," he shouted. "I'm not going out there and get eaten."

"No," nodded Shelby, "none of us are. So get over it. If you want to sacrifice the boy, then you have to take him out there and hand him over to them. And you'd have to fight me to do it. So that's that. We are not giving Dolios to them."

When a measure of quiet muttering replaced the barking of the crowd, he added, "Besides, Melia sent me out here to make you and the wild men be quiet. So pay attention, and then do what I do."

He turned away toward the perimeter beyond the wagons they overturned to make a wall, cupped his hands to his mouth, and shouted. "Hey shut the fuck up! Hey, shut the fuck up!" he yelled through his cupped hands. "Just shut up!"

The citizens looked at him, startled by the sound of his voice, and wondering if they should be amused.

Kratos stumbled up, his chiton awry, bleary-eyed.

"The wild men have been at it for hours," he said. "Do you really think shouting back at them is going to have any effect?"

"No," Shelby said, "but Melia told me to come out here and make them be quiet while she slept. I can't think of anything else to do."

"Hey," hollered Kratos in his battlefield voice, dozens of decibels louder than Shelby. "Shut the fuck up!"

Kratos looked around at his bodyguards, those six seasoned

warriors. "Well?" he asked. To Shelby he said, "Sometimes in battle we will shout together. It carries the orders further."

"Hey!" they shouted together. "Shut the fuck up!"

Signaling with his hands, Kratos stirred the uneasy crowd to join in. Soon, thousands of voices were raised in unison, shouting, "Shut the fuck up! Shut the fuck up!" all on cue, and all together.

The howling stopped.

"Well, that worked," Kratos yawned. "Also it was fun."

"I like how it brought the camp together," Shelby said. "Anytime we can all do something together, we have far more strength and less fear."

"Melia wants to know if you're done now," Rhodia said, coming up with a drum. She was followed by more women with drums and flutes. "If you're done making fools of yourselves, shut the fuck up and let us play."

She plumped herself down on the ground, the drum between her legs, and started tapping a rhythm, slow, even, not very loud. But it was a sound that did not occur in nature, that regular thump-thump-thump, a deep drum beat, steady, compelling. Other women joined her, playing off her rhythm, emphasizing it, amplifying it. Then other higher pitched drums added syncopation, and flutes started, carrying out over the smoldering brush fires. Nearby, groups of people rose to their feet swaying in time to the music, moving in step. Some yawned, but for most the music awakened an energy in them, quelled their fear.

Even when the howling started again, it seemed less intense, less threatening. In fact, Shelby noted, moving away from the music to listen better, it seemed that many voices had stilled. Good, he thought. Maybe they are listening.

With daybreak, the howling stopped completely.

"The howling scares us," Shelby said to Kratos, "but I think they use it to locate one another in the dark."

"They probably do not see well in the dark, not well enough to fight," Kratos replied, despite the attack last night."

"They might, though," Shelby said, taking a piece of flat bread from Alcestis. He turned to her.

"Alcestis, can you shoot a crossbow?"

"Yes master," she said, "I have been doing all the exercises the Meliae do. They have taught me to shoot the crossbow."

"Ah," he said, "I'm glad to hear it. I meant to encourage you to spend more time with them. You are too young to become one of them, but in a year or two you might be old enough to apprentice."

"Thank you master." She handed Kratos a piece of bread and jug of wine, her budding breasts rising with the movement of her arm.

Kratos took the food and looked away at the smoky hillside.

"We need to get higher, to post lookouts," he said to Shelby. "We cannot see far in this smoky haze."

"You're right, and we should do even more to create a barrier."

"That could hinder our cavalry," Kratos said, "but if you think it's a good idea —"

"I think it could free up many of our people to concentrate on building a road for the wagons to move upon," Shelby said. "I think we want the entire wagon train to remain in place until there is enough road to move them. We cannot have more stragglers in this country."

"Agreed," Kratos said. "Also, it will give us a chance to rest some of our horses and men. Good plan."

"The wild men are dangerous, but our biggest danger is this terrain. It's their terrain and they can use it against us, so let's conquer the terrain first. Then we can handle the few wild men."

"You think there are only a few? They sounded numerous last night."

"Melia told me there are not many of them, and I could not count above thirty locations where the howls were coming from. Possibly they have more, but thirty wild men are probably manageable, if we keep our wits about us."

"Maybe," the shorter warrior replied. "I hope you're right."

"I wish I'd been able to watch your fight with that big guy," said Shelby. "How'd you do it?"

"He was just a big bully with a single spear. He didn't even have a back-up weapon or a shield. I knew I could take him the minute I saw him. I've had a lot of experience with guys like that."

"Well, it was a good job. Great fighting. Thanks." He put his hand on Kratos's shoulder.

"For Melia and the goddess," Kratos replied, looking away. "And for my people."

The music stopped about two hours after sunrise, and the women dispersed. They had played for some three hours, and most of the people in the camp had rested, some even dozing. A kind of purposeful buzz took its place as Kratos and others instructed the large camp on improving the perimeter, unloading and roping wagons together to make a picket line. Dolios, somewhat relieved now that the immediate threat from wild men seemed to have eased, made valuable suggestions. As the older and more experienced leaders obviously listened to him, the people, too, began to ease away from their attitude that he should be sacrificed. On this day, at least, he was not to be a scapegoat offered to the wild men.

THIRTY-FOUR

A lucky wind came that afternoon and fanned the burning brush, blowing smoke and embers far into the hills. But the same wind hindered the fire in other areas, leaving the camp exposed. The overturned wagons had spilled their contents, and just the sheer volume of people and materiel was total chaos. Nothing could be found. People remained leery and frightened, and no basic order could be established. Around mid-afternoon, Melia finally lost her temper.

"What is going on around here?" she fumed. "It's like nobody can think! How did we let all our careful plans collapse because of some noise in the night?"

Shelby had seen it coming and moved out of earshot, occupying himself at the far end of the camp, where he attempted to extract some of Hestia's precious tools from a head-high dump of household items: sheets and blankets, furs, benches, low tables, cutlery, piles of chitons, barrels of sandals, and then, finally, a bag with her protractor and ruler, but not her level. Whatever order they had when they began their mad dash from the wild men was completely lost. Just getting the people to understand why they should tie the wagons together, or stake them to the ground seemed impossible. And as far as getting watchtowers constructed so they could see what was coming, forget about it. It was not just that the people were exhausted. They were also frightened, demoralized, and confused. Again, he blamed himself. He had succumbed to fear, and this was the result.

"Do better, be better," he muttered to himself, over and over.

He knew that the largest part of the problem had been his fear for Melia. He couldn't shake the image of some wild man hoisting her pregnant belly to his mouth, preparing to pop it with his teeth like sweet fruit, his large canines dripping with anticipation. The image was like a wolf lurking in his brain, like a madness stalking him. He had been overmatched for the first time; he had met an enemy he could not outfight, even when Kratos demonstrated how it was done.

It infuriated him that Melia didn't understand his fear. She seemed casual, unconcerned by the threat. What did she expect? What did she think he could do? And now this, this awful mess of a camp. It could take weeks to get everything organized, and they were only a day's ride by horseback from the sea.

And all because he had shown fear.

"Melia is on fire," Kratos said, coming up. "She's on fire. Can I help you up here, somewhere away from her?"

"Of course. We're trying to find the rest of Hestia's tools. At least we didn't lose the trebuchets."

"Almost. Some of the people want to set fire to them. Now it's the trebuchets instead of Dolios. They think it's why the wild men are attacking us."

"The wild men are not attacking us, though," Shelby said. "I looked all through this pile of clothing and didn't find a single wild man."

"I haven't seen one all day," Kratos said. "But you're right, you know. I don't want to see one again."

"Not even in a cage?" Shelby grinned. "Can you imagine caging something as large and powerful as that?"

"Our encounter the other evening was bad enough. We would have died if it hadn't been the three of us together, with backups and my body guards."

"Melia says we don't have much to fear because there are not many of them. I think she's wrong," Shelby said. "It doesn't take very many of them to do a lot of damage."

"I think she's right in some ways, though," Kratos shrugged. "But if you don't think so, then you can be the one who tells her. Not me. Especially not today."

"I just hope she's right about them being more propelled by hunger than by revenge," Kratos added a moment later. "If we keep up our defenses and make ourselves difficult targets, they will go back to eating rabbits roasted in the fires. I don't give them much credit for planning or strategy."

"That big guy who spoke to us appeared to have brains and intentions," said Shelby. "Don't underestimate them."

"Well, maybe. Because he's always gotten his way with his size, he never learned fighting strategy. He was just a bully. He acted like a bully and fought like a bully. But I agree. Let's not take any risks. Nobody outside of camp after dark, secure perimeter, mounted patrols, that kind of thing."

"Yes," Shelby said, "and we need fighting paths through all these piles of goods and stores. We need to make it easy for our cavalry to ride the perimeter inside the wagons, and lookouts to spot for movement. I want the perimeter beyond the wagons cleared for fifty paces on all sides. And we might plant sharpened sticks in that cleared space."

"Their physical abilities are largely unknown to us," Kratos said, nodding. "Unlike Achaeans, they have no training, so we cannot get an accurate measure of their capabilities."

"And Melia mentioned something about them bringing their women to the fight," Shelby said, "as though that would be a horror we could not confront."

"We've made an effort to get away," Kratos said, "but that won't satisfy them. We are in trouble, my big brother."

THIRTY-FIVE

🔥🔥🔥🔥🔥🔥🔥🔥🔥🔥🔥

T he large herds of horses and cattle prevented the camp from completely enclosing their perimeter. The animals needed to be grazed and watered daily, and little forage was available in the burned landscape. The camp did not carry large stores of food for them, and much of the grain that they did carry was intended to be sown for new crops. If they fed it to the beasts, then both beasts and people could starve the following year. Eurymedon, Kratos and Shelby organized military escorts for the herders and shepherds, for the people still had a hundred or so of their prized sheep with wool that turned a lovely shade of sky blue when washed and combed. Wild men lying in wait, and at least one wolf known to be prowling close to camp seemed like insurmountable problems, but Shelby saw no alternative. He must split his forces to protect the animals while leaving a defensive force behind. Controlling the animals was going to be a huge problem, he knew, and these people had never needed to evolve working cattle dogs to help with herding. Here on what was essentially open range, just keeping the cattle moving safely to water and feed was going to be tough. Shelby wondered if Eurymedon could learn to use his horses to herd the cattle, the way he had seen it done in the western states of America when he was young.

Melia was not impressed, and continued in her fiery temper. "This is chaos!" she exclaimed. "No order! Everything's jumbled! We can't move a step now and it might take weeks to get these wagons loaded and ordered. What were you thinking?"

Her tone, one he had not heard her use, said a lot more, and it got to him. If she wanted to push his buttons, she was doing a damn good job.

"Fine," he said bitterly. "If you think you know so much, then tell me what to do. Tell me what to do and I will try to do it. But I'm not responsible for this terrain."

"Yes, you are," she retorted. "We are here because of your frantic dash. This is where we stopped. And now look what you've done. You unloaded the wagons and turned them over. You're just not thinking, Shelby. Think!"

Finally he was pissed off. He'd taken a lot of abuse in the last few days, much of it from himself. Her criticism just added to what he was already heaping on himself.

"Well, shit," he said, and got up to walk off.

"Oh no," she said, "you're not walking away. In fact, you're not going anywhere. Sit down right there and keep your mouth shut until I say you can can leave."

He remained standing.

"No," he finally said.

"No? You said no?"

"I said no. I've got things to do."

He turned to go.

"You're not in charge now," she said. "I am. I'm telling you what to do, and you will do it or there will be consequences."

He knew better than to scoff at her threat. From anyone else it would have been empty, but he understood just how far the consequences could go. You don't toy with an absolute monarch, and that's what she was. The whole population of the camp would do what she wanted done, and her justice was swift and revered.

But his fury had ignited in him just as hers had done. He walked back toward her, grabbed his Shrike tomahawk, that nearly useless weapon, and stormed off toward the perimeter.

"Where do you think you're going?" she demanded. The voice was in his head, not his ears. He knew she had that power over him.

Well, she'd hear him if he responded aloud, but what if he just spoke in his head, spoke silently in response. Would she hear that?

"I will not stay here and cower," he said in his head, unsure if he could communicate with her without speaking. "I will not shirk from a fight. I have the duty to go hunting for the wild men."

"You do not. You are under orders from me. Leave the wild men alone."

Her reply to his unvoiced comment proved the mental communication worked both ways.

"I will not hide from an enemy," he responded, pushing the thought aside.

"You will do as you're told, soldier."

She'd never called him that. Why now?

"Your anger is immaterial," her voice continued. "Return and rest. The others will repair and reorder, and you will stay out of the way until you are called back."

"Okay," he said, resigned. He still smoldered, but he knew he could not outrun her voice. "Okay, damnit. I'll go back."

He wheeled around and marched doggedly, looking at no one, returning no greeting, back to the place he had left Melia. She snorted at him with a raised eyebrow and resumed talking to Rhodia and Hestia, pointing him to a spot some ten paces off. He sat down with his back to everyone, and stared at the ground between his feet. He struggled to keep his temper under control, but unbidden thoughts awakened by the insults, the failures, the contrary commands all surged in his head. He closed his eyes, and felt himself nodding forward, his chin going to his chest, his hands clasped around his knees.

* * *

"This is how it will be," Melia was telling Kratos, Eurymedon, Rhodia, and Hestia when Shelby jerked awake, lying on his side.

"I can do that," Hestia said. "It will take some horses to pull the trebuchets into position. That means getting other things out of the way. But we can do it. Maybe by tonight."

"The Meliae will take up positions as instructed," Rhodia said, rising.

"No problems, sister. We just needed a plan. This will get us through the night, but no closer to the sea," Kratos said. Eurymedon nodded.

"We will get to the sea when we get to it," Melia said.

"What are you talking about?" Shelby asked, rubbing his eyes.

"I'll tell you what you need to know later," Melia said. "Don't move from this spot until I send for you. It's not punishment, but you can think of it that way if you want."

She heaved herself up to her feet, helped by Hestia.

"Lie down," Melia commanded. "Put your ear on the dirt and listen. Listen to the earth. I will come for you if I need you."

"I resent your tone of voice," he replied. The others, who had risen when she did, drifted away out of earshot.

"You will obey orders when I give them," she said. "This is not about your feelings. This is about survival and purpose. We need you to be the brave, deadly warrior you are, not who you became after rescuing Dolios and fighting those wild men. Keep your eyes closed. You need rest and recovery in order to clear your mind, and I am ordering you as your priestess, your queen, your wife, and the mother of your unborn child to get that rest. Right now. Also, you might hear something from the earth that helps your mind. It always seemed to help my strange brother Ophion, and he was as great a hero as you. As Kratos, in his own way. Listen, sleep, recover, and learn. I need my Lion, but I need him thinking straight. You protect all of us."

Resigned, he lay with his ear on the ground, a fairly uncomfortable position since his broad shoulders meant that his neck had to endure odd angles. The smell of dirt in his nose, dry, choking dirt, was his first sensation. He was still too pissed to relax, despite his recent nap. After all he'd done, after all the pain and effort he'd made, here he was again, lying in dirt. He had lain in dirt a lot during his years in the Rangers and the smell of this dirt swept images into his brain, of deployment in Somalia, in Iraq, in Afghanistan. He caught a scent of tarmac, of hot dust swirling around his feet, of the vibrations in his torso of screaming jets or of heavy C-130s thundering off the runway over the pub in Kaiserslautern near Ramstein with the sign that read, "Soup of the Day: Whiskey." He indulged himself with a little self-pity. Here he was in some preclassical Bronze Age, with no coffee and no whiskey, and not even any names for days of the week. True, he wanted to be here. The sex was great, and so were the battles. Naked slaves everywhere, some of them quite good-looking. And the baths conducted by nubile young women. Yeah, it had its compensations.

And, Melia, of course, was hot. But not right now. The hot she was at the moment was way different from the hot he dreamed about.

He forced all this away and concentrated on listening. He heard his own breathing. He heard his pulse. He heard his own uncomfortable shifting as he tried to keep his left ear to the dirt. He heard his tomahawk scrape along the ground as he shifted his body away from a little stony projection pressing into his rib cage. He concentrated on the sounds carrying through the earth. He forced himself to relax, that hardest of all tasks, to empty his head of all memories—the second hardest of all tasks—and just to listen. Listen, be still, relax, let go. It was so hard to do.

THIRTY-SIX

W ith his eyes closed, he began to hear sounds. A series of hoofbeats from horses ridden by cavalry. How far away were they? He heard scufflings of people close by, the subdued sounds of the camp, and the faint, comfortable laughter of a woman. Then it grew quieter, as though everyone had moved off, and eventually he entered a waking dream. He was both asleep and not asleep, both in the world and out of it, like floating in the parachute glider from a high altitude. Sound ceased, even the whistling of the wind as he spiraled slowly toward earth, toward sea and mountains. He had control of his dream movements, he could spiral slowly left or right, but he was floating downward, slowly, always downward. Then he was free of the glider's capsule and floating over the ground, from rock to rock to grass clump to gravel. He moved effortlessly, weightlessly, with a sense of his legs carrying him but unimpeded by the weight of reality. He could not stir, did not want to stir from the dream. He was being drawn somewhere unknowable, into some mysterious landscape, both real and not real, both waking and sleeping, both over the earth and on it.

Now upright he entered a gully where blood-red water gurgled from the side of a mountain. Somehow he knew it was a sacred mountain, a place of wonder and terror. He looked up through ancient trees at a distant snow-covered peak. Behind him the valley stretched toward a crystal-blue sea, the stream's red dye spreading bloodily in the seawater where it fell from the land, the long tail of its stain drifting outward forever. He stepped into the stream and felt the cold red water on his naked feet despite his shoes. He was both dressed and naked, both awake and asleep, both alive and dead.

He followed the water course a little way and found a fissure where it came forth from deep within the mountain. He peered into the fissure and something looked back at him, a pair of unwinking eyes glinting in the dark. It's forked black tongue flicked out of the hole.

He panicked and backpedaled from the snake, but the water had risen to his knees and slowed his feet. The slippery stones in the stream prevented secure footing, and he could stumble, even drown, in the fast current. And then the water itself began transforming into the writhing serpent coming at him, its lidless eyes staring at him, coiling larger and larger. Its iridescent skin sparking in the dappled sunlight like diamonds and emeralds.

The snake coiled around him, pinning him, choking him. In a desperate effort, he freed a hand and grabbed its neck, holding the relentless head away from his face. Every time he exhaled, the coils tightened, squeezing him, reducing his breath, and its mouth gaped wide, its jaw unhinging to swallow him, it's teeth angling back into its long gullet, the black tongue flicking at him as it tasted his scent. A huge snake, possibly venomous, maybe a python or boa? No, a bushmaster! "Lachesis," his brain screamed, "the genus of bushmaster! It's a bushmaster!" One of the deadliest snakes in the world. He freed another hand and grappled with the snake, which dragged him underwater. They thrashed in the cold water, twisting over and over, his breath gradually going. He would not be able to kill the snake with his bare hands. Even brain dead, it would continue to squeeze him until it choked him. But he would not surrender.

With one free leg, he pushed himself up out of the water as the serpent threw huge coils around him. Gasping for air, he desperately searched for some weapon. Each coil was as thick as his leg, maybe thicker. What did this snake weigh? he asked his dreaming self. Two hundred forty pounds was the reply.

The snake was getting stronger, and he now needed both hands to hold the hissing mouth away from his head. From its jaws came a sickeningly foul odor, the ugly vulva-like glottis at the base of its tongue clearly visible. Struggling to his feet, Shelby inched farther up the embankment, dragging himself and the looping snake up, up and away from the water. He knew he was dreaming, and he knew he could choose his action, but he didn't know what to do.

But then he sensed that the farther he moved from the water, the weaker the snake seemed to become. It also seemed to grow thinner, somehow less furious. His encoiled leg felt stronger as his bare foot gripped the stony embankment and his toes found purchase.

Panting, he stared back into the unwinking eyes full of reptilian hatred. What had he read about snakes? That there were no plant-eating snakes. All snakes ate living things. That lashing tongue, tasting the air, locating him by his fear and his body heat—where was his knife so he could cut it off? Could he reach it even if he had it?

At last he arrived at the top of the embankment. Ahead of him was a rocky slope dominated by a single stone phallus about four feet tall. Where were they now? Some instinct told him to drag the snake to that stone.

One breathless step after another, trying to hold the snake's fatal mouth away from his face, struggling and failing then struggling again, dragging the long coil with him, the snake's head weaving side to side despite his best efforts. And then he was there.

In the top of the stone was an opening. He battered the snake's head against the hard surface, dashing a thick sheen of ancient reptilian blood over the stone. To get more leverage, he moved his grip down the snake's body and whipped it against the stone, until finally he felt the coils relax in a series of spasms. The snake became flaccid, its head and jaws crushed by his labored beating. Shelby gulped air, re-oxygenating at last, and with one final huge effort, he bashed the snake down on the top of the stone. It uncoiled and began to dissolve, turning to icy water and slipping through in his outspread fingers into the hole in the top of the rock and down into the darkness below.

The dripping water seemed to awaken a thousand female voices, piercing and strident. Panting, he collapsed against the stone, staring at his hands drying in the air, free at last of the snake. Female shapes materialized in the air ahead of him.

Some were beautiful, some terrifying, and all angry at him. They merged together into one being whose face was a knot of writhing, poison-spitting adders. It swooped at him across the rocky ground, glowing green and reptilian, undulating in fury, reaching clawed hands out at him. It was too awful to look at, too awful to listen to.

He backed away in horror, terrified, as it advanced on him. He felt the cold fear striking through him, turning his legs to brittle spindles of ice. His breathing stopped and his mind froze. The creature seemed to be on all sides of him, cutting off escape, flickering first in front and then to the side, then reaching its claws at him. To protect his back, he shrank against the phalluslike stone and waited for it to come at him.

The images dissolved and the shrieking stopped abruptly. Exhausted but alive, he took deep breaths as he carefully took in his surroundings to see if there was any sign of the creature's return. As his body relaxed, he felt the hair on the nape of his neck lie back down.

He shifted in his dream, partially awoke, turned his right ear to the ground, and fell back to sleep. This time, as he drifted off, the dream showed him still crouching next to the stone, but he had the golden shield and the Shrike tomahawk. He reversed the shield so he could look behind him, over the crude rock dome, and in its many reflecting surfaces he saw the green snake-like woman waiting for him. She had remained perfectly silent and still but for the snakes writhing in her face and hair. Her taloned hands still reached for him.

He got his feet under him and slowly pushed himself erect against the stone, watching the creature. The blur of snakes drew back to reveal a human likeness. When she saw him, she began a low scream, her lips drawn back to reveal fang-like teeth, teeth like the serpent's. Her eyes were unblinking, un-lidded, yet human-like. The creature's face was reflected in the hundreds of polished gold panels of his shield, like a multitude of fears.

He moved slowly around the stone watching for any movement from the terrifying creature in his shield. His tomahawk clenched in his hand. She seemed rooted, part of the landscape almost, weaving and unsteady, undulating like the snakes that composed her head. Her shimmering green breasts heaved with her breathing, their dark nipples vibrating in the weak sunlight like olives. She reached out a clawed hand, long and haggard, to the stone, scratching at the drying blood, leaning toward it. Shelby assumed she was drawn by the scent of the snake's blood, hungering for it, and he crept farther around the stone.

Then he was behind her, and with all his strength he swung his tomahawk backward, guiding it in the shield's reflection, and struck off her head. The body crumpled against the stone and the head rolled toward the embankment, toward the creek.

"Must not let the head reach water," he heard himself urging. "Must stop it."

The writhing snakes caused the head to creep aimlessly down the slope toward the red stream. He leapt and smashed the shield on top of the head, kneeling on it, driving the head into the stony ground. The serpents hissed and squirmed, vibrating the golden shield, but he was safe. He had it pinned.

The sunlight brightened on the hilltop and the world came into focus. Looking behind him, he saw the body of the creature dissolving into a green slime, soaking into the earth. He leaned into the shield, feeling it flatten into the earth. The buzzing serpents slowly ceased their rattling.

And then it was over. The shield lay flat on the ground, and he was alone in the sunlight. When he raised the shield to look under it, the terrifying figure of the creature's head was embedded in the gold face like a holograph. The snakes lived in image only, weaving and fanged, but the surface of the shield was flat.

"Master," Dolios said softly, "Master, the sun is setting, and Melia wants me to wake you to join her and the others for something to eat."

THIRTY-SEVEN

T he night was still and quiet, though the sense of menace
seemed to grow with the silence. The only sounds were
the soft crackling of fires interspersed with the occasional
murmurings of guards and groups of gently snoring citizens. The
fires had driven even the insects away. Overhead, a clear sky was
brilliant with sheets of stars like diamonds scattered across a
velvet floor, their light dimly showing columns of smoke drifting
eastward, back toward the mountains they had traversed, back
toward their smothered valley and the immolated remains of
their golden age, barely seen over the jungle of brush and trees,
the dark pines standing sentinel against the mountains, beeches
wearing their new green-gold growth.

Kratos was staring at the shadows on all sides of them from
the top of a hastily erected watch tower, seeing nothing in the
dark landscape. Shelby perched on the railing nearby, keeping
him company and trying not to remember similar nights on the
ground in America's forsaken wars around the globe. What had
the old timers told him on that deployment near—maybe inside—
China? That the term Hindu Kush translated as "killer of Hindus,"
because the harsh Himalayan mountain ranges killed
off the Hindu slaves being marched to new masters. He couldn't
help thinking about it. Those nights came back to him, those
frozen wastes of stone colder than ice, with no snow to soften
the bleak landscape.

"The night is still, brother," Kratos said, his deep voice a
soft rumble.

"It is," Shelby said, in a voice that did not carry, pulled back from the abyss of his memories by the friendly voice. "I wish we could see farther into the shadows under these trees."

"I think they are out there, but I don't know what they're doing."

"Scouting our perimeters, probably," Shelby said, "looking for something to steal. If they're there. These fires may have driven them off."

"Their malice will bring them back, regardless," Kratos said. "Also, possibly they are looking for roasted game in the ashes. That would bring them closer."

"I meant to ask Alcestis about her wolf," Shelby said. "I wonder if she's been able to take meat to it recently. If so, it means the wolf is inside the fire line. And if the wolf is inside, then the wild men have probably found a way inside also."

"I got a good look at that wolf. That is some beast. Those teeth must be as long as my hand is wide. I'd hesitate to have the animal think I had anything to do with raw meat."

"Yeah, almost like that lion we killed."

"You killed that lion. I was frozen," Kratos said. "Magnificent kill. Of course you have done many magnificent things since, but that was the first."

"I was too terrified to think," Shelby said. "I just reacted. It was sheer luck I got the spear up just as the lion jumped."

"The difference between a hero and a dead man is his instincts, brother."

"Yeah, I guess so. It's funny how thinking always slows us down."

"Maybe that's why the wolf is so much faster than we are. It doesn't think."

"Maybe it thinks when it's young, and then learns everything it needs to know." Shelby grinned.

"Maybe we do the same," Kratos replied.

They lapsed into silence, watching the shadows and the night. Somewhere to their north and west was the ocean, and the trackless passages over water to the mountains of central Italy. Somewhere and somehow they would cross that water. Shelby didn't know how. But before they got to Italy, they would need to reach the sea and he didn't want his progressively weakening emigrant city trying to trek across the Dinaric Alps of the Balkans, or through lands already overrun with Achaeans. Or worse. The wild men were bad enough. Encountering more technologically sophisticated brigands might prove fatal.

Being in the comfortable presence of this mighty warrior reminded him of the camaraderie and love he had felt for his fellow soldiers. Nobody lives forever, but you live longer if you have friends protecting your back. The thing about being in the US Army was that the constant training made you expert in a narrow range of activities, all having to do with the army. You learned everything there was to know about mortars, for example: how to pinpoint a target at seven kilometers, whether to use a point detonating fuse or a multi-option fuse, choice of explosives, choice of sizes, sustaining four to five mortar rounds per minute, getting your hand out of the way. A mortar was a simple machine with a lot of complicated options—all task oriented, which was appropriate. Never a question about why the army had such and such a task, or what they were doing freezing their butts off at eighteen thousand feet in the Himalayas or blowing up barren valleys in Pakistan, killing goat herders with minds so simple they didn't know their left hands from their right. No, those questions were for the political leaders who supposedly made the decisions. The GI had a job to do, and he went and did it.

Besides mortars didn't exist in this century. But they had the trebuchets, which were three thousand years ahead of their time. For plunging indirect fire, they functioned very well. A two-hundred-pound boulder falling from a hundred feet in the air turned Achaeans into red pulp. But the Achaeans were massed and unable to maneuver effectively to avoid the projectiles. Here in this brush it was different, and the sparse and dispersed nature of the enemy required different techniques. It was jungle warfare on a brushy Greek hillside.

"I wish Melia would let us go out there to confront them," Kratos muttered. "I'm tired of being cooped up here while we struggle to build roads."

"She may be thinking that they will lose interest in us," Shelby whispered. "But I think she's wrong. We represent too easy a source of food for them. Besides, I'm uneasy about that big guy we saw. He spoke to us with authority, as a leader, or chief."

"I can't stop thinking about him, either," Kratos said. "He was massive, yet he leapt with unbelievable agility. I've never seen a creature so large move so effortlessly."

"He was at least double your weight, too. Maybe double mine. And all muscle with a brain. I bet he could have picked up a horse and thrown it. I hope he was the only one that size."

"If we start hurling stones at them from the trebuchet, we'll just give them loose rocks they can throw back," Kratos said, "not that there aren't plenty of stones out there already. I understand why Melia thinks the trebuchets at the center of camp are a good idea, but it seems ridiculous to start shooting ammunition at our enemies when they can simply turn around and heave it back."

"We have a problem," Shelby nodded. "If the trebuchets make Melia feel more comfortable, then I'm in favor of them. Anything she is in favor of, I'm in favor of. But so far they've not been used, and maybe they won't be. Those piles of rocks Hestia has loaded into the slings are a good idea, and the stones will scatter as they leave the trebuchet at the top of its arc, spreading over a broad area. I don't know how broad, because we haven't tried it, but it's an act of genius if you think about it. If we need those trebuchets in an actual war, loading a large group of skull-sized stones into the sling could be very effective against troops. With all these trees in the way, though, they can't be all that effective."

"Another thing," Kratos said a moment later. "We saw how they could just leap away into darkness and disappear. How fast do you think an archer or one of the Meliae could reload their bows? In the amount of time you would have if they were coming straight for you, you could get off only one shot before he was on you, and if they are all that agile then the chances of even hitting them diminishes. We were lucky they are not sophisticated fighters, or we would already be extinguished."

"Maybe we could buy them off the same way Alcestis feeds that wolf," Shelby said after a while. "We could stake out a cow, perhaps. But I hate to do it. We will need our cattle to survive next year."

"I don't think that would buy them off. I think they would want all of our cattle instead of just one. We need to keep those people away from our people, and staking out a cow won't do that. Besides, the wolf is just as likely to kill the cow as they are, and make short work of it, too."

"Right. Or some other animal."

"Yes." Kratos lapsed into silence again, only his eyes moving over the dark landscape.

"We don't know enough about them to understand their weaknesses," Shelby finally said. "We don't know anything about them, except that they are a mortal danger to us. We don't know where they stay, how many there are, or anything else. We can't fight an enemy we know nothing about."

"We know they are deadly and vengeful," Kratos replied. "They might not have attacked our wagons with such force if we had not castrated the ones we killed."

"I thought that was a bad idea at the time," Shelby said.

"It is how our women fight our wars," Kratos said. "In all the generations of our people, you are the only male who ever taught them anything, and they were still willing to kill you the other day when they thought you and Melia were getting into a fight. I saw that. Your life was in danger from your own students. You taught them well, but you did not teach them to fear you or to avoid you. Perhaps a powerful female cannot be taught those things, as a male can. You arm a female, you have a dangerous creature, more dangerous than these wild men, and without fear of us. You and me, brother, we are lucky they let us live, so we must be useful to them in some way. The day you are no longer useful will be a sad day for you."

They stood together for a long time, looking out in opposite directions under the great wheel of the sky. Finally Shelby stretched and yawned.

"I think I will go to sleep," he said. "Call me if you see anything or need me."

"I do not sleep," Kratos said. "Not since Father's murder. You go and enjoy your rest. I will stay here and brood over my dark thoughts and burning memories."

THIRTY-EIGHT

Several nights later, Kratos and Shelby were again in the lookout tower, scanning the darkened landscape. The people were quiet and nothing was moving in the deep purple shadows of stones and rocky outcrops. The wildfires had burned long distances, but had deflected around a range of barren limestone hills and gone out. The moon shed a pale glow over the mostly open landscape, covered now in ash and smoldering cinders, like some bombed wasteland devoid of life.

Kratos finally broke the silence. "We have outlived our fires," he said. "They have gone out, and we are still here."

"At least we can see more of nothing," Shelby said. "In this country, seeing nothing is a good thing."

"My eyes play tricks on me, brother. Sometimes I think I see nothing. Other times I think I see those boulders and distant hills moving toward us, like great masses of stone giants intent on our destruction."

"We've not seen or heard of wild men for seven days. Maybe they have tired of playing with us," Shelby said.

"Maybe they are hoping we will let our guard down," Kratos replied. "What was it you said, something about eternal vigilance?"

"The price of freedom," Shelby said. "My other favorite saying is that we can only have peace through strength."

"Yes, that was the saying I was thinking of. Peace through strength. That's a nice phrase. It's somewhat more difficult to put into practice."

"All sayings ignore the practical," Shelby replied. "They are at best merely a summary of an attitude. Anyone who says you can have peace through strength is looking for a way to fight. Any way to fight, regardless. It's never about peace. It's always about war."

"Now where's your warrior spirit?" Kratos joked. "You are supposed to keep me inspired."

"I thought I was supposed to keep you drunk and out of trouble," Shelby said, passing the wineskin.

"That too," Kratos grinned. "That, too."

"I have been thinking . . . " Shelby said, trailing off.

"Never a good thing at this time of night," the shorter warrior grunted, drawing the back of meaty hand across his mouth to wipe away the wine.

"What I have been thinking is that we still do not know anything about our enemy," Shelby said. "Melia told us that they travel in small groups, they sleep on the ground without fire, and they hunt constantly. I wonder how she knows that."

"Most likely she saw it in one of those visions she gets from the goddess," Kratos said. "She used that tone of voice, the one she reserves for the divine visions. So my guess is that she knows what she's talking about."

"I didn't have those visions," Shelby said.

"Well, no, you didn't do the sacrifice, either, did you?"

"If I did, do you think the goddess would tell me anything?"

"Are you kidding? Sometimes you are so dense, Icarus."

"What are you talking about?"

"First, you are not female. So, no, the goddess is not going to talk to you about her world. She might talk to you about yourself, as she seems to have done with that last dream you had, the one about the shield. But no, she's not going to help you see anything beyond yourself. Still, you know, that can be useful."

"So I might not learn anything about the wild men, even if I sacrificed to her?" Shelby said.

"You might learn something about yourself, and you might learn something about the wild men only in terms of how you relate to them. But no, you are not going to learn anything useful about them. About yourself, surely, but not about them. How much do you want to know about yourself?"

"Not more than I already know," Shelby replied.

"Right. Me either. I like not knowing more. It's fun to be surprised."

"I'm okay with surprises," Shelby said, "about myself. Other times, no. Other times, I like to have actual knowledge. I'd like to know about our enemies, for example. What can they do? How can they do it? Are they just like flies or mosquitoes buzzing around looking for an opportunity, or do they have strategy and tactics? I'd like to know that."

"Why?"

"So I could make better plans."

"What would you do differently?" Kratos asked.

"I might prepare differently if I knew they could put together an army of fifty or a hundred."

"How?"

"I'd say, 'Kratos, prepare for an attack by fifty wild men.' Then I'd look for a way to help you. Or not." Shelby grinned.

"I am always prepared for an attack of fifty wild men," Kratos said. "It is the day we all die."

"Come now."

"I'm serious. We cannot withstand an attack by that many. They could destroy us all. You, me, Melia, everyone. All our thousands could not defend against fifty of them. They are too formidable."

"Do you have any suggestions?" Shelby asked.

"Do you?"

"I'd like to know more about them so I'd be able to tell if an attack by fifty of them is likely. I don't think they had half that many when they attacked last time. Maybe only twelve or thirteen. Maybe fewer. And we killed three of those."

"How do you propose to find out more?" Kratos asked.

"Go out there and see." Shelby pointed to the wasteland.

"Let's go," Kratos said. "If you think it's a good idea, I'll notify Garanus to keep the watch, and you and I can go now."

"Should I tell Melia?"

"Melia will give you the same advice I will give you. She will say to stay here and be safe. She will tell you that hunting wild men in the dark in their own country is stupid, and that you are asking to get yourself killed. And then she will remind you that you have been forbidden from hunting wild men. And then she will blow up that little brain of yours and you will pray for death just to end the headaches. So why ask her?"

"You mean do it anyway."

"I mean, I'm bored enough stuck in this camp and sitting through the long nights on this watchtower to take my own life. If you want to go out looking for wild men, then by all means let's be off. I'm ready to scream from inaction. I'm close to taking it out on the slaves, and that's bad."

"Well, okay then, let's go."

"Do you want to carry one of those crossbows with you?"

"Not particularly, but I will. Rhodia still leads both of us together in total dead wild men. She shot all those in the back the day they kidnapped Dolios, but Rhodia is, well, you know Rhodia. Sly and fatal. I have now had the unpleasant experience of trying to fight wild men head on, and it did not go well. I'd rather follow her example and ambush them from behind. Together I think you and I are a match for one."

"We weren't the other night. It took three of us to bring that one guy down."

"Yeah, that was close. I can't hit them in the head again. It may kill them, but I'll lose the weapon. Slashing blows with the Shrike is just about the only way to do it, and those are not going to do a lot of damage to men that size. Well, not enough to stop them before they've done worse to me. I've got to have different ways of fighting."

"We all do," Kratos said. "That's the fun of it. Nothing we've known before will work. So we must invent and adapt, or die."

"Right. Creation or death."

"Now?"

"Food? Water?" Shelby asked.

"Wine? Who needs water?"

"I'll gather supplies, you notify the guard to take over for us here. We will scout just to the other side of those limestone ridges. If we don't see anything, we turn around and come back and sleep the rest of the night. If we do, we go on until we know something we did not know before."

"I'll get the supplies and hunt up Garanus. He's used to this from me, so he won't be alarmed."

"Right," Shelby said. "Let's do this!"

THIRTY-NINE

꧁꧁꧁꧁꧁꧁꧁꧁꧁꧁꧁꧁

G aranus climbed nimbly up the ladder of the watchtower while Kratos and Shelby shouldered their scant provisions. No one is ever invisible in a large encampment, and when two well-known heroes and defenders of the city act furtively, they draw more attention. However, their slow, deliberate movements did not telegraph alarm, and no one seemed to notice them hefting spears or strapping into armor. Garanus expressed no concern whatsoever, just saying that he would alert Eurymedon and the cavalry if he suspected anything.

Shelby twinged at that. His conscience told him to include Eurymedon in their exploit, but he did not want the younger brother along. He feared that Eurymedon's need to prove himself, his fearlessness, and his impetuosity might be a burden. Of the three of them, Shelby thought, Eurymedon, as he matured, would have a better future with the city than either he or Kratos. Also, of course, Rhodia was in love with him, which was an important boost to his status. If he and Kratos failed to return, Eurymedon would be a worthy if naive replacement. Meanwhile, if he and Kratos were grouped together, Eurymedon would take risks to prove himself as good as the two of them. And he was as good, on horseback. He was not as good on foot. Eurymedon was one of those lucky souls who was born to ride. Kratos was born to kill.

What was I born to do, Shelby wondered. Ask questions? Defend the weak? He liked the idea that he was born to defend the weak. And that explained why he was setting out in the dark, after Melia was asleep, expressly against her orders, to hunt up some wild men. Sure it did. Maybe he was born to make bad decisions.

The full moon was near its zenith as they eased away from the camp. They walked carefully, sidestepping piles of smoldering cinders still sending up thin wisps of smoke, padding through soft ashes waiting for a rain to wash them away. For the first half mile, they saw nothing in the wasteland they did not expect to see, then Kratos pointed to a series of large footprints. They were the prints of very large bare feet, much larger than Shelby's own feet, which were enormous by city standards.

"They've been inside the fire line," Kratos whispered.

"What have they done? We've had no reports of attacks."

"Scouting? Looking for vulnerabilities?"

"Maybe," Shelby said.

They followed the single line of footprints for several hundred yards, then the footprints were joined by another set coming from the opposite direction.

Shelby looked a question at Kratos.

Kratos shrugged. "They circled the camp, looks like," he said quietly.

"How old are these prints?"

"Hard to tell, maybe just minutes. Maybe yesterday. I think they are more recent than yesterday, though," Kratos said. "The fires have died a lot in the last day. They are no longer a barrier."

"No, and we did not get away in time," said Shelby.

"No," agreed Kratos. "I think we are easy targets for them."

"At least the open ground between us and the unburned brush would let us know when they were coming," Shelby said. He unlimbered his crossbow, checking to be sure it was cocked and loaded.

"Not that it would do us much good. I really am no good at defensive warfare, brother," Kratos said. "My mind does not work that way. The Matrons were always our defenders. They were the ones whose plans and organization helped us build such a magnificent city. Defense seemed to come naturally to them, whereas with me, all I can think about is closing with the enemy with a sword in my hand."

"It's a dual skill, friend," Shelby said quietly. "A good warrior is also a good defender. You cannot be all of one or the other."

"I know. But I always left the other to them. I am for action!"

Shelby nodded, knowing his gesture would be obvious in the moonlight pouring over the burned landscape, the ghostly ashes glowing like liquid silver.

The two sets of footprints had merged, leading off into the unburned brush.

"Should we continue around the camp, or do you want to try tracking them into the brush?" Shelby whispered.

"These prove that they have been stalking us. Looking at more footprints is not going to tell us more about them."

"Agreed," Shelby said, "although it might tell us how many of them are out there. Remember, we are scouting for them, not looking for a fight. If I think we are close, I'll signal and we'll back away as quietly as we can."

Moving as quietly as they could through the brush also meant moving very slowly. They bent twigs out of the way to avoid brushing them as they passed. Patches of dense weeds and brambles made scratching noises on their armor. They stepped between tall burned trees, their black trunks pointed accusingly at the sky, and past smoldering piles of fallen trees in chaotic tangle. They could not move in complete silence, and the best they could hope was that their slow movements would not telegraph their presence. They had to place their feet carefully so as not to dislodge any loose stones or be tripped by branches now lying on the ground. When they emerged past the fire's perimeter, they followed random game paths, crouching to about the height of a goat's shoulder, passing beneath overhanging branches. The moon was already declining toward the west and they had seen nothing since the footprints. But then they came upon a bare patch in the glowing in the moonlight. The relative cover of the brush had been a little reassuring, but crossing into the bare patch meant being exposed. Shelby stopped to consider, surveying the rocky area.

"See something?" Kratos asked in a low whisper.

Shelby shook his head. He had sometimes avoided ambush during his deployments by following his instinct. And now that instinct was flashing yellow and red caution lights in his head. At first he thought it might be a scent on the air, a crushed poppy or wildflower. But he knew better. It was something more threaten-

ing, an odor just below detection, a smell that was almost unde-
tectable.

They remained motionless for minutes, low to the ground,
just observing the slow shifting of the moonlight across the rocks
and limestone gravel. Then Kratos pointed at a spot close by, and
slowly lifted his arm to point at a spot farther away, on the edge
of the clearing. Shelby saw immediately the imprint of a large foot
in the ground, one he had not seen earlier because of the angle of
the moonlight, but he couldn't make out what Kratos had pointed
to farther away. He stared, and then he saw the edge of a bush
rustle a little. No breeze could explain it. Either it was an animal,
maybe a wild boar, or it was a wild man.

He hoped it was a boar. Or a bear. Or even a lion. Anything
but a wild man.

He began to edge around the clearing, staying as low as possible and as hidden as possible, hoping to gain a better angle to
see whatever had made that bush rustle. It could have been a
night bird of some kind. An owl, perhaps, or a nightingale, but he
had heard no bird calls.

Then he heard a low, long snore, followed by a cough. And
suddenly the bush stopped moving. Its leaves hung like so many
tiny slivers of dark glass in the silver light.

Shelby and Kratos froze. A moment passed and Shelby
looked back at Kratos. He nodded. Kratos returned the nod, then
shrugged his shoulders slightly, as if to suggest a question. Shelby
edged closer to the spot.

As he eased ahead, very slight movement on the opposite side
of the bare patch suddenly caught his eye. He glanced at it, not
moving his head so much as his eyes, and froze again. At the very
periphery of the patch, more out of sight than in it, he watched as
a wolf eased ahead on its belly, ears back, nose raised to sniff the
air, baring its upper teeth. It was Calu! Shelby understood at once
that while he and Kratos had been tracking the wild men, the wolf
had been tracking them through the brush. A shiver ran down his
spine. How many other deadly creatures could be stalking them?
And now they were a known location to the wolf. Could they go
ahead to spy on the wild men, who must be sleeping just over that
hill, or had they seen enough? Should they go on? Would the wolf
give them away? Why was the wolf edging closer to the wild men,

just as they were?

Kratos tugged slightly at his back. Shelby looked very slowly back to see Kratos's worried look, his arched eyebrows. Kratos cut his eyes at the wolf, and then he stared past Shelby at the edge of the bare patch beyond the wolf, his spear pointing to the place where the bush had rustled. The bush was still.

Years earlier Shelby had heard of the peculiar habits of the so-called bushmen of Namibia, who sometimes appointed one of their hunting band to go into a trance of protection and awareness while the others slept. The trance acted as a spiritual force field, keeping predators away from the sleeping hunters. Apparently, it worked, even against leopards. Could these wild men have an appointed watcher, whose trance-like meditation might consist of heightened awareness, might alert the others at any disturbance of the local area, sense any changes in the microclimate or sensory field?

It was not worth the risk. They would go back the way they had come, and in the morning they would explore with more warriors at their side.

Shelby nodded at Kratos to signal that they were turning around. An hour later they emerged into the wasteland of ashes that surrounded their wagon train.

"That was close, brother," Kratos said when they could speak again. "I thought you were going to walk right into them."

"The wolf warned me," Shelby said. "What an incredible creature. We've got to keep her well fed, and maybe she will stay on our side. When I saw her creeping forward it was as good as her announcing aloud that the wild men were right there. We might not have been more than twenty paces from them."

"Could you not smell them?" Kratos asked.

"I smelled something," Shelby said. "I took it for crushed weeds, or something more sinister."

"If you smell it again," Kratos said, nodding, "it is the wild men. Go the other way unless you want to blunder right into them."

FORTY

🔥🔥🔥🔥🔥🔥🔥🔥🔥🔥🔥🔥

H aving learned the hard way that they could not outrun the wild men, the city now became even more cautious, expecting attack at any moment. Most days they moved no more than half a mile, and some days they didn't move at all. Instead, they traveled with soldiers on the perimeter, organized into what Shelby referred to as squads and platoons (of course), and patrolled around the clock. When they pitched camp for the night, they circled the wagons for protection and and set bonfires in cleared spaces on either side of the camp. During the days when they stayed put, they attempted with heart-bursting labor to build roads over the cracked granite ground. Alluvial soil washed into stream beds might have made travel easier, but the streams ran in labyrinths south or southeast, away from their goal. And every night after a fourteen-hour day of extreme exertion, they would huddle in the dark listening for the fatal tread of the wild men.

Shelby urged Kratos and the other leaders to allow him to distribute weapons to the citizens, so they could help in an attack. He thought slings and atlatls would be useful, neither of which the wild men appeared to have. But the military commanders were reluctant.

"Our job is to protect," they complained. "We are trained and work as units with the control of command. You cannot expect the citizens to be effective. They could be more a hazard than a help."

"Listen to them," Melia said. "We have had many centuries of experience."

"In my own country, we have a long history of citizen militias," Shelby replied.

"Really?" asked Melia. "And how does that work out when you must fight a war? Do your citizens stop their work and rush to the front lines? Do they have armor and spears? Are they trained and willing to be commanded?"

"We have units that are composed of citizens who train for several days once a month and who are sometimes deployed."

"And who does their work when they are off fighting once a month?" Melia asked. "And another thing. What happens if these armed citizens decide they don't like one another or that they don't like the authorities? Do they rebel, like that group of boys the Achaeans seduced before our city fell, the ones you quelled?"

Kratos had been brooding and now spoke up. "I know, if I were unarmed and the wild men were coming for me, I would want a weapon of any kind. Even a rock. I'm sure the citizens feel the same. But we have always been their weapon, and we have been good at it until the other night. And by the way, sister. Our city did not fall. We tricked the Achaeans into entering it and they were penned inside when the Goddess buried it in fire."

"That's true, Kratos. I spoke too far. Our city did not fall. But the boys still rebelled, and they obtained weapons from somewhere. That made them dangerous."

"An ordered society needs to have clear expectations," said Arktos. "We go to a lot of effort to train our army and our other citizens, and Melia enforces the goddess's will in maintaining those expectations. In this crisis, I do not think we have time to train the citizens to be responsible weapon bearers. They are already responsible caretakers and suppliers and they are essential to our effective fighting. They bring water and supplies, they remove the dead, they care for our wounded, and after the battle our women go out in the night and finish any wounded enemy. It is a good system. This threat from the wild men is unique, but we can deal with it, in my opinion."

"I understand," Shelby said. "I may not entirely agree, but when I look at it from your point of view I appreciate you allowing me to voice my idea. This is not a time to innovate our culture."

"Besides," Melia said, "we have plenty of armed men to deal with these few wild men. They are a threat and are large warriors, but we are powerful also, despite our shorter stature. Kratos, do your job." She stood up to go into her tent, leaving the others staring silently at one another over the dwindling campfire.

* * *

At Melia's suggestion, Hestia replaced the trebuchet weights with waterproof wineskins. They were filled with water every night to provide the potential energy to fire the trebuchets. A test firing was satisfactory, but Hestia tinkered with the design, moving the fulcrum slightly to accommodate the somewhat lighter weight of the water. Draining the water for the cattle lightened the trebuchets considerably, however, and made transporting them much easier. She also redesigned the carriage to be elevated or lowered in the front, allowing the trebuchets to aim closer to the ground, blasting like grapeshot. As artillery, they had their limits. They required time to set up, time to load, time to aim, and meanwhile an enemy like the wild men could be converging rapidly. Trebuchets were just not useful in this kind of warfare, Shelby thought to himself, but he had no ideas that might improve their firepower. Since the city was constantly moving, Hestia could not set up her forges or make new weapons, so he kept to himself his ideas about creating steam engines, steam cannons, and the like. Developing those machines were things they could attempt in calmer times.

* * *

Late one afternoon, Alcestis came to Melia carrying the polished goatskin case that held the golden shield inside. The case was itself an artistic accomplishment. Over the ages, unknown hands had embroidered it with a serpent design, adding tassels like snakes to its fringes. The comforting sweet smell of beeswax used as polish flowed from it.

"Mistress," the slave girl said, "here is the shield you asked for. I have been dusting the shield's case, but I did not open it. All the dust from our travel gets into everything."

"Hmmm," said Melia, taking the bulky case into her lap, enjoying the tactile feel of the leather and its sweet scent, feeling the shield's hard edges through its padding.

"The goddess has been speaking to me about this shield," Melia said. "Why, I'm not certain. I just keep seeing it in my visions, with me holding it before a setting sun."

"I didn't want to open the case by myself, since I know how precious it is," Alcestis said.

"Yes, my father brought it home from his world tour, before he married mother," Melia said. "He never used it, but he valued it highly. It was his most precious possession. I'm not sure where he got it or how, but I always thought it came from somewhere in the west, I think, near the world's edge. Arktos would know. He was with father on the tour."

She undid the ancient leather and gold wire ties, and pushed back the flap. An odor, very different from the sweet honey smell of the waxed case, flowed up and out, almost like an evil spirit, she thought, or the remains of an evil spirit. It was an odor like sodden ashes mixed with rotting meat, old olive oil, and horse manure. She fanned her nose.

"Something dead is in here," she said, recoiling, tossing the flap back over the case, Alcestis helping her tie it.

"Shall I run for Icarus, mistress?"

"Yes, and Kratos. Also Eurymedon. But don't leave me here alone with it. The odor scares me. Get Rhodia and some of the Meliae to come sit with me, or send one of them for the warriors. This is not right. This odor is an insult to the shield's history in my family."

Moments later, Rhodia came hurrying forward, accompanied by five Meliae.

"Shall I run for the men?" asked Amalthea, Rhodia's bulky lieutenant.

"I sent someone already," Alcestis said.

"I think something very odd is going on with this shield," Melia explained. "It has a foul odor it should not have, a smell like fear. Sharp, rotten, frightened, pungent."

A few moments later, the three warriors arrived, Kratos in the lead.

"What new thing, sister?" the ruddy warrior asked, sinking to his knees before her. She sat on cushions with the cased shield upright, facing away from her.

Shelby likewise knelt, concern etching his face, Eurymedon beside him.

"Is something wrong with the shield?" Kratos asked. "Has it been damaged? Stolen?"

"I don't know what it is," Melia replied. "Alcestis noticed it had become quite dusty, but when I started to open it a foul odor escaped. We decided to call you before proceeding."

"I told you not to store your enemies' body parts in there," Kratos said, grinning at Shelby.

"Or your lunch," Eurymedon added, "which might be the same thing."

"It's not funny," Melia said. "If the shield has changed in some way, then it is up to Shelby to be the first to know."

"I did dream about it the other day," he said. "I used it to fight a monster. Rather, in my dream I used its surface to reflect the monster I dared not look at, and that helped me kill it. Then after I killed it, its head was trying to creep away, and I held the shield down on it to smash it until it was still. It was a very strange nightmare."

Melia looked intently at him, her lips drawing into a firm line.

"Was this the dream you had after I made you lie on the ground and listen to the earth?" she asked.

"One of two," he said. "In the first one, I had no weapon or shield and wrestled with a giant snake, a kind of python we call a bushmaster. I killed it by smashing its head on a rock and when it died it turned to water in my hands. The monster and the shield came next." Urged by Melia, he recounted the sequence and details of his dreams.

"You did not tell us about these dreams?" Melia asked, incredulous.

"Well, no, I thought they were just dreams. You know, things going on inside my head."

"Shelby," she said, exasperated, "why were you lying down?"

"Because you told me to listen to the earth."

"And you thought the dreams you had were your own? Really?"

"Well, weren't they?"

"Brothers, take this man away from me and get him drunk. And while he drinks, explain to him what it means when the earth puts visions in his head. I can't believe this, Shelby. After all this time with me, watching me sacrifice, listening to me explain how the goddess communicates with me, you go and have two very important visions like these, and you don't think they are important enough to talk to me about. I can't believe it."

The men got up to go, but Melia summoned them back.

"No, not yet," she said. "I've changed my mind. Let's take the shield out and see what's happened to it. Here, Shelby, you take it and examine it."

He reached for the bag, once more reflecting on how tiny she seemed when she was seated and how misleading it was to think that anything about her was tiny.

The weight of the case with the shield inside felt right. Same heft, same promise of beauty and protection, though its symbolic value as a reward from Phorbus for rescuing Metis and her daughters, Melia and Kalista, carried rich nostalgia for him. Throwing back the flap, however, he too noticed the sharp odor and heard something faintly screaming, very distant, not inside the case but evoked by the case, or the shield, like screams from beyond the horizon. Like the screams of many women full of hate and malice. Screams to evoke fear, to make the blood run cold, the banshee screams of evil female spirits.

He reached inside, found the straps on the back of the shield, and hoisted it out.

The screams dissolved in the afternoon air with a sigh, and the golden surface of the shield caught a ray of sunlight, casting a burning light around the camp. The shield had changed, somehow. He hefted it, thinking it was both heavier and lighter than it had been, both a comfort and a fear, a protection from harm yet giving harm.

"The front of the shield where those arrows struck it that day you fought the Achaeans at the north gate are no longer there," Melia said. "Did you rub them out? Polish it?"

"No," he said, turning the shield over. "Since Eumaeus brought it back, it's stayed in the case."

He looked at the shield's surface, with its fish-scale finish, a thousand little reflecting mirrors of gold. Sure enough, the surface no longer carried any evidence of arrows striking it during that fight. "Do you think Eumaeus repaired it? He could have rubbed out those scratches."

"It was not like Eumaeus to do that to someone else's shield," Kratos said. "Unless instructed. Then it would have been perfect, of course, but he would not presume to do it without orders. If it's been repaired, I don't think it was him. Agala might have done it."

"I don't think so," Melia said. "To her a shield was just an encumbrance, a kind of male extravagance that was a substitute for trust in the goddess. She would have paid no attention to it at all."

"After she returned from those raids with her husband all those decades ago, I don't think she touched another weapon," Eurymedon said. "She did not need to. Her power exceeded every warrior's."

Shelby tilted the shield from side to side, watching the light angling into its shiny surface but also seeing something else. Deep in the light reflected by the shield's surface, something seemed to be moving independently of his hands. Something like a mass of snakes, like the head of that creature from his nightmare. He thought it was imagining it, as though it were a weak kind of holograph embedded in the shield's design, yet he couldn't see it when he looked directly at it. If he let his eyes go slightly out of focus then the image in the shield crystallized with ethereal light, and the screaming head with its snakes and its insanity emerged, its mad eyes boring into his and sending daggers of ice down his spine.

"What is it?" Melia asked.

"Let's put it back in its case," he said. "This object needs to be covered and secured. Alcestis, find a way to box this shield into a trunk with locks."

The slave girl got up to leave, but Melia called her back.

"You did not answer the question, Shelby," she said. The hard edges of her voice cut him.

"I may discuss it with you at a later time," he said. "Right now, I need to think about it."

"Why is it stinking?" she persisted.

"Because embedded in its surface is insanity and fear," he said, watching the eyes of the small group widen suddenly.

"What do you mean?"

"Brother, is this your vision?" Kratos asked.

"Yes, Kratos. It is the dream I had. I may let you look at it to see if you also see it. I may let Melia look at it. But I worry that it could harm our child."

"We need to hear the story of how father came to have the shield," Melia said. "Arktos will tell us later tonight. But you are right. Tie the cords tightly, hero, and let us store this shield out of the way to await its time. Today is not that time. I do not understand it, but I know that much. Give it to Alcestis to store away, and you use the plain bronze shield that Hestia made for you."

"Mistress," said Alcestis quietly, "mistress, I think we should look at the sunset."

In the flaming west, a stream of clouds rushing northwards were convoluting, twisting, spiraling into shapes. One in particular, a large dark thunderhead, was blowing away on the horizon, lit from behind by the burning sun, and limned in radiant glory. As they watched, it gradually assumed the shape of a horse, and from its withers clouds streamed up toward an azure sky taking, gradually but unmistakably, the shape of wings. It was the winged horse, galloping north across the setting sun.

"Shelby," Melia said, "tell me your dreams. Tell them to me every time you have them."

FORTY-ONE

T he sun set, blazing in the west as scudding clouds faded into purple night, the Pegasus-like thunderheads stampeding into the dark north.

"Arktos," Melia said as the stars were coming out and the group settled around a low campfire in the growing dark, "were you not with father when he acquired the golden shield?" Slaves scurried back and forth, tending the fire, preparing food from the dwindling rations.

"Yes," the old warrior said, "but not actually with him at the time. We were mid way through our world tour when he got it. At the time, we were near the burning mountain known as Etna. The three of us and the child Eumaeus had arrived the night before in a little fishing village on the coast below the mountain, a place with hot springs. In the morning, Phorbus told us he was going to climb the mountain for the view, but Amphinomus and I were feeling lazy and wanted to rest. Besides, the tavern keeper's daughter was a very pretty dark-haired girl with bright eyes and long soft arms, and we wanted to watch her. You know that is how men are, so I will not apologize for that."

"I know that," Melia said. "Every woman knows that men at leisure have only one thing on their minds. It's very boring."

"Ah, yes," Arktos said, "so it must be from your point of view. Anyway, Phorbus returned from the mountain with the shield in its case. Eumaeus went with him, carrying food and water. You remember that Phorbus had rescued Eumaeus from pirates when we visited Crete early in our tour."

She nodded. "I remember. And you wondered why Phorbus would want to take such a child who could be of so little use."

"Yes, that's true. It was four, almost five decades ago, but I remember it well. The boy could not have been more than six or seven harvests at the time, yet there was Phorbus rescuing him and then insisting that he accompany us. We all know your father looked deeply into people, and he must have known even then who Eumaeus would become. For most of the trip, I thought it was a mistake that he took the boy, but now look how Eumaeus turned out! Captain of the guard, one of our toughest and most reliable warriors, absolutely dependable, and a genius at defense. Phorbus must have seen that future in the boy from the beginning, and I tell you, I wish Eumaeus were with us today, to help us against the wild men."

Melia and the assemblage nodded. Dolios, the Persians, and other slaves rose and drifted away to fetch wine and bread for an evening meal while Arktos continued.

"All I know about the shield is what Phorbus told me on the day he returned with it, you understand," Arktos said. "I have his word to go on, and I will tell you what he told us, and then you can decide what to believe. For me, it was hard to believe at first, but the shield is the evidence. He went up the mountain without it; he came down with it on his back."

Melia shifted on her cushion and Shelby and Kratos sat next to her. Eurymedon reclined on cushions on the other side of her.

"Phorbus told me that he and little Eumaeus had labored up the mountain from early morning until mid afternoon, arriving eventually at a spot where they could make the summit in a short time. Phorbus said that the views were magnificent, with the whole world seeming to spread out at their feet, so they were eager to get to the next ridge which they took for the top of the mountain, and to look down on the eternal fires smoking there.

"With only a short distance to go, they were suddenly thrown off their feet by an earthquake. Phorbus grabbed Eumaeus by the scruff just in time to keep him from pitching down a steep hillside, and they clung to the ground as the earthquake rumbled and tossed boulders. Then it subsided, and the angry mountain became still again. But a rockslide had exposed an opening in the side of the mountain only a hundred or so paces away from them, across a slope. They saw something white gleaming inside, and were curious because it was completely out of place for something so white to be shining in a dark hole in the side of the fire-blackened mountain. He told Eumaeus to stay put and began inching himself out across the scree. Eumaeus told me many years later he had been ordered to stay put so he could return to us in case Phorbus did not make it across or failed to get back. It must have been a treacherous slope.

"As he got closer, he saw that the white gleam was from a large statue set in a cave, a statue of a crippled male figure. The figure was unclad, his legs short and twisted, and his face held a grimace of both pain and pride. This shield in its case was held by three smaller statues of cyclopes carved into the main statue's base. Many more treasures littered the floor around the statue, and the cave itself was lined with metal that shone like fire. It looked like a temple, Phorbus said, but not of stone. Some of the items on the temple floor moved about on their own. Most did not have eyes, he said, but the single eyes of the cyclopes were alive, staring without blinking like red coals in a fire. He saw a pair of tripods thumping blindly toward the cave's entrance, bearing bright, vibrating thunderbolts. Once he gained the cave, Phorbus went to look the statue in its face, and as he did so, the mountain shook again and a hot, foul wind hissed out at him from the rear of the cave, almost suffocating him.

"Then the statue began breaking apart from the shaking of the earthquake, first the arms falling off, then the head. The base cracked and the statue began to fall toward him. He grabbed the shield and case, and scrambled back across the shifting scree toward Eumaeus. He told us later that night, when we were deep in our cups, that he did not look inside the case all the way back down the mountain, because he was too afraid of the danger they were in, the falling boulders and clouds of ash blowing out of the temple mouth and over the summit of the mountain.

"I can still remember the smell and look of the little house where Phorbus told us all this," Arktos continued. "Goats outside the door, smoke-darkened wooden beams holding the roof, rough tables, stone benches, and everywhere the sick smell of sulfur from the springs. It was late in the night, after we had drunk a lot of wine and the lovely daughter had gone to bed, by herself we think, and all the other patrons had gone home, that he showed us what he had. Little Eumaeus was sound asleep, curled up on one of the benches. He was cute when he was asleep. Also, he was not getting into trouble, but those are stories for a different time. Phorbus looked around the room to be sure no one else was there, then he pulled the case up, lay it flat on the table, scattering the dirty platters and trenchers. He untied the ribbons and eased out the shield.

"Oh, it was a beautiful, magical thing. The gold glittered in the candle light, and its many polished surfaces, like the scales of a magical snake, sent light dancing along the rough-hewn beams in the ceiling. I was glad we were alone, because if others had seen it, our lives would have been in danger. Such an object is worth the risk of a man's life, and many have been murdered for less.

"'What are you going to do with it?' I asked Phorbus. 'Keep it,' he said, 'until it is time to give it away. This shield does not belong to me, but to our people.'" Arktos sat back on his heels. "The shield belongs to our people," he repeated. "That was the last I ever heard Phorbus say about it."

"You've seen Shelby carry the shield," Melia said. "Tell me if it is the same shield that my father took from the cave."

Arktos widened his age-crinkled eyes. "Yes," he said, "it is the shield Phorbus brought back from the burning mountain."

"It is a shield of power," she said. "It is powerful protection, carrying both the spirit of my father and the fear of the goddess, revealed to Shelby by a dream. We will keep it in its case until we know how to use it. Obviously, blocking arrows in flight is not its best use; many other shields can do that. Maybe it will be useful against the wild men, but maybe not. I'm surprised my father never told this story, but perhaps he had been warned by the goddess to keep it to himself. It must be a divine creation."

"Shelby, you are the one who carried it in the dreamworld," Melia said, turning to him. "It is up to you to know how to use it. None of us can help you. You are blessed by the goddess, who brought you here from a distant future, I am pregnant with our child, and you have contributed mightily to our safety and salvation. Many of the things we have done could not have happened but for you. I suspect that the image you saw in the shield is a reflection of your own fear, and a lesson to you from the goddess.

Perhaps she will clarify her intention if you will only learn to listen to her. Just listen, Shelby. But it's not like her to discuss her intentions. I think you will need to reason it out for yourself."

She laid her hand on his knee and looked him in the face.

"Lean down so I can kiss you," she said. And then quietly, to him alone, added, "Welcome home, hero. You see? Being driven by fear is insanity. Be driven by love instead, as the goddess always intended for her creation."

* * *

He saw her to bed, brooding for a while in the dark, then got up silently and went looking for Arktos.

"Tell me the real story of the shield," he said to the gnarled old warrior. "You and I know that none of that happened. What is its real story?"

Arktos stood up, his glare boring into Shelby's eyes like ice-picks.

Finally he smiled, clapped the younger man on the shoulder, and invited him over to a small campfire away from the others. "What is real and what is not?" Arktos asked when they were settled. "Does the story define reality? Is that what you want? A better story?"

"I want a true story," Shelby said.

Arktos rested his hand on Shelby's knee, patting it.

"And about this shield, what is its true story?" Arktos asked.

"Phorbus didn't find that shield in a temple to Hephaestus on the side of Etna," said Shelby. "That part was not true."

"No, but it is a good story isn't it," Arktos grinned. "That magnificent shield deserves such a story."

Shelby stared back. He covered the old warrior's hand with his own.

"Tell me the facts," he said. "How did Phorbus get that shield?"

"We came upon a village being raided by pirates," Arktos said, looking away, "the day we rescued Eumaeus. We stormed the pirate ship and took away the boy, and Phorbus found the shield among the loot buried in that ship. That is what really happened. But the shield deserves a better story. So after Phorbus and Eumaeus went up the mountain and were scared back down by the volcano, he showed us the case with the shield, just as I said. We had seen only the outside of the case until then. When he slid the shield from the case, we knew it was one of the wonders of the world. That is the fact of the shield."

"That is a remarkable story without cyclopses and walking tripods," Shelby snorted.

"But the shield carries a deeper story, does it not?" replied Arktos. "You've carried it. Have you listened to its story? To the story it tells?"

Shelby stared into the fire coals sending up their sparks, listened to the distant creatures of the night, looked at the bright stars in their imaginary constellations, and finally turned back to Arktos.

"It was a good story, old friend," he said finally. "It was a story worthy of the ages. Thank you."

He rose and held a hand to Arktos to help him up.

"Which story do you prefer?" Arktos asked.

"What is my choice?" Shelby answered.

"My advice as an old man to you as a younger warrior is to choose the story that is closest to the truth, closest to the one that gives you life." He grinned. "Closest to the goddess."

Early the next morning, just as the sky over the eastern mountains was graying with the rising sun, wild men silently filtered into camp near the herds, stirring the cattle and horses. A drowsy attendant woke to see large shapes humped over among animals, the penned cattle moving away and snorting in alarm. Then he was dead.

The wild men broke into weird howling, the herds stampeded in their makeshift enclosures and scattered, some thundering in alarm into the camp while others dashed for the open country beyond.

Melia startled awake. Shelby was already rising and pulling his Shrike onto his arm. Alcestis rushed in, carrying an extra crossbow.

"Give it to Melia," Shelby said as he hurried from their large tent. "Kratos!" he called at the top of his lungs.

"Here," Kratos replied. "Guards, prepare for defense. Eurymedon, in the saddle! Hestia, draw the trebuchets! Garanus, form up the troops. Where's Arktos?"

"The horses are scattered," Eurymedon said, hurrying up. "Only mine came when I called. Most are loose."

"Arm your men and form up on left and right. Troops! Behind me! We will take our stand here!"

Over Kratos's head, a large shape rose in the dark like a mighty bear. Shelby leapt at it, slashing with his tomahawk at its face, grappling with it as he cleared Kratos. The bodyguards plunged their spears into the sprawling bodies, then Shelby was up, looking around for other shapes. He was confused. How did it get so close? Where had it come from? Were they already this deep into the camp?

Then he saw them! Leaping the pickets, coming into the camp from the direction of the herds, maybe a hundred of them leaping wagons and tents and slaughtering every living thing, driving the unarmed people in fear toward Melia's large tent.

"They're inside," he roared at Kratos.

"Follow me," Kratos bellowed, plunging toward the huge shapes, his sword over his head.

Shelby took off after him at a run, pursued by Alcestis carrying two crossbows and Dolios carrying his body armor and the lion skin, which he had not had time to put on. He hoped the children would not be killed in the fray. Killed and eaten.

A new pitch of screams sounded, and he looked behind. Dark, smaller shapes were leaping the barriers like baboons, screaming in fury.

"Their women!" he exclaimed to Kratos's back. "Their women are coming up behind us! I'll go that way." He wheeled, grabbing one of the bows from Alcestis and making sure it was cocked. Yes, the girl was thinking.

The first group of furies hurtled toward him, five of them. He dropped one with a crossbow and holding his lion skin over his forearm, prepared to chop at the others. The first one to reach him leapt at his head, and he deflected her with the tomahawk, bashing her skull with the flat side, but three others were on him with claws and teeth, going for his eyes.

They were nearly as tall as he, nearly as heavy. It would be a close thing if he could even beat them off. He felt one of them grabbing at his genitals and whirled to displace her hands, turning his back on the other two. One of them grunted and dragged her nails down his leg as she fell, dying from Alcestis's knife thrust in her ribs. Dolios tackled one from behind, trying to pin her arms, but he was clearly outmatched. At most, a diversion, but at least he succeeded in dragging the female from Shelby's back, and Alcestis disemboweled her.

With one on the ground at his feet, alive and scrambling to continue fighting, Shelby dropped on her with the lion's skin over her head and brought the tomahawk down as hard as he could into her coccyx. He chopped again, feeling the bone separate, then into the small of her back, chopping through muscles, as she screamed and dug her nails at him. Alcestis landed on her broken back with both knees, digging a knife into her thick neck muscles. The savage reached back to rake her face, and Alcestis bit down hard on a finger while sawing into her neck. A moment later, the wild woman stopped struggling as she bled out.

Dolios was leapt on from behind as he tried to catch his breath, and Alcestis was instantly on the savage woman, slashing at her face with her knife. Over and over she feinted and slashed at the woman's eyes and claws, until the woman dropped Dolios and came at the slave girl instead.

Shelby was back on his feet. He dangled the Shrike from its cord around his wrist, and shot the savage woman with the crossbow, the bolt penetrating her left eye no more than three inches from Alcestis's head. She went over backwards, and Shelby tried to re-cock the crossbow but didn't have time before another savage was on them.

In the melee, he worried about Melia. Why didn't he know what she and Rhodia were doing? He could hear Kratos bellowing orders, and glanced up to see him and the bodyguards wheeling in unison toward a huge wild man. Then he looked back to see another ten or twenty females coming up from the pickets, destroying men, women, and children, biting the necks and arms of naked slaves and poking their claw-like fingers into eyes, ripping off ears and hair.

"Not good," Shelby shouted, trying again to cock the crossbow while watching the oncoming gang.

One older city woman standing on a wagon, a club in her hand, bashed right and left at the savage women, screaming at them, a baby at her feet. Slaves cowered under the wagons or ran wailing from the onslaught, thronging about Melia's tent, a chaos of heaving, frightened bodies. Alcestis handed Shelby a cocked crossbow and he headed toward the woman with the baby. Dolios, now armed with a stone-pointed spear, moved alongside Alcestis. He charged one female attempting to scramble up onto the wagon, impaling her ribs from behind. Kidney shot, thought Shelby rushing toward the wagon after him. The female went down screaming in agony just as he got there. Dolios drew the spear with a look of horror on his face as two more women rushed them. Shelby batted one away with the Shrike tomahawk, and chopped into the face of the second, blinding both her eyes. Alcestis finished that one off as Dolios drove the spear into the sprawling savage woman. The chaos of battle rose on the wails of the wounded and the battle cries of the attackers, rebounding in the valley with the sharp clash of metal and stone, confusing everything. Shelby could not see any of the other fighters in the vicious onslaught.

Then Kratos appeared, striding across strewn bodies and debris, bellowing more commands, directing his warriors. Shelby felt the tide turn. The initial surprise of the attack began to wane with the rising sun and the power surged, rushing like a broken dam from Kratos's presence. He had become pure war, pure power and might, his bloodied sword held high, his kingly eyes burning with rage at his people's enemies, so transcendent that he seemed not to even touch the ground as he came forward, and confidence spread over the battle like the sun's warmth. They could do this. They could take on the wild men and their savage women, and they could win. He felt it surge through the people, the certain knowledge that with him leading they could survive.

The rising sun spilled its morning blaze over the mountains, fear melted away with the shadows, and the people rallied. They turned on the savage onslaught like unleashed lions; even slaves crawled out from their hiding places and rushed to enter the fight.

Melia strode from the tent dressed in her golden armor, the magical shield on her arm and Agala's golden idol of the goddess held high in her right hand. The hundred armed Meliae surrounded her. The shield caught the dancing fires of the dawn and reflected across the battle, shining on savage and civilized faces alike. She seemed surrounded by an aura of flame, the air trembling in her presence and the small statue glowing like a burning star.

"For Melia and the goddess!" bellowed Kratos seeing her, his huge voice carrying up into the hills and reflecting back as he banged his bloody sword on his echoing shield.

"For Melia and the goddess!" shouted all the people, over and over. The loud twang of the trebuchets sent stones hurtling overhead into the forest shadows, and when they looked around, the savage people of the mountains were retreating, now shadows, now just distant dark spots, and then they were gone, followed by the hard rain of stones.

"You see, friend," whispered Arktos in Shelby's ear, "there is the logic, and then, there is the magic. In which world do you wish to live? Do our enemies flee from us because they are startled, or do they flee because the goddess drives them? Is there a difference? For me, it is the power of the goddess."

He put his arm around Shelby's shoulder, and wept, his tears mixing with the sweat and mud of his face.

FORTY-TWO

M elia stood frozen like a statue, holding the golden star of the idol high above her head, her eyes unseeing. A myriad of images seemed crowded into the surface of the shield, dazzling in the morning sun and frightening, each of its many surfaces dancing in light and fire and each image contorted by insanity: screaming faces, bared teeth, images of women wrapped in snakes, of fanged warriors, of beasts wild with fury. Shelby felt Melia's glow as much as he saw it, and he knew it arced over the entire camp, summoning every soul from its deep cavern into fearless divine light.

He shook his head to clear his thoughts and glanced nervously around at the camp to look for enemies. Instead of ravening wild men, he saw every person kneeling to Melia, a kind of hum swelling into some ancient hymn.

He alone stood in the rising sun, his war hatchet dripping blood, staring at her. Her body rotated slowly in his direction until she was facing him, her eyes as blank and unblinking as an idol, still holding the statue high.

"Choose," said a voice in his head. It was not her voice. It was a voice he had known his whole life and yet not known. Had heard forever but had not heard. "Choose," it repeated.

In the surface of the shield he watched twenty-first-century aircraft appear out of the swirling insanities, bombs fell, missiles tore into schools and churches, the flag of the United States ripped and burned in nuclear explosions. Behind Melia, Kratos, still kneeling, raised his concerned face to look at him, bloody sweat dripping from his thick brows.

What do I choose? he asked himself. What is my choice? The world became still. Nothing moved but the insanities of the shield and the sunlight glinting from the golden idol, no insects or birds or clouds. Time froze in a silent, stone-like tableau, and he alone seemed to breathe.

Then he saw the unknowable thing and understood it for the first time. "Yes!" he exclaimed.

He sank to his knees staring at her, at her marble-like stillness, and raised both hands.

"Yes!" he cried aloud. "Forever, yes!"

The light came back into her eyes, and she saw him. Her arms sagged, and the shield grew blank, a dead screen of gold, lowered to the ground. She went to her knees, cradling the heavy little idol to her swelling belly, her breath exhaling in a long sigh as she began trembling, then heaving in her withdrawal from the divine presence.

He rushed toward her, but Rhodia was already there. The other Meliae rushed to support her, taking the shield and packing it back into its case, helping her barely conscious body back to the shelter of the tent.

He reached her just as they entered, and she lifted her head.

"I'm glad you stayed," she whispered hoarsely, an effort. "Go clean up this mess. It's time."

"Yes," he said.

"Yes," she replied. "Always the right answer, Lion." She sagged into the arms of the Meliae who carried her listless form to her bed. Rhodia shooed him out.

"You heard her," Rhodia said. "Clean up this mess. We will care for her."

"Do you think the baby is okay?" he asked.

"Did you not just see the baby's power?" she asked. "What a silly question. Now go get busy. We will be along to help after a while."

She dropped the tent flap in his face.

"Icarus!" Kratos bellowed, "You organize the rear-most wagons. Burn the dead. I will get the front organized. I expect we will be ready to move by noon, then follow me out of this hell. It's time!"

"Yes," Shelby said. "Yes it is."

FORTY-THREE

〰〰〰〰〰〰〰〰〰

L ate in the afternoon of the following day, excitement spread through the wagon train. Melia's wagons, moving in the middle and surrounded by a tight cordon of armed men and women, were given a message from Kratos to move to the front to join him and his advance guard. "Come and see a great thing," the message said. "We will pause here for you." The hope that defeated the assault by the wild men the previous day renewed, and even the wounded looked up from their litters with shining eyes, staining to see ahead. Was it the sea at last? Was their tortuous passage through dangerous hills and between forest-darkened mountains coming finally to an end? They believed the prophecy, after all, that until Melia saw the sea they needed to fear the savage men of the hills.

* * *

Alcestis was among the walking wounded. One side of her face had been horribly clawed by a wild woman even as Alcestis was digging between the woman's ribs with her knife, and she hobbled on a deeply cut foot. If Dolios had not rescued her by slashing the savage's face with his sword, she might have been blinded. As it was, she would forever bear the scars on her cheeks, a reminder of life's brutality. Dolios was immensely proud of her. She had been so brave and so ferocious. Practical as always, when it came time to fight she went all in. No hesitation. No fear, no shrinking, no caution. She went straight at them, and her training with the

Meliae had made her formidable. Even for a girl, she was short, but she was fast and agile and deadly. He did what he could, which wasn't much, but she was the leader. She had burned with fury. She ran to meet those horrible female savages, screaming at them and going for their faces. She had been so brave. Dolios had trouble keeping up with her, she went screaming away so fast. He knew he was deeply in love with her and had been for more than a year, but yesterday's fight had cast her in a new light, and he worshipped her for it.

For her part, she was bored with his attention. That's why she preferred to hobble along next to the carts rather than sit next to him as he drove Melia's wagon. At least she could be alone with her own thoughts, deal with the horrors she had survived and the bloody mouths screaming in anger and pain.

Also, she was missing the company of her wolf. She felt possessive of the creature, but it was a wolf. So beautiful and deadly, so unlike Dolios who was all affection and niceties, fawning over her. Calu was not a friend. She was not a pet. And she was not owned. She was wild and free and only what she was, only what she was intended to be. No deception, no loyalty, no restrictions. Alcestis thought that maybe she loved the wolf, and she was prepared to be rejected by her when the time came. Even in that eventual rejection, the wolf would be honest and free. She liked that. She couldn't be that way with Dolios. Too much stuff going on all around her, with everybody's feelings always getting hurt and expectations not getting met, and desires going unfulfilled or, worse, overfilled.

Rhodia was a little like the wolf, more than anyone else in camp. But even Rhodia contended with her own form of slavery. She needed people, desired people, well, some people. Eurymedon. The twins. Both. But at least she was all action. You never had to guess what was on Rhodia's mind. She was blunt and direct about it.

Or was she? Alcestis paused for a moment, watching a butterfly drift in the afternoon sun. The days were growing warmer and longer, and it was planting season. She knew that. Flowers were already appearing all around them. Storks in their great flights were passing overhead all day long, heading where? she wondered. Somewhere north into the lands of the Achaeans.

Overhead now were long skeins of geese and the faster, tighter lambdas of ducks, doing what geese and ducks had done since the world was born. And what was she doing?

If her foot were not hurt, it would be easy to disappear into the brush. They wouldn't miss her for hours, maybe longer. Maybe overnight. She could be gone like Calu, fade into the shadows and run free, living on berries and roots and whatever she could hunt. She could be her own boss, live her own life, never be a slave again.

Her mind drifted on these thoughts for some time, slowly plodding along on her hurt foot, falling farther and farther behind. It hurt a lot and she was limping, trying to stay away from the passing cart wheels, when a strong arm reached down and scooped her up.

"Sit up here, little one," said a kindly male voice. "Let that foot heal. Stay off of it until it's better. You're just making it worse."

She glanced up at the bearded face, one she had seen but did not know. He was in his forties, maybe his fifties, and his beard carried tinges of gray at the tips. His eyes were wide spaced and pleasant, his breath not as foul as the breath of drunks. He lifted her over his lap and sat her on the bench next to him, not looking at her.

She sat silently, puzzled by this kindness but glad it was not Dolios. She liked Dolios enough, but he was boring. This stranger did not appeal to her at all, but she knew she was safe. And yes, her foot was throbbing and probably bleeding more. That witch had cut her right across the arch.

They rode silently for a time. Behind her, Alcestis saw that the cart was filled with supplies of some kind. Pots, skins, and sacks. She smelled the fusty odor of grain.

She crossed her foot over her knee to ease the throbbing, elevate it some. It helped a little, but not much. She decided she would ignore it, the way she ignored her periods. It was just a wound. It would get better.

Eventually the cart driver asked for her name. She wondered at that. Didn't everyone know everyone else?

"I'm Apollo," he said, winking at her. "I'm the Achaean god of the sun. Don't I look the part?"

"If you are one of those gods, then I think you must want to rape me," she replied.

He laughed. "No no," he protested. "I'm just joking. I'm really called Asonius. I have no idea what the name means."

"Nor do I," she said. "We will give your name a meaning. It means 'kind rescuer'."

"That's a nice thing to say, but unnecessary. You were hobbling so badly you were falling behind, and this is slower than a walking pace."

"Yes, I was walking with pain," she said. "But my alternative would have been to ride with a boy who loves me and yet bores me. I preferred walking."

"That was no walk. That was a painful creep."

They rode a dozen paces of the oxen, and then he asked, "So why do you not love this boy?"

"I don't love anyone," she said, hesitating, then adding, "except the wolf."

"That's your wolf?"

"That's nobody's wolf."

"Oh," he said. "I thought you said you loved this wolf."

"I do. She's free. I'm a slave."

"We are all slaves," he said. "The wolf is a slave to her needs. She must eat. She must hunt and kill, and sometimes she is not successful. People try to solve that problem by growing things, but then we are slaves to our fields, and our oxen." He nodded toward the huge beasts plodding along in front of them.

"That's not the same thing," she fussed.

"Yes it is," he said, smiling. "It's different in the particulars, but not different in meaning. We are all slaves."

She folded her arms across her bare chest and looked away, petulant.

"We all must eat," he said finally when she continued to stare out across the sloping hills. "And there are many other things we must do. We have no choice. We must breathe, so we are slaves to air. We must drink, so we are slaves to water. We must make love, although some of us don't feel that so strongly. We must sleep, so we are slaves to sleep. We must walk upon the earth, so we are slaves to earth. And we must stay warm, so we are slaves to fire."

"You are mixing up everything," she said. "Air and water are not the same thing as freedom and self decision. Oh, what's the right word? Not decision. You know. Whatever that is."

"No," he said, "I don't know. All I know is what I see. We must live together, or we die. We are not the wolf, who can survive by her skill in hunting and her ability to live in a hole in the ground. You would be dead within a month of living like the wolf. You are not a wolf. You are a girl. I think you are a very brave girl, and a smart one, but we are all alike. We need one another. Your boy needs you. And I think you need your boy, if only to be bored with. That's what I think."

"Well I think you don't know what you are talking about," she said, sticking out her lower lip.

"I had a teenage daughter once," he said, "back when we had a city. She said the same thing."

When Alcestis looked at him the next time, she saw tears streaming down his face. He did not speak again.

FORTY-FOUR

"Well, old man, what's happening?
Rhodia settled herself next to Dolios on the seat of
Melia's wagon. She shifted her feet to rest on the gunwale of the seat, exposing her freckled knees, which she clamped
together.

"Old man?" asked Dolios. "I'm only sixteen harvests. Maybe
only fifteen."

"But your face says you are ancient," she chortled. "I've seen
such a face on very few people. Once, on a man whose gut had a
knife in it. The other time, on an old man who was told he was
dying, although Goddess knows why he had to be told. It was
pretty obvious. Were you injured yesterday?"

"No. And I'm not an old man," replied Dolios, his temper
rising.

"You fought very well. People have been praising you all day.
How many of those savage females did you kill? You and Alcestis
must have taken down at least six, maybe more."

"So?" he asked.

"So you should be feeling the praise and gratitude of the
whole camp today. You have become one of our best warriors,
and it showed. As we pass, look at how the people smile their
recognition and wave. This should be a day of triumph for you,
so why the face?"

Dolios did not reply. They rode in silence for twenty or thirty
paces, the wagon jouncing.

"For a boy of your age, there's only one explanation."

"Who cares?"

"I care. So do a lot of other people. People keep asking what is wrong with Dolios."

"So what?"

"So change the attitude youngster."

They rode again in silence.

Finally they both spoke at the same time.

"Alcestis," Dolios said.

"Love," Rhodia said.

They laughed, Rhodia clapping her small strong hand on his shoulder.

"I thought so," she said. "It's the only thing that makes youngsters like you look like old men."

"Yeah, well," he said.

"Tell me about it."

"No."

"Yes." Rhodia poked him in the ribs. He jumped, thinking it was her knife. Then he relented.

"She won't have anything to do with me."

"She saved you from the wild men. She tracked them, and then she helped kill them. And she talked a wild wolf into helping her do it. That was for you. Yesterday you two were a fearsome pair, heroic and fatal. Remarkable for persons your age."

"So? We made a pair, did we? But she doesn't like me."

"Oh?" Rhodia wrinkled her nose at him, willing him to look at her. He did.

"Oh?" she repeated.

"She won't sit with me. She won't let me hold her hand. She won't talk to me when I try to talk to her. She won't talk about yesterday, or how she knew what to do. She acts like something's wrong, but I can't get her to tell me what it is." Tears eased down his cheeks and he turned away from Rhodia to pay attention to the oxen hauling the large wagon.

The oxen took another twenty paces, which was plenty of time, and then Rhodia said, "Yes, that's hard."

"So why is she that way?" shouted Dolios.

"Maybe you stink."

She leaned over, put her arm around his shoulder, and pulled him over to her. She buried her nose in the nape of his neck and inhaled deeply.

"Nope," she said. "That's not it." She released him and gave him a little shove.

Dolios thought he would rather be talking to anyone in the world other than Rhodia. She scared him, scared him right down to the bottom of his soul. If he was Prometheus, she would be the eagle coming to eat his liver. He had seen her do absolutely bloodthirsty and dangerous things, and he always shrank when she was around. Literally and figuratively. He became smaller. His penis drew up like a little bird sitting on a nest. He trembled. He would rather have talked to the Persians, whose mindless blather at least did not remind him of Rhodia using her sensuality to lure men into ambush and death. How Eurymedon could endure a relationship with her was beyond him.

"Maybe it's not about you," Rhodia finally said. "Ever think of that?"

Dolios said nothing. He had the wagon to drive, and he pretended the oxen needed his undivided attention. He reached out his switch to brush a fly off the rump of the nearest one.

"Well, what's it about then?" he blurted, suddenly ashamed of himself for opening up to this deadly woman.

Rhodia didn't answer right away. Instead, she looked around, studied the brush, watched some birds flitting from tree limbs near the top of the high ridge to their left, trying to peer into the shadows where the trees grew taller.

"Have you seen her wolf, by the way?" she finally asked.

"No. Not recently." He was sullen. He didn't dare be rude to her, but he he did wish she would go away.

"Me either. I wonder what happened to her." She licked her lips and lifted her chin as if to smell the air.

"I wonder what happened to her," Rhodia repeated a moment later. "That wolf was always around, and then she wasn't. It's not like a wolf to just disappear. They are creatures of habit, and Alcestis had become a habit for her. Did something change?"

"What do you mean?"

"Did Alcestis stop going out to talk to her? Stop taking her meat from the sacrifice?"

"Alcestis doesn't change," Dolios pouted.

"Well, that's wrong," said Rhodia with a laugh. "We all change."

Dolios eased a little. He didn't feel safe around her, but he understood her gesture to be genuine and concerned. Like those of a friend. Still, it's hard to like someone you're afraid of.

"I think she may have stopped taking meat during the fires," he said. "I think she was afraid that wolf would get trapped or hurt by them."

"Did she stop," Rhodia asked, "or do you just think she stopped?"

"I'm guessing. It would be like her to worry about the wolf's safety and not tempt it into the fire."

Rhodia ran her fingers through her rich red hair, causing the curls to stand out from her head a little further. "I wonder if she's doing the same thing with you".

"I don't understand," he replied.

"Maybe she doesn't want you to get trapped or hurt either."

"By what? Not by the fires."

A sly smile spread across Rhodia's face. "Ah, Dolios," she said, her eyes twinkling, "you have a lot to learn about women. Fire is the least of your problems when you are dealing with women." She patted his knee. "Give her some space, young man, and cheer up. Nothing is wrong with you."

"One day, Dolios," she continued, preparing to jump down from the wagon, "I hope you can forgive me."

"I'm trying," he said.

"Smart answer," she said, smiling at him, and then he was alone in the middle of civilization, all of it moving toward the sea.

FORTY-FIVE

I t took several hours for the forward parts of the wagon train to move to the side to clear a path for Melia's wagon to come forward. She was not getting on a horse again until the baby was born, mostly because she was afraid of falling off. She had eased up to the seat to sit next to miserable Dolios, an honor not lost on the people.

After a few pleasantries, they stopped talking. Dolios was expert at guiding wagons, and he concentrated on his job with diligence, guiding the large wagon through narrow gaps between other stopped wagons, avoiding locking wheels, sometimes rubbing axle ends because the space was so narrow. It was slow, but it was steady, and Melia had a chance to read the faces of everyone as she passed, sensing them, sensing their thoughts, balancing her small golden idol on her steadily diminishing lap, her pregnant belly giving the goddess the most appropriate of all cushions.

"Good job, Dolios," she finally said as they squeaked and squealed through one very narrow opening.

"Thank you, my lady," he whispered back, still concentrating on the lead ox. He feared to look at her because he felt so miserable.

"I told Shelby months and months ago that I thought Alcestis would make trouble for you," she said, looking straight ahead.

"No, lady, no trouble. She won't have anything to do with me."

"Ah. So that's it."

"I don't know why. She never has anything to do with me."

"You two were very brave and heroic yesterday. Perhaps you have noticed the people praising you."

He nodded but didn't speak.

"I want to add my praise to that of the people," she went on. "And I want to reward you. Think about what you want, and if I can do it, then I will."

"All I want is Alcestis."

"Of course. That's obvious. But she is not mine to give. Well, I mean I could give her to you as your slave, but I cannot give her heart, and I think it is her heart you want."

He broke down weeping, dropping his head as he sobbed, the oxen veering a little until he jerked them back in line. It was a narrow miss with a dozen pedestrians crowded against a wagon to stay out of their way.

Melia ignored the faux pas. "Think it over and come to me when you know."

"Thank you, lady. I will." His heart rose in his throat to silence him as his eyes burned with tears.

* * *

A mile or more to the rear, Alcestis put her foot across her knee and turned the injury so she could prod it through its bloody bandage. It was beginning to burn, and she didn't see how it could not be infected. In the traffic jam of wagons ahead, their progress finally slowed to a standstill, and one of the healers walked by.

"Alcestis," she said. "How is the injury?"

"It's burning," she replied. "I hope it is not becoming infected."

"It will become infected," replied the healer stepping up into the wagon. "Foot wounds always become infected for a while. I think it is because a foot is so far from the heart. We want to prevent the injury migrating up the leg. Let me look at it."

Alcestis turned sideways, leaning against Asonius, who shifted his arm a little to help her, while the healer slowly and gently unwrapped the injury.

"Hold your foot still," she said. "I don't want you to flex it and make it bleed."

A moment later she had the wound open to the air and bent

down to inspect it and smell it.

"Have you been walking on this foot?" she scolded.

"Yes," said Alcestis.

"Weren't you told not to walk on it?"

"Yes."

"Trying to get away from that boy?"

"Yes."

"Not a good enough excuse, young warrior. Stay off this foot. Were you wearing sandals during the fight yesterday?"

"Yes." Alcestis was beginning to soften, and felt grief rising in her slender chest.

"The blow from that bitch savage could have taken off your foot, if it cut through your sandal like this. I'm glad you had some protection. The arch of your foot is deeply cut, and some layers of muscle might be involved."

"I left my knife in her under belly," Alcestis said. "And I was trying to kick her in the face. Dolios was carving on her other arm, but it was hard to finish her off."

"Very brave," clucked the healer, pulling out her supplies. "First, I will wash it again with vinegar. Then I will place a pad of boiled wool over it. I could sew it together, but I think it will heal better if you stay off of it. Besides, stitches are aggravating. Over the wool pad I will place a flat stick, and then I will wrap your foot very thoroughly to keep you from flexing it. Do you understand?"

Alcestis nodded, glad to avoid stitches.

"This may burn," the healer said. "The vinegar is strong."

Alcestis nodded, steeling herself for the pain. Asonius moved his hand to hers, and she gripped strongly.

"Little one," he said to her, trying to take her mind off the pain, "you've got a good grip. Is that as strong as you can go?"

She looked up in his face blinking away her tears and clinching her teeth as the healer worked. She shook her head.

"Well let's just see how strong you are," he said smiling down at her. "Squeeze with all you've got, and if you make me yell I'll give you my last bit of honeycomb."

She arched her back with pain and squeezed, panting, breathing through clinched teeth.

"Burns," she grunted. "Oh, it burns."

Asonius smiled. "That's pretty good. Can you squeeze any harder?" He squeezed back, watching the healer's progress, and finally said, "Ow. You win! You've got a mighty grip, girl. No wonder you're such a warrior!"

With his free hand, he moved her head to his thigh and patted her cheek. "Bravely done, little one. The healer is finishing up. Rest here for a bit, and then I will give you honeycomb."

She tried to smile through her clenched teeth, panting still but relaxing. Something about Asonius reminded her of being a child again, of being comforted in her father's lap, and she began to unspool years of slavery back to the free days, to the low house, to her large mother, the babies, her dog. She began to weep.

"There, there, little one," the old man said, "this weeping. This weeping is how we heal. You are safe here. Cry those hot tears and be whole again."

FORTY-SIX

ѶѶѶѶѶѶѶѶѶѶѶ

When she awoke hours later, Alcestis realized she had been dreaming of home and freedom but she was also dreaming of Dolios and the future. It had been a pleasant dream.

What woke her was the stillness of the wagon. Asonius's thin thigh had been a comfortable pillow and he managed to keep his leg still enough to let her sleep. But the rocking of the wagon had stopped. She opened her eyes and saw his beard moving up and down.

"Thank you, Asonius," she mumbled, struggling to sit up. He helped her, using both of his gnarled old hands to bring her to a sitting position. Her foot throbbed, but it felt better already.

"You've had a good sleep," he said. "Several hours. I think you must have needed it."

"Yes," she said, "I did. Why are we stopped?"

"The rumor is that Kratos has stopped us to allow Melia to make it to the front to witness our approach to the sea. I hope that is the case. As soon as she sees the open water, then our troubles with the wild men will be over."

"Is that what the prophecy said?" She rubbed her eyes with her knuckles and flexed her legs, willing the blood to flow into them.

"That's what we understood," he said. "I don't know what she understood, and the prophecy was given to her. But that's what we heard."

"Then I hope she wastes no time."

"Isn't that boy Dolios driving her wagon?" Asonius asked. At the mention of his name, Alcestis's mind flooded with images of him, with his scent, with the sound of his voice. It was distracting.

"What?" she asked, sensing that Asonius had been talking to her.

"I was asking you if you would like me or one of these other lads to carry you forward, so you could rejoin Melia's wagon. I've learned that all the rest of us will wait and clear a path for her, but she cannot be going fast. Not with those oxen, and with all the wagons ahead of her."

Alcestis did not like the idea of asking anyone for help. If she wanted to go to Melia's wagon, the one driven by Dolios, she would go on her own feet. Or borrow a horse.

"I think I will stay here a little longer," she said, yawning and stretching, her young, firm breasts rising in the afternoon light, her gold band of slavery around her neck glinting.

"As you will, young lady," he said smiling. "But I think you want to be with Dolios and Melia on this wonderful day."

"Maybe," she admitted. "With Melia, anyway."

"Oh, you want to be with the lad, too." He grinned, working his salt-and-pepper beard at her. "Or you would not have been calling his name out in your sleep like that."

"I did?"

"Yes, you did. Many times. I won't tell anyone, but you need to learn your heart, girl. It's not that hard."

Alcestis was silent for a time, waiting for the wagons to move again. She felt the growing warmth of the hillsides, smelled the bruised wild thyme and lavender, watched the early spring moths and butterflies in their senseless dances from flower to flower, heard the passing bell-calls of wild swans flying north toward home. The beauty of the earth overwhelmed her, the intricacies of trees and bushes, the waving softness of weeds and blooming grasses glowing in the afternoon sun, the little rill of water coming down the hill with a merry song. Her heart swelled, pushing her lungs aside and taking her breath. It was so beautiful! And here was the end at last, or if not the end, then the beginning of the end. The promise of a new life, of a new way of living, of new creatures and hills.

"I will go to the front," she said at last, throwing her arms around Asonius. "Thank you. May I adopt you as my father?"

"My family is gone," he said. "My wife and children went east from the city while I was serving here. I would like a family. If sometimes you will come to see me, I will love you like a daughter."

"Done," she said brightly, spying Eurymedon riding up from the rear.

"Alcestis!" Eurymedon exclaimed as he drew up with the wagon. "Why are you back here?"

"I was walking and Asonius helped me into his cart."

"I'm going forward to join Melia. Want a lift?"

"I do. Thank you, prince."

"Climb up here behind me. Wait, is your foot bandaged?"

"Yes, it was injured yesterday."

"Tended to?"

"Yes, but walking will be awkward for a time."

"Ah, I'll ride up close to the wagon and help you over. Would you rather sit in my lap?"

"Oh no, sir, not in your lap. I'll ride behind you."

"Right, then here you go."

They cantered toward the front, Alcestis turning to wave at Asonius until he was out of sight. The old man waved back, his eyes gleaming with tears. She rode with both arms thrown around Eurymedon's chest, gripping tightly.

FORTY-SEVEN

"We arrive," Kratos said to Melia as the oxen breasted the gentle hill, happy to see the long line of wagons behind her, and to see her. She stood in the wagon when it came to a standstill, flushed and radiant like a goddess herself, her hair uplifted by a gentle breeze that pressed her loose clothing against her pregnant body. Before her lay a gentle green slope descending to the western sea flaming in the golden sunset. Along the shore in the distance lay a hamlet of perhaps a dozen conical stone huts. Farther out, the dark shapes of fishing boats dotted a shallow bay. The afternoon was warm, and it would be a warm night, so much more comfortable than their cold nights in the mountains behind them.

Eurymedon rode up with Alcestis, who leapt into the wagon in a frenzy, searching for something. She found it, and pulled out the golden shield.

"Lady, lady," she called, stumbling over baggage and stumping on her injured foot to come forward. "Here, hold this. Let the setting sun see you."

Melia seemed on the edge of a trance, light dancing in her gray eyes, when she took the shield and ran her arm into its braces. She lifted it to the people, who cheered, and then slowly turned toward the sun. The shield dazzled in the golden light, scattering dancing rays across the new green of the fertile hills, the many concavities of its snakeskin-like golden scales projecting beams of laser clarity against distant hills, against the feet of rugged mountains, and dazzling even the gentle calm of the sea.

While this tableau was etching itself into the cultural consciousness of the people, whence it would become the source of legend
and over centuries be incorporated into myths of the gods and
goddesses, Shelby was at the rear of the wagon train organizing
the rear guard.

Yes, he missed it. He heard about it later, of course, but he
was not there. He was following Kratos's orders to form up a rear
guard, and that was what he was doing. His previously organized
squads, platoons, and companies followed orders—a remarkable
thing in itself—and established a defensive perimeter between
the wagon train and the wild men. Their wagons were ordered
and numbered, the sequence of movement was understood, and
the cavalry and foot soldiers he had been allotted were organized
into patrols with various capacities. No surprise attack could be
launched against the rear, and though the wild men were fearsome opponents, they were not seen. Shelby rather believed that
the wild men had been demoralized by the previous battle, anyway, and would not appear. The loss of their gigantic champion
must have been a blow to them, and it might take the tribes some
time to figure out another way to attack. He frankly doubted that
they had the mental capacity to strategize, so he wasn't worried.
Still, he needed to take precautions. You never know, really, what
your enemy is capable of, so you prepare for the worst.

The soldiers, in particular the heavily armed foot soldiers,
pled with him to let them go forward to witness Melia's contact
with the sea.

"No," he replied every time, "the sea is not going anywhere. I
think you will see more of it than you want in the coming months.
Stay here and defend, until we can move forward."

So it went. Disgruntled but obedient soldiers in the rear,
jubilant citizens in the front. But the excitement from the front
buzzed like an electric current all through the train, and infected
the rear guard with equal power.

Eventually, the wagons began to move again, and Shelby
herded his troops up the long last hill, through brush and short
trees, past thickets of thorns and through fields of trampled rose-
mary and wild onions, until they, too, breasted the hilltop

and peered down at the long, verdant slope spreading before them out to the distant sea.

The last human in the train, he paused to watch the people spreading out over the deep green of the pastures, to see the wagons dispersing into camps, and to gaze with fascination at the unobstructed view of a vibrant west filled with light. Behind him, the shadows had already deepened in the valleys and slopes of the high mountains; the wild men might be gathering for sleep or war council; and the world was turning itself over to the hunters of the night. Ahead of him lay the fertile foundations of an unlimited future.

The sea lay calm and flat in the waning light. Darker spots on its sky-mirrored surface were probably small fishing vessels, but he could not be sure. He inhaled deeply, trying to smell the distant waves and their freedom.

From the top of the hill, he spied Melia's wagon some three or four miles ahead, stopping for the night. Dolios would be driving, of course. He was a superb wagon driver. Perhaps little Alcestis was with them. She and Dolios had fought magnificently the previous day. Magnificently! He wondered what he should do to reward their valor. He'd ask Melia. That was always, he was increasingly aware, the best course of action. Let Melia make the decision.

He saw the oxen being unlimbered to graze in the rich grass, and other wagons drawing up in a large circle around Melia's. He watched the herds of horses, sheep, and cattle being led out by their herders to the fresh grass.

Over to the right, he saw the shadows of the fishing village, fading into dark spots. They would have located there because of the fresh water coming from the mountains, but was there enough water for all of them? That would take time to determine.

Meanwhile, the gradual slope, dense with free grass and flowering weeds, would be perfect for them for a time.

"We've reached the sea at last," he said to himself. "Now I must persuade them to move across the sea to Italy, to become the Etruscans. In this hemisphere, the Etruscans were a long-lived culture, surviving almost two thousand years. And their women were free, not enslaved, holding equal status with the men. That's who these people need to be. Will they go?"

He saw wisps of smoke rising near Melia's wagon as cooking fires and the altar were ignited with the sacred fire brought from their lost city. Soon the sacrifice would be underway, and then the people would have meat.

Yes, they would survive. Melia and the influence of the goddess spread over the assemblage like a golden dome. They would survive.

FORTY-EIGHT

♭♭♭♭♭♭♭♭♭♭♭♭

"**T**onight we rest and give thanks," Melia said. "Tomorrow we begin converting this grassy slope into pasture and fields for grain. We should be able to get one full harvest in and possibly another before winter."

"It has been a tiring business to come through those mountains," Kratos said. "And I still worry about the wild men. But maybe they are frightened by the sea and will not come in sight of it."

The group was sitting together around Melia's campfire as the night shadows advanced across the sea, the peaks behind them still glowing pink in the sunset. Shelby had not rejoined, but Melia was unconcerned. She knew he was tending to the nighttime defense at the top of the slope.

"Alcestis," Melia said, "come here."

As the girl hobbled awkwardly forward, Kratos began applauding and all the people joined in. She knelt in front of Melia.

"First, Alcestis, thank you," Melia said. "You have earned the right to wear clothes and I never wish to see you naked again. You have performed great service to us and to the goddess and deserve to be richly rewarded."

"Yes!" Kratos bellowed, applauding again.

"You were fierce in the fight with the wild women. You and Dolios killed many."

"Three, my lady," Alcestis said, bowing her head. "That's all we could get to."

"But then, despite being wounded yourself, you finished off

several more who were still fighting. Your bravery, your skill so carefully practiced these many months with the Meliae, and your passionate intensity to protect your people and your goddess must be rewarded. I will give you several days to think it over, but ask for any reward you want and if I can grant it, then I will."

Tears welled in Alcestis's eyes as she muttered her thanks.

"Now stay there for a moment." She turned and called Dolios. When he had knelt in front of her, she continued, "Dolios, you too were peerless in your courage and skill during our last fight. I have already told you that you may name your reward."

"Hear, hear," Kratos said, standing and applauding again. All the people rose with him.

"Now Dolios, have you decided?"

"Yes lady, I have," he said.

"Do you wish to tell me what you want?"

"Now?"

"Do you want to tell me in private?"

"I can name it now."

"If you are ready and you think you have thought it through enough, tell me."

Dolios stared around him at all the adults and slaves, and swallowed hard. He clutched his hands together to keep them from shaking and swallowed again.

"Well, lady, as you know Alcestis wishes to be like her wolf, Calu." He kept his eyes on Melia, not daring to look to Alcestis. When he started to speak again, his voice cracked and squeaked. He swallowed again to steady himself, his knuckles turning white. "Alcestis wishes to run free, to pursue game and to travel the wide world as far as her legs will carry her."

Alcestis looked up at him, turning pale, tears glittering on her eyelashes like diamonds in the campfire light.

"As my reward, I wish you to set Alcestis free of her bondage as your slave. That's all I want."

The crowd hushed, holding their breath. Dolios was sacrificing the chance of a lifetime for the girl, and it meant losing her if she took it. It was an amazing act of selfless love. And it was a huge request. Alcestis had proven her worth, one beyond measure, and she was extremely valuable property to her owner. Yet, it was within Melia's power to grant her freedom.

Melia looked from one to another. Her eyes narrowed and then softened as she studied both of the youngsters. She knew that a fourteen-year-old virgin girl would bring a fortune in the world, even this not very pretty one. Although, studying her now with clear vision, she saw womanhood transforming that slender body, those long muscular legs not nearly so bony as several months ago. Her eyes softened as she gazed on the girl, seeing a future for her as a free woman. Even if she accepted Dolios's offer, Melia expected that Alcestis would remain with them.

"Alcestis," Melia said, "you've heard Dolios's offer to you. Do you accept it?"

The girl looked around at all the serious faces, waiting on her to answer. Suddenly she knew she was already more than a slave, more than a negligible person. Suddenly, it was as though a veil had been ripped away and she was no longer ignored by anyone, no longer hidden. She shivered, aware now that she was naked in front of so many people. Goosebumps rose on her arms and legs. She looked back at Melia, as Rhodia came forward to kneel with her, undoing her own chiton.

"I don't, I don't," Alcestis stammered, her cheeks shining with tears. "I don't know! I—oh Dolios!" She looked at his face intently, studying every wrinkle and his downy stubble, inhaling his odor. She reached out to take his hand as he stared straight ahead.

Rhodia removed her chiton and its golden brooches, and gently eased it over Alcestis's head, reaching around the girl's waist to pin the side vents together and then adding her own jeweled belt to hold it cinched, leaving herself as naked as a slave. She sat back and placed her hand on Alcestis's back, a sisterly touch, a demonstration of moral support. Other Meliae crowded forward to kneel behind Rhodia, all of them removing their chitons to hold in their hands, folded. Like Rhodia, in fact like everyone, they honored Alcestis, the wolf girl.

Melia folded her hands in her lap, gently supporting her belly with its newly restless baby. She could feel it moving, maybe turning over in its watery dream, maybe flexing an arm or leg. She waited for several minutes as emotions ghosted through the assembly. Then she turned to Eurymedon.

"Brother," she said gently, "those Persian twins. Where are they?"

"Setting up our bed for the night, I suppose."

"Bring them to me later. I have an idea I want to share with you and Rhodia."

Eurymedon nodded, studying the youngsters still trying to make up their minds.

"Dolios, Alcestis," Melia said, "I think I will give each of you time to think and discuss with one another. No decisions this momentous should be made now. Alcestis, you will remain clothed, and you have a special status among the people that all of us honor. But you have work to do, nevertheless." She rose. "Everyone, let us settle into our more stationary life for the time being. If possible, we will pass next winter here and see what we can do to secure transportation across the water to the land where our Lion will lead us." She clapped her hands once. "Now, let's get going. Alcestis, bring food and drink if you can walk on that foot of yours. If not, get some help. Hestia, help Alcestis get something to aid her walking, a boot of some kind perhaps. Dolios, help me prepare for the sacrifice. Now everyone off. We've got work to do."

FORTY-NINE

T he uneasy occupants of the little fishing village shuffled and muttered to each other as they stared at the strangers who had ridden in. They must have been wondering if their miserable lives were to be taken. Perhaps they would be carried off into slavery, where at least they might have a steady diet. But no one had unsheathed a sword or lowered a spear. That strange man in the lion skin was speaking an unintelligible language to the slim man on horseback.

"I guess we will need to bring Melia over here to talk to them," Shelby said to Eurymedon. "I'm not getting through with any of the languages I know, and I can't understand their mumbles."

"Melia might have a hard time," Eurymedon replied. "We really don't need much from them, except access to their fresh water. And we could trade for some of their fresh fish. I don't think they have anything else."

"Let's give them a few gifts to get their good will, and then we'll leave them alone. The longer we are neighbors, opportunities to gain their trust and help will arise. For the time being, we don't really need anything from them except to follow Dolios's suggestions about damming that creek and creating a diversionary channel to carry off some of the water."

"What do you think Alcestis will decide about Dolios's offer?" Eurymedon asked.

Shelby strode forward to the knot of village residents, smiled, and raised his hand. He tried again to greet them, to show his empty hands. He spoke English, which he so seldom used, asking them about their creek and knowing they would not understand, but his gestures said that they would go over that way. He also hoped those gestures conveyed the sense that he and his small band were no threat to them. But, of course, they were a threat. Even if they did not intend harm, they could cause it. Disease, overzealous warriors, cattle and horses: all of these were dangerous. He realized that he did not see any children in the group, and he made a mental note to ask Melia about it.

He turned back to Eurymedon. "I don't know about Dolios," he said. "I think it doesn't matter to him. He likes the life he has with us. He has opportunity, responsibility, and education. He might choose to stay here."

"Alcestis is not so obvious, but I think she feels the same way." Eurymedon rubbed his chin. "Putting her in charge of the Persians is an interesting idea. They need some intelligent guidance and I'm not up to it."

"Could be more difficult than training a wild wolf," smirked Shelby.

"Training women at all is more difficult than training any other wild creature," Eurymedon smiled back. "Except for you of course, Icarus. You can train women so wild animals will be no problem for you."

"If you underestimate their intelligence and deny them the right to suggest alternative strategies, then yes, it is more difficult to train women."

"We don't need a lot of soldiers thinking for themselves," Eurymedon said. "We need obedience and order, or you have chaos."

"Yes, but sometimes it makes sense to do things the easier way, which means letting women decide what does and does not need to be done." He laughed. "Sometimes."

* * *

Skirting the village, they found the creek in a declivity and followed a path down the low bank to a spot where flat stones stepped down to the flowing water and the buckets used by the villagers had scooped out holes in the creek bed. A clear stream of cold water danced over mossy rocks, splashing and playing under a canopy of hardwoods upstream, where rills and tumbling waterfalls sent out a pleasant sound. The stream seemed vaguely familiar, but perhaps all streams in the mountains of Greece were similar. Nevertheless, it would be interesting to explore. And doing so would relieve him of the incessant demands on his attention back in the camp. The people knew how to set up a long-term camp, and with some innovation from Dolios and Hestia, their water would be sufficient for the flocks and the fields. They really did not need to pester him about every decision.

"What are we looking for?" Eurymedon asked as they rode uphill on their horses. The rest of their small band arrayed to either side to scout and monitor the terrain.

"I just want to follow this creek to see if I can spot places where we can build dams and ponds to provide water to our pastures and flocks," replied Shelby. "I want to know what the terrain looks like, that's all."

"So what about my Persians?" Eurymedon asked after a little while.

"What about them?"

"Do you think Melia is going to take them away?"

"Are you tired of them?"

"Yes and no. Not really tired. They're useful for one thing. And there's Rhodia."

"Forgive me, brother, but it is not my place to advise you about your sexual decisions. If you want to talk, though, I will pretend to listen. Just don't ask for advice."

"I wouldn't take advice anyway," Eurymedon said with a grin. "But you know, I like to talk."

They climbed until Shelby thought they had risen perhaps twenty meters, a sufficient drop to give them plenty of gravity pull for the water. The sides of the creek had become sufficiently steep to allow for easy damming. Also, it was mostly rock and sediment at this place, so the dam would have a good anchor once it was dug out to bedrock.

Shelby swung out from the creekside to see if he could spot the camp on the far slope. He could. It was not that far, but it was far enough to require a lot of labor to construct a dam and an aqueduct. Still, they had a lot of labor. It could be done.

"Hand me a piece of your chiton," he said to Eurymedon.

"Why not all of it?" the warrior replied, stripping off his garment. "Here."

"No, not all of it, just enough to plant a flag so we can find our back."

"Well, we'll post a couple of our soldiers here, then. Let's go fetch Dolios and between him and Hestia everything will get worked out."

"If you're sure you can find the place again."

"Of course. The gray mountain is that way," he pointed, "the village is that way, and here's the creek. We can find this again."

"We will go back to camp," said Shelby, "and we won't leave anyone behind. If you can find it again, we don't need a flag."

* * *

They had been out of sight of the little village for about two hours when they rounded a bend and looked down on the squalid stone huts. Children were playing between the houses and young men were shoving off in their fishing boats mostly made of reeds. The shallow wetland at the mouth of the creek was filled with acres of papyrus, which explained the reeds. One of the younger women screamed when she spotted them, and all of the people disappeared into the closest house.

So that's how they they protect themselves, thought Shelby. They hide from strangers. How did they learn to do that? Pirates?

"Not many ships out there today," Eurymedon commented a few moments later. "Just those reed rafts."

"We may need to hunt for ships," Shelby sighed. "Up and down the coast. Those rafts won't do us much good."

"It's a shame we can't talk to the villagers. They might have some insight." Eurymedon shook his head, continuing to stare out to sea. "It's a big place."

"What is?"

"The sea."

FIFTY

"I plan to take Alcestis and tour the coastline away from the here," Shelby said to Melia two months later, when the weather had grown warm and the grain was knee high. Melia would have her baby in six or seven weeks, before another crop matured. The life of the camp had become regular and calm. It was a good time to explore, and their large pastures and fields had successfully been delineated with defensive walls of dirt and wood. The people felt safe, and so did she. "I want to see if we can find a busier port or perhaps a sheltered cove where we may be able to build watercraft of our own."

"Watch out for the wild men."

"Trust me, I will. It's one of the reasons I'm taking Alcestis. If that wolf of hers joins us, its nose and ears are a thousand times better than even hers, so we will be safer. Ironic, isn't it, when you have greater safety in the company of a wild wolf."

"Will you be gone overnight?"

"I hope not, but I won't know until I see the countryside."

"Send her in here to talk to me while you pack your supplies. Will you wear your lion skin?"

"Not in this heat."

"Wear your armor."

"If you wish. I hope to avoid conflict, though. We will both carry crossbows, just in case. Alcestis has learned to shoot very well."

"It's a wild country. We have wild men in the distance and barbaric fish eaters close by. I can't wait for us to arrive at the land where we can settle and rebuild. Meanwhile, we should be able to harvest in a week or two. We are lucky we've had some spring rain while Dolios and Hestia's workers are completing that, what do you call it? Aqueduct? Silly name. What does it mean?"

"It means a water guide or channel. It guides water from one place to another."

"Why not 'agogos'?"

"What is that?"

"A conduit, for water or whatever."

"I've just always called them aqueducts. We can call this one an agogos if you want." He grinned.

"Are you making fun of me?"

"Never," he swore.

"You might as well. I'm making fun of you."

* * *

Melia spent a long time with Alcestis, longer than Shelby thought necessary, but finally they were on their way. Alcestis was dressed as one of the Meliae in a black fighting outfit, and she still wore the gold band of a slave around her neck. She had not yet accepted Dolios's offer of freedom, but she couldn't tell why. It was too complex to talk about. She was shod, and her lower legs were covered with leather buskins to ward off thorns. Shelby had taken the same precautions.

They both carried water and food, and Alcestis had a freshly killed rabbit in a bag over her free shoulder, in case they saw the wolf. Since they had stopped their flight through the mountains months ago, she had resumed taking a bit of the evening sacrifice up the hill to a thicket and calling to Calu to come and eat. She never waited to know if the wolf had come for the offering, but it was always gone by morning. If they didn't see the wolf, she would skin the rabbit and cook it for them in the evening.

The only easy part of the journey was striding across the fields. Now, though, all hands waged round-the-clock war against predation on their crops by rabbits, wild boar, deer, and even birds. The few children in camp were taught to run around the fields to scare away critters, a healthy exercise at any time, and everyone had learned to use slings to throw stones at birds and other animals.

A few hours later, they ended up along a line of weather-beaten and cracked cliffs, eventually descending to a beach.

"We may make better time along the shore," he said, and they set off along the packed sand and pebbles, the kind of beach the British called shingle. The cooling water lapped over their hot feet, and they were happy for it. He looked out to sea frequently, hoping to see land or a sail, but all he saw was open water.

Alcestis saw something move on the cliffs overhead, however, and exclaimed quietly, "She's back!"

"Who?" Shelby asked.

"Calu. She's up on the cliff, tracking us."

"Or your dead rabbit."

"She is a wild but friendly spirit," Alcestis said. "Be nice to her."

"I will not interfere," he said. "Just remember, she cannot come close to Melia or the child. Not yet."

"She won't. She is wild. They are not. She knows she does not belong there. She wishes to run freely on the world, and sleep peacefully. I wonder if she has found a mate."

"Most women do," Shelby said. "A poet one time said, there's a gander for every gray goose in the pond."

"I don't understand that."

"Most women find mates. Some are good mates, some are not, but they're mates."

"Like Melia found you."

"I like to think I found her, with the help of the goddess, but yeah. She found me. The real me I did not know. And she brought me to life, like grain sprouting in the field in the sun and rain. She is my sun and rain."

"That's a nice thought," Alcestis said. "I'm not sure I agree with any of it, but it's a nice thought. If it's true, then what is the ground?"

"What?" he asked.

"The seed needs to be planted in the ground, so you must have been buried. What were you buried under that would nourish you in the sun and rain? It doesn't make sense to me."

"Oh, shut up," he said, smiling at her with affection.

They strolled along the shore another half mile or so until they reached a place where the undercut cliffs met the surf.

"Let's climb up there and see your wolf, if she will show herself. The shore is too close to the water to build a shipyard or to camp, and a storm would wash water all the way up to the bare stone. We need to keep looking."

"I love it out here," Alcestis said, "in the open air and free like this. I love the birds and the flowers and the sweet smells."

"The sea can have a nice smell when it doesn't have dead fish and human waste polluting it," he said. "Sometimes it is fun to bathe in. This looks like a new shore. The reefs aren't high enough to protect from sharks, so you need to keep your eyes open if you go in."

"I will go in if you will," she said, swiping the sweat from her brow. "Besides, I think I may find some friends out there in the waves."

"Friends?"

"It's just a feeling, like a sense of friendly spirits nearby, in the water. I'm certain of it. More wild but friendly spirits."

"Maybe we can look for them later. We have a lot of sunlight left to explore the shoreline."

* * *

Shelby and Alcestis topped the ridge and stopped when they saw Calu lying in the brush about twenty paces away, watching them, her ears pricked. Her tongue was out a little, which Alcestis knew was a friendly greeting.

"I will go the other way," Shelby said. "You give her the rabbit and speak to her."

Alcestis nodded and approached slowly, talking in a low voice, calling Calu by her name and telling her how happy she was to see her. She pulled the rabbit slowly from the bag and laid it on the ground, about ten feet from the wolf. She then turned, walked a little way off, and sat down with her back to Calu.

After a while, she heard a small squeak, and she slowly looked around. A wolf pup was nosing the rabbit while Calu stood over it, her yellow eyes on Alcestis. Calu licked her lips.

"You had a baby!" Alcestis exclaimed. "Well no wonder I haven't seen you for so long." She put her palms together in front of her face and bowed to the wolf. "Calu, I congratulate you." She made no motion to rise or in any way to come closer to the wolf or the pup.

Calu licked her lips again, dipped down and picked up the carcass. She retreated into the brush, her tail standing high, with the pup tagging along.

"Imagine that," Alcestis said to Shelby after she filled him in on her encounter with Calu. "No wonder she's been hanging around. Something must have happened to her mate, and she was looking for a new pack. I guess she found me."

"I'm impressed by your knowledge of the wolf," Shelby said. "Most people would have been terrified, and they would have frightened the wolf in return. Your body language and your calm voice put her at ease. But for her to bring her pup to meet you is extraordinary. You said before that there was no real connection between the two of you, but this shows you were wrong. I wouldn't say you are bonded, but you are friends. That's as good as it gets with a wolf."

"The fresh meat helps most," Alcestis said. "Every wild thing conserves as much food as it can. Only humans are wasteful."

"I've seen packs of wild dogs destroy flocks of sheep for the sheer pleasure of killing, without eating anything. Humans are not the only ones."

"Then there were too many sheep and not enough shepherds," she replied. "And that was a different form of human waste."

"You're right about conserving energy," Shelby said. "If you live by what you can find, you can go days without finding anything. So you eat when you can. An unplanned life is not an easy one."

She studied him. "I'd rather say that an unexamined life is not worth the trouble of living."

"What do you mean?"

"If you don't know why you are doing something, then you don't know what you are doing. If your whole life is without meaning or plan, it's not worth living. That's my opinion. It's why I haven't decided about Dolios's offer." She held her chin up at him, as though defying him to contradict her.

"You cannot know that in more than a thousand years from

now, a great Achaean philosopher will say the same thing."

"So?"

"So, you're what, fourteen? How do you think that?"

"I'm a slave, Icarus. I spend a lot of time thinking because almost no one but you and Dolios and sometimes Melia talk to me."

"Alcestis, I love to see your mind growing. You will become a famous person in your time."

"I don't care about that. I care about breathing the free air and running in the wind, like Calu. That's what I live for."

"I need to teach you writing and math," he said. "We will start as soon as we get back to camp. It will help your mind grow."

She bowed. Then she looked up and nodded her head toward Calu, who was suddenly alert, her gaze focused away from them.

"Watch her," she whispered, "and get down."

When Calu and the pup moved, they moved too, into a dense covert. When Calu stopped, they stopped. The wolf was ahead of them maybe twenty paces, but she was flat on her belly, a paw on top of the pup to hold it quiet.

A snuffling and grunting came through the brush, and a small pack of boar appeared, rooting the ground. Alcestis signaled to him to stay quiet and low and to wait.

Very slowly and deliberately Shelby removed the crossbow from his back, and Alcestis did the same. They checked to be sure the bolts were loaded and the bows cocked. Then they waited.

The wild pigs caught the wolf's scent, or perhaps theirs, and stampeded right at them. One big sow headed straight for Shelby and Alcestis. With no choice but to be rammed, Shelby fired into the sow's head, dropping her, grunting, to the ground. He quickly reloaded and then remained motionless and waited. Alcestis shot at two others, one a hopeless shot into foliage.

"Calu has not come back," Shelby said quietly after a few minutes.

"She will. She will join us around midnight, I bet, when everything in the world is still except us. I expect she will be hungry again."

FIFTY-ONE

With the light already fading in the late afternoon and sunset coming in less than two hours, and with several miles of rough country between them and the safety of their camp, they decided to stay put. One would keep watch while the other dozed. Some of the boar had been wounded, not killed, and could still be heard angrily stampeding in the brush. A small fire would be some protection against them, but it might be an invitation for wild men.

Alcestis skinned and gutted the sow. She piled the guts on the hide, pulled it to the edge of the cliff, and dumped the mess over. She then returned with the hide.

She disjointed the sow, removed a large ham, cut a slab of belly fat and the tenderloins, and wrapped these up in some leaves she tied with a loop of rope from her pack. She then bundled the meat into the hide and tied it. She made a sling for the slippery hide from the rest of her rope. Then she and Shelby added the carcass and the rest of the dead boar to the feasting crabs below at the water's edge and set off to scout for a safe place away from the bloody slaughter whose odor could attract a variety of unsavory investigators: more wolves, jackals, bears, lions.

As they walked, Alcestis kept an eye out for Calu and her pup, but she didn't see them. Perhaps they were down on the shore feasting on the remains of the boar. Perhaps the rabbit had been enough, but she doubted that a nursing mother would have gotten her fill from one rabbit. If she was still hungry, Calu would find them.

The surrounding brush and scrub stood maybe ten feet high and could serve as dense cover, but it would be easy to get lost if the night were starless. They could miss their footing on the broken ground, too. What she wanted was the companionship of that wolf and her exceptional night-penetrating sense perceptions. It's a strange life when the companionship of a wild wolf was so much easier and more trustworthy than with the man.

"Can we find our way back to the camp in the dark?"

"We had a difficult time climbing over all those cliffs and rocks along the shoreline in broad daylight," Shelby replied.

"I'm not scared of the dark, Icarus. When we find a safe spot, you rest first. I'll watch out for Calu and the pup. Maybe she will join us after all."

* * *

They had an uneasy night, though Calu and her pup came by. Sitting very still, Alcestis let the little pup come close enough to sniff her finger before it was warned off by a low growl from Calu. Then they vanished in the dark.

Shelby's sleep was troubled but quiet. Four hours after closing his eyes he was awake and alert. "Everything okay?" he asked softly.

"I haven't seen anything. Calu came by. She did not appear alarmed."

"Good. Maybe she is lurking somewhere out of sight. You rest now, and I'll watch." He picked up the crossbow and checked the string, the loaded bolt, the cocking. "Sleep with your crossbow across your chest so you'll have it if you need it, but don't waste a shot. Stay steady and calm if we need to defend ourselves."

She lay back and stared at the stars, the divine sisters in their golden homes, protecting the earth. They were not free either. They'd have the same neighbors for eternity. She fell asleep hoping they were happy, so high in the air, remembering Asonius's kind smile and his observation that everyone is a slave. And then Shelby gently shook her awake.

"Time to get up," he whispered. "You can hear the birds from the coast all the way up here. We need to move out."

"It's still dark."

"For another twenty or thirty minutes, and then the sky will begin to gray."

"Did you see Calu?"

"I did. She bedded down with the pup in some grass while the pup nursed and slept. She's gone now."

"Did she take the pup?"

"I don't know. I didn't want to get too close to it, just in case. You gotta give a wolf a lot of respect."

* * *

Shelby led in the general direction back toward the camp. It was still too dark to see much, but it wouldn't be long until there was a little light. They'd just begun following a little stream toward the shore when they heard Calu howling, back toward the mountains, from the opposite direction. It went on for almost a full minute, with that eerie, carrying quality only wolves possess. As she wound down, they also heard the higher-pitched voice of her pup howling. She howled again, and the pup joined in.

"What do you think?" Shelby asked Alcestis.

"I think we better hurry up," she said. "That sounded like a warning to me."

"What do you think she smells?"

"How close are we to the wild men? She might be warning us about them."

"I don't know. I thought we wouldn't see them again once Melia saw the sea. Do you think Calu smells the wild men moving this way?"

"But maybe the prophecy meant that we wouldn't see the wild men again because we would be out of their range. Could we have moved back into their country?"

"If we have, we need to get out of it again as quickly as we can. You and I don't stand a chance against them. Can you keep up?"

She nodded and shooed him with the back of her hand, the way women have done to men since the dawn of time.

Cresting a low hill in the gray light near sunrise, they stopped to catch their breath and surveyed the surrounding landscape, staying low to keep from being seen by any unknown pursuers.

"Wait a bit," he said.

They remained motionless for a time.

The wolf and her pup howled again, now closer but near the shore. More howls joined in, but they came from the other apex predator of the land.

"They're hunting us," he said. "We need to get out of here. Stay low, don't get lost."

They entered a dense thicket, and the dry, hard branches tore at their arms. Shelby twisted and turned and lost his bearings. He glanced up at the angle of the sun and forged ahead. A few yards away, four or five red deer thundered by them in a panic. It was not a good sign. They should have been moving the other way, away from him and Alcestis.

When she caught up with him, he noticed that part of her uniform was gone. "What happened to it?" he whispered.

"Got caught in some brambles. I had to cut it off, but I kept the pieces."

She was bleeding from the numerous scratches on her belly and arms. He held his hand to her, and they moved on.

After maneuvering another quarter mile through the thicket, they broke out onto open rocky ground, well east of the camp at the beginning of a long hillside. There was no place to hide, and the howling cannibals were coming for them. Their only option was to run for it.

They were a mile from the field barricades when the first wild man spotted them and called to the others. Shelby watched them angling out of the brush, running to cut off their escape.

He altered course, putting the savages at less of an advantage. It would take them longer to make the barricade, but it was their only hope.

Alcestis labored to keep up. They'd never make it at this pace. "Quick," he gasped, "this way!" He veered back to the east.

They entered a covert of scrub oak and low brush and dropped to all fours, staying as low as they could. They came to a depression in the ground and stopped to catch their breath.

The howling of the men ceased, and the world became quiet.

Minutes passed. Half an hour. Then a calm voice said through the brush, "Icarus, we have some horses for you if you want to ride back to camp." It was Garanus.

"Thank you," Shelby said, standing. "That was close."

"We alerted Eurymedon's cavalry when we heard the howling and saw the wild men running across the burned ground. We leapt the barricade and came out, and they ran away. Are you alright?"

Shelby nodded and stood. "It's been an interesting night and day," he said.

FIFTY-TWO

S helby was pleased to see the hazy green in the fields. This was a hearty wheat, one of the original strains, not some hothouse variety that was common in his own time. A somewhat taller stand of green was growing in another field. He made a mental note to ask someone what it was.

He could see that Garanus was doing a good job exercising the cavalry as they rode the perimeter of the fields each day, keeping an eye out for the wild men and protecting the ongoing work of erecting barricades and irrigation schemes. But it wasn't the same without his brother-in-law there. He wondered how much longer it would be before Eurymedon returned. He had taken a small group of cavalry and headed for the distant headland, intending to plot a way north from camp and perhaps find other settlements.

Rhodia was busy working with the Meliae in training and fighting: two things warriors need daily. Recently they, too, had added slings to their list of weapons, and spent some of their time rubbing stones retrieved from the creek into nearly perfect spheres. Alcestis remained close-lipped about Dolios's offer, but she was obviously adopted by the Meliae as a younger sister. She trained with them every day when she was not attending to Shelby. Well, actually, to Melia, who was in charge of Shelby's domestic arrangement.

* * *

"I thought the prophecy was that our troubles with the wild men would be over when Melia saw the sea," Kratos said one day. "But then they followed you all the way back here. We cannot possibly live with those savages this close to camp. I think our only safety is in killing them all. They are worse than Achaeans. They're sneaky, they're dangerous, they're huge, and they stink."

"They also eat people," Shelby added.

"And that."

"Raw."

"They are going to attack us when we least expect it. They know where we are, and they want revenge. That was a close chase the other day. Lucky for you that the patrol saw you running."

"Do you have a plan?" Shelby had been thinking along the same lines. In general, he preferred to use force as a last resort, but their encounters with the wild men convinced him that defense and strategy were not going to work. He had seen a lot of wars, and he knew in his heart that sometimes it was necessary to kill people. Perhaps a whole lot of people. This was one of those times.

No doubt they had families, close social bonds, children, and parents they cared for. They had some kind of settlements even if they moved all the time. They probably worshiped some kind of deity, and they probably had some kind of social institutions they were assiduous in maintaining. Of course, baboons had most of that, too. Still, these wild men had survived thus far on the planet, possibly tens of thousands of years, doing nothing different than what they were doing now.

"Our dodecas can defend themselves from the wild men," continued Kratos, "but they can't contain them. The brutes would just side-step away and look for an opening somewhere else. Our trebuchets terrified them last time, but those weapons are no use in killing them because they don't have a location. Except by accident, I mean. We might hit one by accident. This scrubland is perfect cover for them. A hundred of them could be hiding within paces of us and we would not see them. Smell them, perhaps, but not see them."

"They are a very dangerous enemy, even if they do not have arrows. But I've fought enemies like this before, small units easily hidden in the countryside and hard to track or contain. We called them guerrillas."

"How did you fight them?"

The two had turned back from the perimeters and were strolling back toward camp.

"Not easily. We tried destroying all the places that could give them support, but that did nothing to stop them. If anything, it just made them try harder. We never learned enough about them to use food, or medicine, or education to win them over. Generally speaking, we lost every war we fought with them. We killed a great many, but in the end they remained in charge of their land and countries."

"Sounds grim."

"It is. War is a game with rules. When you don't play the game, then you have what we have here: random murder with nothing gained or lost."

"If you kill enough of them, you can take their women and children as slaves, and that diminishes their ability to fight."

"True, Kratos, if you believe in slavery. But do you want any of the wives or children of these wild men? We saw those women fight. I don't want them around Melia or the baby."

"Then it's murder all the way."

"Yes. That's why it's better to think twice before starting a war like that. A band of determined guerrillas will defeat the strongest army."

"There's got to be a way."

"It's a game, Kratos. Both sides need to observe a set of rules and recognize when they are defeated. No rules, no game. Unless they have something we need, and it's something we can take away from them, then we are needlessly wasting our lives and supplies trying to fight them. And these wild men have nothing we want."

"I want them to leave my people alone," Kratos fumed.

"We cannot take that from them. We can only take ourselves away from them."

"How did Alcestis do on your outing?" Kratos asked, changing the subject.

"She's a great shot and not the least bit nervous or jumpy. I've never seen such poise in a warrior. I think she has great promise."

"Maybe I should work with her, teach her some things."

"That's a good idea. I could apprentice her to you for a while. She's not learning much cleaning up my clothes and serving wine, although she trains with the Meliae every day. But you cannot have her full time, because I still need her to do some things, and I want to continue instructing her in math, physics, and writing. She is quite capable, I think. Also, she is occupied supervising Eurymedon's Persians while he is away, and that's hard enough for anyone."

"If she can be trained, Rhodia is the one who can do it," Kratos said. "She has good tactical training, thanks to you. I was thinking more about training in strategy, making logic of the larger picture and learning to read your enemy. Things I learned from my father and have practiced all my life."

"You trust Rhodia to teach tactics?"

"You've fought side by side with her for months. She was a silly girl just a year ago, but being with you has matured her. Give her some credit. She is a dangerous warrior, Icarus, but dangerous the way a woman is dangerous. She's subtle. Quick. No threats. Just swift murder, and then she walks away, job done. She is both more effective and more efficient than either of us."

"She's a weapon, I know that. You're saying she's more than that."

"You and I are similar, but we are male. Her battlefield is much more diverse and subtle than either of us can see. To us, it's about power and dominance. To her, it's about solution. When you become a woman's problem, your life is in danger and you don't even know it. My friend, I think you can learn from her if you will. I know that Alcestis can."

"I don't think I want to learn how to use sex as a weapon."

Kratos laughed at that, slapping Shelby on the shoulder. "But sex is our strongest emotion, my friend. She who controls sex controls everything. It is the fire that drives us."

"I thought war was your driver," Shelby said.

"Only because I have yet to find a woman whose sex matches the thrill of combat. But I know she's out there, and when I meet her we will have a great explosion. Then I will retire to my house and tend my vineyards."

They walked farther from the fields out to the edge of the scrub, studying the brush for any sign of movement.

They were too far for help if they needed it, and Shelby was about to suggest they go back to the camp when Kratos deftly whisked his sword from its scabbard.

"Did you see something?" Shelby whispered.

"Either a wild man or a band of hogs," Kratos whispered. "I hope it's a wild man."

"No, you don't," Shelby said. "Back away."

"Get back here." Melia's voice spoke in his head as clearly as if she were standing next to him. "Bring Kratos."

"Come on," Shelby said, "we've got to go."

"I'm not running from an enemy, Icarus."

"You're coming with me, and I'm running back to camp. Something's going on with Melia."

"Is the baby coming?" Kratos asked, his look turning to glee.

"It's something else. She needs us there now. She's speaking in my head."

"Some of the greatest matrons had that trick," Kratos said as they picked up their pace away from the scrub. "It fits." Kratos punched Shelby in the shoulder. "Race you," he said, and he took off over the broken ground, running like an antelope. Shelby trailed along like a lumbering old saddle-weary horse.

FIFTY-THREE

"Hold it right there," Alcestis said, one fist on her hip and the other hand pointing at them. "You're not bringing those nasty feet into this tent. You're black with dirt all the way up to your knees. Sit down, and take off your sandals."

Kratos looked at Shelby with an expression of smoldering anger mixed with amusement. "Bossy bitch, isn't she?" he stated.

"You too, prince. Remove your sandals, and I'll wash your feet. The others are already here."

"Yes ma'am," he said, yielding and dropping his huge muscles down with a grunt. He leaned in to Shelby and said in a very loud, hoarse whisper, "Some people would flog the girl for such an insult."

"I apologize if you feel insulted," Shelby replied. "I bet she was instructed by Melia to stop us. When we get in, we'll find out. And by the way, you only outran me by a half mile. You can do better than that."

Kratos spat, receiving a baleful glare from Alcestis who dropped his still-dirty foot and moved to Shelby without a word.

"How old are you Alcestis?" Kratos asked.

"Fourteen harvests, sir," she said, not looking up.

"Icarus says he might apprentice you to me for a time so you can learn military strategy and so on. Interested?"

Fire came into her eyes. "Yes sir," she said. "I sometimes dream about it. Battle, planning, moving warriors so they will be most effective. I would welcome the training."

"We will see what we will see," Kratos said. "If Melia approves, we will begin today."

"You know, Kratos," Shelby said, "I never thought to ask, but who are your slaves? Certainly, you have someone caring for you, or several someones, but I've never met them, and you never speak of them."

"Metis, my poor mother, gave me an old toothless man I call Dontia who has been very faithful and efficient. I don't need much. He cleans blood off my armor, gets me a clean chiton every day, and sometimes will rub my sore muscles with olive oil. Every couple of months he cuts my hair and keeps it in a little bag so the sorcerers can't get it. Other than that, I take care of everything else. Why?"

"As close as we have been all this time, I just didn't know. An idle curiosity is all."

She finished with Shelby and moved back to Kratos. This time he behaved, and she finished rapidly.

"Go in," she said, "while I clean these filthy sandals. They will be out here when you need them."

* * *

Melia was sitting cross-legged on a pile of pillows in the middle of the tented room, waiting, her baby-belly resting on a cushion between her legs. Garanus, Hestia, and Dolios were kneeling in front of her. She did not speak. Shelby and Kratos knelt in line with the others and waited, looking left and right. Hestia nodded at him, a serious look on her face, then looked back at Melia. No one spoke.

"There will be no hunting of the wild men," Melia said when everyone was listening. "Leave them alone. We will have no more trouble with the wild men, if we leave them alone. Do not go near them. Do not venture into their lands. Just stay away. Am I understood?"

This was a side of Melia Shelby had rarely seen. She was speaking with the authority of a queen, and it rankled him. She seemed not to care what they thought.

"Kratos, do you have a problem with that?" she asked her big brother.

"I think you invite trouble," he said, "and we will awaken to find them eating us in the dark. But if you want us to leave them alone, we will."

"We have been told that they are no longer a problem. They have seen me with the shield of power. They have experienced our deadly response to attack. Let us not show by our actions that we do not trust the goddess in this. Leave them alone and they will avoid us unless we bother them. Focus instead on getting off this shore as soon as we can. Does everybody understand?"

Everyone nodded.

"Good. Second, it is a bad idea to build boats ourselves because we do not have the expertise or the materials. This is where Eurymedon comes in. If he is successful he will either find a town that already has plenty of boats, or he will bring back a shipwright who can help us build our own. Trebuchets counterweighted with water might be useful in a sea battle."

She paused, looking around.

"The next thing I have been shown is that a great horde of pirates is moving down the coast looking for plunder. They could be here in the next two or three weeks, and our camp might look like an easy target for them. If we do not save these people in the village, they will be overrun and murdered. I instruct you to think of ways to capture these pirate ships, which could help us reach the lands to which our Lion leads us. I want half of the Meliae on the beach with Rhodia in case the pirates strike before we are ready. I want the other half with me. Dolios," she looked at the boy, "when you climbed the hill above the creek, tell me what you saw."

"You can see a long way from up there," he said. "You can see far out to sea, and I saw some boats larger than the ones we've seen here. So we know that transportation is possible."

"Good," Melia said.

"However, if we took over a shipyard in some other town, and added our own workers and supervisors," Dolios added, "we could improve their operations for our own benefit. Hestia and I can discuss this. We might need to conquer a larger city to do that, and that would be a job for Kratos. But first, we've got to find a city."

"Take care of your wolf," Melia said to Alcestis. "Her offspring are destined to become great in our new land. I do not see clearly how we will transport a wolf from here to there, but possibly there is a way. Did I hear a puppy this morning? Perhaps her puppy will be the one who goes with us. Calu has a den in that little thicket where you and Shelby hid from the wild men. Take ten of the Meliae with you and visit her, speak to her about her puppy."

"Yes ma'am."

"And I understand that your master has spoken of apprenticing you to Kratos."

"Yes ma'am."

"Kratos, what is your opinion of that? You cannot abuse her. She is not your plaything."

"If you think she can be a help to us with the instruction, we'll see if she can keep up. If she can't, I'll send her back."

"She does not like to be touched, so keep your hands off of her. Teach her."

"Yes ma'am."

"Garanus, when the wind is favorable from the sea, set more fires in the scrub to expand our border. And no one, I mean no one, is to be alone. Our job is to protect the slaves and everyone else. Let's do our job."

Melia grimaced at the baby's movement. "We have cleared away the preliminaries," she said. "Now let's focus on how to get ready in the event we are attacked from the sea."

"Our best protection is getting in our crops so we can't be starved out," Shelby said. "Everything depends on protecting our crops."

"I think our best choice is to lie in wait for the pirates, then surprise them. I need to envision how they will assemble for an attack. It would be a great thing to kill them and take their ships," Kratos said. "From what I've seen and Melia has foretold, the pirates will plunder everything they can. It's happened here before, which is why the villagers have taught their children to hide in their windowless stone huts."

"Both of those are good ideas," Melia said. "Does anyone else have anything to add?"

"I think we are beginning to run very low on wine," Hestia

said. "If the barley comes in and we have enough, we can make beer to get us through the winter."

"Can you find Eurymedon, my lady?" Alcestis asked.

"Not yet," Melia replied.

"He is our best hope to find another way out. If he can bring ships, even a few, we can begin our exodus," Alcestis said.

"What do you think, Kratos?" Shelby asked. "See what I mean about her?"

"She's fourteen?"

Alcestis ignored him. "Icarus and I went down the coast but found no decent beaches or harbors. This cannot be the only miserable settlement on the coastline of such a rich sea. I think Eurymedon will find another place with better opportunities."

"I agree," Melia said. "Kratos, take Alcestis down to the coastline and discuss with her how to prepare for our defense. Of course, they might not come only from the sea. It's probable, if they have a large enough force, that they will attempt to encircle us and attack from several directions. Get Alcestis to help you think of those scenarios as well. We have some time, but it is limited. Let us all use it well."

Kratos stood. "Thank you, sister, for your wisdom and the prophecies of the goddess. Foreknowledge may be even more precious to us than our crops."

FIFTY-FOUR

🔥🔥🔥🔥🔥🔥🔥🔥🔥🔥🔥

Garanus accompanied Kratos and Alcestis as they went to survey the long coast at the end of their grassy fields. In its ceaseless motion, the sea had thrown up sand dunes, and these in turn had held back millennia of eroded soil from the mountains. The dirt was rich and thick, and friable. It could have been valuable for planting if the sea had not also poisoned it with salt. All along the coast, white sand stretched flat, shadowed gray with seawater washing ashore, and multiple vines and sea-hardy plants had grown in these dunes. Piles of driftwood dotted the shore.

"How deep is the water here?" Kratos asked.

"I'll find out," said Alcestis, and pulled off her sandals to wade out. The gentle waves lapped at her legs, gradually reaching her knees at about fifty paces. She went on until the water reached her waist and her chiton floated up around her. Then she turned and looked back at the two men.

"I counted two hundred paces," Garanus said.

Kratos nodded. "Two hundred four."

"What do you think?" Garanus asked.

Kratos signaled for Alcestis to come back, but instead she started walking in the direction of the village, parallel with the shore. The two men heard snatches of some high song she seemed to be singing, making it up with her steps.

"What's she doing?" Garanus asked.

"She's going to see if the depth is consistent, but we can be sure it is not. That little village is located where it is partly because of the creek, but mostly because that's where the water is deeper.

Let's walk along with her."

"Why is she singing?"

"Hard to say."

"Some of those waves are reaching nearly to her shoulders now. Do you think she can swim?"

"She is not afraid of the water, whether she can swim or not. Fear drowns more people than ignorance. I'm not worried."

They paced along the beach, keeping up with her, observing the quality of the surface, discussing whether it would hinder a mounted attack or their foot soldiers.

Nearer the village, the ground tended to rise a little, and they climbed over a low ridge perhaps six feet high to look down at the village. Alcestis was still in the water.

"Did you get her sandals?" Kratos asked Garanus.

"Yes, when we decided to follow her."

"Good, she's going to need them."

The contours and composition of the beach changed on the other side of the low ridge. Less sand, more stone, some of it black, basaltic pebbles and boulders. The boulders were slimy with sea growth and it was easy to see the tide line. A piece of the shore was a basalt sill, abutting the sea and echoing with breaking waves. Over millions of years the sea had carved into its foundation, giving it an echo chamber for the waves, but it remained stalwart and firm. The ground Kratos and Garanus trod was firm dirt concretized with rock debris. Alcestis was still wading, but she had come closer to shore to keep the water from reaching above her waist. Kratos waved to her to return to land, and she acknowledged.

Soon the three joined on the shore.

"Most of the shore is shallow and flat out to where I was," she said. "I don't know how much water the pirate ships would need to float, but they will not get close to land there."

"No, if they come to attack, they will need to anchor farther out and launch their men in boats or make them wade ashore. That means they will need to guard and maintain their ships at anchor, so they will keep some men on them."

"I don't understand how they anchor those ships, anyway," Garanus said. "It's all sand, right?"

Alcestis nodded. "I felt nothing under my feet but loose sand until I reached that black rock near the village. I assume they will anchor over there and not risk their ships here."

"Good guess, little one," Kratos said. "But they could anchor with the help of lines run out from front and back and to both sides. They would want to choose their anchoring point at low tide, then row out their anchors and drop them, giving themselves plenty of rope to rise on the tide. Otherwise, they could pull the ships right up until they grounded, then prop them up on both sides with their oars to keep them from tipping over. At high tide, the ships would float again and they could oar them off to deeper water."

"The water may be shallow much further out," she said. "I only went so far."

"How do you feel? Are you up for another foray?"

"Sure. Let me warm up for a bit, and I'll go straight out. You can estimate the distance."

"I'll go with you," Kratos said, "if you want company."

"Actually, no," she said. "I like the freedom of the water. It might be selfish, but I don't want to share it."

"I understand." Kratos pulled off a skin he had wrapped around his shoulders. "Dry off and warm up in this while we talk, then if you feel like it, you can go out again."

"We might want to make some surveys," she said. "We could perhaps have a hundred people take a measured number of steps offshore, let Icarus or Dolios measure their height above the average sea water, then walk another hundred paces, and so on. At least we would know what the bottom of this little bay is like."

"Good idea," he nodded. "I also wonder how to defend this beach from them."

"Let's talk about that," she said.

Kratos and Garanus sat on the ground next to her, watching for her to stop shivering.

"The way I see it," she said, "is that the ships will sail in, anchor somehow, and then put men over the side. If they think the sea is shallow enough, they will send their men on foot. If its too deep to wade through, they will hold off. I don't think they will try to launch boats or anything."

"You could be right," Kratos said. "Garanus?"

"I think she's right. If they discover they can ground their ships in shallow water, then that's what they will do. Who do you think they will leave aboard?"

"Probably slaves," Kratos said. "They will chain their slaves to the oars, because they are lazy—like all people. Do you think the slaves will defend the boats if we try to board them?"

"I don't think so," Alcestis said. "I know a lot of slaves. Mostly, looking at the ones I know, they don't think for themselves but wait for instructions. If they have masters to tell them to defend, then they will. But I don't think they will do it on their on. Also, I don't think they will defend, but my reasons are more complex. Basically, I don't think you can depend on your slaves to hold your property. Your property does not mean the same to a slave as it does to you."

"Assuming we can eliminate the pirates themselves, even if slaves are left on board then they would not be difficult to over-power."

"I think that's the idea," Garanus said. "My question, of course, is how to overpower the pirates."

"We have the trebuchets and the cavalry," Alcestis said.

"And many trained soldiers," Kratos said. "But overwhelming force is easily defeated by poor planning. What do you think?"

"We need to know more about the hidden sea bed," Alcestis said, "but in general I believe that the ships will not be able to ap-proach close to shore here. It depends on how much water they need to float. The less they need, the closer they can come to shore."

"I think they do not need more than a short girl's legs," Ga-ranus said. "Not from some of those I've seen. So you may be wrong."

"We will see," Kratos said. "I wonder if there are sand bars or reefs farther out that would keep them from getting to this beach. The only way to know is to wade out there and map it out. Mean-while, let's talk about where to build a defensive wall, how to man it, and where to position cavalry. Do you think the cavalry will be effective on this sand?"

"No," said Alcestis and Garanus together, then laughed.

"I think the sand is too soft," she said.

"I agree," Garanus said, "but it is a question for Eurymedon. He will test the shore with his horses and then we will know. If it is too soft for horses, it is too soft for foot soldiers. We will need to draw the pirates inside. It would be useful if we could slaughter them before their shipmates became aware. Any ideas?"

"This is really the expertise for Eumaeus," Garanus said. "He would have known exactly what to do and it would have been done by tomorrow evening. Perhaps we should ask Melia."

"We should always ask Melia," Kratos said. "And so we will. It would be a good idea to construct defensive barriers that would drive them into places where their congestion and our maneuverability would make it easy to kill them. Funnels of some kind. Perhaps, as Alcestis says, a kind of labyrinth. But it is a flat shore with just these low dunes along it. Whatever we do we will need to build soon. And we may completely mistake the intent of a raid. Maybe these pitiful pirates just want to raid that miserable village again, in case anyone left an infant girl out in the open. Honestly, the villagers have nothing else."

CHAPTER

FIFTY-FIVE

"I think the sand is firm enough," Eurymedon said that evening. "I went and looked at it. I think we can stage charges along the shore near the water. At light tomorrow, I will take twenty or so horses out to test it, but from appearances I think it will hold. Of course it is firmer nearer the water."

Eurymedon had returned from his fifteen-day exploration of the shoreline with disappointing results. In many places the black rock plunged straight into the water without beaches, in others he had encountered dense hardwood forests filled with pockets of impenetrable briars. In all, he had seen two other small hamlets, one made with wooden pickets and thatched or sodded roofs. The other repeated the conical stone of their neighboring village. Neither had more than six huts.

"Cavalry is most effective when it is sudden and a surprise," Eurymedon added. I'm not sure how we will hide our mounted riders. Certainly we do not want to scare intruders back to their ships, so this problem will need some work."

"Would it be wise to keep your horse tracks below the high tide line?" Kratos mused. "If they send a vessel to scout the shore, hundreds of hoofprints in the sand might worry them."

"I agree," Shelby nodded. "What about the trebuchets?"

"We could launch large boulders and small, what do you call it, scattershot?" Kratos asked. "We would need to time the shots just right so we don't hit the cavalry or the ships."

"That's easy for Hestia," Shelby said. "One of us just signals her, and she slings the stones. The question is, what does she fire first? And when? Too soon, and the raiders escape and sail away. Too late, and we do no good. Too far, and we sink the ships."

"Let's go set some flags in the surf," Kratos said. "Then she can get her range."

"I also think we need to go further out," Shelby said. "When I was watching the waves, it appears that there is at least one fairly shallow sandbar just below the surface two hundred or so paces out."

"Tomorrow. Alcestis seems to enjoy it. We will take her," Kratos nodded at the thin girl standing nearby, the gold band of her slave collar glinting in the firelight above her cleverly embroidered chiton.

"Tomorrow I will take a cart into the village," Melia said, "along with some honey for the children and perhaps some bread, if we still have plenty. I want to try to talk to them."

"Your reception last time was not so friendly," Eurymedon said. "They all locked themselves into their huts and refused to come out. At least the first time we went, we met some of the older ones."

"I'll wait," Melia said. "I'll take a few of the Meliae, the ones who can sing, and we will idle there for a bit singing and talking. Our laughter and voices will persuade them to investigate. They obviously have experience with pirates. I will try to get them to discuss it."

Shelby smiled, amused at her concept of feminine power.

"When we draw up plans for coastal defenses, we should also plan to protect the village. It will help to secure our flank," Kratos said.

"Good," nodded Shelby. "What do you have in mind?"

"Tell him, Alcestis," Kratos said, turning to look at the girl.

"A successful commander will control the movement of his enemy," she said by rote. "A successful commander will control the movement of his own men. We must draw our enemies into positions where we can kill them and they cannot kill us."

"What does that mean in this case?" Shelby asked.

"Uh," she paused. "We are discussing it."

He smiled. "What, one full day and you don't have a plan? Tut-tut."

"The principle is where we start, Icarus," Kratos said. "The application to reality is not always so easy. We are discussing screens for the trebuchets, so the pirates can't observe them until they are too close for it to matter. We will dig ditches out to the sea to flood with seawater at the time of the attack. These ditches should turn the pirates inward toward a point where we will have archers and spearmen hidden from sight. Meanwhile, the cavalry can attack down the beach killing stragglers and trapping the invaders between the ditches."

"Why spearmen?" Shelby asked. "Won't they be on the wrong side of the ditches."

"They are backup in case any of the pirates cross over the ditches, which they might do. Construction in sand is not that easy. But Garanus suggests using logs buried in the sand to hold it in place."

"Right, and tie the logs together with ropes. How deep do you think you can make the ditches?"

"They need to be higher than a head," Kratos said.

"Why won't the pirates use them to escape?"

"You taught me that one," Kratos said. "They will be filled with pointed sticks."

"How long will it take to build all this?" he asked.

"My laborers can begin producing logs and helping to plant them tomorrow," Hestia said. "It's not sophisticated work."

"Our troops can dig the ditches by tomorrow evening, I think," Garanus said.

"Who will construct the blinds for the trebuchets?" Shelby asked.

"Everyone else," Melia said. "This is a group effort. Everyone is willing to work, and the grain is just growing. Not much needs to be done."

"Except keep the cattle out of the grain," Shelby said. "Hestia, I wish I had already taught you about steam engines. They would be so useful right now to dig out sand and rock, and to winch poles into place."

"Is it too late?" the wizened old woman asked. "I am not sleepy."

"Neither am I," Shelby said. "Let me take this sharpened stick and blacken it in the fire, and then you and I can use some linen to draw up the basic ideas."

"Master," said Dolios. "I worry about the village. They are gentle, fearful people. They can't help us, but I would like to help design their defenses."

"Oh right of course you should help," said Shelby. "Does anybody else have ideas for defending the village? Alcestis, do you have an idea?"

"I don't know, master," she said. "That ridge of stone between our camp and them, where the wet ground is and the creek runs, might be strategic in the coming fight. At the very least we need to have a group of archers stationed there to observe."

"Agreed," he nodded. "Kratos?"

"Garanus and I talked about that," he said. "We need a reserve force there to prevent a flanking attack against the camp, but perhaps they should be stationed closer to the village. We assume that the major thrust of the pirates will be against our camp, but it may not be. They have always attacked that poor village, and stupid people are always enslaved to their habits. They may be going for the village again. Why would they divert to our camp, especially if they think we are well-armed and prepared?"

"We need camouflage," Shelby said, "or trickery. They will be able to see all of our fields, and probably a lot of our cattle, too. We have had a successful season for calves and lambs and our herds are visible near the top of the hill. We cannot hide them without taking them over the hills into wild man territory. And still, we have turned this entire hillside into pasture and fields of grain. We need to appear defenseless in order to draw them in. Any suggestions?"

Alcestis stepped forward.

"Sir," she said, "Dolios and I have already discussed this. We think we should bring a few sheep down to the sand dunes or just beyond, where the grass is sweeter, perhaps thirty of us, and we should be tending sheep and obviously unarmed. If they see only sheep and shepherds without weapons, they may be encouraged."

"That's a good idea," Kratos nodded.

"And perhaps we can move some of our cattle into the hardwoods on the other side of the village," Shelby said, "to hide them."

"No," Melia said, "we will keep the cattle in sight on the hills, easily visible from the sea. The pirates will invade for the beef alone. That will be a greater enticement than anything."

"We have the beginning of a plan," said Shelby. "Hestia, let's huddle over here out of the way while I explain about pistons, gears, and pressure."

FIFTY-SIX

W eeks passed with no sign of seaborne pirates. Garanus stationed lookouts on the rib of stone, hidden behind blinds where they couldn't be seen from a boat at sea. Ditches were dug and lined with sharpened sticks, coverts were created from sea wrack and driftwood, shooting lanes cut through the dunes. At either end of the long beach, provisions were made for massing cavalry out of sight, including the piling of sand and transplanting of trees. In all, with the prophecy of the goddess helping them, Kratos's people were industrious and efficient. The trebuchets were in position and ranged, stacks of stones of various sizes arrayed about them. The water ballast that powered them was continually checked against leakage. And the crews were close by, each man knowing his part.

Hestia and Shelby made a simple piston from bronze, just a small one, and it was working. Getting the water boiler together, and the piping right, would take another week or two. It was just toy size, but it illustrated the principle, and Shelby was sure Hestia could adapt it to a larger size when necessary. His next plan was to teach her something about hydraulics, about applying force over a distance. Making pipe was not that easy, but if they could create enough pressure with the steam engine, then they could probably extrude softened copper for piping. He was hopeful. Certainly, the rapid hammering of a steam-driven mill could simplify all kinds of metal work.

Various preparations were made around the village as well and viewed with suspicion and misgiving by the villagers. They, in their turn, added more large, flat stones and turf to their conical stone huts. The doors into these huts were low to the ground and narrow, meaning they could only be invaded by a single crawling person. Anyone entering uninvited led with his exposed neck and head, at the mercy of an inhabitant's stone weapons. The heavy roofs of stacked stone could be defeated with enough effort, but only revenge would drive a marauder to such extremes. The villagers and their children were safe, as long as the invaders did not wait around too long and starve them out.

One curious thing Shelby observed was Alcestis wading out to sea. She seemed to really enjoy these excursions, and after her third trip to map the underwater sand dunes, she discovered dolphins. They nosed up to her as she waded, bumping her and playing with her. She giggled and called to them, gave them names, sang to them and tickled their chins. Then she dove underwater with them, rising sometimes astride one or another of them. Eventually, she could stand at the shore and call to them, and they would rise out of the deep, leaping and frolicking. She named them all, and recognized them when they stuck their heads above the water. Their smiling faces suggested that they recognized her, too, and perhaps they had named her as well. Shelby was awestruck by the girl's simple friendship with these wild creatures.

* * *

One day, a vessel with twenty oars to a side appeared around the headland in the north and came their way. It was larger than any they had seen, and its large sail and broad beam suggested that it was a coastal trader. Shelby and Kratos, alerted by their lookouts, watched it approach.

"Our enemy," Kratos muttered.

"Perhaps," Shelby whispered. "I think you are right. I believe this scoundrel will be the scout for others. How he is received and what he learns will determine how many pirates attack us."

"What do you suggest?" Kratos asked.

"I think we should negotiate with him, draw him and his witless brothers in. We might find the fleet we need to emigrate to our new lands."

"I like the way you think, brother," Kratos said. "Should Melia participate?"

"Of course. If he is like all the other Achaeans we know, he will not give much credit to a woman. By all means, let us have her meet him. She will likely confuse him, and possibly anger him. These emotions may serve our purpose."

"I do like the way you think," Kratos said.

They watched as the ship tacked toward them, veering from the pitiful village to their encampment on the hill, with its many tents and fertile herds.

"He seems to have a design," Kratos said quietly.

"Let us hope it is a design for his own destruction," Shelby said. "I will send to Melia to let her know that he approaches. Let us keep him on the seaward side of the dunes, so he will not see our preparations."

"Agreed," Kratos said.

* * *

Melia rode down to the shore in an oxcart driven by Dolios, her pregnant belly resting uneasily. She looked at Shelby and Kratos with a ferocity he had not seen. Her look suggested she was going to this effort out of duty and against her will. Eurymedon and Arktos accompanied her.

They waited on the beach for the pirate to come ashore. Out of sight behind them in the dunes were a hundred Meliae with crossbows. The trebuchets were already ranged behind their screens, and the cavalry had plenty of time to mass at either end of the beach, out of sight. The boat was shallow keeled and pulled close to the beach, just far enough to be afloat again without much effort, and the oars were planted into the beach on either side to prop it up.

"That answers that question," Shelby whispered to Kratos.

"We need to change our plans," Kratos whispered back. "More cavalry and hand-to-hand."

Shelby nodded.

A swarthy sailor dressed in pantaloons, with a shawl of linen thrown across his bare brown shoulders, hopped the four or five feet into the shallow surf and approached them. Shelby raised his hand. The sailor did the same. Melia fixed him with a glare and neither acknowledged his greeting nor returned it.

"Welcome," Kratos said in Achaean. "We are glad you are ashore."

Shelby observed that the sailors on the boat were all armed with spears and bows. They carried shields. He moved slightly closer to Melia, ready to shield her with his lion skin and his life.

"Who are you?" the stranger asked in a common Achaean dialect, smiling. The startling white of his teeth broke his deeply tanned face, with its wrinkled skin and twinkling eyes.

"We have come to this shore over the mountains," Melia said, "through the land of the wild men. Perhaps you have heard of the wild men."

"Yes," he said, "I have. Fearsome cannibals, mighty warriors. They are the terror of the world. How did you come through them?"

"With the power and might of the goddess," Melia said. "And the skill of our warriors."

"You must be remarkably strong," the sailor said.

"Not so much after our encounters," Melia said. "But now we are glad to meet you. We want to purchase passage across the sea to the Deer's Head Harbor. Do you know it?"

The sailor laughed. "Why of course I know it! All people who sail this sea know of that harbor. Why do you want to go there? The people are not friendly, and they resent newcomers."

"Because our destiny is to land there and to travel beyond them into and through the mountains behind them," Melia said.

"Ah," he said, rubbing his hands together. "And what is it worth to you?"

"Do you have anything to trade," she asked. "Wine? Grain? Cattle?"

"I have a few trinkets your people might like," he said. "But no wine or cattle."

"We have cattle, wine, and gold," she said. "We also have a large number of poor farmers. How many could you take in your boat?"

"That depends on what you are willing to pay," he said.

"I see," she said.

A few slaves came to the shore carrying baskets of freshly baked bread, wine skins, and meat from the sacrifice.

"Allow me to serve you some meat," Melia said to him, inviting him to sit on stools provided by the slaves. "Tell us your name and where you are from."

He was barefoot and dressed in baggy trousers that were cinched at the waist with a rope. His broad, white grin was friendly, but anyone looking at him could tell he was a dangerous man. He carried a dagger on a string under his left arm. He walked in a rolling fashion, his bare feet splayed and his legs moving as much side-to-side as they did forward.

"I was not aware meat could be had in this village," he replied with a nod of his head. "I accept your gracious offer."

"We drove our cattle over the mountains from our previous home," Melia said, "setting fires to protect them from the wild men. Possibly you saw the smoke of our passing?"

"You are a remarkable people if you came through their land. Reasonable people avoid them." He smiled and looked at the meat with evident appreciation. Melia served him and the others, and her attendants passed out freshly baked flat bread and poured goblets of wine.

"We had no choice," she said. "We were fighting an Achaean invasion when a volcano erupted and drove us away. We came to this shore, because this is the route we were forced to follow. Now we desire to go on to the west to settle north of the home of the god of fire, behind the Deer's Head Harbor. Now eat, stranger, and tell us your name and where you call home."

"Thank you, lady. My name is Oduze, and my home now is the island kingdom of Ithaca."

Shelby stared at the man for a moment, taking in his whole appearance, the heavy brow, the wind-blown black hair tinged with streaks where the sun had bleached it brown. What was it about the name that tugged at his memory? Something. He couldn't place it, but it was buried in there somewhere. Maybe if he slept on it, he would recall.

"I have seen much of the world," Oduze said, "and I've sailed past the house of the god of fire. I do not wish to return that way, past the Scylla and her whirling friend Charybdis. I have heard her dogs barking in her cave and deem myself lucky to have passed her without losing men and ship. You know you must sail closer to her than to Charybdis, for Charybdis hungers for ships and swallows them whole."

"We have no wish to encounter those demons," Shelby said. "We look for passage to the Deer's Head Harbor, or to the eastern coast of that country. We hope to land at or north of that harbor. Surely you know where that is."

"Oh, yes," Oduze said. "It's straight across the sea from Ithaca. Unless we encounter storms, we can make that journey in a day."

"Overnight?"

"Some people fear to sail at night," he said. "I do not. It depends on the night, of course, and on the winds, and on the time of day you weigh your anchor. In two months, the storms will begin to blow down from the north, and that is a time when wise mariners return to their homes and wait for spring."

"We wish to leave none of our people on this wretched shore," Melia said. "We have cattle and sheep and horses. One voyage in your ship cannot possibly move us all."

"I see," he said. Shelby watched his mind calculating the task.

"How many ships do you think you need?" Oduze asked.

"It depends on how much your vessel can carry at a time. It is hard for us to know the exact number, but many."

"The people of Deer Head's Harbor are grasping and mean. They will not accommodate you."

"Then we will invade," Eurymedon said. "Our patience wears thin, stranded here where the people have no goods to trade and only fish to eat."

Shelby looked at Eurymedon and shook his head imperceptibly. "We have planted crops that we will harvest in two months," he said to Oduze. "If you will undertake to carry some of us to Deer's Head, might you be willing to return in the spring with some fellow mariners to carry more of our people?"

"It goes without saying that these voyages are expensive," Oduze said. "I must pay my sailors, repair my boat, and purchase new sails and provisions. Sails are very expensive. We are constantly at risk of attack by pirates, which is why I prefer the open sea to the shore. Let me suggest that you stage your exodus by traveling first to my island, Ithaca. Then it is a short leg across the sea to Deer's Head. We could make the run and return every few days. Again, however, it is an expensive journey."

"What do you want for it?" Melia asked.

"I need one piece of gold for every horse or cow, one piece of gold for every three people. These prices are high, but for less than that I cannot do it."

"How much would you sell your ship for?" Shelby asked. "Thirty pieces of gold? You could buy another ship easily with that and have a handsome profit without having to spend months transporting us."

"Can you sail a ship?" Oduze asked.

"I do not pretend to be a mariner," Shelby replied. "I am merely curious. And no, I cannot, but I know people who can."

"I will sell you the ship for seventy-five pieces of gold."

"Too high," Shelby said. "For example, we could simply take it from you for much less, but that is not how we do business. Besides, I desire your cooperation and your skill, not your possessions. Let us return to your original offer."

"I offered to transport each horse or cow for one piece of gold and three people for one piece of gold."

"Is this sufficient as a piece of gold?" Shelby asked, producing one of the crudely stamped coins with the eagle on one side.

Oduze hefted it, bit it, looked at his teeth marks and handed it back. "Yes," he said. "This is what I mean by one piece of gold."

"We are not desperate," Melia said. "We can stay here a long time and build our own boats. We have fields, crops, cattle, and an army. We are self-sufficient. We can pay a reasonable sum for our transportation, but we would rather build our own boats and hire sailors than pay an exorbitant rate. Do we see eye-to-eye?"

"You must have a lot of people," he said.

"To make a bargain, both sides must give a little but not too much," she said. "Name a fair price, and we will drink to it. Otherwise, tell us a story, and we will drink to that. I believe the tide is going out, and your ship will be sitting on this shore until it turns again. Let us enjoy one another's company." She stood and raised her goblet, tipped a few drops onto the ground in honor of the gods, and tasted it. She then passed it to Oduze.

He rose to take the cup with both hands. "Lady," he said, "it will be a pleasure to do business with you. I see that my work for the coming year is clear. We can make three, possibly four voyages to Deer's Head before the storms. We can transport most of the rest of you to Ithaca to await the spring."

"We will stay here through the winter," she said. "Return on the spring equinox, and we will resume our transport. Our warriors, Eurymedon and Arktos," she nodded at the two standing nearby, "will travel with the first contingent of twenty armed men with three horses. Is that too many?"

"It will be tight," Oduze said. "The horses can be a problem if they fight the sailors or the ship."

"Our horses will not panic," Eurymedon said. "We have raised them from colts, slept alongside them, and fed them. Where we are, they are calm. Nevertheless, we may have trouble loading and unloading them. I assume you have considered that."

"We have a ramp for heavy cargo. Possibly they will walk up it. The ship is designed for human feet, however, not for hooves. Getting up to the ship is easier than getting them into it, and horses take up a lot of room. I am not sure one gold piece will be sufficient for each animal."

"Who said we were paying a gold piece for each animal?" Melia asked. "We have not agreed on a price yet."

"But those were the terms I cited," he said.

"Yes, that's true. Now I wish you to consider the charge for three horses and twenty armed men with supplies. The men can spell your sailors at the oars, if necessary."

"Twelve pieces of gold," he said. "Three," she said.

He laughed. She did not.

"By your own terms, it would be nine," she said.

"I will do it for nine," he said.

"No," she said. "I will offer you four pieces of gold."

"Eight," he said.

"Four pieces of gold, and a quarter of the steer I will offer at tonight's midnight sacrifice. Think about it until the tide changes, and if you do not find it acceptable, then we must seek elsewhere or make alternative plans." She stood. "Goodbye," she said, and turned to go.

"It has been a pleasure to meet you," Shelby said, standing and extending his hand.

"And you," Oduze said. "Is she the one who bargains for you?"

"She is," Shelby said.

"I may not to be able to do business with you," Oduze said.

"Why not?"

"The terms are too tough," he said.

"Have you bargained with a woman before?" Shelby asked.

"Not for commercial purposes."

"By your own statement, you can make a voyage to and from Deer's Head Harbor and unload cargo every three days. At the end of the first week, you will have eight pieces of gold and half a steer, plus whatever goods you can bring with you from Deer's Head. At the end of a month you will have thirty-two pieces of gold and all the cargo you could trade for from Deer's Head, plus the meat of two large steers. It is not such a bad deal for you. Also, it is likely to continue all summer and into the fall. We have a lot of people, and a lot of gold. In the next two sailing seasons you could make a hundred or more trips, which would also educate the Deer's Head residents to expect you and provide goods for you. It is a good deal for you, and profitable. You could easily have more than four hundred pieces of gold and the meat of a sizable herd of cattle."

"You have that much gold and cattle?"

"We do. And many horses. We are not destitute."

"But she is unreasonable. I can not work with her, no matter the terms."

"It is what it is," Shelby said. "Take it or leave it."

"I think I must leave it."

"Thank you," Shelby said, extending his hand again. "Good-bye."

Shelby and Kratos turned and followed Melia up the beach to the dunes, leaving Oduze to stand on the sand watching them and scratching his head.

FIFTY-SEVEN

🔥🔥🔥🔥🔥🔥🔥🔥🔥🔥

S helby watched the trader's ship back away from shore by oar stroke, then turn and head out to sea. Several hundred paces from land, it set part of its sail, which added the wind's thrust to the oars, and eventually it was cutting through blue sea and throwing up white spray. The draft of the vessel was shallow enough to clear the sandbar, so probably other vessels would do so likewise. The long, rakish hull, despite it's breadth, looked built for speed and he doubted that he had seen the last of it. Oduze would return, with friends, to see if they could take the gold and cattle by surprise. He was sure of it. And he was likewise sure they would come in the night, when they thought no one would be waiting for them.

He discussed his suspicions with Kratos, and they convened a small war council. Their bronze lamps could help signal an arrival, if scouts could spot the ships, but Arktos suggested that they might be moving with slow oars and no sails to catch the starlight. Based on their reading of the sky, they expected the tide and the moonlight to provide optimum opportunity for the pirates in four days. Probably after the moon set on the night of the fourth day.

They would be ready, with scouts posted on shore, in the village, atop the black rib of stone, and at more distant spots along the shore.

"Let's also give some thought to protecting our rear from surprise," Shelby said.

"I hope they try us from the rear," Kratos said. "That means they would need to travel overland through territory we know belongs to the wild men and the wolf."

"The wild men might not be waiting for them, though," Shelby said. "They weren't that night we went looking for them. We need our own guards."

The chiefs appointed Arktos to supervise the rear guard, and Eurymedon to supply and provision scouts. Kratos would organize the defense to respond quickly and quietly. Everything about the operation depended on stealth. No noise, no banging of plate armor or gear.

"Do you think the Meliae will be effective?" Kratos asked Shelby.

"This will be a test of them," Shelby admitted. "We underestimate them at our peril. However, it's best if we do not need to depend upon archery to cut down the raiders."

"I always prefer a swift sword through the neck," Kratos grinned, the veins of his forehead pumping up at the thought and his eyes taking on a wild gleam. "And then to drink wine from the skull that rode that neck. It is a most satisfying drink."

"All wine is satisfying to you, brother," laughed Shelby. "And it is time for wine now. Let's finish another wineskin or two tonight, so we can sober up tomorrow and prepare for battle. If we are successful, we will capture ships to carry us."

"They will leave crew and armed guards aboard the ships," said Arktos. "They never leave the ships untended. They want someone to keep the ship from floating away, so we will need to fight them in the surf, too. This will not be an easy fight."

"It will be a complex fight, in stages," Shelby said. "Eurymedon?"

"The cavalry will ride down the raiders as they come ashore then dash for the ships. Our archery should encourage their surrender. We will board from horseback, and if all the ships are the size of the one we saw, we will also be able to shoot down into the hull from horseback. Especially if we are standing on the horses at the time."

"Don't kill everyone," Shelby said. "We need some left alive to serve us with their skills. A few hangings, a few slow disembowelments, and most prisoners will be willing to work with us. They are not going to be particularly moral or righteous. We can expect them to betray their leaders."

"True," Kratos nodded. "True. Nobility does not go to sea with pirates."

"I want everyone to think through exactly what the scenarios are likely to be and make contingency plans. As for me, I will be preparing the Meliae."

The men laughed at that, as though any male could prepare females to do anything they didn't want to do. But Shelby, though he laughed, knew his was the harder task.

*   *   *

Shelby awoke the next morning listening to the hundred athletic females snoring and farting in the tented room with him and Melia. He lay on his back and stared at the taut linen overhead, taking in the vagaries of dawn color, imperceptibly changing from faint gray to lavender to pink. Hours earlier he had heard Calu's distant howl, and maybe the pup's too, but they were far away.

He had not heard those damned insane operatic jackals in weeks. Perhaps it was because of Calu.

He went outside to relieve himself and stretch in the early morning air. A good run would be nice, about six miles to work up an appetite. Then some calisthenics, maybe some training with the Meliae. He had to prepare them to be on guard perhaps for hours, to be deadly at shooting, and also to be deadly in hand-to-hand combat if that's what it came to. If the star shine was blocked by clouds and the sea was dark, they might not see their targets until they blocked the faint glow of low waves breaking white against the shore. It would be tricky, and even trickier for the cavalry. Eurymedon's boasting about the cavalry might be only that. He might not be able to see the ships either, even if nearly ashore. By the time he got his horses down the beach, the raiders could already be among the dunes. The trebuchets might be no use whatsoever.

But those worries could come later. He wanted to appreciate the stillness of the early morning, the shuffling of the animals and sleeping people.

He walked up the hill above the camp and watched the morning slowly assembling itself from the shadows and the sea. They did not have a way to illuminate the shore, did they? Well, maybe they did. How could they do it without scaring away the raiders? He needed to think about that. He needed to discuss it with Melia and Hestia. Maybe also with Dolios, that brilliant boy. Yes, he reasoned, it might work.

And then, what if some of the Meliae were cavorting on the beach nude? In front of a tall fire or two? Wineskins in full display.

Rhodia had done that before, and now she had a hundred Meliae to back her up instead of fifty.

Overkill? Too suspicious?

Yeah, he thought. *Probably.*

He strolled back to the tent, thinking he should speak with Melia about these concerns. Just voicing them aloud would be a good idea, would include her in the thinking. Knowing Melia, she already had ideas similar to his own, and she might have improvements.

He stuck his head through the tent flap and saw that everyone was still asleep. "Warriors awake!" he yelled. "Out! Now! Time for the morning run! On the double. Get out here!" It might take ten minutes, but they'd come, frumpy and pissed.

He already had his route planned. They'd run north toward the little thicket where Calu might have her den, then along the black rib down to the village, leaping across broken stone and gaps, then wading through the marsh into the village and back up the hill along the edge of the creek, then zig and zag across the hill to the shoreline, then zig and zag again back up to the tent. Afterwards, they'd have an hour of vigorous training among the dunes, and practice shooting at targets. They'd appreciate that. It'd get their blood stirring. Nothing like an easy little six- or seven-mile jog at dawn to prepare you for the day. Tonight, he would have them shooting again at lamps floating in the water. When all the lamps were out, he would set up logs in the surf as targets. Then they would charge the logs. It would be good training for the coming battle.

"Warriors! Out!" he shouted again, in his drill sergeant tone.

Melia raised herself up on one elbow, an unpleasant expression on her face, and looked at him standing in the tent flap. She waved the back of her hand at him and flopped back down on her back, pulling a linen sheet over her head.

"Khloe! Get these warriors out here!" he shouted. He dropped the flap and waited, arms crossed. The smell of baking flat bread drifted through camp, and for the thousandth time he wished he had a cup of coffee. It would be millennia before coffee was discovered by the Western world.

"What do you want?" Khloe sulked, sticking her frumpy head through the tent flap, yawning.

"Everybody's rested. We're going for a run."

"Not another of your famous runs."

"No more backtalk," he said. "Get everybody out here. I could have been a troop of wild men or pirates coming through that tent flap, and you'd all be dead now. This inattention and sluggishness needs to be corrected. This is not how warriors live when they are in the field."

"We're not in the field," Khloe retorted. "We're in a tent. We can run later."

"Get your asses out here and line up," he commanded, sounding like he was on the verge of losing his temper.

Finally, everyone was out, yawning, sleepy, unhappy. But after they had run a hundred yards or so they seemed happier. He kept the pace just fast enough to stir up their blood, to make them break a sweat. It was great joy to be moving, to have a force moving at his back, to feel the power of them all as they moved through the morning.

Khloe caught up with him. "Do we have to do this every morning?" she asked.

"Yes," he said, grinning.

"I'm going to see if Melia will send you away to explore the world," she said, and fell back to join the pack.

When they made it back to the tent an hour later, they were hot and dusty, but they had a sparkle in their eyes.

"Get water and food," he said, gesturing to tables of supplies stacked against the coming invasion, "then come back here. We have training to do."

"We have been training all along," grumped one of the Meliae called Praxidike.

"Then you can show me what you've been doing," he said. "I might like it."

"You won't be able to do it," she said.

"We'll see," he said, and she went off to join her sister warriors, untying her wet hair from her head.

"What are you doing now?" Melia asked when he came near.

She had her forearm across her eyes to block out the light.

"I took the Meliae out for a run, and now we are going to exercise," he said.

"Not in here you aren't," she said. "Leave me alone."

"Yes ma'am," he said, thinking he sounded like everyone else at yesterday's meeting. He went down on his knees, straddling her, and spread her arms apart. He kissed her.

"No, no!" she said, tossing her head from side to side. "Go away. At least wipe your filthy face if you're going to kiss me."

He wiped his face on the pillow and then kissed her, even as she sputtered in protest. The more she protested, the more he kissed. Finally, she put her arms around his neck and pulled him down.

"This is not easy, hero," she said gently in his ear. "This being a queen and a priestess and pregnant and dealing with all of this. And it's not easy for you, either. Thank you for bearing up."

Then she shoved him away. "Now leave me alone." She shut her eyes and turned her head away.

Outside he found the Meliae running circles around each other on their hands, dressed in their black exercise bikinis.

The exercise was great for strength and agility training. He'd wait until they'd finished showing off and then he'd lead them in exercises in slow movement and control.

"I bet you can't catch me," Khloe teased as she breezed by, laughing, her feet in the air.

"Five times around the big tent, all of you," he called. "Then I have new things to teach you. And afterward we will have target practice."

He smiled to see Alcestis running by on her hands like the others. She had been too skinny to do that just a few months ago, but now she had a lithe, strong body with shoulder muscles. A scar across the sole of her foot was the only reminder of their last battle with the wild men, and the injury no longer bothered her. She had run with them in the morning air, and he was confident she would be useful in the invasion. The fearless girl was steady and stronger in heart than body, and her body was strong. He was glad she had chosen to remain with them so far, and he hoped she would stay.

FIFTY-EIGHT

ignals started flashing from sentries near the headland at around midnight on the fourth day. "Large group of ships under sail." Later, the signals flashed from nearer the village. "Sails down on some ships. One group rows to village. Second group rows toward you." From the far end of the beach, a sentry signaled, "About ten ships on this end taking down sails, rowing toward our end of beach."

"Three groups," muttered Kratos to Shelby. "One for the village, one for the bottom of the beach, one to come straight on. Interesting strategy."

"We're ready for them," Shelby muttered back. He signaled acknowledgment to the sentries. He asked for a count of ships.

"All our fingers and toes twice," said the first sentry.

Damn, thought Shelby. He was going to be forced to teach these people to count. Still, all your fingers and toes twice was forty ships. There might be more, but not many more. It would be a nice haul if they captured them all. If they were all the size of the one Oduze landed, it meant as many as eight hundred pirates could be coming ashore. That was a lot of pirates. It would have taken remarkable skills in persuasion to recruit so many. Oduze must have had experience with invasions of this size before.

"Dolios, prepare for land invasion. Possibly a hundred," he signaled. Dolios immediately acknowledged. "Garanus, force headed toward your end of the beach. Expect about two hundred. Eurymedon, ride on my signal." Both acknowledged.

"Now we wait," he said to Kratos.

"Song of fire in my heart," the redheaded warrior replied, his gapped white teeth glinting in the faint starlight.

The pirates had chosen their night well. A hazy overcast obscured some of the sky, the tide was in, the moon had set early, an onshore breeze allowed them to drift to shore. In the end, Shelby and Kratos had discarded the idea of nude women dancing in front of bonfires on the beach. It would look too much like they were expected, like a welcoming party. Melia had already told them how they had come through the land of the wild men. Pirates might be ignorant, but they would respect that and shy away. Their whole strategy was to attack with surprise while their victims were asleep.

"They've lost surprise," he said.

Kratos nodded, testing his sword in its sheath. He looked around at his armed bodyguards with their spears, and nodded. The men were eager. The Meliae were in place among the dunes. Spearmen were lying down, ready to leap up.

Where was Alcestis? Shelby wondered. He had not seen her among the other Meliae.

Then like a ghost she appeared on the shore, alone, walking in her white chiton.

"Alcestis!" he whispered in alarm. He could not see the ships but they could easily be within sound of his voice. "Alcestis! What are you doing?"

She appeared not to hear him over the sound of the waves lapping against the shingle. Midway down the beach she turned to wade out into the night sea, singing her song. Out she went, right toward where the pirates would be landing, her white chiton spreading in the water around her waist, singing her clear song. Then the sea broke around her, and dark shapes rose to the surface.

She had called her dolphins.

From the woods behind the far dunes, the call of a wolf echoed over the land, and then another and another and another, yipping and howling from all directions.

"What's she doing?" Kratos demanded. "What's she doing?"

"I don't know," Shelby said. "She might spoil everything. The pirates might take fright and sail away."

In the dim light, they saw Alcestis suddenly rise from the sea, astride a dolphin whose tail splashed white and phosphorescent in the dark. They disappeared out to sea, Shelby certain that she would be lost to them forever.

Then the pirates appeared out of the dark, the darker shapes of their vessels blanking out the innocent white of the gently breaking waves. They drifted up to ground in the shallow water, planting their oars and jumping off. One by one they splashed down, speaking not a word.

Then the sea erupted behind them as large herds of dolphins splashed around them, knocking them down, battering them with their hard noses. One dolphin took out the steersman, leaping ten feet through the air and battering him overboard, where his body was tossed high in the air again and again. Alcestis rode through it all, singing her song, pointing here and there.

At the far end of the beach, Garanus signaled that pirates were ashore, and under attack by Eurymedon, who was heading their way.

With no clear shot, the Meliae aimed out to sea waiting for targets, but the dolphins were tearing up the shoreline, confusing the pirates, preventing them from re-boarding their ships. Finally, Shelby had enough and charged down toward the beach with his tomahawk, followed the others bellowing their war cries. They waded into the water, slashing at the dead bodies of pirates, and at those still struggling with broken limbs, trying to scramble away from the enraged dolphins. Hundreds of bodies rocked in the gentle waves, many face down.

Shelby found his way to the first boat and climbed aboard, hauling himself up hand over hand, his tomahawk in his teeth. He cleared the gunwale and stared into the ship. A dozen slaves chained to peeled logs that served as seats stared in horror at him. Behind them were three pirates with spears, who bellowed and came at him. The first was cut down by Rhodia, who had followed him into the surf with her crossbow. He avoided the spears of the other two and chopped an arm off. Rhodia used her father's sword to cut down the third. Two more Meliae boarded behind her, but the ship was secure.

On the beach, Eurymedon thundered up with his cavalry, riding out into the dolphin-frenzied sea to peer in the ships, shooting into some of them.

"Icarus," Khloe called from the dunes. "Icarus! Dolios needs help."

Eurymedon raised his head, made a few signals to his men, and took ten with him to ride down the beach toward the village. Kratos signaled Arktos in the rear to go to the village to help Dolios and resumed watching the battle, now almost over.

One ship remained untouched, none of its inhabitants having disembarked. It was grounded on the sand with the receding tide, where it would be at dawn with no water to float it.

Alcestis came wading up the beach, squeezing water from her long hair, which she tossed over her shoulder. She smoothed her chiton against her muscular young body, and approached Kratos, her chin held proudly.

"Well, that worked," she said to the burly warrior. "I wasn't sure the dolphins would do as I directed, but they have a long history of dealing with sharks. It was a simple matter of getting them to understand that the pirates were sharks to me."

Kratos just stared at her.

Finally he spoke. "What manner of being are you?" he asked. "Are you a goddess? You know, the law says you must tell me if I ask."

"Whose law?" she asked. "Not mine." And she winked at him.

FIFTY-NINE

"Sir!" The guard was alarmed.

"Sir, the signals say Dolios is besieged, in trouble."

"Didn't we send Arktos?" Kratos asked.

Alcestis glared at him and then disappeared at a run down the beach.

"Guards, to Dolios!" Kratos cried.

* * *

On the beach, Shelby called out to Oduze, who had remained on his ship. "I see you brought your friends, Oduze."

"These were not my friends," the wily seaman said. "They followed me."

"Of course they did. And why did they follow you in such numbers if you had not told them about the riches from a raid on us?"

"Ask them, my friend," Oduze smiled, looking down on him from the gunwale of the ship.

"I will ask those who survive, if any do," Shelby replied, turning to the contingent of armed soldiers standing by. "Throw a rope over the prow of that excuse for a ship and pull it above the high-water mark. Recruit help if you need it."

"Don't touch my ship," Oduze warned.

"Friend, you will stay with us for a bit. Perhaps a month. I do not expect you to last so long aboard without food and water, but if you try to leave then I will sink your ship." He signaled to the soldiers lining the top of the dunes. A guard turned toward the camp and shouted orders, and Shelby heard the reassuring zip and twang of a trebuchet launching a boulder in their direction. A loud buzz roared overhead, and a boulder landed with a resounding explosion of water in the sea behind Oduze .

"You see, friend, you are not safe aboard your ship. It is time for negotiation."

"What was that?" Oduze was amazed and frightened.

"Again," yelled Shelby.

The next boulder landed a little closer to the rear of the ship, rocking it with its wake and driving it farther up the shore.

"Men, toss the rope around the prow of that ship and pull it ashore," Shelby commanded. "Oduze, we will beach your ship now. If you resist, you and your men will be slaughtered. Surely you would prefer to discuss this predicament. If you wish to die instead, though, we can arrange that."

Rhodia, standing next to him in her wet battle dress, almost invisible in the early dawn, raised her crossbow.

"Just to the right of his right arm," said Shelby, "where the gunwale bends toward the back."

The bolt sank four inches into the oak plank with a loud thud, drawing Oduze's attention. He lowered his own bow and looked at Shelby and his vastly outnumbered force as two hundred warriors began pulling his ship higher on the sand.

"I believe you offered four pieces of gold to carry twenty men and three horses to Deer's Head Harbor," Oduze said, grinning. "I've come back to tell you I accept that offer. Under the circumstances, it appears advantageous and profitable to me."

"I'm glad you are ready to listen to reason," Shelby laughed. "But after this attack, we may need to renegotiate. I will let Melia know you have returned to accept her terms. We will see what she says, given the destruction you and your friends have brought us."

"Is it really necessary for me to talk to her?" Oduze asked. "She is not a reasonable person."

"You have come back to accept her terms," Shelby said. "I suggest you discuss a new deal with her, one that will allow you to survive and also be profitable. Of course, as you may notice in the brightening dawn, we now have a lot of ships of our own, and many of them still have most of their slave labor aboard."

"You yourself told me you cannot sail a ship," Oduze responded.

"And that was no lie. But I also told you that we know people who can. We may have no need of you at all, in which case I might consider whether to release you, or instead kill you now to save the world the trouble. But that depends on Melia, whose word is law among us."

Oduze's serious face showed his concern, but he made no response. He grabbed at a rope leading up to the mast to hold on as the ship jerked up the sandy shore.

* * *

Dolios and his small force had seen the pirates putting ashore at the foot of the village, and they were surprised by how many there were. They were greatly outnumbered, and he advised the men to remain hidden until they had shots at the crowd. But the pirates suspected something and hid themselves behind the conical stone huts, eventually figuring out where Dolios was. They maneuvered carefully, avoiding exposing themselves, seeking to move closer. Some of them crawled into the low openings to the huts, where they crouched looking out, their shields on their backs to protect from attack by those within. Once the signals went out, the archers on the black rib began to take aim at the shadows, but they could not tell who they were shooting at. All they saw were moving shadows in the predawn dark. Some of the shadows were men, some were not.

Then the cries of men attacking one another split the dark night, the clash of swords and the wails of the wounded. The pirates had flanked Dolios on the uphill side, and were driving his men toward the beach, where the pirates hidden among the huts could attack them by surprise. It was a desperate situation, and Dolios lost control of his panicked men, some of whom fled into the hardwood forest.

As dawn lightened the sky, it was clear to the archers that Dolios and his small remaining band were too far away to protect. Then Garanus topped the hill and rode down toward the huts. They were too far away, also, and Dolios looked finished before they could reach him.

Eurymedon came over the rib at full gallop, leaping his horses into the marshy ground on the other side, where they mired and stumbled. He rode his steed down to the ground, urged it back to its feet, and the others did likewise, though two horses had broken legs. Still, he reached the huts just as the pirates closed in on Dolios and caught them from behind.

It was not a sure thing, though. A few men on horseback could not turn the tide of a mob attack at Dolios's position, now circled on a small hill with ten or so remaining men. Then Eurymedon's horses shied away, screaming and bucking, disobeying their riders, struggling to get anywhere else.

The clear howl of a pack of wolves broke through the nightshades of the dense forest, hunting, approaching, on the trail of human blood and meat, frightening away the horses but also driving the pirates into a dense crowd. Men who had fled into the woods reappeared at a dead run, trying to get up to the hilltop to join Dolios and the others, and most made it.

Garanus approached at last, and Eurymedon corralled his horses when the wolves silently withdrew into the shadows, and the terrified pirates threw down their weapons.

Good, thought Dolios, some of these guys will know how to sail a ship. We will convert them to our side, with the help of the goddess, and then we will go on to the land where Icarus wants to lead us.

"Surrender or die," he shouted, saluting Garanus, who circled behind the pirate band. "Put down your weapons, or you will not live to see the sun."

The pirates looked around, and most bent down to place their swords and shields on the damp ground. A few did not, and after Garanus and his men killed three of them, they all dropped their weapons.

Cries from the village distracted Dolios, who shouted at Garanus to round up the pirates. He took off down the hill, reaching the first conical hut. When he realized that the low openings led into a pitch-black interior, he got to his knees and crawled in. About four feet into the tunnel, his hand came to rest on a human leg. No response, so he tugged at it. No response again.

"Somebody pull on my legs!" he shouted. "We've got a corpse here."

Some of the men dragged him out as he grasped firmly the legs of a dead pirate. "Ah," he said, "the others may meet with a similar fate. Let's search these huts until we are sure the residents are safe. We will need them to help us sail."

Several other dead pirates were discovered, all with broken skulls. But in one hut, Dolios found no one. He heard whimpering from the interior, and a rough voice whispering harshly in Achaean. "Shut up!" it whispered. "Shut up or I will strangle you."

Dolios withdrew to discuss with his men, pointing at the smoke hole on the top of the cone. The only way in was through that, or through the tunnel.

"Some of you go up there and start removing the stones. We may be able to get enough light to shoot down. I think I will try going forward again. If I die, pull me out and take my body to Icarus."

Before they could stop him, he was in the tunnel and crawling forward, leading with his spear, his shield on his back.

He could see nothing ahead of him but a somewhat darker square at the end. No light penetrated the hut's floor, or none he perceived. Perhaps it would be different when he was actually inside, perhaps some kind of glow from the graying dawn sky would show him what he was facing. Then his hand brushed the edge of the tunnel, and he was there. Behind him he felt more than heard the shuffling of other men following him, heard their breathing, the soft rasping of their spears along the ground. Ahead of him he heard groans.

Now what? he wondered.

He paused to listen and heard shuffling ahead and to the left, not close. Someone's feet moving. He also heard groans and then the raspy breath of a large body, which he assumed was male.

He eased ahead slowly, gathered his legs to jump, and then exploded into the hut, rolling and flinging himself to the right, away from the sound. He bumped into a low stone curb of some kind and came to a stop. On the side of his face he felt the heat of fire recently covered with dirt, and he saw the glow of red coals through a small opening.

"What was that?" exclaimed a voice. "I swear, I'll kill this child if you make a move."

Dolios did not move, but he did not answer, either.

"Where are you Oeneus, you drunken bastard?" the voice exclaimed. "Dead? Or dead drunk? Did they kill you?"

As his eyes adjusted to the interior of the hut, Dolios saw a darker shape moving against the far wall, obviously dragging something. The child, he assumed. He could hear from breathing along the wall that others were inside, and something stirred nearby. He rolled away, not wanting to be clobbered, but his movement alarmed the figure across the way.

"Who's there?" the voice said again. "You won't get me."

Dolios slowly rose to his feet, holding his spear out level with both hands.

"What's your name?" Dolios asked. "I don't like to kill someone whose name I don't know."

"You won't kill me," the voice replied. "I've got the child. If you come for me, you'll kill the child, and then I'll kill you."

"Look up," Dolios replied. "Hear that shuffling and grinding overhead? Those are my men removing the stones. In a moment, they will have arrows aimed at your head, and enough light to see you by. The tunnel is full of my other men. You are trapped. Surrender and your life will be spared. Try to fight, and you die."

"I'll take this child with me, then," the pirate exclaimed.

"So?" Dolios asked. "What's that to me?"

"Well, we'll see then, won't we!" shouted the pirate, hurling the child across the room in the direction of Dolios.

Dolios anticipated his action before he heard the words, but the child's foot caught the covered fire as it stumbled across, sending up a blaze of sparks illuminating the interior to show a large, swarthy man with full beard holding a sword and a dented shield.

Dolios jumped sideways to avoid the child, a boy of nine or ten, and watched the pirate.

"Why you're a child yourself!" laughed the pirate. "You think you can kill me? I'll suck wine from your skull before the sun goes down today." He charged.

Dolios anticipated that, too, and sidestepped again, causing the pirate to change course. He lost his footing on another stone curb and bumped his head into the incurving cone of the hut's roof. Dolios's spear caught him on the thigh and made a nasty gash, but it wasn't fatal.

The pirate recovered and charged again, his sword overhead, and Dolios dodged toward the wall. The pirate swung hard at him, but the blade caught the rocks of the roof and Dolios rolled away again, coming up behind the man.

Now in the center of the room, Dolios had freedom to maneuver around the low fire, and the pirate had room to swing, and it was spear against sword. The pirate was breathing heavily. Dolios was beginning to enjoy the fight, feeling not the least bit afraid. If Alcestis could not love him, then what was he living for? The outcome of the fight didn't matter because he had nothing to lose.

"Tell me your name!" he screamed at the pirate, "before I kill you!"

The man rushed him again, trying to pin him against the wall of the hut, and Dolios thrust his spear at him. The pirate's shield blunted the thrust, and Dolios leaped past the shield into the center of the room again. The spear's length prevented him from getting it around fast enough to thrust at the man's back, and the pirate wheeled easily to follow him, breathing hard.

"What's your name?" Dolios teased in a sing-song voice, avoiding a renewed rush.

"Your na-a-a-me?" he sang again and the pirate once more failed to catch him.

And then the pirate stopped to catch his breath, his mouth open.

"What's your name?" Dolios asked calmly, not even breathing heavily while the pirate's gasps filled the hut.

"Why?" the man wheezed.

"My name is Dolios. Now you can tell the shades of the underworld who killed you. It's only polite."

"I see him," one of the guards said from the now widened smoke hole overhead. "Dolios, shall I kill him?"

"Oh no," Dolios called back, "I'm enjoying this. Don't kill him yet."

The pirate glared at the faces crowded around the smoke hole, saw the arrows aimed at him, and then turned back to Dolios.

"My name is Clymenus," he wheezed, "and you're dead."

The pirate leapt at him, slashing with his sword. Dolios turned the blow on the shaft of his spear, which he dropped just as the blade struck it, forcing the pirate to overpower the swing and stumble sideways. Before he could recover, Dolios had buried his dagger into the man's diaphragm and ripped upwards into his heart. The pirate was dead even as his body rotated to the floor, gushing blood, where the twitching corpse was instantly impaled with six arrows from above.

In the light from the smoke hole Dolios saw a prostrate form on the floor next to the tunnel, one leg beginning to stir. Over it stood an old man with a stone hammer, and behind the man stood an old woman clutching a knife. The boy was crouched across the room on something that looked like a bed, huddled silently in panic with a young woman and a smaller child. Dolios nodded at them.

"Some of you men out there," he called into the tunnel. "Come in here and help drag out this trash. One of them is still alive. Let's get these people back to their homes and lives."

Soldiers shuffled into the hut, crowding it, silently awed by the pirate dead in the center of the room, one hand smoking in the low fire. They glanced at Dolios with evident respect, comparing the relative sizes, nodding, looking knowingly at one another. Dolios stood off to the side, one hand raised against the inward slanting roof to steady himself, and said nothing, his face immobile, panting, ashen.

He felt a hundred years old.

SIXTY

D olios remained motionless in the hut while the bodies were
dragged out. Now fully dawn, the light streamed into the
hut through the opening overhead, revealing the interior.
On the unevenly paved floor were pools of blood and signs of
scuffle. He went over to the entrance tunnel and bent to shout
out, "Hey, some of you come back in here and clean this mess up!
Bring water."

Then he went over to the boy and kneeled, looking at him.

"Are you hurt?" he asked, reaching for the boy's feet. He
thought they might be burned, but they weren't.

"And what about you?" he asked the young woman, who
might be the mother. Her face was lined and thin, with high cheekbones and stringy hair. He reached his hand across to her, brushing hair away from her eyes, only then noticing that his hand was
glossy with pirate blood. He took it away. "Are you alright?" he
asked again.

She nodded, and grabbed him by the wrist with both hands,
holding him, tears welling from her eyes. She couldn't speak, but
she nodded again, trying to express her thanks. The little girl hiding behind her against the wall peeked out and stared at him with
big round eyes, expressionless.

"Good," he said. "Let me know if you need anything."

Men came in with water and some rags ripped from dead
pirates and scrubbed the floor. It was so dirty that not much progress was made, but at least the pool of blood was mopped up and
most of the stain erased. Dolios watched until they were through

and then went over to the old man on the other side of the tunnel.

The almost toothless gray-headed man went down on his knees and lifted his eyes to Dolios, and his hands, grasping him by the forearms and shaking them. The old woman bowed her head and said, "Thank you stranger. My husband and my family thank you. We cannot repay you but we thank you."

"I seek justice, not profit," Dolios said. "I have been repaid by the goddess." And with that, he ducked out through the tunnel and emerged into the fiery dawn of a new day.

* * *

Oduze was not enthusiastic to see the dawn spreading over the shore and sea. The raid had been an utter failure, and a complete disaster for him. He was clearly not in command of his ship any longer, despite being on it. All he had left in the world was his ability to deceive, which had helped get him out of many tight spots before. He would wait and see what opportunities arose. If these people thought they could sail ships on the open sea without an experienced mariner, they would all drown. That would be a waste of good ships, of course, but it would not be his skin.

And if they thought they could pressure him into sailing to Deer's Head Harbor, why he would just sail them directly into some cove where his vast network of pirate brethren would make short work of them. How would they know until it was too late? Two days at sea out of sight of land and then landfall. He could tell them they were anywhere. Such a plan might work.

He would think about it as he watched the camp on the hill slope, with its green fields and its many cattle grazing in the distance. If they had truly arrived only a month or so ago, they had accomplished much.

But they had not conquered the sea. The eternal sea remained, and they would need him.

* * *

Shelby topped the dunes and looked down at the beached ship, all its mariners sitting in the hull and Oduze pacing in the back. When the soldiers started pulling the ship up the beach, Oduze had unshifted the steering board to keep it from harm, and it was lying across the gunwales at the back. He heard Oduze shouting orders to the mariners, who looked up sulkily, and then casually got up from the deck and went over to untie the ropes bundling the sail to its beams. Shelby assumed that Oduze would occupy them in repairing and restitching the sail. He wondered what it was made of. Wool? It didn't look like cotton or linen. Besides, he reckoned that cotton had not arrived in this part of the world yet. But maybe. Perhaps it was already being cultivated in Egypt. He had not seen any of the fabric among Melia's people, however, so it was probably unknown to them. With their vast stores of flax to make linen, they had not needed it, but now that those rich fields were buried in fire, they needed a new source of cheap fabric. When time served, he would send Eurymedon and Dolios to Egypt to explore.

He half-expected all the ships to be made of reed bundles, but they weren't. They were wooden planks. He wondered where they learned to make wooden-planked ships. The Phoenicians? Were they already active in this era?

He stood for a time gazing down at Oduze and wondering about what would happen next. Melia expressed no hope for dealing with the pirate, but she suggested they wait before executing him. They had his ship intact, after all, and the longer they let him sit on it, who knew? Maybe something would work out. Nobody thought he could be trusted, but with the astrolabe his course could be tracked if Melia decided they would let him transport them. The villagers since Dolios's exceptional performance had all come forward to offer help with the boats, and some of them had sailed in larger vessels. Not all the pirates had been executed, and once they saw the Meliae castrating their dead comrades most of them had expressed a willingness to cooperate.

All in all, things were looking up. In a bit, Hestia would join him on the dunes and together they would inspect the ships. Her beautiful, analytical mind would take in every detail, he was sure, and by day's end she would be contriving ways to improve these vessels.

SIXTY-ONE

B etween carrying meat to Calu and now fish to the dolphin she named "Kymangelos"—wave angel—Alcestis had little time to worry about Dolios. But she did. Part of her feared that her connection with the animals would diminish if she opened her heart to him. Part of her feared that she was hurting him by not doing so. She wanted to be friends with him, but he had become so moody and withdrawn since he gave her Melia's offer. And she still didn't know what that meant. What would happen if she accepted it? Would she lose everything because she was free? Would he expect repayment from her? Did it obligate her to him? Could she give it back? It was so complicated.

And now he seemed to be avoiding her. He was her only friend, after all, not counting old Kratos. Kratos liked her once she had called the dolphins. But with Kratos it was always about power. She had the power to befriend a wolf, and now the power to befriend the dolphins, and he did not have either. He admired her, and his admiration had led to long gazes at her as she came and went. He thought she was a goddess! How silly. He'd seen her foot hurt. Her scarred face was obvious to everyone. Had he forgotten about that? Goddesses don't get cut feet or scratched faces.

Talk about dangerous! Kratos was a blunt package of power and danger. He could do anything he wanted, and no one could stop him. He was far more dangerous than the wolf had ever been. And far harder to look into. With the wolf and the dolphin, the friendship was communal, based on food. But with Kratos? What did he want? At least he kept his hands off of her, unlike some of the others who now, for some reason, found her attractive. How did that happen? Silly males.

She spied Dolios at the irrigation pond, directing a group of workers who were diverting a stream into another part of the field. She headed that way, but he saw her coming and strolled off in the opposite direction. When she finally caught up with him, he was explaining to another group of workers about creating a second pond to pump water uphill to the cattle. She stood around and listened for a while, not wanting to interrupt him but losing patience. Finally she realized he was repeating himself to the workers, who were all nodding and grinning, but occasionally cutting their eyes at her.

"Come with me," she said, taking him by the arm. "We need to talk."

"I'm busy," he said, trying to pull away.

"They know what to do. I'll let you come back before they can get into trouble."

"Go with the girl," said one of the elderly workers. "We can do this. If we have questions, we'll wait for you."

"You understand about the catchment pond?" Dolios asked them, still trying to shrug back.

"Go, go," shooed the old man. "Go on. It will be all right when you return."

"Let's go," she said, tugging him toward the top of the hill, near where the grass was deep and the cattle grazed with contentment or settled on their fattening bellies to chew their cud while looking placidly out to the blue sea.

"What?" he sulked. "What do you want with me?"

"Just come," she said.

She hoped she could say all that she needed to say without breaking into tears. "Come on," she urged, tugging at him.

After a bit they came to a grassy spot chaperoned by the gentle cattle, who moved slowly off to another patch.

"Sit," she commanded, pointing to the ground.

"What if I don't want to?" he pouted.

"Honestly, Dolios, you are the most infuriating human. Sit down or I will throw you down."

"You?" he mocked. "You think you can throw me down?"

"Yes! And break your neck and castrate you before you can

draw a breath. Now sit."

He stood staring at her for a moment. "Try it," he said quietly.

She launched herself at him, hitting him hard in the chest with her body weight, twisting her arms around his neck and pulling him to the ground. She rolled over on top of him, panting, drawing her dagger. He grabbed her arm to hold the knife away, then rolled again, using his superior weight to break her hold, but she wiggled out from under him and got the dagger against his neck from behind. He grabbed her knife hand and pulled her forward over his head, holding her hand into the ground and staring down at her.

"Well, I didn't want to castrate you anyway," she grunted. "Let me up."

"Why?" he asked.

"Because I'm telling you to."

She was breathing heavy into his face, and he drew back a little. Not much, because he liked smelling her breath, something about it stirred him, made him want to hold her down more. But he drew back a little to focus on her, and that's when she snapped her body up into the air and came down astraddle him on his back, forcing him with an oomph into the grass.

Now on top, she grabbed his head and pulled back, exposing his neck. She drove the knife blade into the ground to get it out of the way, and held his head for a bit, her body astraddle his upper back, pinning his arms.

"Are you going to kill me?" he asked.

"No."

"Why not? You might as well."

"What are you talking about?"

Dolios began sobbing. "Because you don't love me."

She released his hair. "You big dumb ox," she said, and cuffed his ear. "Come on, sit up."

She pulled him up into a sitting position and sat next to him, both of them looking at the horizon over the sea, waiting to calm down.

"That was silly, you know," she said.

"What?"

"All of it. Daring me to fight, for one. I've been training with the Meliae for months and months. I can do everything they can do, even the hand-to-hand stuff. Sometimes I spar with Rhodia. Didn't you know?"

"No," he said, "but it doesn't matter."

"And the other thing that was silly was that business about me not loving you. You utterly blind, egotistical, self-absorbed boy! How could you even think that? Who followed you when you were kidnapped by the wild men? Huh? Who?"

He swallowed.

"You," he said finally, wiping the tears from his eyes.

"Right. And I had to persuade that wolf to work with me, which was no easy thing. She absolutely despises to be anywhere the wild men are."

"How'd you do that?" he asked, looking at her.

"It wasn't easy, and I don't know. Maybe I spoke wolf language in her brain. I just know it took a while, and in the meantime I was trying to keep up with those wild men who were running away with you."

"Oh look!" she exclaimed gently, "An imperial eagle. What a beautiful bird! Look at those big wings! I wish I had wings like that."

"So you could fly away?" he asked, his tone edging toward resentment.

"No, silly, so I could fly and see everything. How difficult you are being."

"Not on purpose," he said.

She took his hand and squeezed it. "Okay," she sighed. "Now is the time. I have some things to say to you, and I don't want you take them the wrong way."

"What?" He had turned sulky again.

"First," she said, standing up, "thank you so much for offering me Melia's reward and asking for my freedom. That was the sort of gesture only a really great person could make. You're rather a boy still, but that kind of thing is brighter than gold. You were so, so dear to do that." She knelt in the grass in front of him, to look him in the eyes, just inches away. "Thank you so much. I mean it."

He could hear the implied "but" in her tone. He knew she had more to say.

"And I love you even more for doing it," she added a moment later. "I don't know what love means, but I think it means that I want to always be with you even if we must fight sometimes. I loved you before that, but I loved you even more afterward, if that's possible. Do you understand?"

"No," he said.

"I didn't think you would," she replied. "Of course I love you, you idiot. And when I found out that you had gone into that fisherman's hut after that pirate, alone, with no one to help, and just you against him, I was so angry I was ready to blow up. What if you'd gotten hurt? What if he'd killed you? You have no idea how upset I was."

"It worked out," he said, his emotions hammering at him again and tears seeking a way out of his eyes.

She stood up again.

"It worked out this time. And it was a battle worthy of a true warrior. But you have not been training as a warrior the way I have. You don't have the skill or the strength. At least start training!"

She walked up and down for a minute. Dolios watched her feet lifting, catching glimpses of the scar where she'd been cut, then he watched the pieces of grass clinging to her knees. Her legs were strong and tanned, and so smooth.

She came back and knelt down in front of him.

"So," she said, taking his face in her hands. "Get this into your brain. I love you, I think. I mean, as far as I know. And thank you for the gift. But I want to give it back to you because I don't want something given to me that would change everything. Do you understand?"

She held his gaze.

"Understand?" she asked again.

Dolios's brain had shut off at "I love you," and no longer was engaged. He shook his head slightly.

"I am going to go to Melia and tell her that you and I have talked, and that I have decided to give you back your gift. There, I've said it."

He nodded, his eyes fixed on hers.

"I think we have had enough disruption," she continued. "I don't need any more. Earthquake, murder, volcano, wild men, pirates. Enough. I just want to have some peace with masters I love and food and important things to do. That's all I want. I've thought and thought about it, and that's what I want. I can't accept your gift and keep all that."

She leaned closer to him, breathing on his mouth.

"Questions?" she asked. She could feel his body heat, smell him. She leaned a little closer.

"I love you, too," he finally squeaked, putting his arms around her and pulling her closer.

"I know," she whispered in his ear, falling into him and pushing him backward onto the soft grass.

Overhead, a soft thump and muffled shriek were followed by a gentle shower of dove feathers. The imperial eagle soared away, a helpless bird in its talons.

SIXTY-TWO

"Y ou know the rules, Shelby. Exile or execute. If an exile returns, it's automatic execution. Why is this not easy for you to understand?"

"I thought we might get something of value out of him."

"No. That's not how it works. Exile or execution. Those are your choices."

"But he might have knowledge we need."

"No. He is a wolf and a pirate and a liar and a murderer. He has nothing of value to offer us."

"We are supposed to learn how to sail and navigate and get to our new homeland, and none of us has sailed a boat before?"

"You're missing the point. Prisoners are a waste of resources. Children can be corrected and changed. Grown men are better off dead. We are better off without them. Exile or execution."

"You don't think some men can be educated, changed, made more useful to society?"

"Who are you kidding? Grown men will lie, pretend, do anything they can to confuse the issue. But the issue is, are our women and children safe around him? No, they're not safe. Would you really entrust me or any of us to his care? If you don't trust him to care for me and our unborn child, then you don't trust him. If you don't trust him, then it's exile or execution."

"Give me some time to think about it."

"You've got three days. Then we will execute him. He might be as smart and talented as a god, but if he can't be trusted with women and children, then we castrate him and kill him. Period.

No more wasting of resources."

"Am I the one making this decision?" Shelby pouted, unhappy.

"I have announced my decision," Melia said. "If you can exile him safely, and you think he has a future in the world, then do so. Otherwise, kill him. That's it. Frankly, I prefer that you kill him."

"What about his men?"

"Those idiots? Well, maybe they can be useful as slaves, but I doubt it. I will give you three days to decide about the men, also."

She took his face between her hands. "The goddess says that she doesn't care whether they live or die, but she does care about us. We are to protect ourselves, Shelby. You are to protect us. Do your job."

He closed his eyes. He did not like this assignment, but he saw the wisdom of it. He could not envision himself carrying it out. It was a hateful and despicable task on the outside, but wise on the inside.

"Okay," he finally muttered, "I'll do what I need to do."

"Remember it's about the women and children. Whatever is best for women and children."

She patted his cheek, staring deeply into the distant firelight of his brain that reflected back at her from the blackness of his pupils. "I know it's not easy, but he's not a hero," she added. "He's a scoundrel and a pirate and a liar."

"You're right about that."

In three days, he would find a way to get the lying pirate away from the camp, and away from the women and children. He needed to be sure that whatever solution he came up with would keep him away for good. He could do that. He'd talk to Eurymedon. Maybe he had found a place where they could drop off the wily bastard. The best thing would be to drop him off way out at sea, on a raft.

If he was going to exile Oduze, he needed to make sure it was an exile. Otherwise, Oduze would return to reclaim his ship. He had his homework cut out for him. He needed to know about the prevailing winds, the tides, the currents—one that would carry Oduze far away.

Or he needed to slit the bastard's throat.

SIXTY-THREE

❦❦❦❦❦❦❦❦❦❦❦

"It was a long ride through the woods and over broken ground. We found water, but no food, and the men are terrified of Alcestis's wolf. Again." Eurymedon spat with disgust. "They are afraid of a tame wolf."

"I'm not sure a wolf is ever tame." Shelby shook his head, his brow furrowed. "Do you think we could carry him on horseback to a distant shore and put him adrift?" He had two days to get rid of Oduze.

"I know of a shoreline along the bottom of a cliff."

"How far down?"

"Ten or fifteen paces, at the shallowest. It would be hard to climb back up."

"What if we also threw down some wood for a raft, some rope to hold the raft together, and a little food and water? That way, he could possibly save himself."

"And a fishhook and some line. Then he might survive. If he doesn't break his neck in the fall."

"How many men do you think we need?"

"About twenty, with some spare horses and supplies."

"Today?"

"Sure. Why not? Should I bring Rhodia and some Meliae?"

"That's an excellent idea. Let me think." Shelby looked off at the distant cloud tops piling up over the land of the wild men.

"He's a tricky devil," Shelby finally said. "He will talk his way out of it if he can. You can tie his hands behind his back, but you can't tie his mouth shut, and his mouth is more dangerous than his hands."

"Do you think he would influence the Meliae?"

"I think they would be amused by him, but I don't think they would be convinced. They think of him the way Melia does. He's dangerous."

"Well, that's why I suggested taking some of them. But why do you care whether he survives?"

"I know his name from somewhere. I've been trying to remember where, but my instinct tells me he will become a famous and important person, though his devious nature will not change. I wish I could remember." He trailed off.

Shelby and Eurymedon had been walking through the camp and found Kratos staring at the beached pirate ships.

"What gives, brother?" Shelby asked.

"Ah, there you two are. I'm thinking about that scoundrel Oduze. Melia said you'd make a decision about him today."

"Yes. Exile," Shelby said. "I don't know why I want to keep him alive. Let's go talk to him."

"I'll bring my sword," Kratos said. "This problem might be more easily dealt with quickly."

"And some guards," said Shelby. "We are going to take his men off the ship. Eurymedon, send a messenger to prepare your escort."

They passed the loaded trebuchets, which were crawling with workers. A slave on a ladder inspected the water tank level that served as balance, and another was re-greasing the fulcrum. Like all big machines, the trebuchets required careful attention and maintenance, even when not active.

"Hestia, how is it going?" Shelby waved his hand. In the shade under a cloth, Hestia and Dolios were studying a ship model.

"Dolios has become a genius." She laughed. "Something has happened to him since he killed that pirate."

Everybody knew what had happened to him. They joined in the laughter. Even the busy slaves giggled. Dolios blushed.

"Well, so much for our last virgin slave," grumped Kratos. His broad gap-toothed smile broke out through his red beard.

"Not our last," laughed Eurymedon. "Our only."

"We are going to talk to Oduze, Hestia. Would you like to examine his ship?" Shelby nodded toward the shore.

"I've seen a lot of it," she replied, "but yes. Young man, come along," she said to Dolios. "And bring that model."

"I think we will take everyone off the ship," Shelby said. "Then we will separate Oduze from his men. But first we will feed them."

"Why waste food on them?" Kratos asked. "Are we going to keep them?"

"That might actually be best answered by Hestia," Shelby replied. "If she sees some value in them, they live. But we can't have them mingling with our people. We'll keep them separate, as we've done with the other pirates we captured."

"How many of them are still alive?" Hestia asked.

"We have about forty healthy ones and another six or seven who should heal. The village people are taking care of them."

"Clothed?"

"No, we took away all their clothing. It's warm enough now for them to get into the seawater every day, and that's helping with their smell. Dolios? Did you build a freshwater pond for them to rinse off in?"

"Our workers are doing that," replied the young man.

"The ones who want to work with us will continue to be fed. The others will be fish bait, I guess." Shelby mused for a moment. "Even so, we will need to put collars on them. Hestia, do we have the bronze to make enough neck collars?"

"I think so, but if not I can beat down some of their swords. It might be better to use copper instead of bronze, though. That seems to work better on lice and such. Fleas." She spat. "Keeping them bathed every day will help also, but most of them can't swim. If they go out unsupervised, they will drown."

"No great loss," Kratos said.

"Has Alcestis seen her dolphins recently?" Shelby asked. "I'd hate for those pirates to pollute the water so much that the dolphins abandon us."

"I haven't seen them," Kratos said, "but I haven't really been watching either. I think they prefer to play and have fun, or so it appears, so novel things probably interest them for a while. They are beautiful creatures."

"Yes, yes they are," Shelby agreed.

SIXTY-FOUR

🔥🔥🔥🔥🔥🔥🔥🔥🔥🔥🔥🔥

T he dune was high enough to hide the trebuchet works, but it didn't take Shelby and the others long to scramble over it. Along the beach in front of it were about a hundred soldiers, lounging in what shade they could construct and preventing Oduze and his sailors from leaving their beached vessel. Small campfires sent up their incense, and butterflies danced in the noonday light along the flowering grasses. The dunes were sprinkled with little white flowers and bright poppies. Some of the soldiers were lounging on their spears near the ship, chatting with the trapped sailors. Others had fishing lines running out into the lapping surf, and some were bathing in the water. But the sailors were trapped aboard, sweaty, dirty, and thirsty.

"Oduze!" Shelby shouted. "Let's talk."

The pirate captain appeared above the gunwale, bare chested and deeply tanned. "I'm listening," he growled.

"Come down here. You and all your men get off the ship now."

"No."

"Oduze?" Hestia asked. "Is that you?"

"Who are you, old woman?"

"I knew your mother in Crete. There's only one Oduze in the world. You were the child of Anticlea, grand-daughter, some thought, of Hermes, the trickster god."

"I don't remember you," Oduze said suspiciously.

"Nor do you remember your mother," Hestia replied. She turned to Kratos. "He abandoned his mother on Crete and never returned to her. I heard her weeping the last time I visited our families. Her grief may already have killed her."

"Do you think any of his sailors can be useful to you?" Kratos asked, cinching his sword belt a notch tighter around his middle, storm clouds rising in his face. "Obviously we have no room in the world for a man who abandons his mother."

"Oduze," Shelby said, raising his voice. "If you wish to live, you will come off that boat. Otherwise, we will come and get you, and tonight the crabs will feed on what is left of your body. All the rest of you, you must come off. We have some wine and food on the beach for you, even if your captain would rather have you starve. No harm will come to you if you obey us. Or, if you prefer, we can imprison you on your boat without food and water and watch you starve to death. It's your choice."

Shelby pointed at the slaves arriving with platters and wine-skins.

"Where's that bitch queen of yours?" Oduze taunted.

"Out of range of your abuse," Shelby replied. "But you are not out of range of my revenge. Come off the boat and remain alive, or stay and die. This is the last chance."

Oduze's sailors stared at one another, and some swallowed, their Adam's apples heaving in their throats. One by one, they moved away from Oduze and hopped off the ship into the sand while their leader glared, his arms folded across his chest.

"Good riddance," he spat out. "You traitors."

"Now you," Shelby said, his voice edged with ice.

Oduze disappeared beneath the gunwale.

"We could burn him," Eurymedon said, loud enough to be heard. "You there, bring fire."

Shelby looked at Kratos. Kratos grinned back at him. "This could be fun."

"If both of us go for him, maybe we can keep him alive," Shelby suggested.

"Nah. Who cares?" snorted Kratos.

Shelby leaned over and whispered in Kratos's ear. The burly warrior nodded.

"Don't hurt the mast," Hestia said. "I want to study how it's mounted to the boat."

"And the ropes and things," Dolios added. "We need to study those, too."

"Dolios, do you want to go alone to get him?" Shelby asked.

"Certainly, if you want me to. He can't be that hard."

"Hestia, keep this young man out of trouble if you can," Shelby grinned. He nodded at Kratos and the two warriors sprinted to opposite sides of the ship. Together, they vaulted into the boat, with Kratos yelling "There, in the rear!" and turning a double flip in midair. Shelby vaulted over the gunwale and landed with two feet on a bundle of cloth, which yelped.

"Got him," he shouted.

He knelt on the struggling body, watching for hidden weapons, subduing him under the heavy woolen cloth of a spare sail. Kratos joined him.

"Ready?" Kratos asked, lifting one side of the sail.

"Ready!" Shelby said, leaping up and to the other side. The body stopped struggling.

With a nod between them, Kratos and Shelby heaved the sail and saw a pair of legs swiftly disappearing from sight, under more cargo. Tangles of rope and boxes supporting amphorae full of grain and oil provided a perfect hiding place. Shelby threw himself after the legs, and managed a weak grip on a foot, which struggled loose and disappeared again.

"We are going to take this whole boat apart," Shelby panted.

Kratos signaled to the shore. "Let's get help," he said. "He's not going anywhere now. We can just wait him out if we need to. Sooner or later he's going to want food and water."

"Well, that's not much fun," Shelby grinned. "He might have quite a few hiding places set up. He's had several days to think this through."

"True. And nothing else to do, beached like this."

Eurymedon and Dolios joined them. Hestia waited for some of the soldiers to bring her a ladder rather than clamber over the side like the young men. She climbed it with her arms folded and a scowl on her face, ready, as the senior female present, to administer justice. She stepped off the gunwale into the ship and immediately asked, "Where is the steering board?"

"What?" Shelby asked.

"The rudder, the steering board, whatever it's called. Where is it?"

A dozen soldiers were grunting with the cargo, moving boxes

and piles of rope, sorting through crossed oars for hiding places—
like terriers chasing a rat in a stone wall. He'd been watching
them, amused at the difficulty of uncovering a hiding place in an
open boat. Now he looked around.

"I didn't notice it missing," he said.

"Well, he didn't lose it," Hestia said. "They might lose sailors
and cargo and sails and ropes and anchors, but they don't lose
their steering boards. If you find it, you'll find him."

Dolios was looking at the rigging, studying how the ropes went
up to the mast and back again, bracing it to the frame of the ship.
The sail itself was furled and bulging, and he thought one part of
it was bulging more than it should. He picked up a heavy wooden
pin of some kind and smacked the lump. It gave out a grunt.

"Here he is," he called. He struck the bulge again and got a
grunt and a howl.

"But I saw him crawling away under the cargo," Kratos said.
"I saw his legs down there."

"There's somebody in this sail," said Dolios. "But he's not
going anywhere until we untie him."

"Where in the name of the goddess is the steering board,"
Hestia asked again. "Oduze is the steersman. He does not lose
his steering board. Find that board and you will find Oduze."

"Okay" Shelby said, "that's it. Remove all the cargo from this
ship. Start at the back and move forward. I want everything out
onto the sand. Then if we still can't find him, we'll burn the boat.
Hestia?" he asked, "Will that give you enough time to understand
the construction?"

"The construction is interesting," she replied, "but I can see
several ways to improve it. I don't know why they did not do so
when they first built it. But yes, I think so."

Several of the twenty or so soldiers on board were helping
Dolios unfurl the sail, and finally one of Oduze's men fell out onto
the deck.

"Aha!" Kratos called. "A decoy. Clever. Keep getting that cargo
out of here," he shouted at the men, "and tie this scoundrel up on
the beach."

"No," said Hestia. "Cut off his head. I'm fed up with all of this.
He knew what he was doing."

"Yes ma'am," Kratos said. The head thudded to the sand, and

the body pumped blood over the side of the boat for a minute or more, before stopping.

The sailors already on the beach howled in anger at the execution, but soldiers surrounded them with spears pointed at them and goaded them into a tighter circle.

"False floor," Dolios said, pointing at a section of deck that had been uncovered by the soldiers.

Shelby nodded, and pointed at the clever design, built into the hull of the ship. When soldiers pried the boards loose, they saw an elbow quickly pulled up out of sight. It took several more minutes to pry enough boards away to get to a foot, and then they laid hold and tugged. The chore was made more difficult by knees pressing into the floor of the hull and hands holding onto something.

"Be careful," Shelby warned, "he's armed."

They grabbed the flailing feet, finally, and knotted ropes around them, and then the soldiers tugged on him simultaneously. Finally they pulled him free. He sprawled on the deck cursing.

But it was not Oduze.

"Another decoy," Shelby said, as the pirate was dragged to the gunwale. Kratos did not need to be told twice. Seconds later another human head plopped into the sand.

"Find the steering board," Hestia said. "I expect he will have one more decoy aboard, but if you don't find the steering board then you won't find him."

"Yes ma'am," Kratos said, instructing the men to go back to emptying the ship.

"Do you think that guy was the one I found first?" Shelby asked Kratos.

"We've cleared everything out of the back end of this ship." Kratos chewed on a clump of his beard. "Maybe. Maybe not. You never got a look at him, did you?"

"No."

"Then we will go on until nothing is left on this boat," Kratos said. "I think we should even take the sail out of it."

"Good idea," Shelby said, going over to help roll a large amphora over to the edge of the boat. It slipped anyway, and crashed sideways, cracking and spilling a hundred or more gallons of olive oil around the interior. Some of the pirates on shore laughed at them, making snide observations.

"I guess there are ways to do this better," he observed to his neighbors. "Maybe we just empty it bit by bit into smaller containers until it's all out. Let's do that with all the others."

By evening they had emptied the ship down to its ribs and hull. They found one more pirate hiding in a coil of rope in the front of the boat. His head joined the other two, which were already attracting a parade of small crabs and wheeling sea birds.

But they didn't find Oduze. Hestia and Dolios could stand next to the mast and see every seam of caulk, every rope tie-down—but nowhere in the ship was Oduze.

"He took his steering board and swam away," Hestia said. "It's the only explanation. I suspect if you go look in the sand behind the boat, you'll find his track as he got to the water. He took his steering board with him, and he's paddled way out to sea by now. He's had hours to escape. Only Alcestis riding her dolphins could find him now, but for what? Let him go. He's like a tiger escaped from a cage and returned to the wild world."

"Agreed," Kratos said. "Should I execute the rest of these pirates?"

"Let's feed them first, and then we will let Melia tell us what to do with them," Hestia said. "The night is coming on. Feed them, tie them up on the beach under guard, and tomorrow we will know what kind of justice they deserve. The goddess will tell Melia tonight at the sacrifice. Come Dolios," she said, turning away, "let's go back to the trebuchets and talk about what we have seen."

SIXTY-FIVE

bbbbbbbbbbbb

Dolios and Hestia returned to the beach the next morning as Oduze's sailors were being led away under guard. Melia had ordered that they be grouped separately from the pirates already being held in the little village, but she gave no reason for it. At any rate, they were not to be executed just yet. She wanted to question each one separately before she decided. Hestia and her apprentice strolled down the beach, discussing what they had seen in Oduze's boat, how the planks were secured to the boat's ribs, where the steering board had been located, why the mast was mounted the way it was.

"Let's look at the bigger boats first," Hestia said, resting her gnarled hand on the boy's shoulder. "I'm fascinated by these machines. I'd love to build a few." She gestured at the two dozen ships now beached on the sand, and the dozen or so floating in shallow water.

"I see two problems right off," Dolios said. "First, where to get the timbers, and second, how to seal between the planks. And then there's the whole business of catching the wind to make them move. I don't understand that at all."

"Well, that's the fun of it, isn't it," Hestia said. "We'll ask questions of the pirates. If we're nice, they might cooperate."

"Maybe," Dolios said, suspiciously. "But my stomach is rumbling, and I smell fresh bread. Would you mind eating first?"

"Of course not," Hestia said. "Perhaps we can bring a basket to the pirates. I bet they would like some cheese and fruit, too, if it's available. Run up over the dune and tell some slaves to fetch it.

Get a big jug of wine also. Food may get us more information than we expect, even from pirates. And we might learn a lot from the village people, too."

While Dolios sprinted away, she strolled for a few more minutes, her eyes crinkled with suppressed mirth.

"But you missed the most important part," Hestia said when he returned.

"More important than keeping the boards from leaking?"

"Well, sure. It's how they get the front of the boat formed. I bet there are many shipbuilders along the coast who know that art. I'm not sure you and I are going to do ourselves many favors trying to reinvent that."

"But why is the front of the boat bent like that?" he asked.

"So it will slip through the water. You can't drive a rectangle through the water. You drive a triangle. The sharper the point, the better the water flows."

"I see that, I guess," Dolios said. "Do you want to go over the mathematics of it? Icarus has been teaching me some mathematics, and that might help."

"Of course it helps."

After they collected food and wine from the slaves, they paused to sit on a piece of dried driftwood to study the front of one of the warships.

"See how the boards curve? They curve the same on each side of the boat because they are fixed to a frame inside the hull that is exactly the same on both sides. Let's see what we can learn about that, and meanwhile let's also see what we can learn about how they seal the sides, though I think I know."

"What do you see that I don't see?" Dolios asked.

"What happens when you take two things that have straight edges and then try to mount them so they curve?"

Dolios studied the planking on the side of the ship. "I don't know. What?"

"The planks on the outside, the convex side, have a gap, but the concave side doesn't." She showed him with her hands edgewise on top of one another. "You can close most of that gap by beveling the edges of the wood, but the wood is still going to swell and shrink with moisture and movement. To keep the boat from leaking, the gap on the convex side needs to be caulked. If you look closely, you can see what appears to be whiskers or hairs sticking out from between the planks. I think its bits of rope covered with tar. I bet that's how they do it," she said. "And then they probably paint the sides of the boat with tar to keep the planks from getting waterlogged. But the more interesting thing is how to get started. I bet you have to have that big timber on the bottom first, and then everything builds up from there."

"I bet Icarus has some ideas," Dolios said.

"Certainly he does, but his ideas have more meaning when we have a basic understanding. Let's go on to the village. We will choose a likely looking pirate or two and maybe a couple of the older village men and let them teach us."

The long walk along the shore was pleasant and quiet. Some sea birds called from overhead, or dipped their wings searching the shore for more human heads. The tide had come in, however, and human remains were gone. Even the bloodstained sand had been thrown into the calm surf, with its myriads of small crabs. Smoke from a pyre at the end of the beach where the dead were burned still drifted skyward on the calm air, wiggling from side to side at different heights to show the wandering air over the shore. Later it would dissipate over land as the breeze from a cooler ocean flowed inland with the rising heat of the day.

They found the pirates held in a group in the center of the little hamlet, surrounded by angry village women and stout soldiers with spears. They were naked, but clean. Or cleaner, that is. Some of them were too diseased to be called clean under any conditions. The village women all held knives and shearing implements, intending to cut off the pirates' hair if they had a chance. That seemed more disgusting to them than anything.

"Anyone want to talk to Dolios and me?" she asked the group. The pirates sneered and uttered curses.

"Oh?" asked Hestia. "You won't talk?"

"Give us our clothes," one said.

"Slaves do not wear clothes," Hestia replied. "Slaves wear a collar around their bare necks, and they have their hair cut so they won't infect their masters with lice."

"We are not slaves," cried another pirate.

"Incorrect," Hestia said. "You are either slaves or you are fish bait. At the moment, I am preparing collars for all of you. You will have them welded around your necks later today, those of you who live so long. So I will ask again, do any of you want to talk to me and to Dolios here?"

"I don't like me that one," cried one of the women. "Can I have his ear to bait a hook?" She thumbed her knife.

"And his nose too," Hestia said. "Guards, pull that man out."

Soldiers bashed their way into the group using the butts of their spears, until they reached a man who was trying to elude them by scrambling over other pirates. They dragged him out of the circle of his mates, and four of them held down his limbs while the village woman came forward.

"Wait a moment," Hestia said quietly, kneeling beside the pirate and bending low to whisper in his ear.

A moment later the terrified man nodded enthusiastically.

"I thought so," Hestia smiled as she raised herself up. "Hold him a minute or two," she said to the guards.

"Anyone else want to give this good woman his ear and nose for her fishhook?" she asked.

She was met with sullen, rebellious looks from the group.

"Well, then, how about your penis?" She grinned at them. "You could use a penis for fish bait, couldn't you?" she asked the woman, who laughed shrilly.

"Aye, and love it too!" she howled. All the village women laughed with her.

"No, no, don't love it," scolded Hestia. "If you want to love it, we need to leave it attached!"

More gales of laughter, now from the guards also.

Hestia whispered to Dolios. "We don't need many. Besides, we don't know their capabilities. I'd like to talk to a captain or someone like that, but we don't know these people yet."

"We could learn something we don't know, regardless," Dolios replied. "But these are rough fellows. Let's take some guards with us."

"Of course," she nodded. She turned to the women again.

"Do any of you have men or boys who can teach a thing or two about boats?" she asked.

"Most of them be out fishing," replied a toothless woman, pointing a crooked finger out to sea. "They can talk when they get back."

"I can talk," said an old man coming forward. "This lad saved my life and family. I owe him that. "

"Oh, and then there's this rope maker," said one of the women. "He knows things. Talk to him."

"Good plan," said Hestia.

"My daughter can come, too," said the rope maker. "She knows more about boats than most."

"I like that," said Hestia.

* * *

Hestia decided to tour one of the pirate ships lying on the beach at the village. She led the way on board.

"What do you want to know?" the pirate demanded. "This is our warship. We don't allow women or visitors."

"Well, it's my ship now," said Hestia sweetly. "So this is yours, is it? Here, we brought some bread and wine to make it easier to talk. We just want to know how to build a beautiful ship like this."

"You're not a normal woman, are you?" the pirate replied.

"We're here to admire," Hestia said, and she introduced herself and Dolios.

"He looks like a girl," the pirate said, scratching himself and scowling.

The rope maker's daughter grinned.

"Tell me," Hestia said, "how do you keep the water from coming through the sides of the boat?"

She passed out bread, and Dolios passed around the large jar of wine. Before long, the three were willing to talk, especially since Hestia seemed to have more food in her basket. The girl volunteered information first, explaining about using tar to seal the sides. They got the tar from other settlements along the coast more than two days sail.

"I thought so," Hestia said. "It looked like tarred rope."

For every question they answered, Hestia asked another. She admired this and that, patted them on their shoulders, and joked with them, and the three began to loosen up. The pirate looked with interest at the girl, but her father hoped Dolios would show a greater interest. They showed her the boat's ribs, which held the sides to the keel. They explained how they pegged the planks to the ribs using dowels instead of nails or screws. They showed her rowing ports, and how the mast was fixed into the boat.

"You don't want to pinch the mast where it attaches," the rope maker explained. "That will make it break. You want to set the butt end of the mast into a kind of well so the lower third of it takes the strain of the wind. Lots of people get that wrong." He demonstrated with his fingers.

Hestia was not impressed with the steering board positioned against the side of the boat, and they sensed her disapproval, yet they bragged on the effectiveness of the device.

"I understand that you can hinge it against the side of the boat," she said, "but couldn't you make a better design by putting it behind the boat and moving it side to side with ropes and pulleys or chains?"

"Whoever heard of such a thing?" the pirate replied. "The steersman uses his strength against the sea to make the boat steer. No steersman worthy the title would ever cheat with pulleys and ropes."

"Must be tough in a storm."

"We try to avoid storms," he replied.

"So would I," she said.

She then began asking them about traveling across the open sea, which none of them had done.

"We've been out of sight of land a few times," the old rope maker said. His browned feet and calloused hands showed his long servitude to the sea. "But we don't like it. As soon as we can, we come back to land. It's dangerous out there."

"You know," Hestia said, "I thought so. Monsters and such, I bet."

"And wicked sea gods and storms that come out of nowhere," the pirate said. "We hate it."

"I saw a god rising out of the sea one day," the rope maker said. "He was enormous. He rose up in a huge wave that crashed away from us, destroying a pirate ship. We sacrificed to him for a week after that."

Hestia nodded. "Wise."

"Where do you get your wood to make the ships?" Dolios asked. "There's not much around here."

"We go across up there," the daughter said, pointing northeast.

"It's open water, but we can see both sides, so it's not so scary. We stock up. Mostly pine is what we use."

"Is pine the best?" Dolios asked.

"The Phoenicians use cedar from Lebanon, and it's beautiful wood. It lasts longer, too. Pine rots away in a few years. They have bigger ships than ours, because their planks are longer, and they can get taller masts."

Another few hours, and Hestia and Dolios knew what they needed to know about building the skeleton of a ship, about how the ribs were shaped in hot water, and where to find the best wood.

Finally, Hestia asked who was building boats these days. The father and daughter pointed north.

"Over there," they said, "it's far, and it might not be wise for an old woman and a boy to go there by themselves. Those workers are rough. It is about a day by sea, perhaps three by land."

"Thank you for the warning, you sweet people" Hestia said, beaming at them. "We will pay attention to everything we have learned today. In coming days I hope you can teach us how to sail one of these machines."

They delivered the pirate back to the guarded group and turned to go.

"When we are ready, we will show our model to the rope maker and his daughter," she muttered to Dolios.

"Do I need to be there when you do that?" Dolios asked.

"Why Dolios, you noticed how she made eyes at you!"

"Well, yes, I did. And I'm not interested."

"She is," beamed Hestia, and she giggled.

SIXTY-SIX

〜〜〜〜〜〜〜〜〜〜〜

Nineteen pirates survived their first interview with Melia. She executed the other sixty-three as too diseased or too untrustworthy to allow around the women and children. The smoke from their roasting genitals on the altar and from their burning pyres on the beach hung over the camp for days. The nineteen survivors, well instructed in the law of their new masters, became workers with Hestia and Dolios as they refashioned and improved the captured ships. Oduze's pirate crew were among the first to be executed, of course, and their ship was the first to be launched, the blood stains on the starboard side all that remained of Oduze's trickery. Dolios and helpers searched a month for the perfect wood to replace the stolen steering board, finally choosing a long trunk of ash wood and fashioning it into the right form. And one clear afternoon, she floated again. But they had a ship with a shallow keel, capable of approaching close to shore and of going into estuaries and rivers, but inefficient at wind power.

Visiting with Shelby about it, Dolios and Hestia finally decided a shallow keel might do for a coastal trader, but they would need to redesign the hull for crossing the Adriatic. Hestia, of course, was the first one to grasp the principle of the wind transferring power to the hull and the keel helping to direct that power into a desired direction. When Dolios finally understood about the application of forces, his face lit up and he exclaimed that a keel would allow them to turn the sail from side to side to maximize speed and maintain direction.

"Right," Shelby said, "and to travel faster and also to travel more or less against the wind, too, by using the angles to move side to side in the same way that going up a mountain slope is easier if you don't go straight up. Same principle."

Dolios's face caught fire when he finally understood. It reminded Shelby of how Hestia's face could ignite.

"We can use numbers to understand it even better," Dolios exclaimed.

"And if you take a length of rope with a float at one end," Shelby said, "you can toss it overboard to measure your speed in the water. You mark the rope and then count the time for certain marks to go by. Now let's turn our attention to making a timing device. This could be very handy for crossing open water, because it would tell us how far we were from making landfall on the other side."

"Oh oh oh!!" cried Hestia and Dolios together. "Yes! We see."

* * *

Their joy did not spread to the laborers who were searching for ways to improve the caulking of the ships. On some ships, the staves along the sides of the ship were not pegged or nailed, but sewn, using animal sinews or withies of willow. These ships leaked and required constant bailing to remain afloat. As long as they never got far from land, that worked. But on a long sea voyage of several hundred miles, it meant the ship could sink. These ships were taken apart and rebuilt, and it was hard, finger-breaking work. The stench of tar bubbling in bronze cauldrons replaced the thick smoke of pirate pyres as the weather wore through summer into fall, but getting the tar was itself a difficult feat. Their first seaworthy ships were sailed up the coast to hunt for it, and that brought curious sailors from other locales to barter.

Meanwhile, the pirates and people from the village helped teach sailing skills to Dolios and the others. They taught about tides and winds, about the hazards of a lee shore with the current pushing you toward fatal rocks, and about the changes in weather forecast by clouds and waves. These lessons took months, but Dolios, true to form, was the first to learn. Everything having to do with water and ships fascinated him. His mind was full of questions, and intense. He even attempted to engage Kratos in strategies for naval warfare, but the older warrior could not grasp the necessary concepts other than strategic position, superiority of force, and surprise. How to attain any of those was beyond him, but Dolios saw infinite possibilities.

In the evening, Dolios sought out Alcestis to talk to her. They visited incessantly about subjects like the force of wind and the importance of a keel, about approaching a threatening vessel like a pirate ship and how to board it and capture it. Dolios's mind was afire with these ideas, and the fire was contagious. Alcestis understood and helped in her own ways. But mostly they spent their evenings watching the burning sun set into the distant waves while sitting hip to hip. Sometimes she sang to her dolphins. Sometimes they appeared, as though checking on her. While the water stayed warm even more, Alcestis and Dolios swam out into the gentle surf to splash with them. They were very happy at these times, their simple trust enough to bond them in friendship.

Melia grew gravid and impatient. The first harvest approached and she watched petulantly as the workers gathered their first fruits. No vineyards could be planted, because these would take several years to mature, and the result was that the people would need to drink beer instead of wine. Melia considered beer to be a lower-class beverage, and she was unhappy about that. Still, as long as she was pregnant, she avoided wine, limiting her liquids to clear spring water and sheep milk. That was the wisdom of her people, come down to her generation from time immemorial, and she followed it because she was the one whose actions perpetuated tradition. Not that she enjoyed it. Many restless nights she hoped to have a krater or two of wine to relax, to ease the pressure in her belly from the growing child, to bring Shelby closer and make him more comfortable. But she abstained.

Kratos had his own supply of wine, of course, and his carousing could be heard around the camp late into the darkness after sunset. Shelby and Eurymedon often joined him, Eurymedon seeming to shun his own tent with its pretty Persian love-slaves, and the occasional visit from fiery Rhodia, whose passion burned like a lantern in the darkness of the long nights. The Persians had nothing else to do but giggle and entertain themselves, causing all who saw them to roll their eyes at such worthless behavior. Even Alcestis, who was a stricter disciplinarian than any other female in the camp, despaired of making the pair useful at anything else but their intended purpose, which was to keep Eurymedon sexually occupied and away from other women. But Eurymedon was avoiding them, and avoiding Rhodia, for the time being. Old women in the camp shook their heads in understanding, knowing that eventually change would come to both the Persians and to Eurymedon, but also knowing that no one could predict what that change would be.

"Shelby," said Melia one night, "you must understand this about the goddess. She does not create labyrinths because she likes them. She creates them because that is who she is."

He remembered the statement, but he could not for the life of him remember why she had made it. It was one of the the many mysteries of Melia, he decided. Still, what did it mean to have a divinity who was a labyrinth?

SIXTY-SEVEN

elia gave birth to a baby girl at the autumnal equinox, in the second month after the second crops were planted. She called the baby Polyhymnia, "singer of many sacred songs." Polyhymnia squalled until her daddy picked her up and snuggled her. When he placed her on Melia, she cooed, and both mother and daughter went sound asleep. He thought his heart would burst at the beauty of it, at the love of it.

Of course, the women shooed him out of the birthing room right away, and he went off to visit with Melia's brothers, who were as happy as he was. Late into the night they laughed and drank and laughed some more.

The next day when he went in to see his ladies, Melia took him by the hand and held on for a long time, staring at him. "I'm so happy," she said at last, the baby snug between her breasts. "I'm so happy you came back, and you are still here."

"Me too," he said, his eyes beginning to burn and his throat to close with emotion. He leaned over and kissed both of them, inhaling their beautiful scent, the faint odor of milk, the spice of the new creature who cooed without opening her eyes.

"I'm worried that disease will spread through the camp as the weather turns cold and wet," she said. "We have more visitors now from other places, and they bring diseases sometimes. It is important to prepare for the rainy season with proper drainage to protect our fresh water. I hope you and Hestia are looking into that."

"We are," he said. "Dolios is a big help. He figured out how to run drains, and he may eventually succeed in building an aqueduct to channel fresh water from the springs uphill. Dolios has a genius for water, which is strange for a boy who had never seen the sea until we arrived here in the spring."

"What about Alcestis?"

"Her genius is more subtle," he said. "She certainly has a genius for animals. She understands them better than anyone I know. She's younger than Dolios, but I expect she will be a better student and go further. I don't know what she will be capable of doing, but she will be valuable to us."

"She will be a woman," Melia replied. "She will be valuable to us for that, and she will be capable of doing many things well. I wonder if she might be interested in serving me for the time being."

"I'll ask her, if you like. But most afternoons, she likes to visit the wolf. Calu's pup is growing, she says, and she worries that feeding them means the pup is not learning how to fend for itself. But that is between them. And she seems eager to spend time with Dolios, too. I think we have a romance."

"A summer romance is good for both of them. But I worry about her. We will not be able to bring Calu with us in the ships," she said. "I hope she has prepared her heart for that."

"I'll tell her."

"No, I'll tell her," Melia said. "I can do it better than you." She held up their child. "You hold your baby for a bit while I get up and walk around. I need to move."

"I'm afraid I'll drop her," he said, recoiling.

"Nonsense." She handed little Polyhymnia to him. "Support her head, you fool. You'll break her neck." He cradled the baby like a football.

"For the sake of all that is holy," Melia said. "Sit down, put the baby on your shoulder so she can look around, and don't be so tense. You'll scare her, then she'll cry, then all the other women will come in and fuss at us. If you want to walk around outside the tent with her, you can do that, but be easy at first. She has a lot to learn, and she will not learn it all today."

Melia slipped through the tent flap, leaving Shelby face to face with the incalculable mystery of the female world, who smiled at him. Or burped. Or, quite possibly, pooped.

After a moment, he wandered out of the large tent toward the fields and watched the workers cut irrigation ditches open in places and close them in others. At the far end of the fields he saw Alcestis clambering over the barricades, a troop of Meliae with her for protection, going out to feed Calu.

The grain was tall in the fields and the heads were plumping up nicely. The barley already had long beards, and he expected the next harvest would also be successful if the rains held off. That would be their final crop of the year before winter.

Babies and farming. He had come a long way indeed from the hoo-ra days of his US Rangers, creeping through the red dust of Somalia or up Afghani hills in the dark of the moon. Those days seemed so far away, and, he reminded himself, they should. They were four thousand years in the future and belonged to a man much less mature than he had become in Melia's world.

At least the mountains were quiet. He looked uneasily at the way they had come, through those dark, towering peaks still capped with snow, and hoped for the sake of this child that he would never see or smell another wild man.

SIXTY-EIGHT

T he pirate ships were floated over to the little village, where a ship yard was built with cranes to hoist masts. Over the drumming of rain and the blowing wind during the cold months, the people heard shipwrights hammering and shouting as they worked despite the weather, and smoke from their fires drifted close to the ground some days like wispy serpents crawling toward the upland forests. Hestia taught the shipwrights how to replace the withies in sewn ship hulls with wooden hornbeam pegs hammered through bored holes and secured with wedges hammered into their ends. Other ships had been pieced together with bronze nails, and many of them had worked loose. All of these repairs took time and distracted her from her main project—the building of her own ship.

Eventually, however, Hestia's ship began to take shape, much to the head-shaking and scorn of the fish-eating population. It would be a two-mast affair with a rear rudder, and it was longer and bigger than any ship they had seen. The fishermen didn't expect it to float, much less sail. Just getting it into the water would be a huge chore because of its enormous weight. But Hestia had thought that through, too, and she had constructed the ship on a rail system so that it would slide upright into the water when the time came.

It was Hestia's most ambitious project, required all of her considerable attention to detail, and demanded supervision of the hundreds of laborers she put to work on it. Dolios shone at managing the laborers, his sharp eye correcting and directing them so they would do it right. Soon, "Do it right!" became his mantra. Some of the workers, old enough to be his grandfather, smiled at him and joked, but they did it right, and no one loafed, no one wanted the wrath that came from making the same mistake twice.

Six weeks after little Polly came into the world, Melia resumed daily sacrifices. They had enough food to get through the winter, and had a little success in bartering for wine from up the coast, though they certainly missed the vintages from their old valley. Melia announced that despite the work on the ships, they would remain in this camp for another year to accumulate stocks of wine and wheat before continuing to the new land. Their cattle dwindled, and their poor sheep were not pleased in these strange pastures, but they survived. In this winter, as in all of them, the demand was survival, and for humans, planning for survival.

Through the winter, Alcestis continued to feed the wolf and her pup, now almost fully grown. She harbored no illusions about Calu and did not consider her a pet or even tame, but she depended on the wolf to give her a few moments of privacy from other people, and to tell her, in all the subtle ways the wolf had, whether the wild men were around. Or the one or two pirates who had slipped away from their captors and the hard labor of slavery.

The wild men were not around. Shelby wondered if they had migrated into the distant mountains. As the rains ceased and the first months of spring warmed, they did not reappear. He did not hear their weird calls in the night; he had no sense of them watching. The dark mountains kept them hidden, and he thought maybe they would not return after all.

"No wild men, Icarus?" Kratos asked one day, finding him on the hill where he surveyed the workers in the field.

"Alas, brother," Shelby said, "no wild men. Let's hope we don't see them anymore."

"You make it sound like a challenge," the burly warrior retorted. "They were no worse than hunting a lion at midnight."

"While drunk," Shelby added.

"You might have been drunk," Kratos laughed. "I was not. I never get drunk."

"Not true," Shelby said. "I've seen you drunk."

"You've seen me having a good time," Kratos said. "You've seen me loud and rough and ready to fight, but I am always loud and rough and ready to fight. I am just a little more so when I have had a few gallons of wine."

"The land to which I will lead our people is rich, fertile, and populated with many foes. Those we do not kill will enter into treaties with us, we will intermarry, and over time our people will be happy. But in our lifetimes, my friend, we will fight many battles, build many forts and castles, many roads and walls, and create a nation that will endure two thousand years or longer. That will be the fight to which we go from this place."

"Then let us be gone as soon as ever we can," Kratos said with a grin. "I hate sitting around when the prospect for conquest and glory is just over that little bit of damp earth."

"In time," Shelby said. "It's all about time. We carry the divine fire of the goddess with us, and she will open the world to us in time."

SIXTY-NINE

'm not ready," Melia said, "and I am concerned about you. Would you like to use Eurymedon's Persian slaves for a while?" "What?" Shelby asked. He had just walked into the tent. She was seated on the cushions they used for a bed, little Polly sound asleep at her side.

"The Persian twins," she said. "Eurymedon is not interested in them any longer, and I thought you might be. They might make you more content."

"I'm not sure what you're talking about," he said.

"Sex," she said. "I'm not ready. It will be at least another month before I want to have sex with you. During that time, would you like to have other partners for sex? I think Eurymedon would gladly lend you his Persian twins."

"Are you out of your mind?" he asked.

"Or some of the Meliae?" she asked. "Khloe would love to become pregnant with your child. So would Rhodia, but she's a special case. They all would."

"Thank you for thinking of me," he said. "I appreciate it more than you know. But, no, I am not interested in being with other women. I am content."

"That, hero, is the right answer," she said, grinning. "I expected nothing less. Still, Eurymedon's slaves. You know. They are very pretty, and they are underemployed. You could enjoy them."

"Really, I don't want anyone else. I only feel the fire with you. When you want to have sex again, then I will be ready. Meanwhile, I think I am overwhelmed by you and little Polly."

"Again, hero, right answer," she said, smiling at him. "Come over here."

He approached, and she reached for his private parts, cupping him in her hands.

"Sometimes," she said, "I wonder if we are not missing a good thing." She looked up at him, her eyes wide and dewy. "I mean," she said, "you are so magnificent. We should be getting you to breed with more women, to make more babies who are like you. I don't blame Rhodia for being so hot for you."

"I have no wish to be a herd sire," he said, sighing and lifting her chin so he could kiss her as he settled to his knees. "I'm not sure, really, that I would even be allowed to stay here, in your time, if I loved anyone else. Or," he added, swallowing as he fell into her clear eyes, "made love to anyone else. The fire between us is why I am here."

"You have all the right answers today," she said, her hands still gently squeezing him. "All the right answers. Can you hold me for a bit? Me and Polly?"

* * *

Winter set in with cold rain and winds. Some evenings, they sat huddled around small fires as the rain tattooed on the tents, telling stories and avoiding the dripping water from the seams. Other days, the false warmth of the sun dried out the ground and they could tend to their flocks and beer. By the solstice, roofs of branches and bundled leaves and grasses had been raised over most of the tents just in time for the first dusting of snow. In the distant peaks or the wild men's country, the snow was heavy and they glowed brightly under the moon. It was a slow time until the approach of the equinox, when the quickening world brought out the first faint reds and golds of leaves in the forest and shepherds began shearing their sheep. No one had been idle during the long, slow winter, and Hestia's forges had glowed through the long nights down near the little village. The influx of raw wool provided new labor for spinners and weavers, and the first fields were planted with grain. Life had assumed a steady if somewhat tentative pace as they waited to build their stores before continuing their migration.

One evening they all gathered around a large, warm fire in the open space outside the big tent. Eurymedon and Rhodia came back from their walk into the fresh growth in the high hills, Kratos joined them, carrying a ten-gallon wineskin full of the last wine from the home valley, and Dolios and Alcestis sat around to listen and attend to any needs. Garanus and Arktos were already enjoying the warmth of the fire in the clear spring air, stoking it to keep it bright. In the distance, the workers were still in the fields in the twilight, planting grain and repairing threshing floors. Firelight glittered along the shore from their new shipyard, where workers continued their work. The rope maker and his daughter came to visit, and Garanus eyed the young woman with evident interest, an expression not missed by her or by anyone.

Hestia arrived late, after the sun had set in its blazing glory of thermonuclear vermillion. She was out of breath and angry. "Those damned thieves," she said, plumping herself down. "They steal everything! Now I find they have been trading tools up the coast for whores and wine. I have a mind to drown them all, like rats or unwanted puppies."

Alcestis gasped, putting a hand to her mouth, her eyes widening. "Not puppies!" she whispered in alarm.

"I'm sorry, Hestia," Melia said, little Polly dreamily suckling at her breast. "Why do you think they are stealing those tools? What can they get for the tools elsewhere that they cannot get here?"

"Different women and more wine," Hestia huffed. "Bastards. Motherless scum. Malcontent thieves. Some people steal just because they can, not because they need to."

Shelby nodded, watching the conversation play out.

"Easy enough to kill them," Kratos said. "Do you really need them? We could set them all out to run on the beach while the Meliae shoot them down. Many of your workers were pirates anyway."

"I think the Meliae would like the target practice," Rhodia said, "but I'm not sure they should be used that way. You never know when that kind of thing might go to somebody's head and they just start shooting people they don't like. It's best to keep them under control. And that goes for you, too, big boy." She grinned at Kratos. "You need a woman who can keep you under control. You're as dangerous out of battle as you are in it."

"Might take more than one woman," Eurymedon joked. "Maybe all of the Meliae."

"I don't think the Meliae would be well employed that way either," Melia said. "They are an elite fighting force, not a harem of palace prostitutes. But brother," she added kindly to Kratos, "if you are willing, I might be able to help you find someone."

"Bah!" he retorted. "I don't need help finding a woman. I need help finding a war. That battle in the home valley was wonderful. Very fulfilling. It was everything I hoped it would be—screaming men, the smell of blood in the air, and victory. More intoxicating than wine. Our skirmish with the wild men was not much, and these foolish pirates were no challenge at all. I want an army and a real war!" He poured a large quantity of wine into a goblet, saluted Melia, and splashed a few drops out for the goddess. He drank deeply.

Arktos reached for the goblet when he lowered it and did the same, wiping his mouth and beard with the back of his hand. "I can't wait to make my honey wine again," he said, grimacing at the sour taste. "I've looked all over these hellish hills and can't find a single beehive. Why hasn't anyone cultivated the bees?"

"They're ignorant," Hestia said, still fuming. Arktos passed her the goblet, which she snatched and drank from without toasting either the goddess or Melia. Shelby grinned at her, at the way her anger burned. "I tell you what, Kratos. We would all be better off if we sent you into that damned shipyard and told you chop off all their heads," she said. "Men, children. All of them. I cannot wait to be gone from this place."

"Icarus," Eurymedon said, "tell us what you foresee about our journey to this new land. How will we do it? What does the land look like? You've told us it lies west, at least a day's journey by boat. But we are too many to all go together."

"Yes, Shelby," Melia said. "Tell us the tale of our coming journey."

Shelby stared at the fire for a time. He watched the ashes fall from the logs and the coals in their white-hot burn. "Let's talk first about the home valley," he finally said. "You all remember the distance from the citadel to the southern forest, or from the desolate peaks on the east to the hill forts on the west. Those distances were about about half a degree of latitude, and some of you know how to use the astrolabe to determine degrees. We must travel five degrees north from where we are now, and three degrees west. In other words, ten times the length of the home valley, and almost three times the width. On the ground that does not seem far. On the open sea, in a boat that might struggle to travel one degree in a day, it can be a long way. Simply put, at best it will take seven days of all-day and all-night sailing to reach the new land. Since we do not want to sail continuously, you must double that time. The last leg will be across the open sea and could take two full days if the winds and storms do not delay us. Are you with me?"

They nodded.

"The solution is to make faster boats, Icarus," Hestia said. "More oars, bigger sails."

"Yes, Hestia," he replied. "But we also need supplies. The boats we took from the pirates are a good start, but they can't carry as much as we need even with your excellent repairs. It would take a lot of trips in just those boats to reach that coast above Deer's Head Harbor. Right now, our wood for ships comes from the Corinthian coast. The wood growing in the mountains behind us might be useful, but we could stir up the wild men by going for it."

"Why will you not let me lead an expedition against the wild men, Melia?" Kratos asked. "We could solve a lot of problems if we eliminated them as a threat."

"We could also train them," Alcestis added, speaking up. "I've trained that wolf. We are not friends, but we cooperate. We could do the same with the wild men."

"All I know is that the goddess has a use for those giants at some future time and in a land far away," Melia said, ignoring Alcestis. "Some race of giants used in a war in a far-off land, near Persia or the Mesopotamia."

"But surely our goddess does not mind if we protect ourselves," Kratos said.

"She is very clear," Melia replied, shifting Polly to the other breast. "We have not seen them in months, and we may not see them again if we leave them alone. They are not our business. This is the final word on the matter."

"End of discussion?" Kratos asked.

"End of discussion."

"How are we to get the lumber we need for the ships?" Kratos asked.

"By bartering with the coastal communities," Arktos replied. "That's how it is done. And now that I think about it, Hestia, those thieves of yours might have been doing us a favor. Obviously, the coastal communities desire your tools. Let's make them tools and take supplies in exchange. If we cut out the trade from the thieves, we make the profit, and it doesn't go to whores and bad wine."

"I hadn't thought of that," Hestia said, "but I am constantly running the forges anyway to replace the tools that are stolen. You're right. Let's use our fire to get the things we want."

"And while we're at it," Shelby said, "let's put our craftspeople to work to make other things that we can barter with these people. Eventually, they will come to us and our little harbor will be crowded with trade. By then, we should be well on our way to another harvest. And that reminds me, the fishermen in this little village can also make nets and other fishing tackle to barter up and down the coast. A little supervision will go a long way to making them a useful workforce for us."

"I am tired of supervising ignorant, lazy people," Hestia said, grabbing again for the goblet and swigging from it. "Let Dolios supervise them. He knows what to do. I want to work in the forges and the shipyard and build things we can use."

"How goes your ship?" Arktos asked, reaching for the goblet, taking it out of Kratos's grasp with the prerogative of an older warrior. Kratos stared at him, pretending to be offended, then stood up and refilled the goblet from the wineskin.

"It is a slow process," Hestia said. "Some days the tool you need the most is the very one that's gone. Then I must go out to the forge and cast a new one."

"Cast two or three," Arktos said, taking another swig even though Kratos held his hand out for the goblet. He handed the goblet to Kratos and said, "Take this nasty stuff, then, you villain."

"Make lots of tools," Shelby said. "We'll send Alcestis and Eurymedon along the coast to trade them. They will know what we need and spread the word that the tools can be had more cheaply if people will come to our harbor to get them. By the end of summer, we should have many boats arriving every week to trade with us, and that will be a good thing."

"You make it sound like we are going to stay here forever," Melia said.

"We will stay only until we have what we need to leave," Shelby said. "But that means more boats and more supplies. We need to grow enough extra food to get us through an extra year of migration and we have another set of rocky mountains to go through once we get to Deer's Head Harbor. So we should plan to have two years food supply when we set out. And Arktos is right about the wine from this coast. It's awful." After a moment's pause, he added, "But I suppose we could turn it into brandy. That would be popular."

"What is brandy?" Hestia asked.

"It's wine that is heated up and the vapor caught and condensed," he said. "The vapor, when it becomes liquid again, is much stronger than wine. Much, much stronger. I'll explain the process if you like, but then you will want to build it and that will take away from your boat."

"You don't trust me enough," she said, her eyes catching the firelight and twinkling. "I can do more than one thing at a time. Besides, you've been promising me forever that you would teach me to fly, and here we sit. Maybe you are the one who is not to be trusted."

"Then let us sit up for a time tonight," he replied, "and I will explain the process to you. You can also distill beer. Both products are flammable and useful, and both are intoxicating. Distilled beer might be more popular than distilled wine."

"Is that the special wine you brought that first time?" Kratos asked. "Your first night with us, when I drank some and pretended to be killed by it?"

Shelby nodded. "That's my special wine." He remembered the biting clarity of the cask-strength whisky he'd purchased from the shop near Ramstein.

"That was a good wine," Kratos said. "It gave me the courage to seek out that lion in the dark."

"It has been known to do that kind of thing to otherwise intelligent men," Shelby said, "and worse. A little goes a long way."

"Tell us about the journey," Melia said. "All this talk, and we are still here. Tell us about the journey and the land to which we will go and make our country."

He talked, and he talked. In his mind's eye, he could see them sailing north past Corfu and up the Dalmatian Coast, past lairs of pirates and shoals of fish, until they reached the forty-third parallel. There they would stock the ships with water and replenish food stocks before sailing due west. He visualized the landing on shallow beaches north of Deer's Head Harbor, the trek inland across the Apennines, and the rolling hills on those western slopes that would provide fertile and safe country for the nation.

He spoke long, staring into the embers of the dying fire while overhead the burning stars wheeled away from dawn. Eventually even Hestia dozed off, and he was left alone, staring into the future and listening to the faint opera of jackals answered by the lone howl of a distant wolf. Thin smoke, like the soft shading of an artist's pencil, rose straight up into the heavens, carrying his story to that ancient empire of the gods. Somewhere in the dark land at his back were wild men, but they were silent, and somewhere in the songs of the night was the divine mother in her strength, timeless goddess, older than the fire and the sea.

* * *

"Smoke boasts to the sky,
and Ashes to the earth,
that they are brothers to the fire."

—Rabindranath Tagore, "Stray Birds," #236

* * *

T H E   E N D

No author releases his work to the world without trepidation and a sense of loss. Like a child leaving home, the book strolls through the door waving goodbye, issuing impossible promises, full of hope but nevertheless leaving behind an empty room and the familiar odor of stories not told, of turns not taken, of roads passed by.

This youngster has had some issues with discipline, I admit. Finished once, he proved too fractious and needed serious remediation to the tune of 56,000 excised words. It was almost too late when I realized that he was not ready to make his way in the world, for I had already completed the audio recording and was about to launch the digital edition. But now I believe he has two feet to stand on, and I hope he has legs to carry him.

The Gender of Fire is the third book in a series that began with *The Icarus Jump* and continued with *The City and the Gate*. The familiar characters in unfamiliar situations, new characters added and taken away, new adventures met and avoided—these are the coin of this empire and I remain astonished that the stories emerge from rock like statues escaping stone. I cannot promise to return with these characters, but the story is not finished, and bubbling in the dark inward cauldron of my imagination is an image that might stalk me like a ghost until I give her words.

I wish to thank my ever-patient wife Stephenie, my good friends who labored through the first delinquent version of this story, and my excellent editors, Liz Brown and Jay Hodges. Your support and patience have been true gifts, poorly repaid by my best efforts.

Goodbye, son. Travel far.

— John Yearwood
Austin, Tx, 2019

ACKNOWLEDGMENTS

Special thanks go to Gary Gattis, Megan Biesele, Ann Matlock, Helen Currie Foster, my editors Jay Hodges and Liz Brown, and to Bill Carson who did such a lovely job crafting my poor manuscript into a printable product. Last but not least, I owe deep gratitude to my long-suffering wife, Steffi Yearwood.